REMEMBER THE STRUGGLE

Emmy's Story, Part 12

By
Kenneth Lee McGee

This is for Sheila.
Without the support of my loving wife, this book
would not exist.

I would like to thank Denise and Stephanie for their support and for sharing their knowledge and opinions. I will forever be indebted to the people of WriteOn Joliet without whose knowledge I would have never learned the skills necessary to become the writer I am today.

I want to thank the people from my church who have graciously allowed me to include fragments of their lives as inspirations.

A special thanks to Sue Midlock for creating the cover.

I want to thank my wife Sheila for her suggestions.

Prologue

Emmy pulled into the Colwell's driveway, drove past the house and parked in front of the carriage house. She dodged the raindrops, entered through the service door and dashed up the stairs. She tried the door. *At least you didn't lock me out.* She walked in and tossed her keys and purse on the counter. "Where are you?" When he didn't answer, she checked the bedroom and bathroom. *You did say you would wait out here.* She went back to the kitchen, dug her phone out of her purse and dialed Kenny's cell. She ended the call when she heard it ringing in the bedroom. *Where are you? Should I wait here, or go talk to your parents?*

She set her phone on the counter, bit her lip and tried to stop the tears from flowing. *Oh, Kenny, what's happened to us? Have we lost our focus on what's really important?* She walked over to the couch, sat down, closed her eyes and pictured the way the place looked the first time she braved climbing the stairs. She pictured the cobwebs, dust and the accumulation of fifty years of junk. She opened her eyes and looked into the bedroom. *I remember how tired I was on our wedding night. I'm sorry I fell asleep right after you... we... We have made up for it through the years.*

Kenny increased his pace as his legs warmed up. *I haven't run through Raynor Park since high school and probably never in the rain.* He turned the corner onto Fourth Street and ducked under a tree branch. He slowed his speed as he passed the old playground. *We used to play football here. How did we manage? There isn't much room.* He continued and made his way to Robert T. Colwell Elementary School. *How many years ago did I start kindergarten here?* He stopped quickly, lost his footing as he slid and nearly tripped on the sidewalk. *Holy cow! It's been thirty years ago. How is that possible?* He stared into the building and could see students at their desks. He waited until his breathing returned to normal, moved his feet one after the other and began to jog instead of run as the rain intensified. *I wonder if I would know any of the teachers. Is it possible that Mrs. Prater or Mrs. Saylor might still be teaching? Oh, well.* He glanced at his wristwatch. *I should get back. Emmy is probably there and wondering where I am. What will I say to her? How can I explain?* He jogged to the corner and stopped. He inhaled deeply, held his breath as long as he could and then exhaled sharply. *We have to face the facts. Things have changed. Does she even still love me? We have to figure it out.*

He closed his eyes. "Lord, please give me the wisdom to know what to say. I put my life in Your hands. Everything! My life. The kids lives. Emmy's life if I could do that. I know we can do nothing on our own. We need your strength. I remember reading Jesus went for forty days without eating. The devil offered all kinds of temptations. Jesus resisted all of them. He turned the temptations into triumphs. Help me to turn my temptations into triumphs." He opened his eyes and began to jog again. Faster and faster until he was sprinting through the pouring rain.

Emmy closed her eyes again as she listened to the rain drops on the roof. She moved to her knees and let her head fall onto the couch as she wept. After a time, she clasped her hands together and lifted her head. "Jesus, I know there are things in my life I need to change. You know what they are. You know everything about us. We can't hide things from you the way we do people on earth. If there is anything else I need to change, please tell me. Am I holding something back? If so, please show me. I want to surrender everything to you. I will give up my career if I need to. I will sell the house, the cars, everything. It all belongs to You anyway." She paused and allowed God to speak to her.

She opened her eyes and jerked her head to her left as she heard someone pounding up the stairs. She rose to her feet as the door banged open and Kenny slid into the room. Water dripped from every part of him. He wiped his face and shook his head and hands spraying water everywhere.

"Emmy, I need to tell you something. I need to confess," he said as a bolt of lightning flashed and thunder boomed. "We have to talk about our future." He held out his arms.

Emmy bit her lip. She took a step forward but then stopped. "Oh, Kenny." She closed her eyes. "I don't know if we have a future," she whispered as she turned away.

8

Chapter One

Kenny stretched out his left arm, yawned and slowly opened his eyes after not feeling anyone next to him. He looked up at the antique, hand hewn wooden beams above him. *Oh, right. I'm at the carriage house.* He kicked the sheet and blanket toward the foot of the bed and swung his feet to the floor. He sat there for a moment to collect his thoughts as he stretched both arms above his head. His solitude was rudely interrupted by the annoying ringtone of his cell phone. He grabbed it from the nightstand and peered at the caller ID.

"Hey, Andy, what's up?"

"Apparently not you. Did you forget that today is a workday?" Andy Walker's voice echoed off the two-feet thick brick walls of the carriage house.

"I didn't forget. What time is it?" Kenny glanced at the digital clock next to where a stack of books gathered dust on the nightstand. "It's only seven thirty."

"Exactly my point! The guys will be here at nine."

Kenny stood up and nearly tripped over his running shoes. "Where are you?"

Andy drained his second cup of coffee. "I'm sitting at your kitchen island eating breakfast with your kids who are wondering why you aren't here to take them to school."

"Emmy is supposed to take them to school this week." Kenny walked into the bathroom, rubbed his chin, decided not to shave and took care of business.

"Are you talking to Daddy, Uncle Andy?" Isabella asked.

"Yes, I am, sweetheart. Do you want to talk to him?"

"No, just tell him I learned all of my Spanish vocabulary words. Sofia helped me."

"Did you hear that?" Andy asked Kenny. "Are the girls learning Espanol?"

"Yes, and it helps to have a Spanish-speaking nanny." Kenny walked back into the bedroom and grabbed some clean underwear from the dresser. He picked up the t-shirt he had worn the day before. Smelled it and tossed it toward the plastic clothes

9

basket on the floor in the closet. He missed. *Guess I might as well wear clean clothes.* "I'll be there in an hour. Will you let the guys in if they get there before I do?"

"Anything else you want me to take care of?" Andy laid on the sarcasm.

"Are you going to be on my back, too?"

"I'm not taking sides. You guys need to figure things out." Andy abruptly ended the call.

Kenny stared at his phone. "Tell me something I don't know."

Twenty minutes later, Kenny grabbed his wallet from the kitchen counter. "Where are my keys? I did bring the Civic back here yesterday." He saw them hanging up by the door. "Duh! Emmy always gets after me to put things in the same place."

He drove back to the house in Bristol Ridge and parked in the garage. Instead of going up the concrete steps into the mudroom to enter the house, he walked around the half wall and ambled down the steps which led to the basement.

"'Bout time you got here," Andy said. "Jeff and P.J. are already in there helping Will Consoli set up."

Kenny looked at his phone. "I'm early. Why are you on my case?"

"Do I really have to answer that?" Andy stood up and opened the door for Adam Vicini the newest member of Fridays At Five. "Morning, Adam."

"Good morning, Mr. Walker." Adam smiled.

Andy put his large hand on Adam's back. "I'm not increasing your allowance, so stop calling me Mr. Walker."

"Juliana told me to be respectful." Adam set his briefcase down by the leather couch.

"You tell your lovely wife I said hello."

Dave Persching, the drummer for the band, arrived five minutes later carrying a bag of drumsticks and rolling a case of extra cymbals. "Am I the last one to arrive?"

Andy nodded. *You timed it perfectly.*

"Good. I hate to waste time waiting for the guys."

The members of Fridays At Five planned to use Kenny's

10

state-of-the-art basement studio to record demos for their next project for the Steward Music Group. The band warmed up by playing some favorite old tunes for thirty minutes. This also enabled Will Consoli to set some levels.

"Are we ready?" Kenny asked the guys.

"Let's get down to it," Jeff Rawlings, the bass player, adjusted his headphones.

"I thought we could start with this one." Kenny passed out a chord sheet for "Circumstances Of Life." He played the new song for them on his 1958 Martin D28 acoustic.

"Sounds pretty good," Jeff said. "Are the lyrics finished?"

Kenny studied his lyric sheet. "I'm pretty happy with them, but I want to tweak verse two."

"Could you play the bridge again?" P.J. asked. "You kinda lost me after you stayed on the A. I wasn't paying attention."

Kenny played the bridge again.

P.J. shrugged after Kenny finished. "I should have known you'd go there."

Adam played a progression on his keyboard and drew Kenny's attention. "Did you just come up with that?" Kenny repeated the chord progression on his guitar.

"Yeah, I guess so," Adam grinned and played it again. "Hey, I know I'm the new guy here, but I have a question."

Jeff turned his head to look at Adam. "First day on the job, and he's already questioning the way we work."

"No, no. It's nothing like that." Adam waved a hand. "It's rather petty, but I've never heard you guys call P.J. by his real name. I know it's Paul, but where does the 'J' come from?"

"You want to tell him?" Kenny asked P.J.

"My middle name is Jethro which was my grandfather's name. Mom only agreed to name me that if we never told anyone. I've been called P.J. my whole life."

Adam looked at the other guys. "You're serious?"

The guys kept a straight face for as long as they could.

"Naw! It's James, but I like to tell the Jethro thing to reporters," P.J. explained. "Paul James Joseph."

The guys worked until five.

11

"Not bad," Kenny said. "We've got two demos ready. If we keep up this pace, we should be finished in a couple of weeks."

"Yeah!" Jeff put his bass guitars away. "Then we can spend the next two years doing the actual recording."

Kenny waited until the other guys left and then headed upstairs. "Where are my babies?" he hollered as he searched the first floor. He walked into the kitchen and saw a note on the island.

"Kenny, I took the kids to see Father James. We're going to eat dinner with him."

"Hmmmph! She didn't even sign the note." Kenny flipped the note into the air. "I guess I'll grab something at Darby's since I'll be spending another night in the carriage house."

On Thursday afternoon as the guys were taking a break, Jeremy Lenhart dropped by for a visit.

"How are the demos going?" Jeremy asked as he glanced at Adam. "The new guy working out?"

"He's learning. Yesterday he discovered the black keys," Jeff teased.

Jeremy stared at Adam.

Kenny laughed. "He meant the band. The Black Keys."

They chatted for a time, and then Jeremy mentioned, "Did you guys see the new owners of The Center are shutting it down?"

"No! Really?" Jeff said. "They just bought it a couple of years ago. Why are they closing?"

"According to what I saw online, it's because they couldn't get a liquor license from the city. They claim attendance has fallen off, and they can't make a profit."

"That's always the bottom line. No one wants to lose money on a business," Dave said.

"They'll probably sell the place. That's a shame." P.J. plopped down on the leather couch. "I know Kenny and his partners put a ton of money into rehabbing that old warehouse."

Kenny looked at Jeff and Jeremy. "Yeah, maybe you guys can buy it for a song one of these days."

Later that night, Kenny sat in the carriage house eating a pepperoni pizza from Kerry Lynn's and flipping channels on the

TV when he came across the Bears playing the Packers. *I bet Em's watching this.* He fell asleep late in the fourth quarter and didn't see the Bears lose by thirteen points.

"Let's call it a week." Jeff set his bass in a stand. "It's three thirty, and we've already got nine demos done. We're stuck on this one, so let's come back to it on Monday. Maybe over the weekend something will click."

Kenny stood up and placed his Gibson ES-5 Switchmaster in a travel case. "I agree. I'm getting cranky. I haven't seen the kids for more than a few minutes all week."

"How about Emmy?" Dave did a drum roll and then smacked a crash cymbal.

Kenny glared at him.

P.J. stepped between Kenny and the drum kit. "I wouldn't mind cutting out early today." P.J. often acted as a peacemaker in the group. Because of his size, the other guys didn't challenge him.

"Okay, let's pick it up on Monday at nine," Jeff suggested.

"How about ten?" Dave asked. "I have to take my car in for an oil change."

"I'll be here early," Kenny stated. "I want to work on a couple of guitar parts."

"I vote for ten," Adam voiced his opinion.

Will Consoli listened to the guys. "I've worked in the studio with some other bands, and you guys have always gotten along better than any of them. I hope that's not going to change."

Kenny glanced at Dave.

Dave let his shoulders slump. "My bad, Kenny. I'm sorry."

"It's all right. We're just going through a rough patch. We'll make it through."

The guys headed out. Kenny walked over to the stairs. He paused. *Should I go up, or go back to the carriage house?*

Just then he heard the crash of what sounded like pots and pans. He grinned as he heard someone swear loudly. He sprinted up the stairs, into the kitchen and nearly collided with Emmy.

"Sorry, if I ruined your recording. I was trying to hang these up and they fell. They knocked over those glasses." She pointed. "Be careful. There's glass everywhere."

"You didn't ruin anything. We finished early." Kenny stepped toward her but stopped a couple of feet away. "Are you okay. You didn't get hurt, did you?"

"No! That pan hit me on the head." She rubbed the spot.

"Should I check to see if you're bleeding?" he asked.

She bit her lip and after a few seconds, she nodded. "I don't think I am, but you can look."

He moved close and put his hands on her hair and checked. "Don't see any blood. You have a hard head."

She put a hand to his chest and pushed him away as she backed up.

"Sorry." He held his hands up in surrender. "I didn't mean it like that."

She glanced at the clock on the microwave. "I need to get the kids."

"I could do that if you want."

"No, I need to stop at Mom's."

"I miss them," Kenny said softly.

"I know you do, and they miss you, too. Tomorrow I'm meeting Father James for lunch. If you're not busy, would you mind watching them for the afternoon?"

"I don't have any plans. What time should I be here?"

"Noon. You could fix them lunch."

"Deal." He took a step toward her. "Could I have a hug?"

She looked up at his eyes. *I miss you just as much as you miss me, you know. I'm not going to give in to you because that won't solve our problems.* "Maybe tomorrow. I have to run." She grabbed her purse and keys, dashed out of the kitchen, through the mudroom and into the garage. "You shouldn't be here when I get back," she yelled as she opened the door to the Honda Odyssey.

He followed, stood in the doorway and watched as she got into the minivan and backed out. She straightened out the big Odyssey and gunned it down the driveway. He shook his head as he hit the button to close the garage door. *I should check the pantry and fridge to see what I can make for lunch tomorrow.*

14

Chapter Two

Kenny arrived at the house exactly at noon and walked into the kitchen through the mudroom. "I'm here. Where is everyone?"

"Daddy! Daddy!" Isabella screamed. "I miss you." She sprinted into the kitchen and held up her arms.

Kenny scooped her up and held her tightly to his chest as he smothered her with kisses. "How's my little angel?"

Heather and Kevin ran into the kitchen and wrapped their arms around his legs.

"Careful! You might trip him," Emmy said. She walked around the other side of the island and grabbed her purse and the keys to her BMW X3. "I won't be back until dinner. You can stay all afternoon."

Kenny smiled. "Thanks, Emmy. Tell your brother hi for me."

"I will." *Should I ask for kisses and hugs from the kids, or should I just leave?* She watched the kids with their father and quietly left the house.

"What do you guys want for lunch?" Kenny asked after hugging Heather and Kevin.

"Hot dogs!" Kevin shouted.

Isabella put a finger to her mouth and thought about it. "Sandwiches and maybe some soup."

"No way," Heather hollered. "Pizza! Make us a pizza."

He spoiled the kids by making everything they wanted.

Emmy pulled into the lot at Darby's Dogs and sat in the SUV for a moment. *Oh, Kenny, I can still remember the first time I came here with you. I think I was eight. You bought me a hot dog and some root beer.* She remembered working for Mr. Darby when she turned sixteen. *I hope you're enjoying your retirement in Florida, Mr. Darby. You deserve it.* She closed her eyes and didn't see Father James pull into the lot, park his battered 1998 Honda Civic and walk over to her BMW.

He tapped on the window. "Are you coming in?"

She jumped. "Holy... Jeez, James, you scared the crap out of me." She motioned for him to step back and when he did, she

15

opened the door and jumped out. "I was daydreaming about this place." She poked his arm. "You really did scare me."

"That was not my intention." He took her arm. "Let's go inside. I have a craving for a chili cheese dog and fries."

"Are you buying?" Emmy looked up at her half-brother. *I will never get over how much you look like Daddy.*

"You do realize I have taken a vow of poverty, child." He put his hands together like he was getting ready to pray.

"Oh, cut the crap. You have money." Emmy put a finger to her mouth. "Please?" she asked childishly.

He shook his head. "I bet you've used that look to get whatever you want ever since you were old enough to realize how well it worked. Fine! I'll buy today. You are such a spoiled little sister. You need to say three Hail Marys."

She giggled and then held tightly onto his arm. "You're wearing jeans and a regular shirt. How come?"

"Ssssh!" He put a finger to his mouth. "I'm undercover. I've been told there are lapsed Catholics using this place to feed their vices."

"Not me! I don't have any vices."

"That will cost you a dozen Hail Marys." He held the door open for her.

"Yes, Father James," she said as she grinned.

She waved to Danny Darby as they waited in line. "Did I ever tell you I used to work here?"

"You did mention that. It's a miracle the place is still open."

"Oh, shush."

"And what can I get for you today, Father James?" Danny asked with a grin.

"Bless you, Danny. I crave a chili cheese dog, fries and one of your best root beers."

Emmy stood directly in front of Father James with her arms crossed over her chest and a scowl on her face. "How about me? Am I invisible?"

Father James laughed. "Please put whatever this child desires on my tab."

"Oh, hi, Emmy. I didn't see you," Danny teased.

16

"I would like... maybe..." She read the menu though she knew it by heart. "Oh, just get me the same as my brother." She made a face at Danny.

He rang up the order and took the twenty Father James handed him.

"I'll grab a place in the back," Emmy looked around the crowded restaurant. "Over there!" She pointed and hurried to claim the booth.

"I'll bring your order out in a jiffy." Danny handed Father James his change. The same twenty dollar bill.

"You won't make any money like that."

"Dad told me to never take money from her even though she's rich enough to buy this place a thousand times over. Have a great day."

"Bless you, Danny."

The food arrived within a couple of minutes; delivered by a young teenage girl named Malinda.

Emmy smiled. "Please thank your father for me. I know he won't take our money. How's your grandfather doing?"

Malinda sighed. "I don't know how he can stand the heat, but he loves it down there. I spent most of the summer with him."

"Tell him I said hi."

"I will. Enjoy your lunch." Malinda grabbed the empty trays from the waste bin on her way back to the front counter.

"Should I ask for the blessing, or do you want to pray?" Father James asked. "You do still pray sometimes, right?"

"Are you gonna get on my case, too?" She rolled her eyes. "Can we wait until after lunch before you lecture me?"

"I will wait, but only because this chili cheese dog smells so delicious. You can not find one like this in Kansas."

Emmy took her time eating because she knew once she finished Father James would want to grill her about Kenny. Father James waited patiently after finishing his meal. He even refilled their root beers. Eventually, his patience grew thin, and he grabbed the last three fries.

"Hey! Those were mine," Emmy complained.

"They were cold," he stated sternly. "Now, do we talk here,

17

or would you rather go to St. John's?"

"Could we sit outside?"

"We can do that. It is a pleasant enough day." *I know you're stalling, Emmy.*

She waved to Danny and Malinda as she and Father James headed outside to one of the freshly-painted red picnic tables.

"Okay, now confess."

"Is this covered under priest-parishioner confidentiality?" Emmy asked.

"If you're going to be such a smart-ass, I will leave you here."

"I have my car."

"I meant I will leave without talking to you."

"I'll be good."

"You did call me, remember?"

"Yes, I know. I didn't want to talk to Pastor Tyler or Liz, or anyone at my church." Emmy felt a refreshing breeze on her face. "I know they would keep everything I say in strict confidence, but I would feel guilty. I would be embarrassed knowing they knew everything. They're friends and knowing they knew all my dirty secrets would bother me."

Father James sat with his hands on the table and listened.

"Just so you know, I haven't been fooling around with anyone."

Father James nodded.

"Not in the strictest sense."

"Go on."

"I think this all started when Rory Porter spent a week on tour with me. We didn't do anything. He never even kissed me, but Krissy assumed something was going on." She waved her hands for emphasis. "She told Kenny about Rory being there, so he got upset. I swear we didn't do anything. The only thing I might be guilty of is enjoying his company more than I should."

"You mentioned that."

"Sometimes I feel I missed out on things because I didn't really have many boyfriends when I was younger. I met Kenny when I was seven!" She paused to catch her breath. "There was

18

Tony and Derrick, but I was never serious with them. Shoot! I didn't even sleep with Kenny until we were married. God knows how hard that was."

Father James lifted his eyes but didn't speak.

"Is it okay to talk to you about sex stuff?"

"Yes, it is permissible."

"We did some stuff, but not... you know." She continued to wave her hands as she spoke. "He can't make the same claim. I told you about Becky, right?" She continued without waiting for an answer. "She's really nice and we're kinda friends, but he still slept with her. I know that shouldn't matter, but in a way it does. Not that I want to go out and have an affair, but it bothers me at times."

They both turned as a squad car sped past with lights blazing and the siren blasting.

"Do you still love him?"

"Of course I do! How can you even ask? I love my family..."

"That's not what I asked. I know you love your children. Do you still love Kenny as much as you did before?"

She bit her lip. Father James patted her hand as he noticed a tear careening down her cheek.

"I'm not sure. I love him, and I can't imagine being with anyone else." She looked down at her lap.

"What about Rory? I know you have feelings for him."

"I've known him almost as long as Kenny."

"From what I know about him, I would say you were somewhat attracted to him because of his... shall I say... bad reputation. Is that true?"

"Fine! I admit I had a thing for the 'bad boys' at one time. Especially him." She waved her hands faster. "But Rory wasn't just a wild guy that I lusted after. Sorry, but I did have strong feelings about certain guys. I'm human. He was a friend. He protected me at times. Maybe from myself as much as the unsavory characters I was hanging around. Then he disappeared from my life for a dozen years."

"And you resented that?"

"Yeah! I did!" More tears fell. "I don't now, but I did when

19

I was younger."

"Do you ever picture yourself in a relationship with him?"

"Are you asking if I would ever sleep with him?"

"No, I'm asking about a real relationship. A committed relationship between two adults. I'm not talking about casual sex."

"I might have a long time ago, but not anymore. Maybe I was fortunate he disappeared when he did. If he hadn't, then I probably would have slept with him. I was really lonely the year Kenny was on tour. I do care for him, and I really like having him around, but just as a friend. You know he and Diane were together for a while, right?"

"No, I wasn't aware of that."

"He had the hots for her back in high school, but she didn't feel the same." Emmy made a face. "I probably shouldn't have mentioned that, huh?"

"Is it relevant to your situation now?"

She looked up at two birds doing aerial acrobatics. "Probably not. It was a long time ago."

"Let's get back to you and Kenny."

"Do you think I should let him come home?"

Father James blinked twice but then appeared as calm as before. "Where has he been?"

"He's been staying at the carriage house."

Father James shook his head. "Whose decision was that?"

"His. I didn't kick him out of the house or anything. When he got back from tour, he started staying there."

"Would you let him come home?"

"Yes. I do miss him. I get lonely at night."

"Emmy!"

"For more than that. He's my best friend, and I miss him being around."

"As far as I can tell, nothing has happened that wouldn't be overcome with a little communication. You still love each other, and you have three wonderful children who need their mother and father."

"I'm being a stinker, huh?"

Father James laughed. "I do regret not knowing you all

20

your life. You are a breath of fresh air in a world of pollution."

"That sounds weird."

"So I'm not a great orator like some people. I'm just a simple priest trying to do whatever God commands."

"Oh, don't go all holy on me, Jimmy," she said and then giggled.

"That's Father James to you, young lady, and next time you will have to pay my regular counseling fees."

"Which are?"

"You have to buy the chili dogs and fries."

"Not the root beer?"

"That goes without saying."

Emmy walked over to the soccer fields with Mary Michaelis after school on Monday.

"Can you believe how many kids are in the program?" Mary looked out over the soccer fields in back of the educational building of Crest Ridge United Nazarene.

"I heard they had to limit the registration to 500," Emmy said as she looked for Heather and Isabella.

"The church and school are growing so fast. The junior high enrollment is above expectations."

"Do you think the church will add a high school soon?" Emmy asked. She waved as she spotted Heather and Isabella.

"I'm can't say for sure, but I doubt it."

Emmy sighed, "Too bad. I can't see sending the girls to Roosevelt High where I went. It's full of drugs and stuff."

"Em, the girls are in first grade. You have a few years to decide what to do."

Sloane Bertucci walked up and stood next to Emmy.

"Hey, Sloane, are you here to watch Peter and Dotty?" Emmy asked.

"I am. I left the babies with Mama." Sloane put a hand to her forehead to shield her eyes from the sun. "Which field are the older kids using?"

"The one on the end. Why didn't Tony come to watch? The Bears don't normally practice on Mondays."

21

"He had to run up to Halas Hall today. I guess the coach was upset because they lost to the Packers."

"Sloane, is it true you took a position teaching math starting in January?" Mary asked.

"I did accept a position, but I won't start until next August. I want a little more time to stay home with Coby and Taylor."

"Taylor Beckett will be old enough to start pre-K next year, right?" Emmy asked.

"Yes. Coby will be the only one not in school. Mama will be able to handle him by herself. I see my kids. Talk to you later." Sloane waved at Emmy and Mary and headed for the field to watch her kids.

"I shouldn't say this, but Sloane's a lot heavier than when she and Tony got married," Emmy whispered.

"She's a lot bigger than you or I to begin with and having four babies sometimes does that to a woman. Ma used to be as skinny as me when she and Da got married."

"You won't tell Sloane I said that, will you?"

"Don't be silly."

"Do you remember when all this used to be a cornfield?" Emmy waved at the church property. "Look at it now."

"Of course I remember. There used to be another house over there next to Liz and Pastor Tyler's place. Jonah said the church might buy more land."

"Speaking of Jonah." Emmy grinned.

"We are still dating, but it's casual. We're good friends."

"Uh-huh," Emmy teased.

"Shush!" Mary poked Emmy in the side. "Let's go watch the girls play."

Chapter Three

Emmy checked her email on Sunday morning while the kids ate breakfast. She deleted the junk and then opened a message from Pastor Tyler. *I suppose I should check the order of service for today.* She read the list of songs contained in the outline. "Kevin Michael! Do not play with your oatmeal, and do not throw it at your sisters."

"It's yucky. I hate oatmeal." Kevin dropped his spoon on the table in the breakfast nook and pushed his bowl away.

"Eat it, or go hungry." Emmy continued to scan the schedule. "Shoot! I forgot about the baptism service."

Kevin grabbed his bowl of oatmeal and took another spoonful.

"What's a 'bat-tism' service, Mommy?" Isabella asked.

"Baptism. After people accept Jesus into their life, they get baptized."

Heather and Isabella stared at her with blank expressions.

"Have you ever seen that big thing at the back of the platform?"

"You mean the big bathtub?" Heather asked.

Kevin took aim at Isabella with his oatmeal.

"Yes, except it's not a bathtub. Today it will be filled with water and Pastor Tyler will stand in it..."

"Won't he get his suit all wet?" Isabella frowned at Kevin, who dropped the spoonful of oatmeal back into the bowl.

"He will change clothes. He will meet people in the... bathtub... and tip them back and under the water. That's called being baptized."

"Do they get to swim in the bathtub?" Kevin was now intrigued.

"They don't go swimming."

"Do they drown?"

"No, they hold their nose like this," Emmy demonstrated. "And they hold their breath until they come back up."

"Can they see when they're under the water?" Heather asked. "I can see underwater when I go swimming."

"Do they wear goggles and floaties?" Kevin wanted more information.

"No, now finish your breakfast. I need to text Pastor Tyler."

She pulled her phone out of her purse and sent a text. "Is it too late to be added to the list of people getting baptized?"

A minute later, he responded. "We can always add more people. Are you thinking about the girls?"

"No, me. I just realized I've never been baptized other than in the Catholic church when I was a baby."

"Would you like to be baptized?"

"Yes!"

"Do you want to record a testimony?"

Emmy recalled that in previous baptism ceremonies, people would record a short video about their conversions.

"Could I do that after Sunday School?" she texted.

"Ask Chase to take care of it."

"Thanks, Pastor Tyler. See you later." She tossed her phone back into her purse. "Finish your breakfast and wash your hands. I'll be right back." Emmy ran out of the kitchen, dashed up the stairs and into her bedroom closet. She threw open the dresser draw containing shorts and t-shirts. *I will need dry underwear, too.* She stuffed her clothes in a backpack and then rushed downstairs.

"Are you going to go swimming in the big bathtub, Mommy?" Kevin held up his hands for inspection.

Emmy used the back of her hand to wipe some oatmeal from his chin. "Yes, but it's not... Oh, never mind."

"Will we get to watch?" Heather asked.

"Don't we have to go to church with Pastor Jeremiah and Mia?" Isabella joined everyone after using the bathroom.

"This will be at the end of the service, and all the kids can come back to watch."

"Will you drown if Pastor Tyler drops you?" Heather asked.

"No, but he won't drop me. We need to get going. Everyone out to the car." She watched as the kids raced out through the mudroom and into the garage.

"Will Daddy meet us there?" Isabella asked as she helped Kevin climb into his car seat.

"He should be there." Emmy pressed the button to open the garage door.

"He can watch you go swimming in the big bathtub," Kevin said and then laughed.

Emmy pulled into the line of cars dropping off people at the side entrance. *Timed that right. The first service must be over.* She edged forward and stopped. "You can get out now and go inside."

"We know the drill, Mommy." Heather rolled her eyes. "It's like going to school."

"We know where to go," Isabella said.

"Keep an eye on your brother, okay?"

"I will make sure he goes to the right class."

"Thank you, Isa." Emmy waved to the volunteers who made sure the kids made it inside the building safely. She parked in the back of the building and hurried inside. She dashed into the music suite and nearly bumped into Chase Hillman.

"Whoa! Slow down, Emmy." Chase reached out to stop her.

"I'm getting baptized today, and I need you to do one of those video testimony things for me. Pastor Tyler said you could." She paused and looked up at him. "Do we have time now, or should we wait until after Sunday School?"

"It would be better to do it now, Emmy." Chase checked the time. "Give me ten minutes, and I'll meet you in the production room."

Chase met her a few minutes later. "Sit right there and smile for the camera."

She sat down in front of a blue screen. "What am I supposed to say?"

"We're rolling, Emmy. You can start wherever you like," Chase said and then chuckled. *This should be interesting.*

"Should I start when I was a kid?"

"If you like."

She put a finger to her mouth and gathered her thoughts.

25

"Okay, I'm ready. You can edit this, right?"

"If I have time."

She waved to the camera. "Hi, my name is Emmy Colasanti-Colwell, and I was born in SoHam. Do I have to say when?"

"That is not necessary." Chase shook his head.

"I went to St. John's as a kid, but we stopped going there when I was twelve, I think. Later, I would go to Faith Bible with my husband Kenny. He wasn't my husband yet. He plays guitars." Emmy waved her hands around as she explained some details. "So I would sing with him, and I even came to this church for a while in the summer before my senior year at Roosevelt High."

Chase checked the time again.

"Years later, I was having boyfriend trouble, and Mama Bertucci told me to pray about it. I read my Bible, and one night I got on my knees beside my bed and I prayed for forgiveness. Then I started coming to church here because of Lynette Jefferson. You remember her and Paul, right?" Emmy waved her hands even as tears filled her eyes. "She helped me a lot when I was a new believer. I don't know how I would have made it through those early years without her. My personal life was a mess. I would go to her all the time and dump my boyfriend troubles on her. She never complained." Emmy saw Chase pointing at his watch. "I'll hurry! I started singing with the worship band. Got married along the way. Had three kids." She started talking faster. "I still consider singing here my top priority, but I do go on tours. I have been very blessed and thank God every day for my family and my church family." She bit her lip trying to stop the flow of tears, but it didn't work. "This morning I realized I had never been baptized, so here I am. Is that enough, Chase?"

"I think we can go with this, Emmy." He turned off the recorder.

"I'm sorry if I ruined it. You know how I get emotional at times."

He wiped her tears with a tissue. "I think everyone will enjoy your testimony, Em."

Pastor Tyler ended the second service with a prayer before

26

announcing, "I hope most of you can stay because we have twenty people who are going to be baptized. Wait! Make that twenty-one." He looked over his shoulder at Emmy. "One more person texted me this morning and asked to be added to the list. Please give us ten minutes to get ready. Visit with friends. Have a cup of coffee. Whatever. But be back in the sanctuary in ten minutes."

Pastor Darren Eaton walked to the middle of the platform. "Before Pastor Tyler actually baptizes everyone, we have a video to play. Everyone has been gracious enough to share a little of their story, so let's watch these testimonies while everyone gets ready." He pointed to the tech booth and the video testimonies began. Most were only a minute or two long. Others were slightly longer. Emmy's appeared last.

Tony Bertucci, able to be in church because the Chicago Bears had played on Thursday, poked his cousin Kristen Randolph in the side. "Did you know she was getting baptized today?"

"She never mentioned it to me." She glanced to her right and saw Kenny sitting in the front row with the kids. "He never said anything either."

Sloane Bertucci held almost-two-year-old Coby on her lap and kept an eye on the other five children. "Maybe she was the late addition Tyler mentioned."

"Could be," Tony said and then laughed. "Mama will be sorry she missed it."

"Mom, can Dotty and I go sit with Heather and Isa?" Noemi Claire Bertucci pointed to the front row.

"If you promise to behave, you may," Sloane said. "Taylor Beckett! Sit still and stop getting out of your seat."

He held up a toy firetruck. "I dropped it and had to find it."

Tony glanced at his second youngest child and smiled. "He sure loves his firetrucks."

Emmy joined the six other women, most of whom had already changed clothes, in the large restroom near the music suite.

"Emmy, why are you here?" Mrs. Abraham wrapped her heavy arms around Emmy and smothered her to her ample bosom.

"I need to be baptized."

"I'm getting baptized, too." Mrs. Abraham lifted Emmy off

27

of the floor. "Gracious, child! Have you never been baptized before?"

"Never." Emmy extricated herself. "I need to change clothes. Please excuse me."

Liz Hammond strolled in carrying Zhy, their two-year-old foster child. "Is everyone ready? Tyler and the guys are getting into position."

Emmy rushed out of her stall, threw her backpack in the direction of the vanity, and hopped on one foot. "Do I need shoes?" She hopped to a chair and managed to sit before falling over.

"Good shoes might get ruined. Did you bring swim shoes or flip-flops? Liz asked as the other ladies chuckled.

"I brought some old tennis shoes," Emmy replied.

"Those will work," Liz said.

"Let's show all of these people our appreciation," Pastor Eaton said.

The congregation clapped as Pastor Tyler walked down the steps into the baptistry.

Pastor Darren walked over to the front of the baptistry. "Are you ready, Tyler?"

"Ready as I'll ever be with this many people to baptize."

"Is the water cold?" Darren asked.

"Nice and warm since Bill fixed the pump."

Pastor Eaton moved to the side so he wouldn't block anyone's vision though the image was projected onto the large video screens around the auditorium.

"Ready when you are," Tyler said.

Pastor Darren checked his printout. "We are going to baptize everyone in the order in which they signed up I believe." He glanced up as Tyler corrected him. "My mistake. We are doing the children and teens first."

Pastor Tyler smiled while baptizing six elementary and junior high age kids and then four high school freshmen. "These kids are the future of our church. I love doing this." He watched as the last of the teens moved down the steps. "Wow! How did you ever get so big?" Tyler shook his head as he looked up at all six feet, eight inches and three hundred pounds of Vadim Papadakis. "You might have to help me out a little, Vadim."

"I trust you, Pastor Tyler," Vadim said.

Tyler managed not to drown Vadim, whose face beamed when he stood back up.

"Ten more to go," Darren announced.

Pastor Tyler baptized the next eight without a hitch.

"I don't know if I can fit down the stairs," Bernice Abraham said loud enough for the overhead mic to pick up. "I'm too fat." Her arms jiggled as she laughed heartily.

The crowd laughed with her.

"We will help you get down the steps." The two ladies who had been baptized ahead of Mrs. Abraham helped her negotiate the slippery steps.

She waddled over to the side and smiled at Pastor Tyler. "I weigh over three hundred pounds, Pastor Tyler. You're as skinny as a beanpole. Are you sure you can do this?"

"I've never let anyone drown yet," he replied. Tyler struggled a bit but managed to get Mrs. Abraham upright again.

"Praise the Lord!" She raised her arms over her head and shouted. "Hallelujah! Praise the Lord!" She hugged Pastor Tyler and nearly knocked him over. The same two ladies helped her up the steps.

Pastor Darren smiled as he glanced at the last name on his sheet. "Last, but not least is Emmy Colasanti-Colwell.

"There's Mommy!" Heather shouted.

"Is Mommy going swimming now?" Kevin asked Kenny.

"In a way," he answered.

Tyler held out a hand for Emmy.

"Thanks, Tyler. I should be a piece of cake after Mrs. Abraham."

"Emmy, the mic is on."

She put a hand to her mouth. "Sorry."

"Hi, Mommy!" Kevin shouted.

Emmy waved at the kids and saw Kenny for the first time.

Tyler grinned at her. "This is going to be a real pleasure. Do you remember when you dumped a bucket of cold water on me to raise money for starving children?"

Emmy's eyes sparkled. "Please don't drown me." She bit her lip, took a deep breath and held her nose.

Tyler tilted her back. "Emmy, I baptize you in the name of the Father, the Son and the Holy Spirit." He held her under the water for a fraction longer than the other people. Then he lifted her up.

She coughed out some water and then grinned. "You didn't drown me." She scooted past Tyler and up the steps.

"Mommy didn't stay in the bathtub long," Heather said.

"If we get bat-tised does that mean we don't have to take a bath?" Isabella asked.

"You still need to take baths," Kenny said.

Emmy changed out of her wet clothes and rushed out to find the kids and Kenny.

Tony saw her first. "Hey! There's the drowned brat. Way to go, Em. Tell the whole congregation Mrs. Abraham is fat."

"I did not say that, you creep!"

Tony laughed and tugged on her wet hair.

"Where are the kids?" Emmy looked around.

"I saw Kenny talking to Pastor Darren a minute ago." Tony pointed to the sanctuary. "Here come the kids. Yours and mine."

"Mommy! Mommy! I saw you in the bathtub," Kevin hollered. "Look! I brought my garbage truck to church."

Emmy hugged her kids.

"Was the water cold, Auntie Em?" Peter Bertucci asked.

"No, it was rather pleasant." Emmy watched as Kenny approached. "Tony, would you keep an eye on the kids so I can talk to their father?"

"Sure thing. If you give me the keys, I could take them home." He held out his hand.

"I left them in my backpack in the restroom. Just watch them for a minute."

Kenny and Emmy approached each other cautiously. They stopped with a few feet between them.

"I didn't know if you would be here." Emmy looked down at the carpeting.

30

"Is that why you didn't tell me you were going to be baptized?" Kenny moved close enough to touch her foot with his shoe. "Why are you barefoot?"

"I got my shoes wet."

"Didn't you bring an extra pair?" he grinned.

"Yes, but I left them in the bathroom... never mind. I saw you sitting in the front row. Did you hear the video thing?"

"I did hear it. Everyone loved it, and the kids insisted on sitting in front because they wanted to see you... take a bath... was how Kevin said it."

"They miss you." Emmy bit her lip.

"Do you miss me?" Kenny asked.

Emmy glanced around to make sure no one could hear. "Of course, and not just because I'm..."

"Me, too."

Emmy grinned. "Do you have plans for lunch?"

"Not really. You?"

"The kids want taco salad. I might need some help putting it together. I always forget which ingredient to add first."

"I suppose I could help if you want. Do you have the slotted spoon?" He moved close enough to touch her nose.

She nodded. "I could always send the kids over to Diane's or Uncle Tony's after we eat. Father James told me we need to communicate better."

"It would be a lot easier to communicate if the kids weren't home." He turned around to see Kevin and Benjamin chasing little Grace Randolph through the sanctuary.

"I'll grab the little monsters," Tony said. "Carry on with whatever."

Emmy and Kenny watched as Tony captured Kevin and Grace, but Benjamin eluded him.

"What's going on here, Ben? Is someone after you?" Pastor Tyler scooped him up.

"Papa is chasing me."

"Please hang on to him." Tony carried Kevin and Grace on his shoulders. "He's a slippery little devil."

"How about I return him to the foyer, and you and Sloane

31

can put him on a leash." Tyler hung Ben upside-down over his shoulder and carried him out to his mother and his aunt Kristen. "I found this one in the sanctuary. Does he belong to either one of you?"

"Hi, Mommy. I upside-down."

"Just drop him on his head," Sloane said.

Kenny and Emmy walked out to the foyer as Reed Shafer, the buildings and grounds supervisor, began shutting off the lights.

"I guess that's Reed's way of telling us to go home." Kenny laughed.

Reed chuckled. "You guys can stay as long as you want, but I'm turning off the lights and setting the alarm. You will have to remain motionless until the evening shift comes in to clean." He pointed to a motion sensor.

"Oh, please wait a second, Reed. I need to grab my backpack and shoes." Emmy sprinted to the restroom and returned in a flash. "Thanks, see you on Wednesday."

The Bertuccis, Randolphs and the Colwells headed outside.

"I'll head home and start the taco salad if you can handle the kids," Kenny offered.

Emmy nodded. "Would you stop at the store and pick up some fresh hamburger, please?"

"Sure. Anything else?"

"Actually, could you pick up everything to make the taco salad. I was going to stop, but if you could do that for me, I will greatly appreciate it."

"Geez, Emmy, will you stop flirting with him in the church parking lot and go home." Kristen rolled her eyes.

"I'm not flirting, and he is my husband," Emmy insisted.

"Should I start loading up the kids?" Tony waved goodbye to Kenny.

Sloane counted to make sure she had all six. "Go with your father and don't run in the parking lot."

"Tony, catch!" Emmy threw her keys at him. "I'm parked in the back."

He caught her keys. "Do I look like a valet?"

"There's a tip in it if you bring the car around," Emmy

mentioned. "I drove the BMW."

"Better be at least a twenty." Tony opened the doors to their minivan and loaded up his kids. "Will you help the little ones, Peter?"

"Sure, Papa. If you give me the keys, I can start it up. I know how, and I promise not to drive it around the parking lot again."

Tony stared blankly but tossed Peter the keys. "What did he mean by that?" He asked while walking past Sloane, Kristen, and Emmy.

"He was sitting on my lap, and all he did was steer," Emmy confessed.

Tony shook his head. "Make that a fifty, brat." He muttered under his breath as he walked to the back of the building.

Kristen and Sloane glared at Emmy.

"What?" Emmy shrugged. "The lot was empty... for the most part."

"I'll talk to you later." Kristen held onto Zachary's and Grace's hands as they walked to her Acura RDX.

Emmy made sure Kevin, Heather and Isabella were close but not close enough to overhear. "Sloane, could I ask for a teensy, tiny favor?" She held her fingers close together.

"We can watch the kids if you need some quality time with Kenny," Sloane said. "You should make Sofia work on Sundays."

"She does work most Sundays, but she had stuff to do today, and it's not for that!" Emmy put her hands on her hips. "Never mind. I'll see if Diane and Brady are busy."

Sloane looked down at Emmy. "I'm sorry. Do you and Kenny need time to talk? I can help if you do."

"Does everyone in SoHam know we're going through a difficult period?" Emmy asked.

"Not everyone in SoHam, but everyone in Bristol Ridge does." Sloane put an arm around Emmy's shoulders. "We will watch the kids. I think Tony and John are going to see if Andy Walker wants to come over and watch football."

"Don't they ever get tired of football?" Emmy glared as Tony squealed the tires coming around the corner of the building.

You better not scratch my car. "I might not have time to watch the games this afternoon."

"John seems to have adjusted to life away from football," Sloane said. "Kristen said he's even busier now than when he was playing for the Bears."

Tony slowed down and stopped in front of Emmy and Sloane. He jumped out and grinned. "Here is you car. Do I get my tip now?" He held out a hand.

"I should give you a ticket for reckless driving and speeding." Emmy slapped his hand and then punched his side. "Come on, kids. We need to get home."

Tony put his arm around Sloane's waist as they walked to their minivan. "Do you think we could afford a new car?"

"We don't need another vehicle." Sloane moved his arm away.

"I know we don't need one, but it would be nice to have something with a little pep to it." Tony watched over his shoulder as Emmy quickly accelerated out of the parking lot.

Sloane took a deep breath, held it for a seconds seconds and then exhaled loudly. "You can buy whatever you want, but don't start whining if you get a speeding ticket."

"She drives like a maniac and never gets pulled over." He pointed to Emmy's BMW as it disappeared from sight.

"Are you aware that most SoHam police officers are male?"

"I suppose so."

Sloane shook her head. "She's a lot cuter than you. Get it?"

"That's not fair."

"Get over it, big guy." Sloane opened the driver's door and slipped in. "I'm driving so you don't turn our minivan into a hot rod."

Emmy arrived home before Kenny. "You can play upstairs until the taco salad is ready. I need to shower and change clothes."

"Why, Mommy? You took a bath at church with Pastor Tyler."

"I did not take a bath, young man. I got baptized. There is a difference. Now run upstairs and play until I call you."

34

"Do you need me to help?" Isabella asked. "I can do something."

"Thank you, sweetie, but your father will help once he gets home."

"Is Daddy gonna spend the night? Is he through living at the old house?" Heather opened the fridge and searched for a treat. "I'm starving! Can I have some cheese?"

"You can each have a cheese stick, but only one and that's all." Emmy helped Kevin open his and then followed them upstairs.

She was out of the shower and dressed when she heard Kenny in the kitchen. She dashed down the stairs, but then walked slowly into the kitchen.

"Sorry it took so long. Sainsbury's was packed." He set everything on the granite-topped island and then looked at Emmy. "Did you take a shower? Your hair is wet."

"I needed one."

He grinned and asked, "Even after your bath?"

"You and Kevin are such funny guys." She stuck out her tongue. "Will you help with the taco salad?"

"Yes, m'lady, I will."

She smiled.

An hour later, everyone had finished their lunch.

"Who wants to go for a walk?" Kenny raised a hand.

"I do," Kevin answered. "Can I bring some police cars?"

"Only three." Emmy put the dirty dishes in the dishwasher and then shook her head. "We ate all the taco salad. We'll have to start making a double batch."

"Would you like to go for a walk?" Kenny smiled at Heather and Isabella.

"No thanks, Daddy. Heather and I are going to have a tea party."

Kenny looked at Emmy for help.

"Maybe we can all walk over to see Mama Bertucci. You can have a tea party with Dotty and Noemi," Emmy suggested.

"Do you and Daddy want to kiss? Is that why we have to play with Dotty and Noemi?" Heather asked.

35

How old are you girls now? "Your father and I need some time to talk to each other," Emmy explained.

"It's okay if you kiss Daddy." Isabella carried her empty dish to the dishwasher. "Married people are supposed to kiss each other. I might kiss a boy when I get really old like you guys."

Kenny shrugged but then grinned. "Who's ready for that walk."

"Yeah! Take that!" Andy Walker pointed at the TV as Calais Grove from the Arizona Cardinals flattened Tom Brady. "Awesome!"

"I hate to interrupt your game." Sloane stood in the extra wide doorway to the family room. "Emmy just texted. They're on their way."

"Is Kenny going to watch the game here?" Tony asked.

"No, we're watching the kids so they can talk."

"Talk?"

"Yes, and don't you dare tease her about it," Sloane warned.

"Me?" Tony put a finger to his chest. "I would never. What about them?" He pointed at John and Andy.

"Behave if you want to live." Sloane shook her head and walked back through the kitchen. She opened the door into the garage and pushed a button to open one of the overhead garage doors.

"Did I hear you say something about watching Emmy's kids?" Mama finished drying a skillet and set it on the counter.

"Just for a couple of hours."

"Good! I haven't seen my grandbabies all week."

"Mama, you know they're not your grandkids, right?" Sloane asked.

"Honey, all the kids who live in Bristol Ridge are my grandbabies whether they are or not," Mama said and braced herself as Heather and Isabella bounded into the kitchen.

Heather raced toward Mama and wrapped her arms around a leg. "We're here to have a tea party with Dotty and Noemi because Mommy wants to kiss Daddy," Heather announced. "Will you join us for tea, Mama?"

36

"I would love to have tea with you young ladies. Should we go upstairs and find Dotty and Noemi?"

"Yes, please," Isabella said as she took Mama's hand.

Kenny and Emmy walked into the kitchen with Kevin, who promptly took off to find Ben. Emmy stopped by the island. Kenny moved close behind her and put his hands on her shoulders while he glanced at the freshly baked cookies on the countertop.

"Thank you so much for watching them. We really appreciate it, Sloane."

"It's all right. I'm sorry for being a bit snippy earlier. How long will you need?" Sloane asked. "Help yourself to a cookie."

Emmy blushed. Kenny grinned. Sloane laughed.

"We're just going to talk," Emmy finally said.

Kenny held up a hand and raised his fingers. "Two hours. Three at the most."

"Take all the time you need. We will be fine. The girls are having tea, and the boys will keep busy."

Emmy heard a commotion from the family room. "What about the bigger boys? Who's watching them?"

Sloane rolled her eyes. "They're watching football. They're on their own. I'm going to get the younger ones down for a nap and then, hopefully, take one myself."

"We'll come back to fetch ours later," Kenny said.

Kenny and Emmy strolled down the driveway from Tony and Sloane's house. Their hands brushed against each other a few times. They waited for a car to pass before crossing the street. Kenny brushed a hand against Emmy's and this time she held onto it.

Just like the first day of high school, Em. Kenny squeezed her hand and they crossed the wide street and walked through the open gate of their driveway. They ambled slowly up the long, winding drive. Emmy listened to some unseen birds singing to each other. Kenny watched the leaves rustling in the fall breeze.

He pointed up. "Some of the leaves are turning already."

"Do we need to rake them up?"

"Not really. I want to keep this part of the property more natural."

She grinned. "Kevin likes to play in the woods with Ben and Caden. He told me they built a huge fort last week."

"Sometimes the older boys play, and they even let the girls join in."

"I love my house, but I would even live in the guesthouse if we needed to."

"We would have to find another place for the band's office," Kenny said.

"Right. I forgot about that. How's Jana doing? Is she seeing anyone special?" *She's such a pretty young lady. I'm sure she has her pick of men.*

"I don't know, Em. I don't pry into her private life." He stared in the direction of the ranch house he and Emmy had occupied while the main house was built.

They came around the final bend in the driveway and kept going to the back of the two-story, brick and stone dream house. Emmy glanced at the swing set complete with a slide and tree house.

"We could sit on the deck and talk, Em. It's such a pleasant day."

"Okay. I love the fall better than any other season."

"Me, too, I think."

She pointed and said, "Let's sit at the picnic table."

They sat on opposite sides of one of the numerous picnic tables scattered around the property.

"Thirsty?" Kenny asked.

"No, you?" Emmy replied.

"Hungry?" he asked a moment later.

"Not really."

They listened to the sounds of the woods for a moment.

"Recording going all right?" Emmy asked.

"Better than normal."

"The girls are enjoying school."

"They're growing up so fast."

Emmy glanced at Kenny but turned away when he looked at her. For several minutes they avoided looking at each other.

"Are we going to talk about it?" Kenny asked.

"We should."

"I like Rory..."

"Nothing happened!"

"I know."

"I like him, too. He's a good friend."

"Yes, he is."

"You and Jana?"

"Friends, Em."

"Good friends?"

"As good as possible considering I'm kinda her boss."

"She's pretty."

"You're prettier."

She bit her lip. "You still think I'm pretty?"

"The prettiest girl in the world, m'lady."

"You are such a dork!" She climbed onto the table, scooted to the edge and held out her arms.

He stood up and squeezed her.

"I can't breath," she whispered.

"I'm going to fall over if I let go."

She released her grip on him. "Maybe we should go inside?" She put a finger to her mouth.

Kenny sat down and pulled her onto the bench beside him. "Will that solve our problems?"

"It will solve one of them," she said and then giggled.

"You are so bad."

"We have to make a point of communicating better."

"Because Father James said so, huh?"

"He is pretty smart."

They stood up and held hands while walking into the house. He stopped at the bottom of the stairs.

"Have you changed your mind, Kenny?"

Not at all." He picked her up and carried her up the wide staircase. He used a foot to open the door into their bedroom. "I think I've done this before."

She giggled again. "We've done it many times."

"I meant I've carried you across the threshold before, m'lady."

"Yes, I remember now. You are such a dork at times, but I wouldn't change that for all the tea in China."

"Or the coffee in Columbia?" He carried her to the bed and tenderly set her down.

"Dork!" She reached up and pulled him close. "Shut up and kiss me."

Three hours later, the landline rang. Emmy picked up the extension from the nightstand.

"Do you want your kids back? Is it safe to bring them home?" Tony asked.

"Give us ten minutes."

Tony laughed. "You've already had three hours to talk, brat."

"Creep! Ten minutes." She pressed the button to end the call as hard as she could.

"I suppose we need to get up, huh?" Kenny grinned.

"Yup, the honeymoon's over. For now."

Chapter Four

"We aren't supposed to have a fire drill today, are we?" Liz Hammond looked at Emmy who was helping out at the school for the morning.

"Not that I know of. Should we treat this as a real emergency?"

"Yes, we're supposed to," Liz said. "All right, children. Let's line up in a straight line and march outside."

"Mommy, what's that noise?" Heather stood next to Emmy with her hands over her ears like many of the other children.

"It's the fire alarm. I want you to hold Isa's hand and line up to march outside." Emmy checked to make sure Zachary, Caden and Noemi lined up.

"All right, kids. Follow me! We're going outside." Liz smiled for the children and then nodded at Emmy. They marched the children outside to their designated spot in the yard.

"Okay, now I want everyone to sit on the grass in as small of a circle as you can. We're going to play a game." Liz and Emmy grouped the first graders in a circle. Liz counted to make sure all sixteen children were present. "They're all here, Emmy. Would you go over there and talk to Tyler. Maybe he knows what's happening."

"Okay, Liz. I'll be back as soon as I can."

Emmy hurried to where Pastor Tyler, Reed Shafer and several other adults waited near the east entrance to the education building. She stood beside one of the other volunteers.

"Hi, Emmy."

"Do you know anything?" Emmy couldn't recall the lady's name.

"I heard Mr. Shafer mention a small grease fire in the kitchen," she answered.

"Oh, no! Was anyone hurt?"

She shrugged. "I can't say for sure, but I heard one of the cooks might have suffered a slight burn to her hand."

"That's terrible. Burns can really hurt," Emmy said.

"The fire department is on their way, but the fire is already

41

out. Here they are now." She pointed to Canton Lane.

Emmy watched two SoHam squad cars and two units from Fire Station 5 pull onto the road leading to the education unit with sirens blaring and lights blazing. Four firemen and one of the police officers exited the vehicles. Reed and Tyler met them and led them to the entrance.

"We will take it from here," one of the firemen said.

"I better get back to my kids." Emmy put her hand to her forehead to block out the sun as she searched for Kevin's pre-K class. She spotted her son and rushed toward him.

"Mommy! Mommy! Look!" Kevin jumped up and down along with Ben Bertucci.

"Are you all right, Kev?" Emmy held him hand.

"Firetrucks! Police cars!"

"I see, buddy, and here comes an ambulance." Emmy pointed as a rescue unit arrived.

"Look, Ben!" Kevin pointed. "Ab-u-lance!"

Emmy picked up Grace Randolph, made sure she wasn't scared and then rejoined Liz and the class.

"Do you know what happened?" Liz asked.

"I heard it was a small fire in the kitchen, but they put it out already. One of the cooks might have been burned."

The ambulance quickly transported the injured cook to St. Bart's. Tyler walked to Liz and explained what happened.

"So no major damage, huh?" Emmy looked up at Pastor Tyler.

"We will have to replace that stove but that's all. The fire suppression system knocked it out in a matter of seconds." He snapped his fingers.

"What about the cook?" Liz asked.

"She suffered a minor burn, but she will be okay. There was some smoke damage. I've already made the call to ServPro and talked to Jerry Wright. He's the guy who handled the flood in the sanctuary. Remember that? They will probably have the damage cleaned up by this afternoon."

"Good thing it's a beautiful day," Emmy said.

Thirty minutes later the firemen finished their inspection

and gave the okay for the teachers and students to return inside. One of the firetrucks remained behind and the kids marched past it much to the delight of the younger boys. Emmy smiled as Kevin and Ben stood by the firetruck talking to the fireman, who happened to be a member of the church.

"How was school today, Kevin? Anything exciting happen." Kenny grinned as the family sat down in the breakfast nook to eat dinner that evening.

"I saw two firetrucks and two police cars and one ab-u-lance." He held up both hands and all of his fingers.

"Did you see any firemen?"

"I talked to a real fire man! He let me and Ben touch his helmet."

Heather and Isabella listened patiently as their younger brother jabbered about his exciting day. Kevin finished and began playing with his small red firetruck.

"You need to eat your spaghetti, Kevin Michael." Emmy cut the pasta into small bites for him. "Use your fork."

"Daddy, we had to march outside and sit in a circle. We weren't scared because Mommy and Miss Liz were with us," Heather explained.

"I was a little scared because of the loud noise," Isabella confessed. "But after we went outside, it wasn't as loud. We played games, but then we had to go back inside and have class again."

"Can I see more firetrucks tomorrow?" Kevin took a bite of spaghetti and had red sauce dripping down his chin.

"Let's hope that doesn't happen again." Kenny laughed.

"Now I don't want to hear another peep out of you, Kevin Michael. It's almost nine o'clock and you have school in the morning." Emmy tucked the blanket around him and kissed his forehead. "Go to sleep."

"Tomorrow is Saturday. No school."

"Not quite. Tomorrow is Wednesday." Emmy shook a finger at him. "You have three more days of school this week."

"I need a drink," he said.

"No, no, no!" Emmy waved a finger at him. "You had a glass of water. I'm turning off the light. Do you want the door open or closed?"

"Open." He pulled his stuffed moose closer and lay on his back.

"Close your eyes. See you in the morning." Emmy left her son's room, walked down the hall and peeked into the twin's room. "Time for lights out. Put the books away and go to sleep."

"Night, Mommy. I love you." Isabella placed her newest Junie B. Jones book under her pillow and pulled the sheet up tight to her chin.

"Heather! I said lights out."

"I only have a few pages left. I want to finish tonight." Heather kept her attention on her book and didn't look at Emmy.

You are more stubborn than I was at your age. Emmy sighed. "No, I said lights out, and I mean it. Put the book away, or else I will take it away."

"Just a few more pages."

Emmy took a step into the room. "I said no. Do I have to use the flyswatter on you?"

"Life is totally unfair! I'm not a baby anymore." Heather tossed her book in the direction of the bookcase and turned away from Emmy.

Emmy closed her eyes. *Lord, give me patience and wisdom.* "You can finish the book in the morning after you get ready for school. Good night, girls. I love you." Emmy flipped the light switch and headed downstairs.

"Did they give you any trouble?" Kenny paused his laptop as he looked up from his recliner in the family room.

"No more than usual. Heather is going to be a handful in a few years." Emmy picked up a couple of magazines from the table in front of the couch. "Have you seen my laptop?"

He pointed. "In the den."

She plopped down on the couch. "How can they be twins, but yet be so different. They're like night and day."

"Good and evil?" Kenny grinned.

"Not that bad. Heather is a good girl but kinda stubborn." Emmy put her bare feet on the front edge of the couch and held a small pillow to her chest. "Does she remind you of Diane at all?"

He set his laptop on the side table. "Diane?"

"You're a stinker! She's a lot more stubborn than I was."

"If you say so."

Emmy thumbed her nose at Kenny. "Sometimes I worry she will turn out like Diane once she reaches puberty and discovers boys."

"And Isabella will be like you?"

"I was never as wild as Diane. Isa is quieter and listens better."

"Sometimes it's the quiet ones who rebel."

"I never rebelled," Emmy insisted.

"You were a perfect little angel, huh?"

"Fine! I might not have rebelled as openly as Diane. I hid it better, I guess."

"Why are you worried about this now?" He started the video on his laptop again. "We have a few years before we have to deal with it."

"It's a fact that children learn more in the first three years than all the years after that. If we don't teach them now, it will be too late later. Might be too late already."

"I don't think we have to worry too much. They will have the advantage of growing up in the church."

She moved her feet to the floor as she glared at him. "Do you think Diane and I would have been different if our parents took us to church?"

"Definitely. Church would have made a difference."

"Church or Jesus?"

"Definitely Jesus, but I think just going to church would have changed you guys." He sat up straighter. *I'm not going to argue with you, Em.*

"Todd Delaney went to church all the time as a kid. Look how he ended up." She waved her hands in the air. "He murdered Amy Porter and maybe even others. Church didn't make a difference for him."

"I'm just saying..."

"I know what you're saying. Diane wouldn't have slept with Craig and Owen and who knows who if she had been going to

45

church. What about me? How would I have been different? I didn't sleep around." She stood up and threw the pillow at him. "Maybe I should have."

Kenny sighed. "Don't think like that, Em."

She sighed and exhaled as her shoulders slumped. She bit her lip as she looked at him. "That kinda got me in trouble before, didn't it?" She moved around the table and over to his recliner. "I'm sorry for getting riled up."

He opened his arms and she sat on his lap. "I forgive you," he said and then grinned. "Are we going to kiss and make up now?"

She kissed him but then got up. "Maybe later, but I need to read my devotional book. I didn't have a chance this morning."

"Maybe we should get up earlier."

"I got up at six. That's early enough." She touched his knee as she walked toward the den. "If you go upstairs before I do, try to stay awake."

He grinned. "I can do that."

She laughed. "You're such an adorable dork.

"That I am."

She found her laptop on the roll-top desk in the den, booted it up and sat in one of the recliners. She checked her email and was about to open the BibleGateway site she used to study the Bible when her cell phone chirped. She grabbed it out of habit and checked the caller ID.

"Hey, Barry, what's up. Long time no see, no hear from. I thought you might have forgotten about your best and oldest friend."

Barry cleared his throat. "I'm sorry, I must have dialed this number by mistake. I meant to call Emmy Colasanti. Please forgive me."

"You're a goof. How are you and the kids? Did Fen start college yet? Is Hattie married? Are you a grandfather already?"

"Anything else? Go ahead and let it all out."

"No, I'm good now. So what's up?"

"Linda and I are expecting number three."

"For real!? It's about time you guys caught up with us. Give me all the details." She didn't hear or see Kenny pop his head into the den.

I guess you're busy. See you later, Em. He headed upstairs.

Barry adjusted his position on the couch in the basement. "She's three months along. Her due date is March seventh, and it's too early to know the sex."

"I hope you have another girl. Congratulations, Barry. I shouldn't say this, but you are a good father."

"Do you mean I'm not a nerd anymore?"

Emmy laughed. *You walked right into this.* "You were never a nerd. You're a geek. There's a big difference."

"Yeah, whatever."

"Geeks and dorks can be good fathers."

"And you're still a... What is it Tony always calls you? Oh, I know. You're still a brat," Barry teased her back. "What's that rock star husband of yours up to? Is he on the road?"

"They finished the tour, and now the guys are recording demos in the basement. They're trying to put together a new project."

"Lucky you. You get to have him home everyday."

"It is good to have him here." She thought about the time he spent at the carriage house. "Everything okay with the house? Do any painting or remodeling?" She pictured the house Barry and Linda had purchased from Mama Bertucci.

"Painted the basement. Fixed up the garage a bit. Redid some of the landscaping. I have to turn the spare bedroom into a nursery."

"Marco's old room, right?"

"Yeah, I guess so. I didn't really know Tony's brother."

"How's work? Is Sennco Systems still giving you a paycheck, or did they finally realize they don't need you?"

"As it so happens, I earned a promotion last month."

"At the Burger Bob's?"

He ignored her teasing. "I am now the vice-president in charge of product research and development."

"You mean you have to develop new burgers and fries?"

"My office is in the new company headquarters in

Newcastle. It's a longer drive, but the money is worth it."

"Good for you."

"I'm waiting for the punch line," Barry said after a moment of silence.

"No kidding. I'm happy for you. You have turned your geekness into a career."

"Such a riot, Emmy."

"Does Linda still hate me?" Emmy asked.

"She doesn't hate you, Em." He sat up on the couch.

"She doesn't like me. She never has. I used to think it was because she thought we were more than friends, but even though she knows better, she still doesn't like me."

"She has always been a bit resentful of people she perceives to have more material possessions than her," Barry explained. "Do you still have a nanny for the kids?"

"Yes, but Sofia only works part-time. You guys are doing all right. You have a decent job. That house will be there forever. Is she still working part-time?"

"She's been working full-time since Hattie's in school all day. She's actually managing her mother's beauty salon in the Mayfield neighborhood. My mother-in-law owns four of them now. But that will change once the baby is here. She wants to keep working a few hours a week, but I'd rather she stay home. We'll have to see." He shrugged.

"Can you believe how fast the kids are growing up? The twins were babies just a year ago and now they're in first grade."

"It goes by fast, Em. I should let you go. I wanted to let you know about the baby before you heard it from someone else."

"Thanks for calling, Barry. Tell Linda I said hi. Or don't tell her. She might get mad that you talked to me."

"She doesn't hate you, Em," Barry insisted.

Chapter Five

"Hey, Dad, happy birthday," Kenny called early on Thursday morning. "The big seventy, huh?"

"Thanks, son. I don't feel that old. Your mother told me a few days ago that seventy is the new fifty, or something. Are we still on for dinner tonight?" Mr. Colwell asked.

"Yeah, but Emmy kinda forgot about worship band practice. Could we move dinner up to say five? We need to be at the church by seven. Sorry."

"I don't mind. We usually eat around then anyway."

"If that's Kenny, ask him if we're supposed to bring anything," Mrs. Colwell refilled her coffee. She pointed to her husband's cup.

He waved his hand to indicate he didn't need a refill. "Your mother wants to know if we need to bring anything."

"Emmy said to bring a healthy appetite."

Carter shook his head at his wife. "Don't bring anything."

"Okay, Dad. I wanted to make sure it wasn't a problem to eat early. I'm on my way to the basement. The guys will be here soon. See you tonight."

"See you later. We might come early to see the kids."

Sofia Talford, Emmy's part-time Peruvian nanny, picked Kevin Michael and Benjamin Alexander up from school at noon. Ben climbed into the car and scrambled into his car seat behind Sofia. She stepped out of the car, strapped him in and got back inside.

"Sofia, I didn't see any firetrucks today. No police cars." Kevin climbed into his car seat and one of the volunteers buckled him in.

"I'm sorry, but that's a good thing." Sofia waved to the volunteer and pulled away. "You guys make sure to watch for firetrucks and police cars."

"I stayed on green all day," Ben said proudly.

Sofia glanced in the rearview mirror. "That's good. How about you Kevin?"

He didn't answer.

49

"Kevin, were you on green all day?"

"I had to go on timeout 'cause I took a toy away from someone," he confessed. "Are you going to tell Mommy?"

"I won't tell her, but what will you do if she asks?"

He thought about it while staring out the window. "It's wrong to lie."

"Yes, it is."

"Maybe Mommy won't ask."

Emmy did ask and Kevin told the truth.

Emmy sat on the couch with Kevin. "You need to share the toys. You share your toys with Ben. Why can't you share at school?"

"Ben is my cousin and we're friends," he explained. "I don't like all the kids at school. Some of them are mean."

"You need to get along with everyone even if you don't like them."

Kevin jumped down and faced Emmy. "Why? You don't."

"I do so!" Emmy insisted.

"You said Mrs. Thompkins was an old fart and smells funny."

"I did not."

Kevin grinned and nodded. "Did so. You said that to Auntie Kristen." Then he took off for the stairs and stomped to his room.

Emmy looked at Sofia. "He may be right."

"They hear more than you think," Sofia said. "Did you decide on dinner yet?"

"Kenny and Andy are going to grill some steaks and stuff. I'm going to make potato salad and baked beans with bacon and onions. Dad Colwell likes that. Might throw a salad together."

"I can help if you want, but I've never made potato salad before."

An hour later, Emmy put the large bowl of potato salad in the fridge. "I will need to put the beans in around four thirty. Now I need to clean."

"I can help with that. I've been cleaning for my mother since I was ten." Sofia smiled.

Emmy shook her head. "You don't need to help clean. You're the nanny not my maid."

"I don't mind. Kevin is taking a nap. What else am I supposed to do?"

Emmy and Sofia divided the chores and finished cleaning in time for Emmy to pick up the twins and Carson and Caden from school. She pulled into Brady and Diane's long driveway and dropped off her nephews.

"Thanks for the ride, Auntie Em." Carson helped his younger brother Caden get down from the Odyssey.

"See you in the morning," Emmy waited until the boys were clear and then turned around and sped down the driveway. She paused long enough to wave at Brady Robertson who was getting his mail.

"Hi, Emmy, thanks for playing taxi," he said while sorting through the mail.

"You're welcome. Tell Diane it's her turn next week." Emmy glanced only long enough to make sure there was no other traffic on the lightly-traveled street and gunned the Odyssey.

"We need to finish wrapping our presents for Gra," Isabella reminded her mother.

"Would you mind if Sofia helps you? I've got to shower and get ready."

"We don't mind," Heather said. "We can practice reading in Spanish."

"Where are my favorite grandkids?" Mr. Colwell hollered from the kitchen. "I know we're a few minutes early. Is dinner ready?"

"Oh, Dad, they're your only grandkids," Emmy reminded him. "Happy birthday." She opened the oven and set the baked beans inside. "Kenny and Andy are outside. They made hot dogs for the kids, and they're about ready to grill the steaks. I told him you like yours medium well."

"Thank you." He smiled as three kids jostled for position around him.

"Happy birthday, Gra. Mommy said you are really old now," Heather held his hand.

51

Isabella grabbed his other hand. "Is seventy older than my other grandma?"

"No, it's not, Isa." Emmy rolled her eyes.

Kevin held up his hands. "I can count to seventy, but it takes me a long time." He began to count.

"We have presents for you. I can help you open them if you want," Heather said.

"Presents have to wait until after dinner." Emmy opened the silverware drawer and grabbed a handful of utensils. "Who wants to help me set the table?"

The kids hustled Gra out of the kitchen.

"We can't, Mommy. We have to take care of Gra. It's his birthday," Heather shouted over her shoulder.

"I'll help," Mrs. Colwell said. "Are we using these plates?"

"I thought we could use the good stuff from the china cabinet."

"Not for the kids?" Mrs. Colwell shook her head. "I'll set three places for the kids."

"Thanks, Mom."

Sofia walked into the kitchen. "Hello, Mrs. Colwell. It's good to see you, and I already set the table, Emmy."

Emmy hugged her. "Oh, Sofia, you didn't need to do that, but thank you."

"The steaks are done." Andy walked into the kitchen with a platter of sizzling steaks. "To perfection if I say so myself." He set the platter on the island and licked his lips while taking in the aroma wafting through the air. "I'm starving. How soon can we eat?"

Kenny followed with hot dogs.

"How many did you make?" Emmy looked at the steaks.

"One for each adult." Andy winked at Mrs. Colwell. "Oh, did you want a steak, too, little cuz?"

"You are such a riot. Didn't your doctor tell you to cut back on red meat?"

"He did." Andy put his hands on Emmy's shoulders and squeezed. "That's why I only made one steak for me."

The oven timer beeped.

"The beans are done. We can eat in a couple of minutes." Emmy ducked under Andy's arms. "Kenny, would you gather everyone to the dining room, please?"

"Kevin, why do you always eat your hot dog without the bun?" Gra asked.

"Buns are just bread shaped like buns. I like the hot dog better."

"Sounds reasonable to me," Gra said and then laughed.

"Make sure your hands are clean before you get down," Emmy reminded him.

Kevin looked at his hands and licked the mustard off as best he could. "See! Clean."

Mom Colwell pointed to his plate. "Finish your beans and potato salad."

Kevin shoveled a spoonful of beans into his mouth. "Beans are good for you, Me-maw. They make you fart!"

"Kevin Michael! Where did you hear that?" Mom Colwell asked.

"Mommy said so," Kevin answered with a grin.

Everyone turned to stare at Emmy.

Emmy shrugged. "Well, it's true."

"You are supposed to be the adult," Kenny said and tried not to laugh.

Emmy stuck out her tongue at the men, and then turned to Kevin. "You're a traitor. You weren't supposed to tell anyone."

"Who needs more beans?" Andy scooped another helping from the casserole bowl.

"Can Gra open his presents now," Isabella asked. "He might fall asleep if we wait."

Emmy checked the time. "We should open them now. Daddy and I have to leave in a half hour." Emmy wiped the counter one more time and then tossed the wet towel at the sink faucet where it landed perfectly.

"Come on, Gra! We can open presents now," Heather shouted.

Everyone gathered in the family room.

Emmy patted a spot on the couch. "Sit by me, Sofia."

"Which one should Gra open first?" Isabella asked. "Does it matter?"

"You can choose, Isa," Kenny said.

She picked out one and handed it to Gra. "This is probably clothes."

"I need clothes, Isabella."

"I can read the card for you if you need help."

"Thank you, sweetie. Who is this from?"

She read the card. "It's from Mommy and Daddy."

Mr. Colwell opened several presents. All clothes.

Kevin picked a present from the stack of three remaining. "Open this one, Gra. You can play with it." He wrinkled his nose at the pile of clothes.

"Who is this from?"

"It's from me," Kevin smiled.

Mr. Colwell opened the small package.

"It's a firetruck, Gra! It was mine, but you can keep it. I have other ones."

"Why, thank you very much. I need a red firetruck."

"The doors open and there's a fire man inside. He drives the truck. We can play later."

Mr. Colwell opened the last couple of presents. "Thank you all for making this a special birthday."

Heather and Isabella climbed up next to him on the couch. He put an arm around each of them and they snuggled against him.

"We love you, Gra," Isabella said.

He kissed the top of their heads. *Not nearly as much as I love you girls.* He clenched his jaw to keep from crying.

"We need to get going, Em." Kenny checked the time and stood up. "I hate to leave, but we really have to be at practice tonight. Chase said it was a mandatory meeting."

"Can we stay with Gra and Me-maw?" Heather asked. "We don't want to go to church."

"Yes, you can stay here tonight. Sofia will put you to bed later. I don't want to hear about any fussing."

"I need to go to the church with your mom and dad, but I need hugs and kisses first." Andy stood and held out his arms. He had been roped into working with the tech team for rehearsal sessions.

"Bye, Uncle Andy." Isabella allowed herself to be picked up and hugged. She kissed his cheek. "Do a good job at practice."

"I'll try, sweetheart." He set her down and repeated the process with Heather.

"Do I get a hug?" Andy asked Kevin.

"I'm too big for hugs, Uncle Andy. Men shake hands."

Andy laughed and then held out a hand. "I will see you later, Mr. Colwell." Andy ruffled Kevin's reddish blonde hair.

"Come on, Gra! We can play fire man."

Andy, Kenny and Emmy walked into the music suite and Emmy saw Chase in his office to the right. They took seats next to Tyler and Liz.

"Are we late?" Emmy whispered to Liz. "We had Kenny's parents over for dinner."

"You're right on time. Was today his father's birthday?" Liz asked.

"Yes, and I feel bad about leaving them, but Chase said this was a mandatory meeting."

Chase walked out of his office and into the large practice room. He studied a printout as he took his place at the front of the room. He set the paper on a music stand and smiled. "We can get started now, since Emmy has finally arrived."

Emmy made a face at Chase. "We were not late. You just like to tease me."

"You're so easy to tease, Emmy."

Yvonne Hillman joined her husband at the front. "Stop it."

"Thank you, Yvonne. He's being mean to me again," Emmy said.

Kenny frowned at her, so she crossed her arms over her chest.

"I want to thank everyone for taking the time to be here," Chase started. "Quite a number of you have expressed concerns over the scheduling, and I agree I could have done a better job. It's not easy to schedule for three services."

"Especially three different services with different music.

55

There's a huge difference in what the Saturday night crowd expects and the early Sunday service," Cam Frees said.

Bobby O'Connor laughed. "The Sunday morning people would have a nervous breakdown if they came to the Saturday night service."

"What I'd like to accomplish tonight is breaking down the team into three units. I have surveys from everyone except Micah Hurst and Emmy Colasanti..."

"I turned mine in last week," Emmy claimed.

Yvonne handed Chase a sheet of paper.

"Sorry, I must not have seen it. Micah, if you could fill one out now, I would appreciate it."

Micah, who played bass in Emmy's band and was a new member of the worship team, filled out his survey as Chase continued.

"These units are not set in stone, and should be fluid depending on everyone's circumstances. We have to adjust for vacations and certain members of the team have obligations which require extensive travel." He smiled at Kenny and Emmy.

"Hey! I can't help it if I married a rock star," Emmy said and then nudged Kenny in the ribs.

"I meant your band, Emmy. Kenny has figured out a way to maintain his touring schedule without being gone on Sundays."

"I'm here most of the time." Emmy crossed her arms over her chest again.

"Now that Hank has retired and moved south, is there anyone without access to a computer?" Chase glanced around the room.

Miles Goossens raised his hand. "My computer crapped out last week. I kinda need a new one."

"Laptop or desktop?" Andy Walker pointed to Miles.

"Either one," Miles answered.

"We got you covered. Talk to me after the meeting," Andy said.

"Anyone else?"

No one else raised a hand.

"All scheduling and service orders, the whole shebang will

56

be online. I have upcoming message themes from Pastor Tyler, so the song committee should be able to pick out songs at least a month ahead of time."

"Am I still on that committee?" Emmy asked. "If so, could I be excused."

Yvonne checked her laptop. "I believe Heidi and Regina offered to take your place, Emmy."

"Thank you so much, ladies. I haven't had the time to do an adequate job picking out songs."

"You have your hands full writing the songs, and we thank you for that," Heidi said.

Regina added, "And taking care of the kids takes a lot of your time."

"Tell me about it," Emmy said and then sighed.

"I'm going to pass this out. Please take a look, and we can discuss any changes that need to be made." Chase handed out the team assignments.

Bobby O'Connor stared at his sheet. "Why do I have to be on the same team as Emmy? It's bad enough I have to tour with her. She's such a diva."

Emmy made a face at her drummer. "I know how to solve that issue."

"You can't fire me. You need me. I attract the young girls," Bobby said.

Adam Vicini and Mich Hurst began to cough.

"Hey! I can't help it the young girls find me irresistible."

"Please," Emmy dragged out the word into three syllables.

"I'm sorry, Bobby, but someone has to play the drums for Emmy's team," Chase said with a straight face. "You have the least seniority. Deal with it."

The worship team perused the new assignments for several minutes.

"Any changes or questions?" Chase asked.

"Why don't we try scheduling one team for the whole week instead of having all three teams work every week?" Regina Collins wondered.

"That was one of the questions on the survey, and the

57

majority voted to only play for one service," Yvonne stated. "Some of the comments I read, especially comments from people with young families, indicated it might be a hardship to be there for all three services as well as the rehearsals."

Emmy stood up. "I voted to play at one service for that reason. I can't expect the kids to be here for over three hours on Sunday."

"You have a nanny to take care of them," Heidi Knapp reminded her.

Emmy replied rather harshly, "Yes, we do, but Sofia doesn't work on Sundays unless I absolutely need her."

"Do we need to discuss this further?" Chase glanced around the room. He could hear people murmuring.

"I'd like to say something." Steve Van Zant stood up. "Now that Hank and John have moved away, and I moved back from Nashville, I guess I'm the guy who's been on the team the longest." He motioned to the front. "Along with Chase and Yvonne."

"Your opinion matters a lot, Steve," Kenny said.

"I don't come to the Saturday services, but there are times I stay for both Sunday services even when I'm not playing. I know the sermon might be the same for all the services, but the music is drastically different. Maybe drastic is too strong of a word, but there are differences." He looked around the room. "I struggle at times with the newer music. I feel more comfortable playing on Sunday morning. I guess I'm showing my age, but that's how I feel. I'd prefer not to play for three services." He sat down.

"Thank you, Steve," Chase nodded. "Anyone else have a comment?"

Cam Frees rose from his seat, adjusted his Buddy Holly glasses and straightened his long, angular frame. "I volunteered to play keyboards for the Saturday service, and I like playing. I happen to enjoy the light show if you want to call it that. Since Lindsey and I are here for both services on Sunday because she teaches a class, it wouldn't matter if I play in the early service in addition to the second one, but that makes for a long morning. My vote is still for the three units and playing every Sunday."

Pastor Tyler stood up. "I'm not a regular member of the

worship team, but I can fill in."

"We appreciate that, but you have enough responsibilities already," Chase said. "We have been blessed with an abundance of talented musicians, and we'll work out the kinks in the system."

The meeting broke up, and Chase quickly rehearsed with the Saturday night musicians.

"I'm heading home," Andy Walker said. "I want to see if one of my old computers will work for that new guy. What was his name?"

"Miles," Kenny answered. "He's pretty good, and he's only been playing for a couple of years, I think. See you later. I gotta find Emmy."

Emmy walked out with Liz Hammond. "Who's watching the kids?"

Liz braided her long blonde hair as they walked. "Mom and Dad have them. They were in Colorado for a convention and stopped on their way home. We're leaving in the morning for Jason's wedding. You guys are still coming, right?"

"Yes, but not until Saturday morning. I want to talk to Dany about school." Emmy felt a hand on her shoulder.

"Pastor Tyler mentioned ice cream. You interested, Em?" Kenny asked.

"Is he buying?"

"You can buy your own ice cream," Kenny said.

"Fine! I'll buy."

They met at Robbins Old Fashioned Ice Cream Parlor.

"What would you like, Em?" Kenny asked. "The usual?"

"What does she usually order?" Tyler asked. "Liz likes mint chocolate chip ice cream."

"Emmy craves hot fudge sundaes with whipped cream, but not a cherry on top," Kenny answered. "I'm buying by the way."

"In that case I'll take a large shake with cookie dough ice cream. They make them the old fashioned way here."

Kenny placed the order and the guys joined Emmy and Liz at a table.

"Do you think Heidi was mad at me?" Emmy asked.

"No, I think she might have expressed a tiny bit of envy,"

59

Kenny responded. "I don't think she was mad."

Their treats arrived within a few minutes.

"Thank you, sweetie," Emmy took a bite of the whipped cream.

Liz smiled. "Thank you, Kenny. This is yummy."

"Maybe I shouldn't mention this." Emmy scooped some of the hot fudge into her mouth and looked at Pastor Tyler. "But I heard Chase has been offered a position back in Toledo. Can you comment on that?"

"I really can't comment." Tyler knew he had confirmed the rumor.

"Do you think he'll take the offer?"

Liz wiped her mouth. "Tyler can't say anything, but I will. Yvonne talked to me about it. I think there's a strong possibility they might be leaving, but it wouldn't be until after the end of the year."

"I'm not surprised. He's been here a long time," Emmy said. "Anna will be graduating in January, and Jada is only a freshman. It's almost the perfect time to leave."

"Emmy, you can't say anything to anyone," Kenny informed her.

"Did you already know about this?" Emmy poked Kenny in the side.

Kenny grabbed Emmy's hand. "Chase mentioned it, but made me swear to keep it a secret."

Tyler finished his shake. "Nothing has been decided. We have to allow Chase and Yvonne to leave if God is leading them elsewhere."

Emmy grinned. "How come you are so smart for someone as young as you?"

Tyler chuckled and said, "Just lucky, I guess."

Chapter Six

"How much longer will you be?" Liz called Tyler, who was finishing his Sunday sermon at the church.

Tyler glanced at the large digital clock in his office. "I need twenty to thirty minutes. Maybe less. Are your parents getting anxious to leave?"

"You know them. They're taking their sweet time, but they need to be getting out the door. The rehearsal is supposed to start at six thirty Michigan time."

"Relax, Liz. There's plenty of time. It's only a little after eleven. Are the kids going with your parents or us?"

"Natalie wants to go with Grandma, but we'll have Grayson and Derby with us. Should we put Derby in her cage for the trip?"

"I think we need to take the cage, but we might need to put Grayson in it," Tyler said.

"We are not putting our son in a dog cage!"

"Just kidding. We can take the cage, but I bet Derby will want to sit on your lap. She's a baby. She's only four months old."

Tyler and Liz were preparing to travel to Hillsdale, Michigan, for Liz's younger brother Jason's wedding.

"I'm so glad the school let me take today off," Liz said balancing the phone on her shoulder while she emptied the dryer. "Larry had to work today. North Park College can be so unreasonable at times. He and Allie aren't leaving until later. I hope they make it in time for the rehearsal."

"One of the perks of teaching at a Christian school."

"Especially one where my husband is the senior pastor." She laughed and then turned around. "Grayson! Stop that! Do not pull Derby's tail and watch out for her water dish."

Tyler heard a crash.

"I gotta go. Grayson dumped Derby's water and food all over the floor. Hurry home."

"Do you need some help, Liz?" Dr. Dusty Kimmerle asked as he walked into the kitchen pulling a suitcase.

"Yes," Liz answered. "Could you grab Grayson and hold him while I clean this mess?"

Grayson chased Derby into and through the kitchen.

"Grayson! Where are you going?" Dr. Kimmerle asked.

"Me chase Derby." Two-year-old Grayson paused only a moment to answer.

"I'm not sure I can catch him, Liz."

Liz sighed. "It's all right. The damage is already done."

"What's wrong, Lizzie?" Karen Kimmerle entered the kitchen with Liz and Tyler's nearly five-year-old daughter Natalie.

"Nothing, Mom." Liz wiped her brow.

"Something has you frazzled." Mom pulled Liz to a chair and they sat down. "Tell me."

"It's this house." Liz waved at the small kitchen. "It was fine before the kids came along, but now it's too small. Especially with Derby running everywhere. I know the church provides it for us, and I don't want to sound ungrateful, but..."

"I can see your point."

Dusty returned from loading the car and took a seat. "Did I hear something about this house?"

"It's too small, Daddy."

To prove her point Derby raced through the kitchen and knocked over the plastic garbage bin by the back door.

"There is a simple remedy," he said as he smiled.

"What?" Liz slumped lower in the chair.

"Buy a bigger house."

"Houses are expensive around here, and we would need a down payment." Liz tried to grab Grayson as he darted past. "We're talking thousands of dollars."

"This is exactly what your grandparents envisioned when they invested in mutual funds for their grandkids. Have you looked into using part of that money?" Dad asked.

"Not really. Would Grandma mind?"

Mom put an arm around her older daughter. "She would be thrilled for you and Tyler. You should look at houses. You must have a Realtor in the church."

"We do and we have talked about it. One of the ladies on the worship team is selling real estate now. Heidi Knapp."

Her parents shrugged with blank expressions.

"You'd know her if you saw her. Anyway, she used to work for Robertson Industries, but left the company a few months ago."

"It's something to consider. Are we ready to go, Dusty?"

"The car is packed. Are we going to stop for lunch along the way?" he asked.

"McDonald's!" Natalie suggested while bouncing on her toes. "I need Nuggets."

"All right, but you have to drink milk." Liz stood up and hugged her parents. "I'll walk you out. Grayson! Come and say goodbye to Grandma and Grandpa. They're leaving now, and taking Natty with them."

Grayson scampered into the kitchen and wrapped his arms around his grandparents one after the other.

"Natty is leaving, too. She needs a hug," Liz said.

"Bye, Natty. I wuv you."

Natalie hugged her little brother. "Stay out of my room, and don't touch my dolls," she ordered.

Tyler walked in just in time to say goodbye to Natalie and his in-laws. "Have a safe trip. We'll be leaving soon."

"I talked to Mom and Dad about the house," Liz said as they pulled onto I-80 to leave SoHam thirty minutes later. "Daddy suggested we buy a bigger house."

"Did you mention the down payment?" Tyler looked in the mirror at Derby. "I hope she doesn't get carsick."

Liz checked on Derby. "She should be all right. Dad suggested we take money from the mutual fund. Mom thought it would be a good idea."

"I'm ready to look."

"Should we talk to Heidi about it?" Liz asked. "Grayson, do not try to pull Derby's tail. You should try to take a nap. It will be three hours before we arrive."

"Don't need nap. Need drink," Grayson insisted.

"She would be a perfect choice. She might be new to real estate, but she knows a lot of people. She knows all about budgets and financial matters."

They talked about what they would look for in a house for a few minutes.

Liz looked over her shoulder at Grayson and smiled. "He's zonked."

After making a stop in Indiana to let Derby out to do her business, they arrived in Hillsdale ahead of schedule.

"We're here, Grayson."

He squirmed in his car seat. "I want to play."

"Hang on a second, buddy. I'll let Derby out and come back for you," Tyler said. He grabbed Derby's leash and let her out. "Good job, Derby. We didn't have to put you or Grayson in the cage." He secured Derby to a chain under the shade of the large Eastern White Pine. *The leaves are changing already.* He noticed as he glanced up.

Jason and his fiancee, Michelle Dayscomb, strolled out of the house arm in arm.

"Hey! You aren't supposed to see your fiancee before the wedding," Liz shouted.

"I believe that applies to the day of the wedding, and that's so old-fashioned. Does anyone even follow that tradition anymore?" Jason asked while he laughed.

"I didn't see Tyler before the wedding," Liz twirled a finger through her long blonde hair. "Does that make me old-fashioned?"

"You said it, not me," Jason replied.

Liz walked up to Michelle and hugged her. "Did you get your hair trimmed?"

"I did. Do you like?" Michelle twirled in a circle.

"It looks gorgeous," Liz said. "Do you want a hug, Jason?"

"Certainly." He leaned over to hug his older sister just as Dany Kimmerle walked out of the house holding hands with Natalie.

Natalie let go and scampered to Liz. "Mommy! Grandma has nine cats now. I counted them with Dany." She knelt before Derby and wrapped her arms around her. "Derby, I haven't seen you for hours. I missed you so much."

Tyler chuckled as he helped Grayson out of his car seat in the Ford Flex. "You saw him three hours ago."

"Hi, Tyler. You're early," Dany put an arm around her brother-in-law. "How was the trip? Did Grayson behave?"

Grayson wrapped his arms around Dany. "Dany, I miss you."

Dany reached down to pick him up. "How's my little man? I miss you, too."

"What time did you get here, Dany?" Liz asked her younger, and much shorter, sister.

"I didn't have any classes today, so I drove home last night." She pointed to her new Toyota Prius. "I love the gas mileage."

"I knew you would. We love ours."

Grayson released his aunt and said, "Dany, I want to play."

"Let's go inside, Grayson. I think Mom made some sandwiches to tide us over until tonight."

Larry and Allie drove straight to the church from SoHam and arrived just in time for the wedding rehearsal.

"Did you run into a lot of traffic," Tyler asked his brother-in-law. "That stretch across Indiana can be a royal pain."

"I've seen it worse, but we had an emergency at the office," Larry mentioned. "I had to put out the fire."

Tyler tilted his head. "You work in the registrar's office. What kind of emergency did you have?"

"Computer meltdown. Some class schedules vanished into the Ethernet."

"That's why you get paid the big bucks," Tyler said. "Hi, Allie, if you're looking for Liz, I think she and Dany are with Michelle in the sanctuary."

"Thanks, Tyler. Where are the kids?" Allie Kimmerle pushed a stroller with daughter, Lorraine, sound asleep inside.

"Back at the house with Grandma. She agreed to watch them tonight."

Larry walked into the sanctuary of Hillsdale First Nazarene and stood next to Jim Hammond, Tyler's father and the piano player for the church.

"Hi, Larry. Glad you made it. Jason was getting worried."

"I texted him. He knew we were running late." Larry waved to his younger brother on the platform.

"Everyone's here now, Pastor Mortland. We can get

started," Michelle's mother announced as she glanced at everyone.

"I'm sure most of you know how this works since you were in Liz and Tyler's wedding," Pastor Mortland said.

Forty minutes later the wedding party left for the rehearsal dinner at Johnny T's Pizzaria. They gathered in a side room to eat.

Michelle's phone buzzed. She checked the text message. "Oh, no! This is awful."

"What is it?" Liz asked.

"That was from Phyllis. She is supposed to sing tomorrow, but she's sick. Who am I going to find at the last minute?"

Liz grinned. "I have an idea."

"What? Who?" Michelle asked.

"I'll ask Emmy. She and Kenny will be here tomorrow."

"You can't ask them. That would be too much of an imposition." Michelle shook her head. "I hate to impose."

"Nonsense! I'll text her right now. She owes me a favor," Liz said.

Back in SoHam, Emmy checked her phone. "Shoot!"

"What is it, Em?" Kenny looked up from his book.

"It's from Liz. The lady who was supposed to sing tomorrow is sick. She wants to know if I can fill in." Emmy bit her lip.

"You could help them out."

"I suppose. I owe Liz a favor, and she's calling it in."

Kenny waited for more of an explanation, but Emmy didn't elaborate. She texted back and forth with Liz and learned which songs she would have to sing.

"Are you going to sing?" Kenny asked.

"Yes. Tyler's father will accompany me. He's played with our worship band before. He's good. He knows the songs. I just need to practice a little."

"That's so sweet of you to help out."

"Yeah, now Liz might owe me." Emmy grinned.

"She'll sing tomorrow," Liz told Michelle and Jason. "I knew she would. She's such a sweetheart."

Tyler looked at Liz and cocked his eyebrow. "Are we talking about the same Emmy?"

66

Liz poked Tyler's arm. "Yes, and you better not tease her tomorrow."

An hour later, the party was winding down.

Liz said goodbye to Jason and Michelle. "Remember, you guys aren't supposed to see each other tomorrow until Michelle walks down the aisle."

"We were going to have breakfast together at the Pancake Palace," Jason said without cracking a smile.

Liz waited for him to laugh, butt he didn't. "You better be joking."

"I'll be home as soon as I drop Michelle off at her parents' house."

"You are being rather gullible, Liz," Tyler said. "All of the guys are getting together to play football in the morning."

"Are you really, or are you teasing?"

"We want to play football to kill time," Jason said. "After football we're going to play ping pong."

"How about only playing ping pong? It's safer," Liz suggested.

"We'll see," Jason said.

"Did you print out directions to the hotel and church?" Emmy asked Kenny as she finished packing Saturday morning.

He used one hand for support while leaning against the bedroom doorway. "Don't need to. We have navigation in the Odyssey." He laughed as Kevin ran down the hall in his birthday suit followed by Sofia.

"I don't want to get dressed," Kevin hollered.

"Kevin Michael! You get dressed this instant." Sofia squeezed into his bedroom before he could close and lock the door.

"This suitcase is ready to go. Did you remember to pack a tie?" Emmy zipped her suitcase and pulled it off of the bed.

"I packed two in case you don't like one. I'll take this to the van, and we'll be ready to hit the road."

"Kevin has to get dressed first. Where are the girls?" Emmy asked.

"Finishing breakfast," Kenny answered. "I told them to

wash their hands and brush their teeth and be ready to go."

Emmy bit her lip. "I hope we get there in time to practice with Tyler's father."

"You could sing those songs without rehearsing. You've sang them plenty of times," he kissed the top of her head and laughed.

"Why would they pick two of my songs to sing at their wedding?" Emmy asked.

"Well, they are about love and being true to each other. They kinda fit. I bet there are lots of people using those songs at weddings." Kenny put his hands on her shoulders and kissed her neck.

"Stop it! We don't have time for that now. I hope they never use any of my songs at funerals."

Sofia knocked on the open door and grinned at Emmy and Kenny. "Kevin is dressed and ready to go. Do you guys need a few minutes?"

"No, we're ready." Emmy stepped away from Kenny. "Take this downstairs." She pointed to the suitcase. "We should be back Sunday afternoon. Do you and Niles have anything planned for the weekend?"

"Not really. He has to work today, and tomorrow is church. I still have to prepare my Sunday School lesson," Sofia realized.

"Have you ever thought about giving up your class? There are other people who aren't as busy as you."

"I love the kids too much, and there aren't any other Spanish-speaking teachers with the time." Sofia tried to comb Kevin's hair but he resisted.

"One of these days the church will have to build a new building for the Hispanic congregation," Emmy said. She heard her phone chirp. "Hey, Kristen. What's up? We're about to leave for Michigan."

"Have you talked to Christopher or Maddy lately?"

"No, why?"

"She called me and guess what?"

"Are you going to make me guess?"

"They are expecting!" Kristen shrieked.

"Cool! When?"

"In April sometime. I'll talk to you later. Have a good time at the wedding."

"Oh, Barry called me. They're expecting, too. In March."

"It's about time they had another baby."

Dusty Kimmerle looked out the kitchen window and saw the guys still tossing a football back and forth. He walked outside and caught the football.

"Nice grab, Dad," Jason smiled.

"Don't you guys have somewhere to be today?"

"What time is it?" Larry asked.

"Eleven thirty, and I believe you need to be somewhere by one." Dr. Kimmerle tossed the football toward Jason, but Tyler intercepted it.

Tyler tossed the football over his shoulder and continued running into the house. "I got dibs on the shower."

"Some of you can use the bathroom in the basement. I suggest we leave for the church by twelve thirty. Maybe sooner." Dr. Kimmerle checked his watch.

The ladies arrived at the church from the hairdressers and began getting ready under the supervision of Mrs. Dayscomb and Mrs. Kimmerle.

"Try not to sit down once you are wearing your dress. This material wrinkles so easily." Mrs. Dayscomb fussed over all the ladies, but especially Michelle.

"Mom, we can't stand up until the ceremony."

"I'm trying to make sure you look your best."

Mrs. Kimmerle smiled at Michelle. "Don't worry, dear. You look beautiful."

"Oh, Karen, I am so nervous," Mrs. Dayscomb lamented. "I need a Valium or something."

"You will be fine, Nancy. Just close your eyes and take deep breaths. Everything will be okay," Mrs. Kimmerle advised.

"What about that singer?" Mrs. Dayscomb wrung her hands nervously. "Is she here yet? What if she doesn't get here in time?"

Liz held Nancy's hand. "Emmy could sing those songs in her sleep, and she just arrived. Would you like to meet her?"

"Yes! I want to make sure she knows when she's supposed to sing." Nancy nodded. "I will be right back, Michelle. Don't sit down."

Liz and her mother escorted Mrs. Dayscomb to the sanctuary.

"There she is!" Liz pointed to Emmy, who had her back turned while she talked to Jim Hammond about the music.

"Good gracious! She's a child!" Mrs. Dayscomb staggered and nearly tripped. "She's wearing a t-shirt, and are those shorts? She will ruin Michelle's wedding. I need to sit down. I can feel my blood pressure spiking."

"Have a seat here, Nancy." Karen helped Nancy into a pew. "Lizzie, would you bring Emmy here, please?"

Liz scurried up to Emmy and put her hands on Emmy's shoulders. "You made it. Thank you for filling in at the last minute."

Emmy turned and hugged Liz. "You owe me big time."

"I need to introduce you to Mrs. Dayscomb. She thinks you are a child, and she's about ready to have a nervous breakdown."

Emmy rolled her eyes. "I'm not a child. Just petite."

"Mrs. Dayscomb, this is my friend Emmy. She actually wrote the songs Phyllis was going to sing. I think she will do all right as a last minute replacement."

Mrs. Dayscomb stared at Emmy for a moment. "You really wrote the songs?"

"I did. With a little help from Kenny." Emmy purposely used her most childlike voice.

Liz bumped hips with Emmy.

"Do you have a dress to wear?"

"I thought it was casual," Emmy said and then looked up at Liz.

Liz frowned. *Please don't joke. She's close to a nervous breakdown.*

"Oh, I did bring a dress for the wedding. We drove over from SoHam, so I didn't want to wear it in the van."

"Everything will be perfect, Nancy," Karen assured her. "Liz will show Emmy where she can change. We should get back

70

to Michelle." *And I am not giving you a Valium. Deal with it!*

Liz waited until her mother led Mrs. Dayscomb out of the sanctuary and then turned to Emmy. "You're a stinker for teasing her like that, but she has been driving Michelle up a wall." Liz put a hand to her mouth. "I almost started laughing when you said you thought it was casual. That was priceless."

"Should I have really brought a dress to wear?" Emmy put a finger to her mouth.

"I know you better than to fall for that," Liz said. "Come on. I'll show you the room we're using to change."

A few minutes after one, Julian Dayscomb escorted his only daughter down the aisle, and the ceremony ensued. Emmy smiled at Mrs. Dayscomb when it was time to sing.

"How did I sound?" she asked Kenny after sitting down.

"You sounded like an angel. Just like always." He squeezed her hand. "You even remembered all the lyrics."

"I wasn't sure because Michelle's mother started crying."

The guests moved to the large multi-purpose room for the reception while a photographer took pictures of the wedding party and their families.

"You did a good job singing, Mommy," Isabella said.

"Thank you, sweetie." Emmy checked the seating chart. "We're at table twelve. Could you find it for us, Isa?"

Later Tyler and Liz entered the room and Heather and Isabella jumped down from their seats and dashed over to them.

"Miss Liz, you are wearing a princess dress," Isabella grinned. "You look beautiful."

"You look so precious, Isa. Is this a new dress?"

Heather grabbed Tyler's hand. "Mommy said we could afford new dresses. Are we going to have a party now?"

"We are going to eat and Jason and Michelle might open their presents later," Tyler said.

"Where is your mother?" Liz asked.

"Over there." Isabella pointed.

"I need to thank her for singing today."

Isabella took Liz's hand and dragged her over to Emmy. "Mommy, look! Miss Liz is wearing a beautiful princess dress."

71

"I see. Maybe you should let go of her and sit down."

Liz hugged Emmy. "Thank you for singing. I've heard Phyllis sing before, and you sounded tons better."

"Mrs. Dayscomb started crying. I thought maybe I was singing in the wrong key," Emmy grinned.

"You're still a stinker. I'll talk to you later. I think Tyler and I are supposed to walk in together to be introduced."

Hillsdale First Nazarene did not allow dancing or alcohol, but none of the guests complained. Two large video screens displayed photographs of Jason and Michelle growing up.

"Kenny, did Jason and Michelle know each in grade school like Tyler and Liz did?" Emmy asked.

"I believe so. Both families are from this church. It's kinda like you and me, huh?"

"That's right! I did know you when I was a little girl." She stuck out her tongue as Mrs and Mr. Dayscomb approached.

Mrs. Dayscomb nudged her husband. "See, Julian, I told you she was a child."

He laughed and then stood beside Emmy. "I'm sorry we didn't have a chance to meet earlier. I'm Julian Dayscomb. Michelle's father."

"I'm Emmy and this is my husband Kenny and those are our kids." Emmy pointed.

Kenny stood up and shook hands with Julian.

"Kenny, will you watch the kids for a bit. I want to talk to Dany?" Emmy asked a few minutes later.

"Sure thing. We might get some more ice cream."

"Yeah! More ice cream, Daddy." Heather grinned.

Emmy walked over to the table where Dany Kimmerle sat with a couple of younger cousins.

"Hi, Dany. How have you been? Liz said you're working on your master's degree in child development."

Dany patted the chair next to her. "I have one more semester to go, and I already have a solid lead on an internship for a medical group in SoHam."

"Does that mean you'll be moving here? There? You know." Emmy's eyes sparkled.

"It does!" Dany exclaimed. "I will love being close to family. I can spoil my nieces and nephew even more."

They talked about Dany's time at Olivet Nazarene University, and then Emmy brought up the subject of relationships.

"You can tell me to mind my own business if you want, but Liz mentioned that you broke up with your boyfriend." Emmy scooted closer so they could whisper to each other.

"We did break up at the beginning of my senior year," Dany admitted. "He decided not to finish at Olivet and moved to Philadelphia to finish college."

"Were you shattered?"

"Not completely. He had talked about Philadelphia for about a year. I admit it took me some time to get over it, but I kept busy with classes."

"I remember what it's like to break up with a guy. Even though Kenny and I have been friends since I was seven, we didn't start dating until I was almost ten," Emmy said and they both giggled.

"Liz and Tyler have known each other forever, but they didn't start dating until high school. They were together in a school play." Dany looked across the room at her sister and brother-in-law. "Look at them now. They're like an old married couple with two kids and a dog."

"You must think Kenny and I are really old, huh? Emmy asked.

"I didn't mean old in years, but in maturity. You still act like a kid, and I mean that in a good way."

"I'm just yanking your chain. Have you ever thought of becoming a doctor like your parents?"

"I would probably specialize in psychiatry or something in research for kids, but, yeah, I have thought about it."

"Not to totally change the subject, but can you beat Tyler at tennis?"

"I win a game here and there, but I can never win a set from him. I can beat Liz, though," Dany laughed. "She's not as athletic as me, and I played on the tennis team in high school."

"I used to play quite a bit in my younger days."

73

"You're still young, Emmy."

"Kristen's brother Derrick went to college on a tennis scholarship. I would play against him. He would let me win occasionally."

"Tyler never lets me win. He's so competitive. I would have to earn it."

"We should play sometime. There's an outdoor court at... It's Derrick and Amber's house now, but it's where Derrick and Kristen grew up. Mr. Robertson has an indoor court at his place. They live down the street from us."

"Sounds like fun." Dany pointed at a young man coming their way. "Here comes your son, and he looks like he has ice cream down the front of his shirt."

Emmy turned and shook her head. "That's Kevin Michael. He is all boy. I better rescue Kenny. It's been so good to see you again."

They hugged briefly.

"I'll call you the next time I come to see Liz and Tyler."

"Mommy! Mommy! I ate more ice cream, and it made my head hurt, but I feel better now."

The reception officially ended at six, but some people stayed to help with the cleanup. Emmy and Liz helped in the kitchen. Tyler, Larry and Kenny helped the local people put away tables and chairs.

"Are you still going back tonight?" Emmy asked Liz.

"Yes, hopefully the kids will sleep on the way home. I think that will be easier than trying to wake them up early. Derby will sleep, too. Are you staying overnight?"

"We checked into a room at some motel. I don't remember the name. The kids want to go swimming." Emmy tossed some paper plates in the trash. "What time are you guys leaving?"

"Nine at the latest. We're going to visit with Mom and Dad for a while and then head home."

"Have a safe trip."

"You, too. Have fun, and we'll see you when you get back."

Chapter Seven

"Mary, do you have a minute? I need to talk to you," Pastor Jonah Galves held her hand as they walked toward the sanctuary from the educational wing.

"Okay, but the second service will be starting soon. I'd rather not be late." Mary Michaelis flipped her long, straight brown hair over her shoulders.

"It's kinda important." Jonah smiled as he led her into the main office and down the hall to Pastor Tyler's small office.

"What if Pastor Tyler needs to use his office?" Mary asked.

Jonah chuckled. "He's never in here. We have some privacy." He put his hands on Mary's slim arms.

"And why do we need privacy?" Mary asked with a hint of her Irish accent. "You better not try to kiss me in the church like you did after school on Friday." Her brown eyes sparkled.

"I'm not going to kiss you. Not right away, I mean." He reached into a pocket of his brown suit and pulled out a small black box.

"Jonah," Mary whispered and put a hand to her mouth.

"Mary, I love you with all of my heart. Will you do me the honor of becoming my wife?" He said and then opened the box to let her see the ring.

She barely glanced at the ring before wrapping her arms around his barrel-size chest and holding on tight. "Yes, I will marry you."

"I'm glad," he said and then kissed her.

"Did you think I would refuse?"

"I was pretty sure you would say yes. Do you want to try on the ring?"

She held out her hand. "You're supposed to put it on for me."

He slipped the ring onto her finger. "Do you like it?"

"It's perfect!" She stared at the gold band and small stone. "Does anyone know about this?"

"I told my parents, but no one else. I didn't tell my brothers."

75

"So Ma and Da don't know yet, huh?"

"They might suspect it if they see the ring," Jonah smiled. Then he kissed her again.

"Should I take it off until after church?"

Jonah shook his head. "I don't want you to ever take it off, Mary Ellen."

"We better go sit down. I hear the worship band playing." *I love the way you use my middle name. No one else ever does except Ma at times.*

They scurried through the back hallway and entered the sanctuary on the far side. Mary spotted her parents and two brothers and her sister sitting in their usual spots. Mary sat beside her sister, and Jonah covered her hands with his.

Fifteen-year-old Dahlia Michaelis poked Mary in the side. "Where have you been? The service has started."

Pastor Darren Eaton was praying at the moment.

"Hush," Cora Michaelis frowned at her daughters.

"Jonah needed to talk to me. That's why we're late."

Dahlia looked into Mary's eyes. "You're holding out on me."

Dylan Michaelis leaned forward from his seat and the end of the row and stared at his daughters.

"I'll tell you later, Dahlia."

Jonah kept his hand on Mary's through most of the service. No one had spotted the engagement ring until he sneezed and used his hand to cover his mouth.

Dahlia glanced down and spotted the ring. "Oh, my God, Mary! Is that what I think it is?"

Mrs. Michaelis touched her older son's knee. Darian poked his younger brother Eli in the ribs. Eli bumped Dahlia's arm and relayed the message, "Hush."

Dahlia stifled a giggle. Something not easy for fifteen-year-old girls to do even in church. She grabbed Mary's hand and covered the ring until Jonah returned his hand to Mary's. Dahlia grinned at Jonah, sat back, folded her arms across her chest and smirked.

"What is your problem," Eli asked.

76

"Nothing. Pay attention to Pastor Tyler."

Eli stretched his arm over the back of Dahlia's chair and tugged on her ponytail. He received an elbow to the ribs for his effort.

"That was a good message, Cora." Dylan said after Tyler dismissed the congregation.

"I appreciate the way he applies his lessons to daily life. Some preachers just try to impress people with their knowledge. Pastor Tyler is very intelligent, but knows how to get his point across."

"Ma, Da, Mary needs to talk to you." Dahlia scooted past her brothers will Mary in tow.

"Hey! Watch it, little sister. You stepped on my foot," Darian complained.

Dahlia teased back, "It's difficult to miss it. It takes up the whole row."

"What is so important that it can not wait until we are home, or at least in the car?" Mrs. Michaelis asked.

Dahlia grabbed Mary's hand and held it up. "Notice anything new? Besides the red nail polish she's not supposed to wear at church."

Darian and Eli shrugged. Mr. Michaelis shook hands with a visitor. Mrs. Michaelis picked up her purse from the floor.

"Ma! Look!"

Jonah moved behind Mary and placed his hands on her shoulders.

Finally, her parents looked at Mary's hand.

"Is that a ring?" Mrs. Michaelis asked.

Dahlia rolled her eyes. "Duh! Of course it's a ring. It's her engagement ring. You guys! They're engaged!"

Mrs. Michaelis looked up at Jonah and Mary and asked, "Is this true? Are you officially engaged?"

"Yes, Ma. Jonah proposed just before the service started."

Darian slapped Jonah on the back. "'Bout time you asked her to get hitched. You've been dating long enough."

"We've only been dating since last July," Mary said. "Some people date for years before they decide to get married."

"I haven't been dating anyone for more than a year," Darian said.

Eli smiled down at Mary. "Yeah, but you're not getting any younger."

"I'm only twenty-five," Mary said. "That's about the average age to be getting married these days."

Ma reached out and hugged Mary hard enough to squeeze the breath out of her. Da vigorously shook hands with Jonah.

"Welcome to the family, son." Mr. Michaelis continued to shake Jonah's hand while using his left hand to hug him.

Dahlia bounced on her toes. "Isn't this super great! I can't wait to tell my friends. I'm going to post it on Facebook."

"Dahlia, you have to wait," Mary insisted. "I have to tell my friends first."

"What about my friends here at church? Can't I tell them now?"

Mary shook her head. "No, you have to wait."

"Okay, but you have to do it today. I'll simply burst if I can't tell my friends."

"Are you and Jonah coming for dinner, or do you have other plans," Ma asked.

"I didn't make any other plans because I didn't know he was going to propose," Mary smiled at Jonah.

"Then I think you should bring Jonah home for dinner."

Mr. Michaelis tossed Darian the keys to the family van. "Would you bring the van up before Dahlia bursts. If we don't get her home right away, I'm afraid she will spill the beans and spoil Mary's surprise."

"Oh, Da! I'm not going to blab to everyone." Dahlia wrinkled her nose at her father.

"Girls, we have to get out of the pool now. We have to change clothes and check out," Kenny helped Kevin out of the pool and made sure Heather and Isabella were following.

"Thank you for letting us swim again, Daddy," Isabella wrapped a towel around her shoulders.

"You're welcome, Isa." He glanced over his shoulder. "I mean now, Heather."

"Fine!" Heather reluctantly got out and stomped toward the door.

"You need to towel off before you leave the pool area." Kenny tossed a towel at her.

They headed back to the room.

"Let's get a move on," Emmy shouted. "We have ten minutes to check out. I'm not paying for another day in this place."

"I'll check out if you help the kids change clothes," Kenny offered. "Where are the suitcases?"

"In the Odyssey. I packed up while you guys were swimming again. I've been busy working while everyone else has been playing." Emmy made a face at Kenny. "I'll check out since I don't have to change. There are dry clothes for everyone on the bed. Throw all your wet clothes in that garbage bag." She pointed to the white bag on the table and left the room.

"Do we have to throw our clothes away because they're wet, Daddy?" Kevin shrugged. "Why? I like my police swimming trunks."

"We're not throwing them away, Kev." Kenny helped him change out of his wet clothes while the girls used the bathroom to change.

"Do we get to stop for lunch somewhere?" Heather asked while stuffing her bathing suit in the garbage bag.

"I think we'll stop along the way, but no McDonald's."

Ten minutes later Kenny backed the Odyssey out of its parking spot and they headed for SoHam.

"We're starving, Mom!" Heather shouted. "I really, really have to eat soon, or I will starve to death."

Kenny whispered to Emmy, "I said no McDonald's, so don't let Heather persuade you otherwise."

"If you can wait a while, we can stop at a nice family restaurant," Emmy suggested.

"I want a burger and French fries," Kevin hollered.

"Milkshake," Heather announced. "Chocolate!"

"What would you like, Isabella?" Kenny asked.

"Fish sandwich."

Emmy sighed and then looked at Kenny. "Fine! We might

as well stop for fast food. It will save time."

Four and a half hours later Kenny pulled the Odyssey into their garage.

"We're finally home," he said.

"How do you feel, Kevin. Is your stomach still upset?" Emmy looked back at her son.

"I don't have to throw up anymore," he answered.

"Let me out of here!" Heather insisted. "It stinks like throw up."

Kenny opened the doors and helped Kevin out of his car seat. The twins unbuckled themselves, scrambled out of their booster seats and scurried into the house.

"I guess we shouldn't have let him have that milkshake," Kenny said and then shrugged.

"Ya think!" Emmy held her nose. "Can you take this thing to the car wash today?"

"I can't run it through the car wash with the doors and windows open, Em."

"No, but you can vacuum it out and use some air freshener. I have to use this thing to haul the kids around, and I don't want it smelling like puke."

"Can I take the suitcases in first?"

"Just put them in the mudroom, and I'll unpack them. I need to throw a bunch of clothes in the washer anyway."

It was ninety minutes later when Emmy finally had a chance to sit down and relax. She booted up her laptop to check her email.

"Hey, there's one from Mary with 'call me urgent' as the subject," Emmy mentioned to Kenny, who had returned and was watching football in the family room.

"What do you think it might be?"

"Don't know. Left my crystal ball in Michigan. I hope it's nothing serious. I better call her." Emmy frowned at Kenny.

"I'm sure everything's okay." Kenny raised his hands as Peyton Manning threw a touchdown pass to bring the Broncos closer to the Texans in the fourth quarter.

"I'm going to call while the kids are upstairs being quiet."

80

Emmy walked into the den, sat in Kenny's new black leather recliner, put her feet over the arm, leaned back and dialed Mary's cell phone.

"Hey, Mary, I saw your email. What's up? Everyone okay?"

"Are you sitting down, Em?"

Emmy bolted out of the chair. "Yes! No! I was, but now I'm standing. Tell me what happened. Is it really bad news?"

Mary laughed. "No, but you should sit down."

Emmy plopped into the recliner. "Okay, I'm sitting."

"Jonah and I were walking out of the education building between services..."

"Did he fall and hurt himself? Did he break his arm again?"

"No, he's all right." Mary shook her head and laughed. "Are you going to let me tell you what happened?"

"Yes, I won't interrupt again."

Mary knew she had to make this quick because Emmy would keep interrupting. "He pulled me into Pastor Tyler's office."

"Was Pastor Tyler in there? He usually doesn't use his... Sorry. I interrupted again."

"Jonah proposed!" Mary blurted out.

Emmy jumped out of the recliner again. "He did what?"

"He pulled out a ring and asked me to marry him. Oh, Emmy, I'm engaged. Are you happy for me?"

"Kenny! Kenny! Guess what?" she screamed as she ran back to the family room.

She startled Kenny and caused him to spill his Coke on the couch. "What, Em?" He tried to wipe off his jeans.

"Jonah asked Mary to marry him! Isn't that great!?"

"He did? When did this happen?" He asked a little too casually.

Emmy stopped in front of him and frowned. "Did you already know? Don't lie to me."

"Well..."

She kicked his foot. "You are a real stinker! How did you know before me?"

"Sorry, but I opened Facebook, and saw that Dahlia had

81

posted it. I knew Mary would want to tell you herself, so I didn't say anything."

"How long have you known?"

"Ten minutes, so it's not like I knew yesterday, or last week."

"Why am I always the last one to know whenever anyone gets engaged?" Emmy plopped down next to Kenny. "Yuck! What is on the couch?"

"I spilled my pop, and you just sat in it."

"Great! These are new jeans." Emmy rolled her eyes. "So why am I always the last to know? Are you still there, Mary?" Emmy put her phone on the speaker.

"I'm here, Em. It sounds like you are having a rough day."

Emmy explained about the trip and Kevin getting sick in the van.

"So why am I always the last to know?" She crossed her arms over her chest. "People knew I was getting engaged even before I did."

"What?" Kenny asked.

"Kristen knew you were going to propose before I did. Same thing with most of our other friends."

Mary laughed. "Maybe it's because if you know ahead of time, you would tell everyone."

"Would not," Emmy proclaimed. Then she bit her lip. "Maybe I would. Oh, Mary, I'm so happy for you. What does the ring look like? Is it a massive diamond. He better have bought you a diamond ring."

"I'll let you see it tomorrow at school if you want."

"I definitely want," Emmy said and then giggled. "Did he kiss you after you accepted?"

"Emmy," Mary drew out the name. "I'm not talking about our love life to you. You would tell everyone."

"Would not," Emmy said though she knew Mary was right.

Chapter Eight

"Let's go, girls. We have to leave for school in three minutes." Emmy combed Kevin's curly, reddish blonde hair. "You need a trim, little man."

"Do we have to take Caden and Carson to school with us?" Heather grumbled as she grabbed her backpack. "Caden is starting to bug me."

Kenny laughed. "And just how is he bugging you, Heather'?"

"He is always trying to sit by me, and at recess he tries to play with me. He's a boy. He should play with boys."

"I always played with the boys at recess," Emmy confessed. "I liked sports. Especially football. I tried to get Barry Newton to play ball, but he was a klutz."

"What's a klutz, Mommy?" Isabella asked. "Is that the same as a dork?"

Emmy laughed and grinned at Kenny.

He rolled his eyes. "Go ahead, Em. You know you want to."

"There's a difference, Isa. Your father is a dork. A lovable dork, but still a dork."

Isabella and Heather stared at their father. He shrugged his shoulders.

"Barry is a klutz because he's uncoordinated and not very good at catching a ball. Does that help?"

"I can catch a ball," Kevin insisted. "I can catch a firetruck, too. I'll show you." He tossed one of his many firetrucks in the air and it landed in the sink.

"See what you started, Em." Kenny retrieved the firetruck from the sink and handed it back to Kevin. "No more throwing firetrucks in the house. We will play catch with a ball after school if you want."

"Time to go," Emmy said.

She picked up Carson and Caden, drove to the Crest Ridge United Nazarene church where the kids went to school, dropped them off and then parked the Odyssey. She hustled inside to Mary

Michaelis' kindergarten classroom. She waited until Mary had a moment to talk.

"I'm so thrilled for you." Emmy hugged Mary. "Now let me see the ring."

Mary held out her hand. "Did Dahlia spoil the surprise? The little stinker posted it on Facebook before I told her she could."

"Kenny actually saw it, but he didn't tell me. Were you surprised he proposed?" Emmy held onto Mary's hand to inspect the ring.

"Not really. Maybe by his timing, but we had talked about getting married."

Emmy let go of Mary's hand. "I don't suppose you've had a chance to set the date, have you?"

"Not specifically, but I would like to get married as soon as school is out." Mary glanced around the room to make sure her students were behaving.

"You want to be able to take a long honeymoon, huh?" Emmy grinned.

"Stop that! Jonah would only be able to take two weeks of vacation." Mary smiled at one of the students and helped her off with her jacket. "Find your seat, Danisha."

"I bet Pastor Tyler would let him take an extra week," Emmy said. "I should go. Call me. Maybe we can get together this weekend and do something."

"I will. Maybe you can help with some of the planning for the wedding."

"I'd love that, Mary. The girls will be so thrilled when they see you in your wedding dress."

"You mean my princess dress?" Mary grinned.

"I'll teach them the difference. Call me." Emmy held her hand to her ear as she scooted past some of the students and out the door.

"Thanks for coming to the office this evening," Heidi Knapp smiled at Tyler and Liz. "It will make it easier for me to pull up some listings.

84

"No problem," Liz said. "Your office is only two minutes away."

Tyler glanced at some photos of homes for sale that were spread out on the table.

"What do you absolutely need to have in a house?" Heidi asked.

"We made a list like you suggested," Tyler said. He checked the list on his phone. "We need four bedrooms because we are in the program to be foster parents. At least two bathrooms."

"More would be better," Liz said.

They mentioned a few more items.

"I took the liberty of pulling a few listing from the area close to the church. I can eliminate some because they only have three bedrooms."

Heidi went over the listings with Liz and Tyler, and they picked out three to visit.

The next evening Heidi showed the three houses to Liz and Tyler. The first home reeked of cigarette smoke, and the second didn't meet their criteria closely enough.

"I have one more. It's a bit cheaper than the other two, but newer. The neighborhood is not far from the church. It might be a better fit." Heidi sounded hopeful.

Heidi drove them to the Leechmont Glen subdivision.

"This one is empty, and would be available for a quick closing," Heidi said while checking her information sheet.

Tyler and Liz went through the house without commenting.

"What did you think?" Heidi asked as they walked out the front door.

Liz looked at Tyler and shook her head.

He chuckled. "I know carpeting and wallpaper can be changed, but that blue shag carpeting was hideous."

"Why would anyone paint the bedrooms such an ugly shade of yellow?" Liz shivered as she thought of the colorful bedrooms. "The basement isn't finished at all. The kitchen cabinets were green."

"I haven't shown that listing before. I should have done

85

more research on it. I'm sorry," Heidi apologized.

"The backyard was large and fenced in," Tyler said.

"Doesn't make up for everything else." Liz hurried to the car. "We would have to change too much."

"Let me do some more research. When would you be available to look again?"

"Not tomorrow. We have Wednesday night service," Tyler said. He looked at Liz. "Could we see a couple of houses on Thursday after school and before worship band practice?"

"If I can find someone to watch Natty and Grayson," Liz said.

"I'll try to set up something for Thursday," Heidi said.

"Hi, Mary. Are you enjoying being engaged? Silly question, I know," Emmy said and then giggled.

Mary sighed and answered, "Jonah and I have been busy. There is so much to do in order to have a wedding."

"Tell me about it. I was fortunate to have Kristen and Paula Kratzsky helping because I actually went on tour for several weeks. Kenny and the guys were gone, too," Emmy recalled. "Sorry, I shouldn't bore you with my stuff. Are you and Jonah busy this Saturday?"

"Sorry, Emmy, but we are. We're spending the weekend in Milwaukee. It's his parents fortieth anniversary."

"You need to be there for that. Maybe we can get together the following weekend," Emmy said.

"I'll tell Jonah not to plan anything else."

Heidi met Tyler and Liz at the church Thursday afternoon.

"I have three more homes that might work better." Heidi showed them pictures of the three houses.

"I like this one," Liz said.

Tyler glanced at the information. "It's a bit out of our price range."

"It might be too far from the church, but I have been inside it. It's a gorgeous home."

They visited that house first, and although it was as

86

beautiful as Heidi had mentioned, the location would not work.

"I don't want to be ten miles from the church," Tyler said as they walked out of the house.

They rejected the second house because the floor plan felt too claustrophobic.

"I have one more. This one is only five miles from the church," Heidi informed them. "I checked it on Mapquest. It's only five years old. The taxes are rather high, but average for the area. There is a three-car garage which would be a bonus. Four bedrooms, three bathrooms and the basement is partially finished."

Heidi turned into the Cinder Ridge development, and Tyler and Liz gawked at the large homes.

"It's this one." Heidi pulled onto the concrete driveway.

Tyler and Liz jumped out of the car. "This one has great curb appeal," Liz said with a smile.

The inside of the home kept them smiling.

"It's almost perfect." Liz ran her hand along the granite countertop of the kitchen island. "I love these cabinets and the stainless steel appliances."

"I like the idea of being on a cul-de-sac. Less traffic. The bedrooms are large enough." Tyler opened a door. "Liz, look. There's a walk-in pantry that's big enough to use as an office."

"Maybe for you." Liz poked him in the arm. "Are you hoping the pool table in the basement stays?"

"I could get used to a pool table. Don't need the wet bar, though."

Liz and Tyler went through the house one more time. They walked out into the backyard and saw one of the neighbors, who smiled and waved.

"Could we have a minute, Heidi?" Tyler asked.

"Certainly, I'll check my phone."

"I like this one," Liz sat on the built-in bench on the large deck.

"Five miles is not that far from the church. I wouldn't want to be any farther away. This is actually in SoHam, and I think Kenny and Emmy's house is over there a ways."

"Do you want to make an offer?"

"It's in our price range. We wouldn't have to change a thing to move in."

"I might want to paint the master bedroom. I might get tired of that lavender," Liz said.

They talked about it, and even closed their eyes, held hands and prayed.

"I feel good about this one, Liz."

"Me, too. Should we let Natty and Grayson see it before we make an offer?"

"No, I think we need to make an offer right away. This one could go fast."

They told Heidi, and she drove them back to the office. She drew up the offer. Tyler and Liz signed it, and Heidi faxed it to the listing agent.

She smiled at Tyler and hugged Liz. "We should know by Saturday if they accept your offer."

Monday afternoon Heidi got back to Tyler and Liz with news about the house.

"There are two other offers. I'm afraid you might be in a bidding war," Heidi said.

"How much higher would we need to go?" Tyler asked.

"Too high, I'm afraid. I don't know for sure, but the listing agent gave me the impression the other offers were higher."

"I'll talk to Liz, but we might have to let this one go," Tyler informed Heidi.

"I understand. You have a budget to consider. I'll keep my eyes open in case we have to find another house," Heidi promised.

Tyler talked to Liz, and though they both loved the house, they decided not to make a higher offer.

"God will provide the right house, Tyler. As much as we liked this one, it wasn't meant for us."

"God's timing is sometimes much different than ours. It could take several months to find a house."

"I'm sorry to bother you so early on a Tuesday. I know you have a Bible study at ten, but I have to tell you about a property

88

that's going to be listed later today." Heidi's enthusiasm bubbled over. "Do you know where Vine Ridge is?"

"Isn't that a street off of Essington?" Tyler thought.

"It is! This house is three minutes from the church. Tops! Maybe less. It fits all your criteria, and it's owned by one of the agents in this office. They built a new house and are ready to move to that property. He described the house to me, and I definitely think it's worth a look. Is there any way you and Liz could meet me there this morning?"

"I could see if Liz could get away at lunchtime for a few minutes," Tyler answered. "I'll text her and get back to you as soon as I can."

Liz was able to get away for thirty minutes. She and Tyler met Heidi at the house.

"It looks good from the street," Liz said. "I love the landscaping and the mature trees."

Five minutes later Tyler and Liz knew this was the house for them. An hour later they had placed an offer.

"I feel good about this one," Tyler told Liz after she and Natalie returned home from school.

"Have we heard back from Heidi?" Liz rubbed Derby's ears and gave her a treat after she did her business outside.

"Not yet. We need to be patient. God knows whether or not we will get this house. Are you hungry?"

"I'm almost too nervous to eat, but the kids will need something." Liz opened the pantry. "You have a taste for anything in particular?"

"Not really," Tyler answered just as his phone rang. He looked at the caller ID. "It's Heidi. Maybe she has some good news."

"Congratulations! The seller has accepted your offer. I have a signed contract in my hands." Heidi waved the document at the phone.

"Liz! We got the house."

"Don't kid me about that." Liz twisted her hair.

"I'm not. Heidi has a signed contract."

"See! I knew God would provide the right house," Liz said.

Heidi talked to Tyler for a few more minutes.

"Once the seller learned you were the pastor at Crest Ridge, he accepted your offer without trying to counter it."

"I wonder why," Tyler asked.

Heidi explained, "He told me why. Do you remember Mrs. Gerl from the church?"

"I've heard the name, but... " He tried to remember. "Oh, that's Mrs. Capista's sister. She passed away several years ago if I'm thinking of the same person."

"Yes, and the seller happens to be her son. Doesn't God work in mysterious ways at times?"

"I believe He does." Tyler chuckled.

Heidi helped set up an appointment for the house inspection. Tyler accompanied the inspector two days later. No major problems were discovered.

"What do we do next?" Tyler asked.

"We have to set a time for the closing. You need proof of homeowner's insurance." Heidi explained everything that would happen over the next couple of months.

"I can't believe we are going to be homeowners, " Tyler said as they got ready for bed that night.

"You said that God's timing is different than ours. Maybe he was teasing us with that other house."

"You believe God has a sense of humor, huh?" Tyler asked.

"Of course He does. Go to the zoo, and you'll see all kinds of examples of His sense of humor. Zebras, giraffes, anteaters..."

Chapter Nine

"What time should we come over?" Mary asked Emmy on Saturday morning.

"Why don't you guys come over for lunch? The girls and I will be here, but Kenny is taking Kevin to the zoo. I'm not sure when they'll get back," Emmy replied.

"Should I bring anything?"

"Just Jonah and your engagement ring. The girls will want to see it," Emmy said. "Just buzz yourself in. I'll probably be in the kitchen."

"We'll be there by noon," Mary said, hung up and then kissed Jonah. "Will you be finished by then?"

"Soccer games should end around eleven. I don't need to be at the church any later than that." He checked the time. "I should get going. Please thank your mother for inviting me to breakfast."

"I will. You can pick me up whenever you finish. Have I told you that I love you lately?" Mary asked.

Jonah put his arms around her waist just as Dahlia entered the living room.

"What are you guys doing? You're not married yet," Dahlia teased.

"I can kiss him if I want."

"Dahlia! You let them have some privacy," Mom hollered from the kitchen. "You can help me load the dishwasher."

"Coming, Ma," Dahlia grinned at Mary and blew Jonah a kiss.

Jonah made it through the security gate at the entrance to Bristol Ridge after getting hassled by the guard.

"I didn't think he was going to let us in for a moment," Jonah wiped some sweat from his forehead.

Mary grinned.

"Why do you think it's funny?"

"He knows me, and I bet Emmy called him and told him to give you some flack." Mary pointed. "Take a left here."

Jonah pulled into the gated entrance and drove up the winding driveway.

91

"You can park in front of that garage bay. That was my spot," Mary directed him.

"You can't even see this house from the road, and it's huge." Jonah parked and got out.

"Please don't say anything to Emmy about it. She still feels guilty about living in such a big place."

Mary punched in the code to open the service door and pulled Jonah in with her.

He glanced around. "The garage is bigger than my parents' house, and they raised five kids in it."

"Shush." Mary led him up the steps and into the mudroom. "Now hush about the house."

He nodded and zipped his mouth shut.

"Em! We're here. Where are you?" Mary hollered as she and Jonah entered the kitchen.

"Be right there," Emmy answered from the family room.

Heather and Isabella rushed into the kitchen.

"Hi, Mary!" Heather shouted. "We miss you." She looked up at Mary and grabbed her hand. Then she smiled at Jonah.

Isabella grabbed Mary's other hand. "Is this your ring? It's looks beautiful. Look, Mommy," Isabella held up Mary's hand.

"Hi, guys. I know it's beautiful, Isa. I've seen it before."

Jonah looked around the kitchen and then at Emmy. *This kitchen looks like it could be in a five-star restaurant. The house is humongous, and you're wearing old, faded jeans with holes in the knees and that Fridays At Five sweatshirt looks so faded. It must be twenty years old.*

Emmy grinned at Jonah. "Did you have any trouble finding the place?"

Mary turned and smiled at Jonah. "You should have seen his face when the guard started giving him a hard time."

"I'm sorry, Jonah. I couldn't resist," Emmy said and then hugged Mary. "Are you hungry? I can put some sandwiches together."

"Sandwiches are fine, Emmy." Mary pulled Jonah around the island and they held hands while sitting on barstools.

"Kenny texted a few minutes ago. They'll be home soon."

Emmy opened the fridge and grabbed some lunch meat and a couple of packages of sliced cheese. "I've got ham, turkey and some sliced roast beef." She waved the packages at Jonah. "I know Mary likes turkey. What would you like, Jonah? I could make tuna salad."

Jonah grinned. "I'd like ham and provolone on rye bread with honey mustard, please. Oh, and a sliced dill pickle."

Mary poked his arm. "We aren't in a restaurant."

Emmy laughed. "It's okay, Mary. He's getting back at me for the security guard thing. Let me see if I have any rye bread." She checked the breadbox. "You're in luck, and it doesn't look too moldy. I could scrape off this section."

"Have you eaten?" Mary asked Heather and Isabella, who were standing at the side of the island.

"We had chicken noodle soup and bologna sandwiches earlier," Heather answered.

"Heather, would you and Isa run upstairs and play in your room for a while. I want to talk to Mary and Jonah."

"Come on, Heather. We can play dress up and pretend we're getting married," Isabella yanked on Heather's hand, and the girls giggled as they ran out of the kitchen.

"They are so darling, Em," Mary watched the twins leave and then turned back to Emmy. "I've seen pictures of you at their age. They look almost exactly like you."

"Their hair isn't as curly as mine was, and their eyes are darker. Brown like Kenny's."

Emmy made the sandwiches and pointed to the breakfast nook. "Let's eat in there so we can talk. Anyone wants chips?"

"Sure, whatever kind you've got is okay," Jonah said.

"What? No special request? How about sea salt and vinegar?" Emmy asked.

"Sure, whatever."

Emmy grinned at Mary who was making a face. "You will have to learn about Mary's likes and dislikes. She can't stand the taste of vinegar."

"I'm sorry," Jonah said. He kissed her cheek. "What flavors do you like?"

She stared into his eyes. "Just about anything else."

"How about sour cream and onion?" Emmy didn't wait for an answer. *You guys are so in love.*

They moved to the breakfast nook. Emmy prayed and they ate.

"Have you set a date?" Emmy asked.

"June first, and we're getting married at the church."

"And the reception?"

Mary looked at Jonah and smiled. "Do you want to tell her?"

"There's this old hotel in downtown SoHam."

Emmy didn't let him finish. "The Lincoln Hotel? For real, Mary?" Emmy squealed with giddiness.

Mary nodded. "We've both been saving money, and Ma and Da are paying for most of it."

"That is fantastic. Have you hired a wedding coordinator?"

"Not really. We thought we could plan it ourselves," Mary answered.

"It's more difficult than you think. We used Paula Kratzsky. She is super."

"She's kinda expensive, Em."

"Would you use her if the cost wasn't an issue?"

Mary looked at Jonah. He shrugged.

"I suppose so," Mary said.

"I'll call her and make sure she's available," Emmy said. *She better be available, or else I'll get after her.*

"Emmy," Mary said slowly.

"No arguing, young lady. You are like part of our family. You can consider it part of our gift to you guys."

Mary reached across the table and squeezed Emmy's hand. "Thank you," she whispered.

The girls came downstairs, holding hands and each wearing a dress they had borrowed from Emmy's closet.

"What are you doing?" Emmy tried to say sternly but couldn't.

The twins giggled and the Heather said, "We're getting married and these are our princess dresses. Do you like them?"

94

"You both look like adorable princesses," Mary reached out to hug them. *You will always be so precious to me.*

"This works better," Emmy told Kenny as they entered the Sunday School classroom. "I'm glad Chase changed the schedule." She waved to Kristen Randolph and hurried past some people to sit next to her.

"I'm glad you don't have to play for both services, Em. I feel more comfortable when you're in class with me."

"Why?" Emmy asked. "You've been coming to this church for ten years."

"I know, but you know more about the Bible than I do. I study my Bible, but I can't remember specific verses the way you do. I'm afraid if I have to say something, I'll make a mistake."

Emmy squeezed Kristen's hand. "Don't be silly. You're smarter than me, and no one would laugh at you the way they laugh at me when I say something goofy."

Pastor Tyler and Liz scooted around the table and sat on the side by the windows.

"Morning, everyone," Liz said with a smile.

"Hey, guys. Are you going to tell everyone about the house?" Emmy asked.

Tyler chuckled. "Well, I suppose we might as well."

"Shoot!" Emmy put as hand to her mouth. "Did I spoil a secret? I'm so sorry."

"It's all right, Emmy," Liz said. "We were going to tell people today."

Don Williams finished outlining the lesson on the whiteboard and faced the people. He flashed his cheery smile at Emmy. "Do we need to talk about something before I begin the lesson?"

"No, sir," Emmy answered. She respected the part-time pastor who had started the sports and athletic program several years before.

"We can talk after class," Liz said.

"I have the feeling I will not have your full attention unless we talk about whatever is on your mind," Mr. Williams said. He unbuttoned his black suit coat.

Emmy developed a sudden interest in the missionary book on the table and kept her eyes down.

Liz checked with Tyler who nodded. She smiled and then spilled her news. "The seller has accepted our offer. We're homeowners. Well, in November. That's when we close."

"Congratulations, Tyler and Liz. Buying your first home is always a major step for a young couple," Mr. Williams said. He clasped his large, strong hands together in front. "Do you want to tell the class more about the house?"

Liz twisted her hair. "I'll tell them after church. We don't want to take up anymore of your time."

Mr. Williams looked at Emmy. "Should we pray first?"

She glanced up at Mr. Williams and then closed her eyes. *I don't know why I feel so intimidated by you. You're such a gentle man even if you look like a football player. You remind me of Otis Wilson who used to play for the Bears.*

Mr. Williams prayed and then began the Sunday School lesson.

Emmy, Kristen and Liz walked out together after the class.

"Why are you so quiet, Emmy?" Liz asked.

"Is it just me, or does Mr. Williams scare you guys, too?"

Liz laughed. "Why would you feel intimidated by him? He's like a big teddy bear."

"He reminds me of a high school principal or the dean of a college," Kristen said. "He's always wearing a suit and his shoes are shiny enough to be a mirror."

"You guys are goofy," Liz chuckled.

"Are you going to tell us all about the house?" Emmy asked.

"Can I wait until after church? We'll have more time then. Or do you have to hurry home to watch the Bears?" Liz asked.

"They aren't playing today, so Tony better be here unless he wants me to get on his case."

"After church works for me," Kristen flipped her long blonde hair over her shoulder. "I'll meet you later, Em."

Tony snuck up behind Emmy after church as she talked to

Mary and Jonah in the lobby. He tugged on her hair and then squeezed her shoulders.

"It's a good thing you're here and stop pulling my hair. I don't have a ponytail like I used to." She turned to face Tony. "Do you and Sloane have plans for lunch?"

"You'd have to ask her. I just eat it." Tony shrugged and then smiled.

"You're a big help." Emmy rolled her eyes. "If you aren't busy, Liz and Tyler are coming over for lunch. She's going to tell us about the house."

"I'll ask the boss," Tony said.

"Have her text me." Emmy heard a commotion. "Never mind. I'll ask her myself."

Sloane approached with six kids in tow. "No, Peter! You can't go over to Carson's house to play. You are grounded for fighting with your little brothers."

"You're so mean. Ben hit me first," Peter whined.

"He's four. You're twice his size. I don't want to hear another word," Sloane said and that settled the matter.

Emmy saw the frown on Sloane's face. "Are the kids getting on your nerves again?"

"No more than usual, but the big one is asking for trouble." She looked at Tony.

"I hear ya," Emmy said. "Tyler and Liz are coming over for lunch. You guys have plans?"

"Sorry, Emmy, but Mama is making lunch. Maybe another time." Sloane picked up Coby who had started to fuss.

"No problem. Make him help you with the kids. Don't let him be a couch potato and watch football all afternoon." Emmy poked Tony in the arm.

"I help with the kids," he claimed.

"You could help more. See you guys later. I have to round up my brood." Emmy waved and left to search for the girls and Kevin Michael.

An hour later Emmy announced, "Lunch is finally ready. Sorry I took so long."

"It's okay," Liz said. "I gave the kids a snack."

Kenny and Tyler came up from the basement where they had been listening to tracks in the studio. "Are we too late for lunch?" Kenny tried to grab a sandwich.

Emmy pulled the platter of cold cut sandwiches away from him. "Those are for the kids. If you guys are hungry, you can make your own. There's roast beef and ham left in the fridge. Could you grab a high chair for Grayson, please?"

Kenny brought one of their old high chairs from out of a closet. He counted the chairs around the breakfast nook table. "We have seating for seven now."

"Thank you, sweetie," Emmy kissed his cheek. *Such a dork.*

Kristen arrived with Zachary and Grace. "Are we too late? Did you already eat?"

"You're timing is perfect. Lunch is ready. Where's John?" Emmy asked.

"He had to meet with the foreman of that project in Newcastle. It appears they are having trouble with a couple of the subcontractors."

"He's busier now than when he played for the Bears," Emmy said.

"Tell me," Kristen sighed. "He's working seven days a week and is putting in twelve hour days. Sometimes even more." She looked at all the kids. "We're missing a kid. Where's Zhy?"

"She's on an overnight visit with her father," Liz said. "I'm afraid we might not have her for much longer."

"Do you have a preference, Tyler?" Kenny pulled out the roast beef and ham. "It's understandable. Bertucci and Keasling Construction is one of the biggest in the state."

"Yeah, and John feels that since he's new to the company, he has to prove he can handle it." Kristen leaned down to answer a question from four-year-old Grace. "Yes, you can play with the girls after we eat."

"I'm good with either," Tyler answered.

Emmy, Liz and Kristen managed to get all the kids seated with a plate of food and something to drink.

"It's not easy to feed seven kids," Kristen said.

98

"Sloane has to feed six every day. At least she has Mama Bertucci to help her," Emmy reminded them.

The adults gathered around the island. Kenny prayed and they started to eat.

"Okay, I want to hear about the house," Emmy said with her sandwich halfway to her mouth.

"Em, let them eat first," Kristen said.

Emmy waited patiently for fifteen minutes. By then the kids were finished eating. The mothers inspected the kids hands and faces.

"Okay! Everyone march upstairs and play nicely. I don't want to have to come upstairs and give spankings," Emmy said.

"Oh, Mommy, you don't spank us. You put us in timeout," Heather said and then the kids giggled.

"Does anyone want coffee, or something more to drink?" Kenny asked as Emmy herded the kids up the stairs.

"Water is okay with me," Tyler said.

Kenny waited on everyone who wanted a beverage.

"Should we move to the family room? It's more comfortable than the island." Kristen headed in that direction and everyone followed.

"Now can Liz tell me about the house?" Emmy asked as she sat on the arm of Kenny's recliner.

"You can sit on the couch with us," Liz patted the spot next to her. "Tyler doesn't bite."

Everyone got situated and then Liz began, "It's a two-story house. Four bedrooms. Three baths. Full finished basement."

"What do you see when you walk in the front door?" Emmy asked.

"Liz, it might be easier if you show Emmy the video you took," Tyler suggested.

Kristen said, "I thought it was illegal to take pictures or videos of houses you were seeing."

"The listing agent got permission from the owners," Tyler said.

"I have an idea," Kenny grinned. "How about I hook up Liz's phone to the TV, and we can watch it on the big screen."

"Great idea."

"I come up with great ideas every so often." Kenny ran to the basement to grab the cable he needed.

"It's true," Emmy said with a straight face. "He has a great idea every ten years or so."

"He married you, Em. Was that one of his great ideas?" Liz teased.

Emmy nodded. *Sometimes I wonder if he still thinks that was a great idea.*

Kenny returned, hooked everything up, and they watched the ten minute video.

"It's a beautiful home," Kristen said.

"We might want to paint the master bedroom. I'm not a big fan of that lavender color, but otherwise it's ready as is."

"A turn-key place," Kenny said.

Tyler checked the time. "We should get going. Zhy is supposed to be back at three."

"Thanks for lunch, Emmy." Liz gave her a hug as Tyler rounded up Natalie and Grayson.

"I realize Zhy should be with her biological father, but you will feel sad if she leaves," Emmy said.

"That's the hardest part of being a foster parent. We love Zhy, and will miss her terribly," Liz admitted.

"I'm sure you will get more kids soon. The program knows you are conscientious foster parents unlike some who are only in it for the money."

Chapter Ten

Diane called the next Thursday. "Emmy, I'm going over to see Mom. Will you come with me? I won't be there long."

Emmy sighed. "I know I should go see her more often, but I've been so busy."

"So come with me today. What are you doing right now?"

"Nothing too important, I guess."

"I'm picking you up. We'll be back before Kevin Michael is out of school," Diane said.

"Kenny said he would pick up the kids from pre-school."

"It's hard to believe Kevin is already going to school."

"So are Ben and Gracie. Gracie is so little, but she's smart. She can already say the alphabet and count to like a million," Emmy said.

"So, no excuses. You're coming with me," Diane ordered.

"Fine, but we have to be back by eleven."

Diane drove down the street and picked up Emmy.

"You're being rather quiet," Diane said on the way to Sunrise Garden. "What's on your mind? Everything okay between you guys? You aren't fighting, are you?"

"We are doing just fine, thank you. I was thinking about when we were kids. You and Mom fought all the time. You couldn't wait to move out, and look at you now. You go to see her two or three times a week. You have her power of attorney stuff. You're dealing with everything because I don't want to, so I feel guilty."

"For some reason now that Mom is losing her mind..."

"That's not funny, Diane." Emmy frowned.

"You know what I mean. She and I get along. It's like I'm the mother now, and she's the child."

"The last time I went to see her she didn't remember I was married. She got after me because I wasn't at school," Emmy recalled.

"She asked me last week if you had a new boyfriend. She said she knew you and Rory would sneak out at night."

Emmy's eyes sparkled. "She did not!"

Diane grinned, "She did."

"Do you think she really knows? I didn't think she ever knew about Rory."

"She obviously knew more than you realized."

"I never did anything with Rory," Emmy insisted.

"What do you consider anything? Obviously you guys did some things together." Diane waited at a red light. The light changed and car in front of her didn't move. "Move it! It won't get any greener."

"That was a long time ago, and I never did anything really bad with him."

Diane smirked, "Uh-huh, sure, Em."

"Can we change the subject, please?" Emmy crossed her arms over her chest.

"You do realize that Mom will get worse, right?"

Emmy bit her lip. "Will she get as bad as Aunt Betty?"

"Who knows? Betty's mind is totally gone, but she's in good health. She's six years older than Mom, but it wouldn't surprise me if Betty lives to be a hundred like Grandma Isabel."

"That would suck big time to live that long without your memory," Emmy said.

"I hate to sound morose, but I doubt Mom will last as long as Betty. Her heart just isn't as strong." Diane pulled into Sunrise Garden and parked. "You okay, Em?"

Emmy wiped her nose and dried her eyes. "I'm okay. Promise you won't tell Mom about Rory and me."

"What can I tell her? I don't know for sure what you guys did. Not back then, or just recently when he joined you on tour."

Emmy stopped walking. "We didn't do anything on tour."

"Good. Come on. I don't want to be here all day."

They took the elevator to the second floor, turned left and walked down the wide hallway, passing one of the caretakers pushing an elderly man in his wheelchair. The caretaker smiled and greeted them.

"Have you seen her today?" Diane asked.

The caretaker nodded. "She was upset earlier about something your father did."

102

"Great! Thanks for the warning."

"Why would Mom be upset about Daddy?" Emmy fell behind as Diane continued down the long hallway.

Diane stopped and turned around. "Because she still thinks he's alive. Now hurry up."

"I'm coming."

Diane pulled out her keys and opened the door to their mother's apartment.

"Are you going to wait in the hall?" Diane frowned at Emmy.

"You go in first."

Diane rolled her eyes. "Stop acting like a baby." She pulled Emmy into the apartment.

Patricia Colasanti sat in her recliner and stared intently at her TV. She glanced over her shoulder as Diane and Emmy approached.

"How are you doing today, Mom?" Diane asked and then sat on the couch.

Emmy picked up two Care Bears and then sat in a rocking chair on the opposite side of the room.

Mom ignored Diane and looked at Emmy for a moment. Emmy bit her lip and squeezed the bears.

"Emily! Why aren't you in school? This is a school day."

Emmy didn't answer as she looked at her mother and then at Diane.

"Emmy doesn't go to school anymore, Mom. She's older than she looks... and acts." Diane smiled at Mom and then frowned at Emmy. "Will you say something?"

"Hi, Mom. What are you watching?" Emmy shrugged.

"Some rerun. There's never anything good on this TV." Patricia used the remote to change channels. "Are you still seeing that boy from down the street? Your father doesn't like him or his brother. He thinks they're only interested in one thing, and you better not be giving it to him."

"Mom, Emmy is married to Kenny. She brought her girls to see you a couple of weeks ago," Diane said. *It was a couple of months ago, but you won't remember that.*

103

"My girls have dark hair, too," Patricia said and then stared at Diane. "You look older than the last time I saw you. How old are you now?"

"I'm only thirty-four and Emmy is thirty-two." Diane pointed to Emmy.

Patricia tilted her head and continued to stare at Diane. "You look a lot older."

Yeah, like ten years older than that. I'm going gray because I have to take care of you. "Thanks, Mom. Did you get your hair done?"

"They have a beauty shop here in the hotel, but they charge twenty-five dollars, and then they expect a tip. What a bunch of crooks!"

"You don't have to worry about money, Mom. You can get your hair done every week if you want," Emmy said.

"Not at that price! You need to learn the value of a dollar, Emily." Patricia flipped to another channel.

"Did you eat breakfast, Mom?" Diane asked.

"I think so, but don't ask me what I ate. I'm not hungry, so I must have eaten." Patricia stared at Diane.

"Do you need anything? Paper towels? Kleenex?" Diane walked into the bathroom and took a quick inventory. She made a note to buy more shampoo and a few other essentials.

"You should bring those other kids back sometime, Emily." Patricia pointed at the Care Bears. "They liked playing with those bears."

"I will, Mom." Emmy began to fidget in the rocking chair. "We should get going. I'll bring the kids over soon."

"Okay, but make sure you don't miss too much school, and tell her," she pointed at Diane, "to buy me some more of those cookies I like and a bottle of wine."

"Okay."

Diane walked up to Patricia. "We're going to leave." She noticed the empty phone base on the end table next to the recliner. "Do you know where your phone is?"

"No, I think it's back at the house."

"Em, would you check the bedroom?"

104

Three minutes later Diane hollered, "Found it!"

Emmy walked out of the bedroom. "Where did you find it? I found some cash and an old sandwich in the closet."

"Mom, this is your phone. It's supposed to go here so it can charge up. It doesn't belong in the refrigerator." Diane placed the phone in the base.

"I didn't put it in the fridge. Her father probably put it there. I know where my phone goes," she replied angrily while frowning at Emmy. "You stay away from that boy down the street. He's nothing but trouble, and you'll end up like your sister."

"Okay, we'll come back and see you soon," Diane said. "Let's go, Em. I need to get home and make a few calls."

Emmy walked over to her mother. "I'm gonna go, Mom. I'll bring the kids over soon." She leaned down and kissed her mother's cheek.

Diane made sure the apartment door was locked as she and Emmy left.

On the way out to the car, Emmy asked, "Why does she call me Emily, but never calls you by your name?"

"Why do you think?"

"Doesn't she remember who you are?" Emmy got in and buckled her seatbelt.

"I'm not always sure if she does or not. The last time I was here she did call me Diane, but she didn't today. One of these days she won't remember you either."

"That will be difficult to handle," Emmy said.

"We better be prepared for spending the money to put her in the memory care building. It will probably double the cost."

"We can afford it, Diane."

"We better be prepared to spend the money for several years."

A couple of Sundays later, just before the second service was about to start, Dave and Cathy Behren slipped into the building and sat near the back of the sanctuary. The former senior pastor had not been back to the church in over a year since resigning to take the position of president of Bellchester College in

Bellchester, Indiana; his alma mater.

As the worship band kicked off the first song, and Emmy clapped her hands to get the congregation to participate, Dr. Behren felt a tap on his shoulder. He turned and smiled at Jim Rosek.

"Hello, Jim."

"All righty then. It's a beautiful thing to see you."

"I'll talk to you after the service. We need to plan a trip around the lake."

"For sure. My motorcycle is getting rusty."

By the end of the service word had spread through the building that the Behrens were in attendance.

"I want to talk to Dr. Ausland," Dave whispered to Cathy as Tyler prayed to close the service.

Herb Ausland and Dave Behren had been friends for nearly thirty years, and Dave had succeeded Herb as the senior pastor.

"I'll meet you in the foyer later. I have some people I'd like to talk to as well," Cathy answered.

Dr. Behren made his way to the front of the sanctuary by slipping down the side aisle. He waved to people and shook a few hands before putting his hand on Herb Ausland's shoulder.

Herb turned, smiled and said, "Dave, it's good to see you. How are things in Bellchester?"

"The situation has improved considerably since last year."

Dr. Behren had taken the position after the sudden death of the previous college president and inherited a financial mess.

"That's good to hear," Dr. Ausland said.

"How's the kid doing?" Dave looked in Tyler's direction.

Herb chuckled as he patted Dave on the back. "He is wise beyond his years. I believe the church board made a very smart decision when they accepted the person God intended to lead this church without considering his age to be a negative factor."

"Having you back must have eased the transition," Dave said.

"I promised the board I would work with Tyler and Darren for two years, but I'm no longer needed. Those men are leading the church without my help. I'm going to retire for good soon. I'll let you visit. I think there are some people who would like to talk to you."

"I'll send you an email. I might have a position that would interest you." Dave shook Herb's hand again and then smiled at Chase Hillman and shook his hand vigorously.

"Hello, Chase. How are you? How are Yvonne and the girls?"

"Yvonne is upstairs in the booth. The girls are growing up too fast," Chase said.

"That will happen. I remember when my daughters were about that age."

Pastor Tyler finished talking to some people and walked over to talk to Dave.

"I didn't know you were here," he said as he shook hands with his former boss.

"I've been in the area for a conference. Cathy is here somewhere. We didn't want to interrupt your service, so we sat in the back. I enjoyed your message, and the band sounds better than ever." Dave waved to Kenny Colwell. "I see that Emmy is still singing and dancing around."

Tyler chuckled. "She is."

Kenny put his hands on Emmy's shoulders and turned her around.

"Hey! I was talking to Liz," Emmy complained.

"There is someone here you might want to see," Kenny pointed to Dr. Behren.

"Holy... moly!" Emmy put a hand to her mouth. She grinned and ran down the platform steps and stood beside Tyler.

Kenny smiled at Liz. "Emmy was pretty close to Dr. Behren like she was with Pastor Herb. They are sorta father figures to her. You and Tyler are more like good friends. I don't mean that to be disrespectful."

"I understand, Kenny," Liz answered.

Dr. Behren smiled at Emmy. "Tyler, I see the worship team still has to put up with this young lady. I'll keep praying that the Lord sends a more mature singer your way."

"I appreciate that, Dr. Behren."

Emmy refrained from making a face or sticking out her tongue. "What are you doing here?"

He explained the reason. "I wanted to see my friends. Is that okay with you?"

"I didn't mean it like that," Emmy said and then bit her lip.

"I'm teasing. How are you?" he asked and then waved to Kenny. "When are you coming to Bellchester? It appears that some of the students are fans of yours. I can't understand why."

"I'll talk to Andy and see if we can fit you in sometime," she teased back.

"How are the kids?"

"Growing like weeds. How many grandkids do you have now?" Emmy asked. Kenny walked up behind her and shook hands with Dr. Behren.

"We have seven grandkids."

"Will you excuse me, please? I need to talk to some people." Tyler headed to the foyer.

Emmy waited until Tyler was out of range. "I cried for a whole week when you left, but I understand why you had to go. I prayed the church would hire Pastor Tyler to replace you. I was kinda selfish."

"It was not an easy decision, but I love the college. I can see Tyler being your pastor for a long, long time."

"I hope so," Emmy said and then hugged Dr. Behren. "I still miss you even though we love Tyler and Liz."

"I miss all my friends here."

"I don't want to keep you from mingling with other people, so I'll let you go. I'll see if we can schedule something at the college soon."

That afternoon as Kenny and Kevin were taking naps and the girls were playing in their room, Emmy's cell phone rang.

"Hey, Rory. What's up?"

"You busy?"

"No, the guys are napping and Heather and Isa are playing in their room. Why? You wanna do something?"

"I do have something to tell you, and I'd rather not tell you over the phone."

108

"That sounds serious."

"Can you get away for a bit?"

"Yeah, I'll tell Kenny I have to run out. Where should we meet?"

"My place okay? I haven't eaten. I had to work until two. I'll grab something from Burger Bob's. I'll buy you a root beer and maybe some fries if you want," he said with a smile.

"How can I pass up such an offer," she teased back. "Meet you in thirty minutes."

"I'll be here."

Emmy ran into the family room where Kenny had fallen asleep watching football. She sat next to him and touched his shoulder.

He opened one eye. "Is the game over?"

"The second one hasn't started. Would you watch the kids so I can run out for a while?"

"Where are they?"

She explained.

"I'll try to stay awake."

"They'll be okay if you fall back to sleep. Should I pick up anything on the way back?"

"I'm good."

She kissed his cheek and raced out to the kitchen, grabbed her purse and keys and scampered into the garage. She drove at her normal pace—never less than fifteen miles above the speed limit—and made it to Rory's in twenty minutes. She sprinted inside and knocked on his door.

That was quick," he said.

She scooted past him, removed her old army jacket and tossed it in Rory's direction. He caught the jacket and hung it in the closet. She kicked off her sneakers, plopped down on the couch and asked, "So what's up?"

He stood in front of her and said, "You aren't going to like this, Em."

"Tell me. I'm a big girl. I can take it."

"Tomorrow I'm giving my two week notice," he said.

She patted the couch. "Sit down. That's no big deal. There

109

are lots of other places to work in SoHam."

He shook his head and sat down.

She bit her lip and then whispered, "You're not staying in SoHam, are you?"

"No, sweetie, I'm not."

"Where are you going? I'm assuming you already have another job."

"Tampa, Florida."

"Florida! Why are you moving so far away? I won't ever get to see you."

"It's only a few hours away by plane." Rory took her hand. "I'll be making more money, and I just need to get away from SoHam. There are too many bad memories here."

She pulled her hand away. "I'm here. Does that mean I'm one of your bad memories?"

"Come on, Em. You know that's not the case."

"It better not be."

"Did you tell Kenny where you were going?"

"I didn't mention anywhere specific."

Rory sighed and stared at the ceiling. "You should have told him."

"I'll tell him if he asks. I won't lie to him, but I don't always volunteer information."

"You want a tasty beverage?" He walked into the small, open-to-the-living-room kitchen, yanked open the fridge and pulled out a beer.

"Better not, but I'll take water." She moved her feet underneath her and sat with her back to the end of the couch.

Rory handed her an Ice Mountain and sat at the opposite end.

"Are you leaving SoHam just to get away from me?"

Rory grinned. "Yes. I'm leaving to get away from you."

She wrinkled her nose at him. "You're a stinker."

Rory put his feet on the faded, brown-fabric ottoman, stretched his arm along the back of the couch and took a long drink of his beer. "Wanna watch TV?"

"No, I want to talk to you." She closed her eyes and leaned

110

back. "You moved away in high school, and I didn't see you for a thousand years. Now you're leaving me again. It's so not fair."

"I'm not leaving you, Em."

She opened her eyes and sat up straighter. "You know what I mean." She moved her feet and tried to kick Rory's leg.

He grabbed her foot. "I had to leave the first time."

"You thought you had to leave because of that girl."

"Her name was Leanne Garcia."

"Whatever. She tricked you into thinking you got her pregnant. All the time she knew it was some other guy's kid."

"I admit it could have been mine."

Emmy bit her lip. "Would you have stayed in SoHam if you'd gotten me pregnant?"

"There was no way I could have gotten you pregnant," Rory said and then finished his beer.

"There would have been a way." She put her foot on top of his thigh. "You didn't ever try hard enough."

He moved her foot away. "You were sixteen when I left."

"Diane started..."

He shook his hand. "Don't even go there. I screwed up my life. I wasn't about to mess up yours, too."

Emmy grinned and then put a finger to her mouth. "We came close to messing up our lives."

"Did not!" he insisted.

"Did so," she said and then giggled.

"When?"

"One night at Grafton's party."

"No! No! No!" He wagged a finger at her. "You were going to do something, and I stopped you."

"What was I gonna do?"

"You know full well what you were gonna do. Just because some of the other girls were... showing more than they should, didn't mean I was gonna let you."

Emmy stared at him and grinned. "I can't believe it. Rory Porter the notorious Don Juan of Raynor Park is embarrassed."

"Hush your mouth, little girl."

"Or what? You gonna swat me?"

111

"No, but I might make you leave."

"Like you're gonna toss a female out of your apartment."

"You're a real riot, Em. You make it sound like I was as bad as Owen."

"You're late brother was the biggest player in the entire city." She spread her arms out wide. "He seduced so many innocent girls. Including my sister."

"Hey! Diane was not very innocent."

"Okay, I'll give you that, but there were others."

"He tried to get you to go up to his room," Rory recalled. "I wasn't there, but Amy told me."

"I never let him so much as kiss me. You know that."

"I would have beaten him senseless if he tried anything."

"You were my protector, Rory. My fearless knight in shining armor," she said and then sighed.

"I thought Kenny was your hero."

"He was but in a different way. You were the one who beat up that guy who made a pass at me."

"He deserved it. What was his name? You remember?"

"Nope!" She shrugged and shook her head. "But I remember he missed two weeks of school."

"I shouldn't have done that, but you were my friend."

"Just your friend?"

"You know what I mean. I cared more about your reputation than I did my own sister."

"No disrespect, but Amy was a little promiscuous."

"Yeah, I know." He thought about Amy for a moment. "It's been over two years since Delaney shot and killed her, but it seems like a month ago."

"How are her kids doing?"

"Fine. I hate to say it, but they're better off without her."

Emmy kicked his thigh. "That's so cruel."

"True, but it's the truth."

Emmy bit her lip and didn't say anything for a moment.

"What?" Rory asked.

"You thought of me as a friend, right?"

"Yeah."

"Did you know how much of a crush I had on you?"

"Get out! You were in love with Kenny, and you know it."

"I loved him, but I had a crush on you. You were one of the school's bad boys and that attracted me to you."

"Good thing we never let that get in the way of being friends, Em."

"I used to feel disappointed because you didn't think of me like one of your other girls. You were only interested in girls with better bodies. I was like a kid to you."

"Hey! You were petite, but you were prettier than almost every other girl at Roosevelt High."

"Liar!" Emmy grinned.

"There might have been a few cuter but not many."

"Puppies are cute," she teased.

"You know what I mean. Want another water?"

"I'm good," she said and then grinned.

"Stop it."

"What?"

"You're flirting, and I won't allow it in my apartment."

"So, you don't want to kiss me?"

"I want to kiss you, but I don't want to ruin Kenny's trust in me." He jumped up. "I'm getting another beer."

Emmy laughed. "You are afraid of me. It's so funny."

He grabbed another beer and stayed in the kitchen to drink it. Emmy turned and sat facing him.

"It's not fear that keeps me from kissing you, Em." He looked at her but then turned away.

She bit her lip. "Oh, Rory, are you trying to say you love me?"

"Not like that. Maybe I love you as a friend. I love your kids."

"Come on, admit it. You love me." Emmy got up and walked into the kitchen. She held out her hands and hugged Rory.

"Fine! I love you." He hugged her back.

"I knew it."

"I've heard you say a million times we are supposed to love our neighbor as our self. That's why I love you."

113

"Good! I love you as one of my best friends. Maybe if Kenny hadn't lived three houses away, things might have been different."

He kissed the top of her head. "God knew who you were supposed to fall in love with. It wasn't me. Perhaps, there is still that special person out there somewhere for me."

"I hope you meet her soon. You're not getting any younger, and I think you're putting on a few pounds." She nudged his belly.

"Too many lunches at Burger Bob's." He laughed and then released her.

"I should be going. Will I see you before you leave?"

"I'll be here for two or three weeks, Em."

"Good. You have to come over for dinner again. The kids will be disappointed if you don't."

"I certainly don't want to disappoint them."

"Do you really have to move to Florida?"

"Yes, sweetie. I have a new job, and a bigger apartment. I can actually fit a queen-size bed in the bedroom."

She put her hands on her hips and looked up at him. "Do you have a girlfriend in Florida already?"

"Not yet, but I'm going to be actively searching for one."

"Maybe you should find a church and look there. You should avoid the bars."

"Yes, Mrs. Colasanti-Colwell."

She called Kenny on the way home. "Need anything?"

"I'm good, Em. Are you on your way home?"

"Be there soon. I have bad news. Rory is moving to Florida."

"Are you sorry?"

"I will miss him, but it might be for the best."

You might be right, Em.

Chapter Eleven

"Heather, will you stop pestering Uncle James. You have asked him a thousand times why he looks like Grandpa." Emmy sighed and pointed in the direction of the family room. "Go! Find Isa and change out of your good dresses. We'll be eating soon."

"Okay, Mommy. Are we going to have taco salad again?"

Father James laughed. "You can blame me for that, Heather. I asked your mother to make it today."

"I don't mind. I like it except for the black olives. I like green ones better," Heather said and then left the kitchen.

"I prefer green olives as well," Father James replied.

"Too bad. I use black ones. How did mass go today?" Emmy asked her half-brother. "And why haven't you called me for a month or more. I haven't seen you in forever."

He held up a hand and tilted it back and forth. "So, so. And I called you last week. How was your church service. Lead any lost souls to our Lord today?"

"Don't make light of it. God might decide to punish you." She opened the taco spices packet and dumped it into the bowl.

He clasped his hands together as if praying. "I have confessed all of my sins. My heart is at peace. How about you, dear child. Is your mind at ease, or would you like for me to hear your confession? I bet you have some doozies."

She put a finger to her mouth and then grinned wickedly. "I do need to confess a few sins, Father. For starters I have committed several acts of a lustful nature with a very sexy man."

"I don't want to hear about your sex life, Emily. Is that the correct spoon to use for stirring the taco salad?" he asked.

She waved the old, slotted metal spoon at him. "Don't you start that crap with me. It doesn't matter which spoon I use, or what order I add the ingredients. Don't listen to Kenny."

"Tsk! Tsk! I know better than that." He waved a finger.

Emmy rolled her eyes and turned her back to Father James. She glanced at the hamburger browning on the stove and then stirred the beans, cheese, black olives and other ingredients that made her taco salad special.

"You didn't answer my question about lost souls."

"Contrary to what you might believe, Father, not every service is an evangelical one. Sometimes Pastor Tyler doesn't preach about getting saved." She turned back to face him. "You should come to a service sometime."

"Should I wear my clerical collar or my cassock to let everyone know I am a man of the cloth?" Father James asked without batting an eye.

"Are you sure you're a real priest?" She turned down the heat on the hamburger. "Sometimes I think I better pray for you."

He shrugged. "They pay me the big bucks to hold services and drink the communion wine. I try to buy a good year."

"You are going to end up in hell if you're not careful. You should come so you can hear the worship band play."

"I've listened to your CDs. I love your sweet voice."

"And? What's the catch?" She stared at him. "I know you well enough now to know you're teasing me."

"Far be it from me to make light of a gift God Almighty has bestowed upon you." He made a sweeping gesture and then held out his hands.

"Yeah, keep it up and you won't get any taco salad." She turned off the stove. "Speaking of my voice, would you listen to some new tunes after lunch. I want your opinion on them."

"Why me? You do realize your husband, the one you have lustful relations with, is a professional musician of sorts."

"I don't want him to hear these demos yet. The lyrics are rather personal."

"Personal, huh? Are they about your lustful relations?" He lifted his bushy eyebrows. "I have all afternoon, but aren't you going to watch the Bears? Who are they playing today?"

"They play tonight against the Texans. I doubt if I watch any of the other games. I'm not as fanatical about it anymore."

"Does that have anything to do with this being your friend Tony's final season, and why do the kids call him Uncle Tony? Don't they realize he's not really your brother?"

"They know. The girls know. Not sure about Kevin Michael, but they call John and Brady uncle, too."

116

"Brady Robertson is actually their uncle. He's married to your sister Diane. You are aware that..."

"I am fully aware that Diane is my sister," she frowned.

He pointed at the stove. "No, I meant are you aware the hamburger is burning."

She turned to the stove. "Shoot! I thought I turned it off."

"Is it ruined?"

Emmy checked it. "Not quite."

"Thank you, Lord, for your blessing upon us your holy servants."

"Knock it off before I slug you."

He laughed and then became serious. "I am indeed grateful I finally met you. I wish I had been able to watch you grow up."

"Most people would tell you they are still waiting for me to grow up," she said. "At least you are here for Heather and Isabella. They remind me so much of myself."

"Thank you for cleaning up the kitchen, Kenny." Emmy hugged him from behind later. "I'm going to take Father James downstairs and force him to listen to some demos."

"I take it you don't want me to hear them yet, right?"

"Yes, that is correct." She looked over her shoulder and saw that Father James was watching her, so she swatted Kenny on the backside.

"That will cost you, young lady." Father James shook his head. "Lead me to the studio before something else happens."

She patted Kenny's bottom again and then marched around the island. She stuck out her tongue and then giggled. "If you would be so kind as to follow me, Your Grace."

"Ten more Hail Marys." He followed Emmy to the control room of Kenny's state-of-the-art basement recording studio.

"You can sit there. I have to sit at the board so I can play the tracks." She put a finger to her mouth. "Now which button do I push?"

"Do you actually know how to operate this... whatever?"

"It's a digital mixing board, and I know enough. I don't mess with all of the settings, but I know how to record tracks and play them back. The real technical stuff I leave to Kenny or Will.

117

He's the sound guy. He's been with the band since the beginning."

Father James settled into the black leather recliner, closed his eyes, placed his hands in his lap and got comfortable.

"Ready? These are the lyrics if you want to follow along." She handed him a folder with the lyrics to four new songs. "Hey! Open your eyes. You can't take a nap."

"It's extremely important that I get enough rest to care properly for the sheep in my flock."

"You mean so you can fleece them, right?"

"You must have inherited your sense of humor from your mother. Our father would never resort to such low puns."

"Like you would know," she said and then put a hand to her mouth. "I'm sorry. That wasn't very nice. Please forgive me."

"I only forgive people during office hours. Now let me hear these songs, so I can take a nap."

She played the first track and then the second one before pausing. She spun her seat around. "Well, what do you think?"

He studied the lyrics. "You're right. These are personal. They're about you and Kenny. Did you really feel this way?"

She nodded. "I did at one time, but things are getting better."

"You were really going to end your relationship?"

"It was heading in that direction. Let me play these two tracks. They explain a bit more." She turned back to the board.

He listened to the next tracks without speaking. He closed his eyes, and Emmy thought he was actually praying.

She waited until he opened his eyes. "Well?"

"You definitely have a way with words and getting your point across without actually coming right out and saying it. Do you understand what I mean?"

"Yes, Kenny tells me I use symbolism and other stuff more than he does."

"Are you sure you want everyone to listen to these songs? They are rather personal."

"But not everyone will know. Lots of people have gone through struggles like this. It's important to remember the struggles for a relationship to grow. I will always remember the struggle."

Chapter Twelve

"Kenny, would you mind watching the kids this afternoon?" Emmy walked into the den. "You're going to be home, right?"

He set down the *Billboard* magazine. "I wasn't planning on going anywhere, but I did want to work on a guitar part. I came up with a new lick I want to try."

She walked up behind him, placed her hands on his shoulders and kissed the top of his head. "Couldn't you do that when I get back?"

"I suppose so. Where are you going, or shouldn't I ask?"

"I told you a few days ago that Rory would be leaving this Sunday. I want to see him so I can say goodbye."

Kenny leaned back and looked up at her. "Will you be gone long?"

"An hour tops," she said. "Just want to run over there and say goodbye in person."

"You're going to see him no matter what I say, so go ahead," he said and then began reading his magazine again.

"Don't be like that. He's a good friend, and he's moving to Florida." She moved in front of the recliner and put her hands on his knees. "I could see if Krissy will watch the kids if you want to go with me."

Kenny laughed. "You don't want me to go with you, so don't pretend you do." He shook his head but then smiled. "I'll watch the kids as long as you remember he's just a friend."

"I will. Cross my heart," she said and then actually crossed her heart. "I won't be gone too long. An hour or two at the most."

Emmy pulled into the parking lot of Rory's apartment building and saw him loading boxes into an older-looking white minivan. She parked and walked over to him.

"Hey, Em, you're just in time to help load up."

She looked into the back of the van and saw a bunch of boxes, his TV and a recliner. "Where did you get this old thing, and what is it?"

"I sold my car."

"Get out! You sold your Camaro?"

He nodded. "I can fit a lot more stuff in here. It's a 2001 Dodge Grand Caravan. I figured if it got me to Tampa I could either keep it, or buy a decent used car. I was kidding about you helping load it up."

"Good! I didn't come over here to work," she said. "I can't believe you sold the Z28." She followed him inside, took off her coat and tossed it on the kitchen counter. She removed her shoes while standing up and kicked them out of the way.

"I've got a few more boxes to load up later, and I'm taking that stand for the TV and my couch." He pointed toward the worn, faded couch.

"Who's gonna help you with the couch? It's too heavy for me. I'm just a little girl."

"The guy across the hall agreed to help me. I gave him some of the extra kitchen stuff."

She stood in the open doorway and glanced into the bedroom. "What about the bed and dresser and that ugly end table?"

"I sold it to the guy taking over the lease." Rory walked up behind her and put his hands on her shoulders. "It's a cheap bed, and I can pick one up in Florida. I grabbed that end table from the curb. Someone was tossing it out, and I needed something for my alarm clock."

"I'm glad you didn't pay any money for it."

"Hey! You used to buy second-hand furniture."

"I would now if I spotted a bargain. Make sure you buy a good mattress." She spotted two large suitcases next to the bed. "Have you packed your clothes?"

"I will in the morning," he said and then released her shoulders. "Want something to drink? I have a few bottles of water, and I need to clean out the fridge."

She scooted past him and moved into the kitchen. She opened the fridge door and laughed. "All you have in here are some bottles of water and three beers. What are you gonna eat tonight?"

He opened the freezer. "I have two of these small Home

120

Run Inn pizzas. I can pop them in the microwave. You can have one, and I'll eat the other."

"Thanks, but I told Kenny I wouldn't stay too long. Those pizzas are small. You should eat them both. In fact, you should save the water for tomorrow. I'll have a beer with you and we can sit on the couch and talk about the old days back in Raynor Park." She pulled two bottles of Sam Adams from the fridge. "At least you buy the good stuff."

"I'd offer you a glass, but my kitchen stuff in packed away already."

"I can drink from the bottle." She handed one to him. "I always have, remember?"

"Ah, so true. I think you were nine or ten when you started sneaking your father's beer." He opened the bottles and led her over to the couch. "Have a seat. I'd turn on the TV so you could watch football," he said with a shrug. "But it's in the van."

"I'd rather just talk." She sat at one end of the couch and he sat at the other end. Just as they had the last time she came over. "Shoot! I just thought of something."

"What, Em?"

"Our church is a Nazarene church, right?"

"Yeah, you mentioned something about that. Why?"

"The Nazarene church has a manual."

"A what?"

"It's called the church manual."

"Is it like a rule book you have to follow? You know, do this, don't do that."

"In a way. I think it's mostly rules for ceremonies and stuff. I don't know for sure, but Kristen told me that we have to change some things."

"Like what?"

She held out the bottle of beer. "We aren't supposed to drink alcohol."

"Get out! For real?"

Emmy nodded.

Rory laughed. "How are you going to follow that? You've been drinking since we were kids."

121

"I don't drink much anymore. I never did, you stinker." She kicked his leg and stuck out her tongue. "This might be the last beer I ever have."

"What about wine? Is that taboo also?"

"Guess so, but I don't see anything wrong with having a glass of wine once in a while."

"Didn't Jesus change water into wine?" Rory asked.

"Yes, but the Bible also cautions against getting drunk. You know Sloane, right?"

"Tony's Sloane?"

"Yeah. She and Cam and Lindsey Frees were all raised in the Nazarene church. I know Sloane doesn't allow alcohol in the house, and I doubt if Lindsey and Cam do either. Tyler and Liz don't ever drink alcohol."

"Should I take it away from you? I don't want you to get kicked out of your church."

"Don't be silly! They won't kick me out," she said and then laughed. "They will pray for me."

"That's not something to laugh about." Rory pointed a finger at her. "That's serious."

"I'm not making fun of praying. I pray for you all the time. One of these days you will accept Jesus," she said and then smiled. "You may not believe it now, but it's true."

"Could happen, Em. I do go to church once in a while."

"Yeah, you're what we call a CEO."

He grinned. "I know. Christmas, Easter and occasionally."

"Andy Walker used to be a CEO, and look at him now."

"What's he doing now?" Rory asked and then finished his beer. "You done?"

She handed him her empty bottle.

"Do you want to save this since it might be your last one?"

She shook her head. "It probably won't be the last one, but I'll try."

He stood up, walked into the kitchen and deposited the bottles in the trash.

She turned on the couch, got on her knees and faced the open kitchen. "Andy's more involved in the church now. Since the

122

band isn't touring, he has more free time."

Rory rejoined her on the couch. "What's he doing?"

She sat back down with her feet under her. "He's actually built some new computers for the church, and he works in the tech booth."

"I didn't know he could build computers."

"After he got out of the Navy, he went to college. He worked for the government for a while before he got into the music industry."

"That's quite a change."

"He's always loved music even though he can't play an instrument or sing on key."

Rory rested his left arm on the end of the couch. "Did I ever tell you that I used to listen to you and Kenny practicing?"

"Yeah, you said you would hang out in the alley and listen. You should have come inside." She put her arm on the back of the couch.

"No way! I didn't want to interrupt anything." He put his arm on the back of the couch and touched Emmy's hand.

"We were practicing music," she insisted.

"Uh-huh."

"Stop grinning like that," she said and then slapped his hand. "I'm not telling you about anything else that might, or might not, have happened in the carriage house."

"Good." He intertwined his finger with hers.

She scooted to the middle of the couch, still holding his hand. "We waited until the wedding."

"I'm happy for you, and I don't want to hear anything else."

She pulled his arm around her shoulders, bit her lip, but then grinned. "You probably thought that would have been impossible because of how I sometimes behaved with you."

"Why would I think that? You weren't that bad. You talked about sex a lot, but I knew you were still innocent in most ways."

"I wouldn't have been if you hadn't dropped out of sight," she admitted. "Maybe I shouldn't have mentioned that."

"You loved Kenny, and not me."

"You won't ever understand how I felt," she said softly.

123

She leaned against him and neither one spoke for a time. Rory closed his eyes and could smell her shampoo. She snuggled closer to him and rested her head on his chest.

"Are you crying, Em?"

"Just a little," she admitted.

"Please don't cry, sweetie."

"I can't help it. I'm gonna miss you."

They held onto each other for a time.

"What time is it? I told Kenny I wouldn't stay too long."

Rory looked over his shoulder. "I can't see the microwave clock."

Emmy turned around and saw the time. "I should get going."

"Will you say goodbye to Kenny and the kids for me?"

She nodded.

Rory stood, took her hand, helped her up and they stood facing each other. "Promise?"

"Yes, but you should come back to SoHam every so often to see them."

"Them?" he asked.

"And me." She put her arms around his waist.

He rested his chin on the top of her head. "I'll try, Em."

"You better do more than try."

"I'll use all my vacation time to come and see you," he teased.

"Not funny." She poked his side. "If I ever get to Tampa to do a show, I'll make sure you have tickets and a backstage pass."

He retrieved her coat and helped her put it on. He moved some of her hair away from her face and tucked it behind her ear. He looked into her eyes and took a deep breath. *You sure aren't making this easy, Em.* Then he walked her out to her BMW.

"Remember you are in my thoughts and prayers." She poked a finger in his chest. "I will remind the girls to pray for you, too."

He smiled. "We can keep in touch with emails, texts, Facebook and even Skype once in a while Em. I'm not going to disappear from your life like before."

124

"You better not."

He opened the door for her and watched her drive away.

Emmy walked into the family room and plopped down on the couch.

Kenny turned his attention from the football game to Emmy. "Should I ask how it went?"

"It went okay. He's pretty much all packed and leaving in the morning. He wanted me to tell you and the kids goodbye."

"Anything else I should know?" He patted his legs. "Sit with me."

"He sold his car and bought an old minivan. He's only taking his couch and a recliner. He sold his bed."

"Is he taking his clothes?" Kenny patted his legs again.

"Duh! Of course." Emmy got up, moved over to the recline and sat on his lap. He held her close, and she began to cry.

"It's all right, Em. I know you care for him."

She stopped crying after a moment and sniffled. "I love you."

"I know, and I love you more and more."

"He promised to stay in touch and not disappear like before. It will be easier now with all the technology."

"Like telephones and mail service," Kenny teased.

"Don't make fun of me while I feel sad," she whispered.

Kenny brushed some hair out of her face and kissed her eyes. "Did you ever really try to find him all those years ago?"

She thought about it. "No, I guess I didn't because I was in love with you."

He kissed her, and she kissed him back as she melted into his arms.

Chapter Thirteen

"Look at you!" Mama Bertucci smiled at John Randolph. "I haven't seen you in such a fancy suit since you stopped playing football." She smoothed his jacket and adjusted his red tie. "Nice material."

Sloane walked back into the kitchen after letting John in the front door. "Today's the day the company learns if they got the contract to build the new hospital, right?"

"Yes, and I still think we have the best shot at it. The other companies are from out-of-state. One is from Dallas. I think being an established local company is an advantage. The company did one of the additions to St. Bart's."

Tony appeared wearing jeans and a sweatshirt.

"Papa! Uncle John is all dressed up," Ben pointed. "You should wear a suit to football."

Tony picked up Ben and held his feet to the ceiling. "I wear a suit when I need to."

Sloane shook her head and put her hands on her hips. "Will you put him down before you drop him?"

"I like being upside down, Mommy. Papa won't drop me."

"I better do what Mommy wants," Tony said. He set Ben down and picked up Coby and Taylor. "How are my other little men today?"

"Don't hang them upside down," Sloane warned.

Mama finished packing lunches for the four older kids.

"Mama, we don't have school today. It's Thanksgiving," Peter said but then grinned.

Mama laughed. "You can't fool me, young man. I know this is Monday. Thanksgiving is three days away."

"Can I have chocolate pudding, please?" Dotty asked.

"You can have pudding if there is any in the pantry," Sloane said. "Get four of them, Dotty. Ben will eat lunch at school today."

Six-year-old Noemi Claire finished her oatmeal. "I want vanilla pudding, Dotty."

"What kind do you want, Ben?" Dotty asked.

126

"Chocolate! Two of them," he answered.

"One is enough, Benjamin," Mama said sternly.

Dotty found the pudding and brought them out to Mama.

"Did you get me one?" Peter asked.

Dotty held up a package. "I know you like chocolate."

"Thank you, Dotty."

Mama smiled at her two oldest grandkids and thought about their birth mother, her daughter Heather, who had passed away suddenly seven years ago because of a brain aneurysm. *Dotty, you look so much like Heather did at eight. You have Heather's eyes and her round face. It warms my heart that you and Peter are so close, and such a big help to Sloane. I know you're both old enough to understand what happened.*

Heather passed away, and Peter and Dotty's father Alex Khryzman had not been able, or willing, to deal with the children at the time. He later perished in a one-car accident. He had been drinking and crashed into a tree and died instantly. Tony and Sloane adopted Peter and Dorothy and then had four more children.

"We have to leave for school in five minutes," Sloane announced. "You need to wash your face and hands, grab your book bags and put on your coats."

The kids scrambled to get ready while Sloane talked to Tony and John.

"How can you be so calm?" Sloane asked. "If the company is awarded this contract, it will mean secure jobs for years to come and several million dollars. I'm more nervous than you guys."

Tony wrapped his arms around his wife's expanding waist and smiled. "Remember John and I have been in the Super Bowl twice. We know a little about how to handle pressure."

"So true," John said. "Can you imagine the flack we would have faced from Emmy had we lost the Super Bowl? This is a piece of cake compared to that. It's only a mega-million dollar contract to build the new hospital. Super Bowl losses are remembered forever."

Sloane and Mama loaded the kids into the minivan for the trip to school.

127

"Do we need to pick up Zachary and Grace?" Mama asked.

"No, Kristen still insists on taking her kids to school everyday. I told her I didn't mind alternating weeks, but she said no."

"But she takes your kids to school occasionally," Mama reminded Sloane.

"That will probably stop soon. She doesn't like to drive their minivan. She prefers her new Acura and it isn't big enough to hold all the kids."

"I'm sure she has her reasons." Mama buckled Ben's car seat and then waited until Sloane left to go back inside. *Yeah, she doesn't want anyone to drive her kids around but her or John.*

Sloane paused at the end of the driveway as Emmy drove past with her kids and Diane's boys. *Maybe the school will have bus service one of these years. I won't have to worry about this next August since I'll be teaching at the school.*

Tony poured a cup of coffee for John, and they sat at the breakfast table.

"Do you really believe we have a chance?" John asked.

"We spent a lot of time on that bid. We did everything we could, John. Now it's up to God, and the wise people making the decision."

"I hope they're wise," John said.

Tony finished his coffee. "I hope they're Bear fans." He got up and set his cup in the sink. "I gotta run. Text me if you hear anything."

"Will do." John finished his coffee, set his cup next to Tony's and slapped him on the back. "Have fun sitting through meetings today. I don't miss those sessions at all."

"I would have the day off if we hadn't got blown out by the 49ers. Coach was pretty upset on the plane ride home last night. He never likes to lose and we've lost two in a row."

"I will be pacing around the office until I hear from the committee. I'd rather be scrimmaging on the practice field."

Kenny called Pastor Tyler's cell phone at eight thirty.

"Hello, Kenny, did you hear about the truck?" Tyler asked.

"I just got off the phone with Paul Yakel, and he has one of the trucks and eight guys lined up to work. Levi and I figured that would be enough. It will be easier to maneuver one of the smaller trucks on your street than trying to turn one of the semis around."

"That's true. We might have to make two trips, but probably not. I've got some stuff loaded into the Flex already."

Kenny chuckled. "Your new house is less than five minutes away. If we make more than one trip, it won't be a big deal."

"I really appreciate this," Tyler said.

"I'm glad we could help. The guys are on the payroll, so Paul likes to keep them busy."

"Who is Paul exactly?"

"Paul started out as my assistant on one of the tours. He moved up the ladder and he's now in charge of the logistics for the tours. He works with a couple of the other bands signed to Steward Music. You might recognize him if you see him tomorrow. He wears granny glasses and has a bushy Afro-style hairdo."

"I think I've seen him before. He's white, right?"

"Yeah, he reminds me of Jerry Garcia, but you probably don't know who he was."

"Not really."

"What time is the closing?" Kenny asked.

"Liz and I have to be there at nine. The sellers have already signed everything. They were leaving on vacation."

"If you would like, I can have the guys bring the truck over around eight. They can be loading up while you're at the closing."

"Are you sure we should? What if something happens and we don't close?"

Kenny grinned. "Not gonna happen."

"That would save time. Everything will be packed other than some clothes, so I guess it's all right."

"See you in the morning. I told Paul to have the guys meet at your old house at eight. Is that too early?" Kenny asked.

"Not at all. You know I get up as soon as the sun comes out. Sometimes before."

"Has Derby been to the new house?"

"I actually took her for a walk in the new neighborhood. I drove over there first," he said and then chuckled.

"That's good. Canton Lane is a busy street and there are no sidewalks along that stretch."

"If there were, I would ride my bike to the church every day. I still might ride some of the time." Tyler paused and then chuckled. "Can you believe there is a corn field along Canton Lane? It seems so out of place."

"There's a place like that in SoHam west of the Cathedral area. Some farmer still plants corn there every year," Kenny said.

John arrived at the main office of Bertucci and Keasling Construction at nine that morning.

"Good morning, Mr. Randolph. You look mighty handsome today. Is that a new suit?"

He brushed some imaginary lint away. "Yes, it is, Mrs. Posey. Are you going to start calling me John?"

"I will if you stop calling me Mrs. Posey. You may call me Gladys. Daniel Keasling and Peter Bertucci, rest his soul, always called me Gladys. I began working for the company after I married Roy, and that's been too many years ago to recall. Would you like some coffee?"

"Not now, thanks." John waved a hand dismissively. "I'm going to pace around the office until I hear something."

"If you weren't wearing that new suit, I would suggest you run out to the site in West Bartlett. They are falling behind schedule. You might have to kick some butt."

"I hate that part of the job," John said as he tried to loosen his shirt collar.

"So did Daniel. He tried to avoid it if at all possible," she grinned. "On the other hand, Peter Bertucci didn't mind getting after the guys. He was more hands-on than Mr. Keasling. That's why they made such a good team. They complimented each other perfectly."

"Do you remember much about Mr. Bertucci? He's been gone for a long time. Tony only has vague memories of his father."

Mrs. Posey let her eyes drift upward before returning her attention to John. "It will be thirty years next year, and I remember him as clearly as if he were standing here. Marco Bertucci looks a lot like his father except Peter didn't have a beard."

John glanced at the large photographs of the two men who founded the company. One of them being his father-in-law. "I can definitely see the resemblance. I'll be in my office."

Mrs. Posey buzzed John around eleven. She sounded excited. "Mr. Randolph, you have a call on line four. You might want to take it."

"Hello, this is John Randolph."

John listened for a moment and then ended the call. "Yes!" He yelled loud enough to startle Mrs. Posey as he pumped his fist in the air and stomped his feet. "Mrs. Posey!" he hollered as he jumped out of his chair and dashed out of his office. "Mrs. Posey, we got the contract!" He paused and was about to hug the white-haired secretary before he came to his senses. He smiled at her. "We got the contract."

She held out her hands and hugged him. "Was there ever any doubt?"

"We thought we had a chance, but there were other bids."

She backed up and waved a hand in the air. "Those other companies never had a chance," she said with certainty.

"Why do you say that?" John asked.

"I wasn't supposed to say anything, but my sister-in-law works for the law firm that reviewed the bids. I talked to her on Friday, and she told me we had the contract all but wrapped up. You will learn that it's the executive secretaries who really run the companies," she said with a grin. "I'm sure the fact she was a bridesmaid in Peter and Maria's wedding all those years ago had nothing to do with the decision."

John smiled at the gleam in Mrs. Posey's eyes, ran back into his office and called Kristen.

"Did you get the contract?"

"Yes! You might have to come back to work. We need to hire a ton of people, and I will need you to help with personnel."

"What about Two Bears Landscaping? You haven't had much time to take care of that business."

"Yeah, I know. The last time I mentioned it to Tony, he said we should sell it to the Quezada brothers. Alberto and Luis are actually running the business anyway."

"You should talk to Derrick, and go ahead and sell it to them. Neither one of you guys knows as much about landscaping as they do."

"You're right. I should let you go. I need to inform Tony about the contract."

John texted Tony the news, but Tony's phone was turned off. Tony finished practice and saw the message.

"Thank you. Lord. I know you are in control."

"What's up, Bertucci?" one of the other players asked.

"Good news about our construction business," Tony answered.

"Sounds like you are getting ready for retirement."

"Can't play football forever," Tony said and then chuckled.

Tyler Hammond watched a truck back into the driveway. He walked out of the garage as the truck stopped and Kenny jumped down from the passenger side.

"You guys are early," Tyler said.

"We didn't want to be late." Kenny turned to look as two cars pulled in and seven guys got out. "If you show them what has to be moved, they can get an idea of how best to pack everything. You'd be amazed at how much they can fit in a truck."

"Good morning, Pastor Tyler. I'm Levi Sayer, and I'll try to keep these guys in line."

Several of the guys chuckled.

Kenny smiled. "Levi is in charge of the road crew. He may look young, but I assure you, he runs a tight ship."

"Let me show you what we've got," Tyler said.

Liz walked out carrying a sleepy Grayson. "I'm going to take Grayson to the church. Jody said she and Darren would watch him all day if necessary. I promised to return the favor someday."

Tyler walked up to Liz and tickled his son. "See you later, buddy. We're going to move into our new house today."

"Is Derby moving, too?" Grayson asked. "And Natty?"

"Yes, we're all moving. We won't leave anyone behind."

"Tell Daddy goodbye for now," Liz said.

Grayson waved and scooted out of Liz's arms. "I can walk

132

to the church, Mommy. I know the way."

"Show me the way," Liz said to Grayson and then turned to Tyler and Kenny. "To the best of my knowledge all the boxes are labeled with the room they need to go to. There's a map on the kitchen counter with numbers of the bedrooms and stuff."

"Sounds like you've been very busy," Kenny said. "Emmy was kinda like that when we moved to the ranch house. She labeled everything."

"We need to leave by eight forty," Tyler reminded her.

"I'll be back and ready to go as soon as I drop off Grayson."

Tyler took Levi and Kenny inside.

"Are you taking the clothes with you?" Levi asked.

"We had planned to."

"I brought two wardrobe containers. You could hang clothes up in them and the guys can load them last."

"You think of everything, Levi." Kenny patted the large young man on the back.

"I try to be efficient, boss. We are pros, remember?" he joked.

At ten o'clock Kenny's cell phone rang. "What's up, Em?"

"Have you heard from Tyler and Liz? Are they finished with their closing? I'm on my way to the house."

"I haven't heard yet, but the truck is loaded. We're just waiting to hear from Tyler. You should see Levi," Kenny said.

"Why? What's he doing?"

"He's making the guys clean the house. He's got guys scrubbing the kitchen and bathroom. Lucas is vacuuming."

"Good!"

"Hang on, Em. I've got another call. Could be Tyler."

"Call me back."

Kenny answered the other call.

"We are officially homeowners. I'm holding the keys in my hand," Tyler said.

Kenny could hear him jangling the keys. "Fantastic. The truck is loaded, and the guys can be there in fifteen minutes." Kenny ended the call and walked over to Levi. "They are finished with the closing and should be at the house shortly."

"The new house must be in pretty good shape. Some people like to paint before moving in," Levi said. He walked through the house and smiled. "This is about all we can do here, boss."

"It looks great," Kenny said. "The sellers moved out last Wednesday, and they allowed Tyler and Liz to come in and paint the master bedroom. That's the only thing they really wanted to change. They loved the rest of the house. You'd never believe it was built around 1990. Everything looks brand new."

"I guess we'll see it soon enough," Levi said. "All right, guys. We've got ten minutes to be at the new house."

"We're ready now," Lucas said. "Who's gonna lock up?"

"I'll take care of that." Kenny held up the keys.

"See you guys in a couple of minutes," Levi said.

The guys got into the cars and left. Kenny rode in the truck with Levi, and they headed down Canton Lane to Vine Ridge.

Levi stopped in the street. "There's Emmy, and the garage door is open."

"Let me jump out and I'll guide you in."

"I think I'd rather leave the truck in the street. That's a concrete driveway, and I don't want to take a chance of it cracking."

"Good thinking, Levi." Kenny ran up the driveway. "Why is the garage door open?"

"I called Liz, and she gave me the code. They won't be here for ten or fifteen minutes. I thought the guys could get a head start."

"Good thinking," Kenny said. *Why is everyone around me so smart?*

By the time Tyler and Liz arrived, the guys had unloaded half of the truck.

"Isn't this great?" Liz hugged Emmy. "I'm going to love my house."

"I gave myself a quick tour. Hope you don't mind."

"Not at all," Tyler said. "What did you think?"

"I love everything except for the master bedroom," Emmy said. "If this was my house, I would paint the master lavender."

134

"You're such a goof, Emmy." Liz shook her head.

"Once we get everything in the house, I'll help Liz in the kitchen. You keep the guys out of there and don't bother us unless it's an emergency," Emmy ordered.

Kenny saluted her. "Yes, ma'am."

A few minutes later Darren Eaton and Herb Ausland walked into the house.

"We knocked but no one heard us," Pastor Herb said as he peeked into the kitchen.

"Come on in," Liz said. "Tyler is in the basement, I think."

"We'll find him." Pastor Darren smiled at Emmy. "You have some dirt on your face. Right here." He wiped her cheek.

Emmy grinned and wiped some dirt onto his face. "I've been working. Now scram! Liz and I are organizing the kitchen."

Darren and Herb headed downstairs, but Tyler and Kenny met them at the top of the stairs.

"Looks like you have everything under control," Darren said.

"Thanks to Kenny's crew. They even cleaned up the old house."

"We stopped over there, but no one was around," Herb said. "The place is going to be empty for a while."

"Maybe not," Tyler said. "This is not for certain, but it's a strong possibility. Chase and Yvonne might be leaving. If they do, we will have to hire a new worship pastor, and that house would come in handy."

"It would at that," Herb said. "We should get out of your way. Let us know if you need anything."

"Thanks, but we're fine."

Tyler supervised and the guys moved the furniture into position, set up the beds and even hung up the clothes.

"Liz, exactly how did you want the living room arranged?" Tyler asked.

Liz and Emmy walked out of the kitchen. Emmy had her hands on her hips as she frowned at Kenny.

"Em, we want to get it right the first time."

Liz checked her tablet. "Whoops! I forgot we don't have

135

Internet." She eyeballed the space and made up her mind. "The couch goes against that wall. The recliners can go over here and the TV and stuff goes against this wall. Okay with you, Ty?"

"Sounds like a plan."

Two hours later Tyler shook hands with all the guys. "Thanks for all your help. Are you sure I can't buy lunch?"

Levi shook his head. "Already taken care of. Let me know if the guys damaged anything."

"Well, thanks again. You guys are welcome to come to church sometime," Tyler said to the guys in the crew.

Levi grinned. "Thanks for the invite, Pastor Tyler, but we've all heard Emmy sing lots of times. She's such a diva."

Emmy stuck out her tongue. "I heard that, Levi. I'm going to tell your mom and dad."

"What are you going to tell them, Emmy?" Tyler asked.

"Not sure, but I'll think of something." Emmy walked up to Levi and hugged him. "Your mother trained you well. She was a miracle worker when it came to organizing everything at the church. I wish they would get transferred back to the area."

"I'll pass that along."

The guys waved goodbye and got in the cars. Levi and Lucas climbed into the truck and headed back to the Fridays At Five warehouse.

"What's for lunch, Em?" Kenny asked.

"Liz and I have been busy. We thought you and Tyler should take us out for lunch," Emmy said.

"Anywhere special you want to go?" Kenny asked and then turned to Tyler. "She's gonna say Darby's."

Tyler chuckled. "I wouldn't bet against that."

"You know where we want to go, Kenny Colwell," Emmy said and then she and Liz giggled.

"Fine! Darby's it is." Kenny smiled.

Chapter Fourteen

"Did you have enough to eat yesterday?" Kenny asked as Dave Persching entered Kenny's basement studio.

"Macy and her mother made an enormous turkey, and I had to carve the giant beast," Dave sat on one of the couches in the lounge area.

"Did you celebrate Thanksgiving back in England when you were a kid?" Jeff asked though he knew the answer. He opened a bottle of water from the fridge.

"No, and we didn't celebrate the Fourth of July either. Though I suppose we should. We got rid of you pesky colonies."

"Come on, Dave. Get over it. That was a thousand years ago," P.J. said.

Adam Vicini the newest member of the band quietly observed his bandmates.

"When was the last time you were even in Great Britain?" Kenny asked.

"Not counting a tour?"

"Yeah, when did you last go over there to just visit?" Jeff asked.

Dave inspected the ceiling as he thought about the question. "Probably ten years ago when my great-grandfather passed away."

"How old was he?" Kenny asked. *I know you. You're going to come up with a crazy answer just for Adam.*

"As near as anyone could tell, he was 107 years old."

"Get out!" Jeff exclaimed. "You said he was 103 the last time you told this wild story. Which is it?"

"New information surfaced that proved he was older than everyone thought." Dave shrugged. "What can I say?"

"Did your great-grandfather know Queen Victoria?" Adam asked.

"No, but he knew Henry the Eighth." Jeff laughed.

"Is this pick-on-Dave day?" P.J. wondered. "If so, I didn't get the memo."

"Fine! Have a good laugh on me." Dave leaned back and put his foot on his knee. "You guys have always been envious of me because of my extraordinary good looks."

"So true," Kenny said. "We should tell Macy about some of the..."

"Let's not get too radical."

After clowning around for a time the guys got serious.

"I've listened to all the demos several times, and I don't think there's a filler track among them," Kenny said.

Adam asked, "How many tracks do we have?"

"Twenty-five," Kenny answered. "I know most record companies don't like to put out two CD sets, but I think we have enough good tracks to consider it."

"We could do what we did before and put out one CD early in the year and the second one in the fall," Dave suggested.

"Nah, I don't want to go through that again." Jeff shook his head. "We had to go through two press conferences and two of everything. I'd rather put out one disc. If all the songs are good enough to be included, let's include them. So what if it's one or two CDs."

"We could always hold some back for the next project," P.J. suggested.

"Let's wait and see how it turns out. Maybe six months from now we'll have a better idea as to how many songs are really good enough," Kenny said.

"Which studio are we using?' Adam asked.

The Steward Music Group complex included four different recording studios. Number four being the newest.

Jeff drained his water and tossed the bottle toward a recycling bin. "We better be using number four. Our recordings have probably paid for it." He walked over and picked up the plastic bottle. This time he didn't miss.

"We have number four for three months except for the last couple of weeks in December and the first two in January. I assumed we would be taking a break then." Kenny checked his calendar.

"What if we need more time?" P.J. asked.

"I imagine we can probably get more time if we want." Kenny pulled up the schedule on StewardMusicGroup.com. "There is a band using the studio in March. Should we book three more months?"

"Wouldn't hurt," Jeff said.

The band spent two hours listening to the demos they had recorded, and then called it a day.

"Ten o'clock Monday morning, huh?" Dave put on his knee-length gray wool coat and his matching fedora.

"Do you think you can get up that early?" Jeff teased.

"I can wake up and get to the studio okay, but I'm not sure I'll know which end of the drumsticks to use."

"I didn't think it mattered." Emmy grinned after slipping downstairs unnoticed.

"Shows how much you know about being a professional musician, little lady." Dave doffed his hat to her and then opened the door leading to the stairs up to the garage.

"We have leftovers in case any of you guys are hungry. I can make turkey sandwiches," Emmy offered.

None of the guys took her up on her offer.

"Sorry, Emmy, but Frances made a ham, and I love leftover ham sandwiches. Say hi to the kids for me."

"How about you, Adam? Did Juliana cook yesterday?"

"She helped Mom with dinner, but we ate at my parents' house," Adam answered.

"How is your father doing? Does he miss being one of the Plaintiffs?" Emmy referred to Dixie Case's band.

Adam laughed. "He claims to be content to stay home and run the music store. He's always saying he's too old to travel with a band. He's actually giving drum lessons again."

"I talked to Dixie a month or so ago. He's doing enough gigs to make ends meet, but he's looking for a new label deal," Emmy said. She bit her lip as she thought about the handsome man who traveled with the original Crest Ridge Worship Band. *He's more of a rock star than Kenny. I bet the women are throwing themselves at him.*

"Yeah, I don't blame Steward Music for dropping him. The first two CDs sold decently, but the last two didn't make the charts. Any charts. Dixie needs to refocus on what kind of music he wants

139

to play." Adam picked up his coat and gloves. "I hope it doesn't snow tomorrow. I'm not ready for winter."

Jeff and P.J. got ready to leave. Everyone walked out to the garage together.

"See you guys on Monday." Kenny watched them head out to their cars. "Hey, Em, it's starting to snow a little."

"I'm with Adam. I don't like winter as much as when I was a kid."

Kenny laughed. "I know one person who's ready for winter."

Emmy shook her head. "Cousin Andy is nuts. He likes thunderstorms and would be happy if it snowed every day."

"Kenny, did you notice how many empty seats were filled by invisible people tonight?" Emmy put her feet on the dashboard of their Odyssey as they drove home from church.

"That's a rather unique way of putting it, Em," Kenny said and then laughed.

"I'm serious. Fewer and fewer people are coming to the Saturday night service. It must cost quite a bit to have the church open."

"I'm sure it costs more, but there are some people who have to work on Sunday mornings."

"Ha! I bet most of the people come on Saturday night so they can have their Sundays free. They don't have to go to Sunday School, either."

"Are you upset because we have to come on Saturday night and Sunday morning?"

Emmy sat up straighter and bit her lip. She looked over at Kenny. "That might be part of it. Maybe we should let some of the other musicians take over Saturday night."

"I thought you liked the Saturday service. You help choose the music, and you get to dance around a bit more than on Sundays," he grinned.

She frowned and poked his arm. "It's not totally like a concert."

"Not totally, but it's getting closer."

140

"Can we stop somewhere for ice cream, please?"

Kenny looked out the windows. "Em, it's freezing. All of the ice cream places are closed until spring."

"Not the Robbins place. It stays open all year round."

"You really want to go that far for ice cream? We have some at home. I could make you a chocolate shake," he suggested.

"Will you make it extra thick?"

"Thick enough you have to use a spoon to drink it."

"Okay, that's better than going all the ways to Robbins."

By the time they arrived home, Kevin was sound asleep and Sofia had the girls ready for bed.

Emmy walked into the twins' bedroom after checking on Kevin. "Why are you still up? It's past your bedtime."

"We were reading in Spanish, Mommy," Isabella said.

"Okay, but now it's time for bed."

"Will you read us a story first? Or let us read one to you?" Heather asked.

"I think you've done enough reading for tonight." She tucked the girls in bed, kissed them goodnight, turned off the light and left the room.

"Mom, we didn't say our prayers," Heather said.

Emmy stopped and sighed. She entered the room. "All right, but tonight you have to say your prayers in your beds."

The girls prayed longer than usual, but Emmy didn't interrupt.

"Okay, now go to sleep." *Should I let you keep praying for Scout? I suppose God listens to prayers about family pets. He created everything after all.*

"Night, Mommy," they said and then giggled.

Emmy joined Sofia and Kenny in the kitchen.

Kenny poured the milkshakes. "Did you get them down?"

"Finally."

"I'm sorry I let them read longer than normal. It's my fault," Sofia apologized.

"It's not that late, and they like to see Emmy before they go to sleep."

"I thought this was supposed to be so thick I would have to

141

use a spoon. What gives?"

Kenny grinned at Emmy's chocolate-milk-mustache. "I made it as thick as I could."

"It's delicious."

"How was the service tonight?" Sofia asked.

Kenny shook his head.

Emmy rolled her eyes. "Don't get me started."

"That bad, huh?"

"I don't think there were a hundred people there."

"There were a lot of empty seats filled with invisible people," Kenny repeated what Emmy said earlier.

Sofia stared at him. "I don't understand."

Kenny pointed at Emmy. "She said it first."

Emmy walked out onto the platform with Liz to get prepared for Sunday's second service. She handed Liz a wireless microphone and pulled her own from the stand. They moved to the front and then Emmy nudged Liz.

"Who are those men in suits talking to Tyler?"

Liz looked to the floor of the sanctuary and smiled. "The one on Tyler's left is Dr. Schofield. He's the DS for the Chicago Central District. Tyler's boss."

"I've heard of him, but never seen him. Who's the other one?"

"I'm not sure. I'll have to ask Tyler."

The worship band finished and Emmy and Liz scurried back to the music suite. They were still there when Tyler introduced Dr. Schofield to the congregation. Dr. Schofield in turn introduced the man neither Liz nor Emmy knew.

"Before I begin, I would like to welcome and introduce a surprise visitor." Dr. Schofield turned a bit and held out a hand. "Dr. Keck, would you please stand?"

The man stood and turned a bit so the congregation might see him better.

"Some of you might not be aware, but the Nazarene church is led by six General Superintendents, and Dr. Keck is one of those men. It's a pleasure to have you with us, Dr. Keck. Would you like

142

to say something?" Dr. Schofield waved for Dr. Keck to come up to the platform.

"I don't want to intrude on Jaren's time, but I certainly want to congratulate this church for being a vibrant and thriving church." Dr. Keck spoke for a couple of minutes. Just long enough to be speaking when Emmy and Liz returned to the sanctuary. Liz joined Tyler and Dr. Schofield on the front row. Emmy saw Kristen and Sloane and slipped in next to Kristen.

Dr. Schofield returned to the platform and Dr. Keck sat next to Liz and Tyler. Dr. Schofield prayed and then began his message.

A few minutes later, Emmy whispered to Kristen, "He's certainly an energetic speaker. Do you know he's Tyler's boss?"

"I am aware of that, Em."

"Who's the older man that was talking?" Emmy asked.

"I didn't catch his name, but Dr. Schofield introduced him as a General Superintendent."

"Does that mean he's kinda like the Pope?"

"Hush, and listen to Dr. Schofield. You might learn something."

Dr. Schofield finished and turned the service back over to Pastor Tyler.

Tyler prayed and then held up a hand. "Before I forget. Our new sign is installed and functioning. Check it out as you leave."

"What sign?" Kristen asked.

"The one by the entrance. It's one of those new digital ones. The guys don't have to change it by hand anymore."

After the service Emmy was talking to Kenny when Tyler, Liz, Dr. Schofield and Dr. Keck walked up behind her.

"Hey, guys!" Liz smiled.

Kenny put his hands on Emmy's shoulders and turned her around. Her eyes opened wide and she bit her lip when she saw who was with Tyler and Liz.

Tyler chuckled because he could tell Emmy was going to by shy around the two leaders of the church.

"Dr. Schofield, Dr. Keck, this is Kenny Colwell and his bashful wife Emmy Colasanti-Colwell," Tyler said knowing that

143

would embarrass Emmy even more.

Dr. Schofield shook hands with Kenny. "It's a pleasure to finally meet you. My son is a fan of your music."

Dr. Keck stood before Emmy.

She looked up at him and bit her lip even harder. *Please don't talk to me. I'll just die if you ask me something.*

Dr. Keck smiled. "I enjoyed hearing you sing in person. I recently listened to one of your CDs. I believe the title is *The Carriage House Sessions*. My daughter recommended it to me, and I thoroughly enjoyed it."

Emmy's eyes opened even wider. *Holy crap! You're joking, right?*

"I appreciated the lyrics. They are more than repetitive worship songs. They show deep insight into human nature," Dr. Keck said and then smiled.

Emmy stared at him without speaking. *Shoot! What should I do? Do I have to kiss his hand? Do I curtsy?*

Kenny put an arm around her waist. "Dr. Keck, I do believe you have performed a miracle. You have completely silenced Emmy."

Tyler chuckled. Liz braided her hair.

Emmy broke out of her trance and elbowed Kenny in the side. "Thank you, sir. Am I supposed to call you something special? I was raised Catholic. I've never met a Nazarene General Superintendent before."

Dr. Keck grinned. "Most people call me Ed."

144

Chapter Fifteen

Emmy picked up her laptop from the kitchen island and headed to the den. *I have the whole house to myself until Kevin gets home.* She plopped into one of the leather recliners and booted up her computer. She deleted a bunch of messages and then sat up straighter. She opened the email from Rory Porter.

I'm settled in my apartment. All unpacked and even bought some furniture. I started my new job, and I like it. I'm in charge of a dozen therapists. Can you imagine that? I have Sundays and Mondays off. Say hi to Kenny and the kids. Take care.

She read it again and then sat back and closed her eyes. She opened them quickly and reached for her phone. She bit her lip as she punched in Rory's number.

He answered after three rings. "Em, is that you?"

"In person. I was checking email and came close to adding a certain message to my spam folder, but decided to open it instead."

"I'm pleased to be on your list of non-spam contacts. How are you?"

"Enjoying a morning of peace and quiet. The kids are at school. Kenny is at work. I have the house to myself."

"You guys should get a pet. You need a few cats and dogs to keep you company," he suggested.

"Not possible. Kevin is allergic to pet dander according to the doctor. He sneezes every time we go over to Tony's. He plays with Scout and then suffers later. How are you? Are you home?"

"I am. I just finished breakfast and cleaning the kitchen."

"Do you have Internet?"

"I do. Cable TV and high speed Internet. Why?"

"Wanna Skype?"

He thought about it, "Yeah, sure. I need to turn on my laptop. Are you decent?"

She giggled before answering. "Skype me and find out."

"You're dressed. I know you better than that." He walked into his spare bedroom, grabbed his Dell and turned it on.

"Stay on the phone until we get the Skype working, Rory,"

she said. She opened the program and waited.

"It's booting up now."

A few seconds later she heard the familiar ping.

"Can you see me, Rory?"

"It's kinda fuzzy. You look like you're wearing an old sweatshirt and your hair is a total mess."

"You're so funny." She ran her fingers through her hair. "I love having it short. Show me your apartment. I want to see it all."

He stood up. "Okay, but it's just a two-bedroom apartment. Nothing special about it."

"Show me anyway."

"Okay, this is the spare bedroom that I'm using as my office." He pointed the laptop at his computer desk and then turned around. "And I found this couch thing that doubles as a spare bed in case I have a guest."

"Are you inviting me over?" she asked and then giggled.

"You are welcome anytime you and Kenny are in the Tampa area."

"Party pooper," she teased. "Show me your room."

"I didn't make the bed."

"I've seen your bed before. I don't care if it's not made."

"This is a used bedroom set, but it's in great shape. I have a walk-in closet and a private bathroom."

"Don't you have a tub?"

"Not in here. There's one in the other bathroom," he said.

"Get out! You have two bathrooms!" she shrieked.

He teased back, "And I even have central air and heat. The electricity works until eight at night, and I even have a garage in case I buy a car."

"Haven't you bought a car yet? What about the minivan? Did it make it all the way?"

"Nope! It died somewhere in Georgia, and I carried everything the rest of the way."

"You're such a creep. Why do I even like you?"

"Because of my charming personality and overall sexiness, I suppose."

"Ha! I might have considered you sexy at one time but

146

never charming. Show me the kitchen."

He showed her the rest of the place and even walked out onto his patio.

"How's the weather up there, Em?" he grinned.

"Stuff it, Rory." She stuck out her tongue and frowned at his image. "I didn't put on a coat to see the kids off to school, and I about froze my butt off. It's definitely too cold to be wearing shorts and a t-shirt like you."

"That's a shame, Em."

"Go ahead and laugh now, buster. Wait until summer when it's 120 outside, and you burn your hand opening the door."

"I'll never leave the air conditioning." He moved to his couch and stretched out. "Anything else going on?"

"Are you asking if I caught grief from Kenny for going over to see you before you left?"

"Not specifically, but did you?"

She sat Indian-style in the recliner. "No, but I did sit in his lap and ended up crying."

He looked at her image for several seconds before responding. "Did you really? No, wait. I know you did. You can't hide your emotions. Not possible. It's a good thing you don't have anything to hide and don't ever play poker."

"He knows I care about you. Do you have any ceiling fans?"

Nice way to change the subject, Em. He laughed and said, "I have two. One in here and one in my bedroom. So I touched a nerve, huh?"

"Did not," she insisted.

"Hey! You're talking to me, kid. I've known you almost as long as Kenny. He just didn't disappear for ten years."

"More like fourteen years, and I'm not a kid anymore." She leaned forward and rested her chin in her hands.

"The cameras are so good on these computers now that I can see your eyes sparkling. Just like they do whenever you get excited."

"Do you have a girlfriend yet?"

"Yes, and she should be here any second."

147

"What's her name?" *I know you're kidding, Rory.*

"It's Francesca, and I met her at... at the grocery store. She's French and about six feet tall. She has long black hair down to her butt with gorgeous dark eyes that just stare deep into your soul."

Emmy rolled her eyes. *Give me a break.*

"She is slim and is one of those supermodels you see on the covers of magazines."

"I think I know who you mean. She has one of those beauty marks on her cheek, right? And a big tattoo on her butt."

"That's her." He laughed. *I know you know I'm making her up.*

"In your dreams, Rory Porter," she said, paused a moment and asked, "What's your middle name?"

"Don't have one," he said without sounding convincing.

"You're lying. What is it? Mine's Olivia."

"I know that and Kenny has a whole bunch of names."

"Tell me!"

"If I tell you, I'd have to kill you." He sat up, swiveled and put his feet on the floor while holding the laptop on his legs.

"Not working. Tell me, creep."

You have to promise never to tell a soul," he insisted.

"Why? Is it something really weird?"

"Not weird, but I've always hated it."

She raised a hand in a mock salute. "I swear on my honor as a Girl Scout to never reveal it to..."

"You were never a Girl Scout."

"No, but I knew some, and I bought some cookies."

He shook his head. *You are so fumy, Em.* "All right. It's Clarence."

"Clarence! For real!?" She sat up.

"It was my father's name."

"I'm going to call you Clarence from now on."

"Not if you want to remain my friend."

"How about Owen? Did he have a middle name?"

Rory laughed. "He did, and he would beat the snot out of anyone who ever used it."

"Tell me." She stopped laughing and looked serious.

"Hubert."

"Herbert?"

"No! Hubert." He spelled it for her.

"Poor Owen," she sighed. "That's even worse than Clarence, Clarence."

"Go ahead and call me that if you want me to disavow any knowledge of your existence, Olivia."

"I was named after a great-grandmother, if I remember right. Sometimes I use Olivia if I want to be incognito."

"Oh, are you a spy? Is that your cover? You're Olivia something-or-other."

"Porter. Olivia Porter, and I work for the C.I.A."

"Get out!"

She bit her lip. "Sometimes on tour I use that name to check into a hotel. Sometimes the guys in the band call me that if they are trying to tease me. Especially after you spent that week with me."

"Aw, Em, you really do love me," he said.

"Oh, shut up and wipe that silly grin off your face." She maneuvered in the recliner and ended up on her back with her feet up in the air and the laptop on her stomach.

"Does Kenny know?"

"No, and I'll kill you if you tell him, Clarence."

They laughed and then stared at each other's image.

"I'm gonna miss you, Em. You're so much fun to be with."

"I'll miss you, too, Rory," she admitted.

"Will Kenny mind if we stay in touch?"

"He better not. I know he and Becky email each other once in a while, and their relationship was more... more."

"Physical?" Rory asked.

"I was gonna say intimate, but physical works."

"I should let you go, Em. It's been good to see you."

"You, too, Clarence. Say hi to Francesca for me," she said as she grinned.

"I will, Mrs. Porter."

"It's Ms. Porter for your information, and don't blow my cover story. Should we try to Skype every Monday?"

"At least every other Monday."

"Deal. Take care, Rory, and stay out of trouble."

"You, too, Em. Don't get caught up in any spy rings."

"Never! I'm like a female 007."

"Better not be. He sleeps around."

"I didn't mean it like that," she shouted.

"I know. Have a good week, Olivia." He ended the session before she could reply.

She remained in that strange position on the recliner and stared at her computer for a time. She slid off of the recliner and ended up on the floor with her feet still on the recliner. *I will miss you, Rory, but it's for the best.*

"All right, Brady, stop pacing around and tell me what's wrong." Diane set down her fashion magazine. "You've been antsy all week."

He ran a hand through his thinning hair and sat down in his extra-wide black, leather recliner. "There's only so much I can do with my hobbies. I love photography, but I'm never going to be very good at golf or tennis. I need more. I need a challenge." He raised his arms in the air.

"How old are you now?" she asked.

"Don't you know? I'm forty-seven."

"I know. It was a rhetorical question."

"Your point?"

"I'm perfectly happy to stay home and raise the boys and take care of Lily. I keep busy taking care of Mom's stuff and doing some charity work." *Who would ever believe I would be on some of these committees with society women.* "I hate doing housework, so thank you for letting me hire a maid. You, on the other hand, are not a homebody." She stood up and sat on the arm of his chair. "You have to use your mind to solve problems."

He grinned and put a hand on her thigh. "Are you saying I should be a math teacher?"

"Only if I can be your student." She leaned down and kissed him.

"You can be my teacher's pet."

She stood up. "Spill it. I know you have a plan. You are a meticulous planner." *I bet you plan a week in advance when you want to have sex.*

"Okay, this is it."

She sat down on the couch.

Brady stood up and began pacing again. "I happened to go through some of Dad's old files and came across a patent that wasn't sold along with the company." He proceeded to explain the patent in great detail.

I don't understand any of this, but keep going.

"I think I could use this patent to start a new company. Nothing too big or too risky, but something to challenge my mind. I mentioned it to Bennett, and he thought he might like to join me."

"Do you want to start a business with your brother?"

"I've always gotten along with Bennett." He stopped pacing for a moment. "Can you believe Spencer is twenty-one already?"

"And little Abigail is about ready for college." Diane laughed. "Get used to it, Brady. Kids grow up a lot faster than we think they should."

"Would you mind if I research this a bit more deeply?"

"Not at all. Promise me you won't risk all of your money."

He waved a hand. "No! No! The initial capital investment would only be a few million. Certainly less than ten."

Diane waved a hand in front of her face. "Goodness gracious, Mr. Robertson. Why would you bother me with such a trivial amount. I assumed you might need several hundred million."

He laughed. "You got me."

"You have my permission to return to work if that will make you happy."

"I never dreamed I would be retired in my forties. Dad still keeps busy consulting for companies all over the world, and his father worked until the day he passed away. He was eighty-five."

"Would you have time to take the boys Christmas shopping? They don't want me to take them. I think they want to buy me something special."

"But it's Saturday. Won't the shops be packed?"

151

"The longer you wait, the worse it will be. It's the beginning of December. If you take them today, you will be finished."

"Did you tell them what you would like? Are they searching for something specific?"

"I gave them a list."

He pulled out his wallet and checked his cash level. "Will this be expensive? I don't have much money."

"You are such a riot, Brady Robertson."

"Must be why you love me so much," he said and kissed her again. "What should I do with these special gifts? I can't wrap a present to save my life."

"You are hopeless. Take them over to Emmy's. She will wrap them for you."

Brady called his team of attorneys together for a meeting Monday morning. He passed out a folder with twenty pages explaining his intent.

"I know this is short notice, and it's nearly Christmas, but I'd like to get this company started as soon as possible."

One of the attorneys chuckled. "This is an unusual name, Brady. It sounds more like a law firm than a tech company."

One of the other attorneys tilted his head. "I must be missing something."

"Carson and Caden are Brady's stepsons."

"What about Lily? And what if you and Diane have more children? Will you change the name of the company?"

Brady smiled and shook his head. "No, I will start another company. Maybe one named for each kid."

Chapter Sixteen

Emmy stomped into the music suite Thursday evening without talking to Kenny who followed at a safe distance.

"Hi, Emmy, is Kenny with you?" Chase asked.

"He's here somewhere," she spat.

Chase tilted his head and watched as she took a seat and crossed her arms over her chest. *Whoa! Someone must have had a rough day.* He looked at the folder in his hands. *She might not want to sing this song.*

Liz sat down next to Emmy. Emmy looked up at Liz, but then back down at the floor. She kicked at the chair in front of her.

"Are you okay? You look like you're about to bite someone's head off. Did I do something?" Liz asked.

"You didn't do anything, Liz," Emmy said and then sighed. "This has been a horrible day. I went to see Mom, and she's just totally out of it. Complete bonkers! She thinks Daddy is still alive, but he's avoiding her. She thinks I'm ten and got after me for missing school. She threatened to ground me. The kids wouldn't listen this morning when I told them to get ready for school. Kevin Michael threw a fit because I wouldn't let him take a firetruck to school. Heather and Isabella were asking so many questions about goofy stuff that I snapped at them and told them to go bother their father." Emmy put her elbows on her thighs and rested her chin in her hands. "I almost stayed home tonight, but Kenny made me come. I didn't talk to him on the way here. I stared out the window and ignored him."

Liz put a hand on Emmy's back and massaged it. "It's all right. You are allowed to have a bad day once in a while."

"I wish having my tubes tied got rid of my periods but it didn't. They've never been regular, but when they come, they really bother me."

"Sorry, I forgot about that," Liz said.

"It's all right. I usually deal with it better, but not today."

Chase looked at the people in the room to see if he might need to wait for someone. *Bobby and Skip aren't here, but they told me they wouldn't be here this weekend. Robby doesn't mind*

153

playing drums for all three services. Steve told me Miles agreed to cover him on bass. He moved to the front of the room and everyone knew this was his cue for them to take a seat.

"I received a text from Heidi this afternoon. Her mother is in the hospital. She thinks her mother might have had a heart attack. I think we should pray for Heidi and Ross and Heidi's parents before we start. She told me her father needs constant care now, and this has put an immeasurable strain on her mother." He looked around the room. "Are there any other urgent requests for prayer?"

Regina Collins raised a hand. "My grandmother is back in the nursing home. She fell again, but didn't break any bones."

"Any other needs?" Chase asked.

Several people raised hands indicating unspoken requests.

"Let's spend some time in prayer."

Some people knelt in front of their chairs. Others sat still. Others used the piano bench as an altar. Freddie and Marshall Bender paced at the back of the room. Emmy sat in her chair with her chin in her hands. Chase led the group in the beginning, and then others prayed.

Emmy listened. *Why can't I pray like Chase or Cam or Regina? They are so eloquent. If I pray out loud, I sound like a kid taking to a friend. I don't use all the fancy words they do.*

Chase closed the prayer and everyone returned to their seats.

"I hope everyone has been checking online for the songs and order of service. I do have one change, but it only affects the second service on Sunday." He glanced at Emmy and saw her sitting with her arms crossed over her chest. He held up the folder which contained the chord charts and the lead sheets for the song. "It's an older song, but... Well, it's 'Yolanda's Song.'" He looked directly at Emmy.

Emmy stared back at Chase. *Why? You know I have trouble singing that song at church. It's all I can do to get through it in a concert. We'll have to talk about this.*

"Emmy, do you have any thoughts about singing this song? I know it means a lot to you personally."

154

"I'd rather not do it, Chase, but you already know that. Why didn't you ask me before you added it to the service?"

Everyone stared at Emmy.

"What's up with Emmy tonight?" Robby asked Regina. "She's usually so easygoing. I've never heard her use that tone of voice with anyone."

Chase set the folder on the podium. "We'll talk about it later, Emmy. Right now I'd like to split into two groups. Those of you who are on the schedule for Saturday can use the sanctuary to rehearse, and I'll go over Sunday's songs in here. We'll join you in the sanctuary in fifteen or twenty minutes. Will that be enough time for you, Cam?"

"That should be plenty of time." Cam adjusted his black-rimmed, Buddy Holly-style glasses. "There are no new songs."

Emmy rose from her chair and frowned at Chase. She turned on her heels and quickly headed to the sanctuary.

Chase looked at Kenny.

Kenny shrugged. "Sorry, Chase. Don't take it personally. She's had a rough couple of days."

Fifteen minutes later Chase and the rest of the team entered the sanctuary. He didn't see Emmy, so he asked Kenny where she was.

"She needed to take care of something. Women stuff."

"Oh, sorry I asked."

Emmy stomped in a minute later and sat on the front edge of the riser for the guitar players without speaking to anyone.

"Are you going to sing at all tonight, Emmy?" Chase asked in a calm manner. "I would appreciate it if you did."

"I'll sing the other songs." She grabbed her microphone.

Chase rehearsed the songs for both Sunday services. He liked to familiarize all the musicians with all the songs in case they needed to adjust the schedule. They rehearsed all the songs except for one.

He looked at Emmy. "Could we run through 'Yolanda's Song' once, please?"

"You guys can play it if you want. I'm not in the mood to sing it," she said defiantly. She placed her mic in the stand and

155

turned to walk away, but Kenny grabbed her hand and stopped her.

"Emily! Stop it."

Emmy ripped her hand away from Kenny. "No, I won't sing it."

Everyone stopped talking. They glanced at Emmy and then at each other. Emmy felt the tension in the room. Kenny touched her hand again.

"I'm sorry for being a diva tonight, Chase. If you want me to quit the team, I will." She broke away from Kenny and ran toward the hallway behind the sanctuary.

"You're not going to resign from the worship team, Em," Chase said softly. "Kenny, would you run through the song while I talk to Emmy."

"No problem."

Chase left the sanctuary and found Emmy in the entryway to the music suite.

"I'm sorry, Chase. I'm sorry," she said. "I really should quit. I acted like a spoiled child, and now everyone will hate me."

Chase put a hand on her shoulder. "Let's use my office to talk. I need to tell you something."

She followed him into his office and closed the door behind her.

"Am I fired?" She slumped into one of the chairs that faced his desk.

"Don't be ridiculous." He moved a couple of photos and then sat on the front edge of the desk. "I haven't told anyone other than Tyler and Pastor Herb, but Yvonne and I are leaving."

"What? No way! You can't leave! What will we do without you?" Emmy said and then bit her lip.

"The church will survive without us."

"Where are you going? When?"

"I've received an offer from the church I grew up in back in Toledo. We're not certain exactly when we will leave, but it will be after the holidays."

"Is that why you want me to sing that song?"

"Not really. I don't choose the songs by throwing darts at the wall," he said with a grin.

156

She managed a weak smile. "I know that. You put them all in a bingo thing and draw them out."

"I can't explain it, but the Holy Spirit has been telling me to have you sing that song this Sunday."

"Why?"

Chase shrugged. "I don't know, Em, but I always try to obey what the Holy Spirit asks of me, and in this case I've felt the need to do this song all week."

She slumped in the chair.

"It's been a long time since you sang it in church," he said. "I looked it up on the computer, and it wasn't even on the list. Remember how we used to use those folders for every song?"

She nodded.

"Then we started tracking it on the computer. Much easier. I pulled the folder and guess when you last sang it."

"I can't remember."

"May 6, 2007. Ring a bell?"

Emmy looked around the room and then back at Chase. "Was that when Lynette and Paul left for Iowa?"

"Yes, that was their last Sunday here."

Emmy brushed away a tear. "Lynette told me that was her favorite song because she actually knew Yolanda."

"It's been a long time, Em. Five and a half years. I don't understand why, but we need to sing this song this Sunday." He closed his eyes for a moment. "I remember the first time you sang it. That was over ten years ago, and I can recall it as if it was last week."

"I'll bawl like a baby if you make me sing it."

"No one will mind if you do," he assured her.

Emmy bit her lip. "Are you sure it was the Holy Spirit and not something you ate?"

He grinned. "I think I can tell the difference, Emmy."

She took a deep breathe, held it for a time and then let it all out. "Fine! I'll sing it."

"About the other thing, Em?"

"I have to keep it a secret, right?"

"Please don't tell anyone until we announce it."

157

"Can I tell Kenny?"

"I don't want you to keep this is a secret from him if that would cause a problem." Chase got down from his desk.

Emmy stood up and waved a hand. "It's okay. I have some secrets from Kenny. I won't mention it to anyone. Promise."

"Should we go back to the sanctuary?"

"Yes, I need to apologize to everyone. I behaved like an..."

"Like a diva," he interrupted her.

She grinned.

They returned to the platform and Chase gathered everyone close.

Emmy glanced at the floor but then raised her head. "I want to apologize to you for acting like... like a diva tonight." She glanced at Chase. "I've had a really horrible day, and I let that affect my attitude. I'm sorry, and I hope you will forgive me and not fire me from the team because I really love working with you guys." She stopped as the tears flowed.

Liz hugged her. "I suppose we'll give you a second chance."

"Jesus did say we have to forgive people 490 times," Emmy said softly.

"I think you've used up a couple hundred of those, Emmy," Chase teased her.

She wrinkled her nose at him. "I'll run through the song now if you want."

He waved a hand dismissively. "No need. I'm sure you know the song by now."

Natalie and Grayson were standing on the couch in the living room looking out the large window on Friday evening.

"How soon will she be here, Mommy?" Natalie looked over her shoulder at Liz. "I can't wait to see her."

"It won't be long. She said she would be here by six."

Natalie turned back to watch out the window. Grayson began jumping up and down as a white Toyota Prius pulled into the driveway.

"Mommy! Mommy! Dany is here!" Natalie jumped down

158

from the couch, dashed to the front door, opened it and ran over to the car before Dany Kimmerle could even get out. "Dany! I missed you. What took you so long?"

Dany stepped out of the car and hugged Natalie. "I got here as fast as I could, Natty."

Liz carried Grayson outside, but then he squirmed to get down and ran to Aunt Dany.

Dany picked him up. "Look at you! You are getting so big, Grayson. Give me a kiss."

"It's a shame they aren't excited to see you," Liz said.

"How long can you stay?" Natalie asked.

Dany looked at Liz as she let Grayson get down. "That's up to your mother."

"Mom, can Dany stay this long?" Natalie held her arms out as wide as she could.

"She can stay as long as she wants, but Dany is going to look for a place of her own. She's going to be working... What is the name of that company?"

"Hampshire Medical Group." Dany held Grayson's hand as they walked back to the house. "They specialize in child development."

"Tyler, would you grab the luggage for Dany, please?"

"It's all in the trunk, Ty," Dany said. "Thank you for letting me crash here."

Tyler chuckled. "The kids and Derby would be upset if you didn't stay with us."

"How would Derby know?" Natalie asked.

"Derby is the smartest dog in the world, Natty. Let me prove it." Tyler pointed at Derby. "Derby, roll over."

Derby cocked her head to the side and sat down.

"Derby, shake hands."

Derby rolled over.

"Derby, sit."

Derby raised her paw.

"See?" Tyler smiled.

"But, Daddy, she didn't do any of the tricks right." Natalie shrugged.

"She's a procrastinator. Most dogs don't understand the concept of procrastination. That proves how smart Derby is."

Liz and Dany shook their heads, and Dany moved a finger in a circle around her ear.

Natalie tugged on Dany's hand.

"What is it, Natty?"

"Dany, Zhy doesn't live with us anymore. She went to live with her real daddy, and I miss her so, so much. Is it all right to still say prayers for her?"

"Of course it is. You can always pray for whoever you like." Dany looked at Liz.

"It was last week."

"Will you have any contact with her at all?" Dany asked.

Liz shook her head. "Unfortunately, no. Her father has requested we not maintain contact. That's how the system works."

Dany sighed. "I could never be a foster parent. My heart would break every time I had to give a child back."

"Tell me," Liz said. "You are like that with cats."

"Oh, shush. Mom is the one who keeps all the stray cats."

"Did you eat?" Liz asked.

"Not since lunch. Did you guys eat already?"

"I fed the kids, but Tyler and I haven't eaten. I made a cold spaghetti salad."

"Oooh, yum. I haven't had one of those in months." Dany followed Liz into the kitchen and looked around. "I love the layout of the kitchen and family room. It's open so you can be working in here and still see the TV."

Tyler struggled with two suitcases in each hand. "How much stuff did you bring?"

"Most of my clothes. Well, everything from my apartment at school. There is some stuff left at home."

"Where should I put this, Liz?"

"In the guest room unless you're going to make Dany sleep in the basement."

"Let me help you, Tyler." Dany grabbed the smallest suitcase, looked up at her brother-in-law and smiled. "This is going to be fun."

Chapter Seventeen

After the second service on Sunday morning, Emmy made her way down the steps to the main floor of the sanctuary and glanced around for Kristen and Sloane. She turned toward the side and was immediately approached by Dany Kimmerle.

Dany hugged Emmy as tightly as she could. "Thank you so much for singing that song." Dany squeezed Emmy for a few more seconds before letting go.

"Dany, you're crying. What's wrong?" Emmy held Dany's hand and pulled her to the chairs in the front row. "Sit down and talk to me."

Dany dried her tears and sighed. "It's nothing."

"Tell me, or else I will ask Liz."

Dany sighed. "When I was still in high school, I had a friend named Samantha Dykstra. We were the same age."

Emmy bit her lip and felt tears forming in her eyes.

"Sammy was killed by a drunk driver just like Yolanda, and one of our friends sang that song at her funeral. I've listened to your versions on the CDs a million times, but I've never heard you sing it in person until today." Dany hugged Emmy again. "Thank you so very much, and I'm sorry if I made you cry."

"It's all right."

Liz noticed them crying and knelt in front of them. "Are you guys all right?"

Emmy nodded but then shook her head.

Dany sniffled, but then answered Liz. "I told Emmy about Sammy. You remember Sammy, right?"

"Yes, her brother Gary was my age. I don't remember her other brother's name," Liz said. "Wait! It was Clark."

"Right," Dany replied.

"Wasn't Samantha killed in the winter?" Liz asked.

"December," Dany said. "The ninth, I believe. Yes, it was. What's today's date?"

Emmy sobbed harder, and Liz put her hands on Emmy's head and pulled her close. She looked up at Dany and mouthed the words, "The ninth."

Chase walked over a few minutes later and saw Liz and Emmy standing together.

"Are you all right now, Em?"

"I'm fine. I'm sorry for being such a baby."

"It's okay. I'm going to see if I can find Tyler and the kids." Liz left.

"What's wrong, Emmy?" Chase asked. "I can tell you've been crying. Was it just because of the song?"

"I'm so sorry I fought against singing that song. I should have known better than to doubt you." She hugged Chase and didn't care if anyone saw.

"It's okay, Emmy. I thought you sang beautifully, by the way."

Emmy took a moment to explain about Samantha. "Did you know this before?"

Chase shook his head. "No, Em, I had no idea. I've never really talked to Liz's sister."

"So it really was the Holy Spirit telling you I needed to sing it today, huh?"

"I knew it wasn't the spicy burrito."

"You are a stinker." She pulled his head close and whispered. "I'm not even gonna miss you when you leave."

"Emmy!" he drew out her name.

"Fine! I'll miss you a little, but not as much as Yvonne and the girls."

Liz found Dany in the foyer. "Have you seen Ty?"

Dany pointed. "He went that way."

They walked around the corner and Dany was nearly run over by a tall young man.

"Excuse me. I should pay more attention to where I'm walking."

Dany grinned up at him. "No problem."

Liz noticed the smile on her sister's face. "Dany, this is Darian Michaelis. He's Mary's brother. Darian, this is my sister Dany. I have to find Tyler and the kids. Wait for me, Dany."

Holy cow! You are the prettiest girl I've ever seen. Darian grinned. "Now I'm not so sorry I wasn't paying attention."

162

Dany smiled. *Thank you for running away, Liz.* She held out a hand. "It's a pleasure almost being run over by you. I know your sister."

Liz watched from the end of the hall. *I might as well take my time finding Tyler. That will give Dany a chance to talk to Darian. He's quite a remarkable young man.*

Darian and Dany chatted and discovered a few things about each other.

"My brother works at North Park. Do you know him?" Dany asked.

"I've met him, and talked to him, but mostly at church. I've done some flying, too."

"Larry loves to fly. What do you do at Aberdeen Investments?" *You are so tall I almost can't see your eyes.*

Darian explained some of his duties at the investment company owned by Mr. Robertson.

"That sounds interesting," Dany said.

"I'm just starting out, but it's a great company." Darian stared into Dany's big brown eyes. "Where is Hampshire Medical Group?"

"A couple of blocks away from St. Bart's."

"How do you like it so far?"

Dany waved at Tyler who was at the other end of the hall. "I actually don't start until January. I've been there several times and have an idea of what I'll be doing to start, but for now I'm on vacation. I'm going to stay with Liz until I find my own place."

Darian put a hand against the wall and leaned that way. "Natty and Grayson will love having you around."

"They are adorable." Dany smiled and each time she did Darian became more infatuated.

"So what are your doing until you start work?"

"Watching the kids. I have lots of free time." *Let's see if you get the hint because I've never asked any guy for a date.*

His hand slipped, and he had to move his feet or risk losing his balance. "So, Dany, uh, would you be interested in maybe grabbing some lunch or something one of these days? You do like to eat, right?"

She grinned and said, "I do eat occasionally." *I shouldn't do this but I want to see how long it takes you to come right out and ask me for a date.*

He suddenly found the paint texture quite interesting, but then looked at Dany again. "I'm off on Wednesdays. Would you like to grab something to eat? My treat." *Geez, I sound like a total dork. I've never had this much trouble asking a girl on a date before, not that I've dated a lot of girls.*

"What time?"

"Uh, any time would be all right with me," He scratched at the paint. "Is there anywhere special you would like to go?"

"Darby's. We don't have anything like Darby's back in Hillsdale."

"I love Darby's. Would it be all right if I pick you up at noon?"

""I'll be ready. Do you know how to get to Tyler and Liz's house?" Dany saw that Liz had joined Tyler and the kids. "I need to get going. Do you have a cell phone?"

He pulled his cell phone out.

She took it, punched in her name and number and handed it back. "Call me sometime, and I'll see you Wednesday." She looked back over her shoulder and waved as she walked toward Liz and Tyler.

"Dany! We're going to Emmy's house to eat. Isn't that great!" Natalie grabbed Dany's hand. "Heather and Isa have lots of dolls."

Liz looked at Dany to see if her expression would give anything away, but it didn't. "Well, did Darian ask you out?"

Tyler looked at Liz and then Dany. "Huh, what?"

Liz poked Tyler in the side. "You do realize Dany is grown up, right? She is allowed to date without a chaperone."

"I know. Darian Michaelis?" Tyler asked.

"He's a nice guy. Why shouldn't he ask Dany out?"

"I can beat him at tennis with one eye closed." Tyler motioned like he was hitting a tennis ball back across the net.

Liz looked at Dany, and they both made a motion indicating Tyler had lost his mind.

164

"What are you going to make for lunch, Em? Do we have enough to feed Tyler, Liz and everyone?" Kenny pulled the Odyssey onto Canton Lane and headed home.

Emmy laughed. "You make it sound like I will need to make enough to feed an army. I'll find something for the kids, and I thought we could make a pot of chili for the adults."

"We?"

Emmy sighed. "Liz will help me. You and Tyler can watch football or whatever. Dany will keep an eye on the kids if we let her, so tell Heather and Isa not to pester her."

"What about Grayson and Kevin?"

"They might play together. Kevin Michael can show Grayson his cars and trucks."

"He might bonk Grayson in the head with a firetruck. I'll keep an eye on the boys."

"Thank you, sweetie. Oh, I have to tell you later what Dany told me."

"Can't you tell me now?" Kenny pulled up at a red light.

"Not now. I will later when we're alone."

"Okay." *What could it be that you want to tell me in private?* He stared at Emmy until she pointed to the green light.

Dany helped Natalie into her booster seat while Liz strapped Grayson into his car seat.

"Are we ready?" Tyler checked that Liz and Dany were buckled in.

"We're ready, Daddy."

Liz turned in her seat to look at Dany. "Are you going to tell me?"

"He is taking me to Darby's for lunch on Wednesday."

Tyler looked in the rearview mirror. "I love Darby's."

Liz poked his side. "You are not going to Darby's with Dany and Darian."

"Could you bring me back a chili dog?"

Dany grinned at Tyler. "What's it worth to you?"

"I'll let you stay with us until you find your own place."

"Liz will let me stay. No deal. Anything else?"

"Pretty please," Tyler tried.

165

"I'll think about it." Dany tapped Liz on the shoulder. "Can I ask you something about Darian?"

"What?"

"Do you think he's too tall for me to consider dating? Assuming the first date isn't a disaster."

Tyler chuckled and said, "He's taller than me."

"He's pretty tall, but I can think of several couples like that," Liz said.

"Like who?" Tyler wondered.

"Dany, did you know Emmy used to date Tony Bertucci?" Liz asked over her shoulder.

"The football player?"

"The very one," Tyler said. "Now there's a difference in size. He's built like a tank, and she's a tiny tricycle."

"I'm going to tell her you said that," Liz frowned.

"I thought she and Kenny were like a lifelong couple. She really dated Tony?" Dany glanced over at Grayson. "He's asleep, you guys."

"She's known Kenny since she was a little girl, and they were friends. I don't think she met Tony until later in high school, and they didn't date too long," Liz explained.

"When I see them together now, I think of them as brother and sister, or at least close cousins." Dany kept an eye on Grayson. *Such a sleepy boy.*

Liz looked at Grayson. *Maybe we can get you in the house without waking you up. You need a long nap.* "They tease each other a lot. More than you and Tyler tease each other."

Tyler stopped at the security gate, and the guard recognized him immediately, waved and raised the gate.

"Can you imagine living in a place like this." Dany looked back at the guard house. "I love the natural look of the woods."

"In your dreams, Dany."

Tyler drove up the winding driveway and parked in front of one of the garage doors.

"How many cars will fit in here?" Dany asked.

"Not sure. These are custom garage doors. They're wider than a normal door, and the one on the end opens onto a wide area

166

where you could park at least three cars."

"Is it true that Kenny drives an old Civic?"

Tyler laughed. "Ask Emmy about that. She always claims Kenny is the dorkiest rock star in the world."

"He does seem really normal to me." Dany jumped out and then helped Natalie. "Your brother is sleeping so try to be quiet."

"I will, Dany." Natalie saw Isabella standing with Emmy and shrieked.

"So much for being quiet," Liz said.

Tyler carried Grayson inside without waking him. "Where can I deposit a sleeping child?"

"You can put him either in Kevin's room, or in Sofia's, but her bed might be too big for him."

"I'll put him in Kevin's." Tyler carried Grayson upstairs and returned in a minute.

"I turned on the intercom. We'll hear him if he wakes up," Emmy said.

"I think he's going to be out for a couple of hours or longer. Can I help with lunch?" Liz asked.

Isabella tugged on Emmy's dress. "Mommy, can we play in our room until lunch is ready?"

"Yes, but you should change clothes. You don't want to get you Sunday dresses dirty."

"We won't. We want to play school, and we need to wear dresses because we're the teachers," Heather explained.

"Okay, but you have to suspend school for the day when lunch is ready," Emmy informed them.

"What does suspend mean?" Natalie asked as the girls ran upstairs.

"It means stop," Isabella answered.

"I thought I could make chili for the adults, but what should we make for the kids?" Emmy checked the pantry.

"Sometimes we have soup and sandwiches on Sunday," Liz suggested.

Tyler stood behind Liz. "When did we ever have soup and sandwiches on a Sunday?"

"We have. You can watch football with Kenny."

167

Kenny looked at Dany and then Emmy. "Do you need my help with anything, Em?"

Emmy turned to face Kenny and let her mouth open wide, as if surprised. "Can this be? You're actually offering to help get lunch ready during football season?"

Tyler laughed and Dany grinned.

"Aw, come on. You're the one who's always been a football fanatic. Just because Tony is retiring doesn't mean you'll stop watching."

"I still like football, but I have other priorities now. I'm more mature." *Crap! I shouldn't have said that.*

"True, you are much more mature now, Em. You are as mature as the twins," Kenny said with a straight face.

"Get! All of you. Go now!" She pointed toward the family room.

"Dany, do you want to stay with us, or watch football with the men?" Liz made men sound derogatory.

Dany sat on one of the island barstools. "I'll stay in here and listen to you guys." *I want to hear if you talk about Darian.*

Emmy and Liz got lunch ready quickly for the kids. Emmy threw together the chili and warmed up the oven to make cornbread. They arranged the kids around the breakfast nook table, and sat at the island to wait for the chili and cornbread.

"Mom! My soup's too hot," Kevin Michael whined.

"Blow on it and let it cool. You're not a baby."

"Emmy, how much do you know about Darian Michaelis?" Liz asked and received a poke in the side from Dany.

"He's good at basketball. I know he played for Lincoln High, and he might have played at North Park. I've seen him slam dunk. I wish I could do that."

"I was thinking more about his character," Liz said and then grabbed Dany's hand. "Don't hit me again."

"Why? What's going on? You know Darian is a super good guy."

Liz looked at Dany and waited.

Dany squinted her eyes and made a face at Liz. "He asked me out. We're going to Darby's for lunch on Wednesday."

168

"Cool! Can I go with you guys?" Emmy glanced at the kids and saw Kevin blowing at his sandwich. "I love Darby's."

"You are as bad as Tyler," Liz said.

"Why? He likes Darby's, too."

"You can't go with Dany on her date," Liz stated emphatically.

"Duh, I get it now. Sorry, Dany. I'll sit at a different booth," Emmy said. Then she and Dany giggled while Liz rolled her eyes.

"Do you think Darian is too tall for me?" Dany asked while helping Natty and Kevin Michael finish their lunch.

"He's just a bit taller than Tony, and I dated him. Tony, not Darian." Emmy checked the twins faces and hands. "Go!" she pointed to the powder room next to the mudroom. "Wash your hands and faces and then go upstairs and play nicely. Help Natty and your brother."

"So I heard," Dany said. "What was it like to date a celebrity?"

"He wasn't all that much of a celebrity in high school. Kinda, but on a smaller scale. He did draw attention from the high school girls. Don't ask me why?" Emmy looked at Dany and then slapped her forehead. "Darn it! You got me. I always forget that some misguided people in this world think Kenny is some kind of rock star. You know him well enough to know he's a dork. If he wore glasses, he could be a college professor teaching some boring class like European History in the 1600s."

Kenny walked into the kitchen a second later. "Isa said the chili is ready. Is it? And what is wrong with European History?"

Emmy looked at Dany and shook her head. "See?"

Liz ran upstairs to check on Grayson as Emmy and Dany set the table for the grownups.

"He's still sleeping. We might just make it through lunch without any interruptions."

They did, but just barely. Grayson started to cry just as Emmy cleared the table.

"We should get going, Em. Thank you for lunch."

"You're welcome, Liz." Emmy hugged Liz and then Dany. "I promise not to show up at Darby's on your first date with

Darian, but if you guys go there again, I make no guarantees."

Darian arrived exactly at noon on Wednesday. He got out of his car and was about to ring the doorbell when Natalie opened the door.

"Are you taking Aunt Dany on a real date like Mommy and Daddy?"

He stooped down to her level. "I would like to, Natty. Do I have your permission, and why aren't you at school?"

Dany rescued Darian from further interrogation. "Come on in. I'm sorry, but I have to wait until Tyler gets here. Shouldn't be too long."

Dany led Darian into the living room. He sat on the couch, and Natalie sat next to him.

"I had to stay home because I'm really sick." She coughed to prove it. "Are you going to kiss Dany on your date? I heard Mommy tell Dany she shouldn't let you kiss her on the first date. I'm never going to kiss a boy. They're gross."

Darian smiled. "Am I gross?"

"No, but you're not a kid. If I was real old like you, I might kiss a boy."

"Natty, maybe you should go upstairs if you're really sick," Tyler said from the living room doorway. "Sorry, Dany, but I had to visit someone in St. Bart's. Hey, Darian, ready for another tennis lesson?"

"Yeah, but after that we have to go one-on-one on the basketball court." Darian shook Tyler's hand. "Do you really want a chili dog?"

Tyler chuckled and then smiled at Dany. "I do, but Liz threatened me with bodily harm if I interfered with your date in any manner. She specifically included asking you to bring a chili dog home."

"Grayson had his lunch, and he's napping. See you later." Dany grinned as she walked past Tyler.

"You want to grab a booth while I place our order?" Darian asked.

"Sure," she replied, walked away and chose a booth.

Darian set the tray on the table a moment later.

"Is that who I think it is?" Dany pointed to the pictures on the wall.

Darian laughed. "I guess you wouldn't have any way of knowing this, but we are sitting in Emmy and Kenny's favorite booth. The story is that he brought her here when she was eight or nine and they sat in this very booth. That's why there are photos of Friday's first gig here."

"So is that Emmy?"

"Yep!"

"She looks so young and tiny. Not that she's changed a lot."

"I remember coming here with my parents when Emmy worked here. I was probably six or so. If I'd been older, I would have had a crush on her." He looked up at the photo and then quickly back at Dany. "I didn't though. Never had a crush on her."

Dany laughed.

They ate their food and then talked for two hours. Dany talked about life at Olivet and Darian told her about commuting to North Park from home.

"Mary said your parents are doctors. Do you have any interest in becoming one?" Darian asked.

"My goal is to become a doctor and specialize in children with special needs, but that might be several years in the future."

"Would you like another root beer, Dany? The refills are free."

"I'm good. I can see why everyone loves this place. I can picture eating lunch here everyday. It's not far from St. Bart's."

"It's only a couple of blocks from where Emmy and Kenny grew up," Darian mentioned as he finished his root beer.

"Do you know where they lived?"

He nodded. "Would you like to see?"

"Yes, please, if it's not too far out of the way."

Darian made sure he opened all the doors for Dany without making a big deal about it. He pulled out of Darby's and made his way to East Fifth Street. He stopped in front of the two-and-a half-story brick home where Kenny grew up and where his parents still lived.

171

"Is that it?" Dany stared at the immaculate home. "I love that porch."

"The Colwell family has lived in that house for over a hundred years."

Dany stared at him.

"Not Kenny or his parents, but the family. You know what I mean, don't you?"

"I'm teasing you."

"Do you see that carriage house back there?"

"Yes."

"That's where Emmy wrote the songs for that CD. It's actually the place where Kenny and the guys started the band."

"Is it like a historical place now?"

"Some people think it should be. Emmy told Mary that she and Kenny actually met in the alley behind the carriage house."

"That's so romantic," Dany said and then sighed. "Where did Emmy live?"

"It's just up the street, but... I'll let you see for yourself."

He pulled up in front of 16301 East Fifth Street.

"Is this it?" Dany covered her mouth with her hand.

"Hard to believe the difference, huh?"

"That house looks like it should be torn down. Are you pulling my leg?"

Darian shook his head.

"Wow!" Dany sat back and closed her eyes for a moment. "I can understand why Liz says that Emmy still clips coupons and is rather frugal."

"I suppose it's no secret. A lot of people at church know she grew up in a rather poor household."

"Didn't her parents work? Were they divorced? It's none of my business." Dany waved a hand.

"I've heard her father worked for one of the utility companies, but he had a problem with alcohol. Emmy told Mary he sometimes wasted his paycheck at a bar around here. Please don't say anything."

Dany zipped her mouth closed. "That might be, but look at her now. She's a celebrity even if she would deny it vehemently.

172

She's a wonderful mother, and shes lives in a dream house."

Darian laughed.

"Don't you think so?"

"I'm not laughing about that. You know Mary was the girls' nanny, right?"

Dany nodded.

Mary would tell us how Emmy would clean that gigantic house by herself, and never treated Mary like an employee. More like a sister. Mary loves those kids and Emmy and Kenny. Please don't say anything to Emmy or Kenny, but they paid for most of Mary's college and helped me. They're paying for part of Eli's, and they have a trust set up for Dahlia."

Dany's mouth dropped. "Really?"

"Dahlia's not so little anymore. She's fifteen and bigger than Mary."

Dany grinned but then looked away.

Darian laughed. "You got me again. I like that. You're funny."

Dany fought back a tear. "Would you take me home now, please?"

"Sure, did I say something wrong?"

"No, but I need to go see Emmy and hug her again."

Darian escorted Dany to the door. He happened to see Natalie watching from the living room window.

"Thank you for a lovely lunch and everything, Darian."

"You're welcome. Would you be interested in dinner or maybe a movie sometime?" *Please say yes.*

"I would like that very much."

Darian refrained from a fist pump by exercising great willpower. "I'll call you. I won't try to kiss you because Natty is watching."

"I saw that. I'll take care of her," Dany said.

Darian waved at Natalie, waited until Dany was inside and then pumped his fist.

Chapter Eighteen

"Are you sure you won't get fired or anything?" Emmy turned in the front passenger seat of the Odyssey to talk to Father James.

"I covered my butt. I got one of the young priests from St. Raymond's to handle everything today. He needs the experience, and he is always looking for a chance to get away from the bishop. I don't blame him. The bishop is a son of a... you know."

"A female dog?" Emmy laughed. "I probably shouldn't hang out with you too much. You use some naughty words, and I might accidentally repeat them in front of the kids."

Father James laughed. "I've heard some words come out of that pretty mouth of yours that would not be acceptable even at St. John's. Not to mention your holiness church."

"Do you know much about the Nazarene church?" Kenny asked without taking his eyes off of the car in front of him.

"I like to study other religions. I may be a Catholic priest, but I like to believe we serve the same God." He glanced at the large van festooned with Chicago Bears logos beside then on I-55. "Is the traffic always this bad?"

"It will ease up a bit once we get past Walker's Grove. Then once we get close to Soldier Field it will get worse again. Don't worry, James. I'll get us there in time. You won't miss any of the game," Kenny assured him.

Kenny made good on his promise, and they pulled into their VIP parking spot a few minutes after eleven. Emmy led Father James to their seats while Kenny stopped to buy pretzels, Cokes and a beer for Father James.

"Well, what do you think?" Emmy waved to some people she recognized. "Pretty impressive place, huh?"

"Not bad, but have you ever been to the Vatican? St. Peter's is pretty impressive, too."

Emmy sat down and pulled her half-brother down into his seat. "Will you stop being a priest for one day. You're wearing jeans and a Fridays At Five sweatshirt. No one is going to recognize you with that baseball cap and sunglasses on."

174

"I wanted to look like Kenny. Don't people recognize him?"

"Not as many as you might think. Would you recognize the lead singer from The Black Stripes? They're a famous rock band."

"Heard of them because I confiscated one of their CDs from a kid at school, but I would not know any of the band members if they walked up to me and handed me a beer and a pretzel. Thanks, Kenny. I'll buy the next round."

"You're welcome." Kenny sat beside Emmy. "But I'll buy. You wouldn't believe the price of concessions."

She took a sip of the Coke Kenny handed her and then continued her conversation. "Maybe I'll introduce you to him. He's the guy in that purple hoodie three rows in front of us." Emmy pointed to the guy.

"Are you... kidding me?" Father James asked.

"I kid you not." Emmy laughed. *I wonder what Pastor Tyler would say if he heard you swear so much.*

"So people don't hassle Kenny? Or you for that matter? You're a celebrity of sorts."

"Get out! I'm not a celebrity."

"Have you ever been to a pro football game, James?" Kenny asked. "Ever been to Arrowhead Stadium?"

"Never sat in the stands and watched any kind of football game in my life. My parents were very strict, and did not approve of any sports. They thought football was created by the devil because of the violence."

"Do you know the rules?" Emmy asked. "I can't imagine anyone not liking football."

"Of course I know the rules. You score a goal when you kick the ball through those poles, but I thought there would be a net."

Emmy laughed, "Are you confusing football with soccer?"

"Oh, is this an American football game? You are aware the rest of the world calls soccer by its proper name, right?"

"I thought you didn't know anything about sports. What gives?" Emmy asked.

"Never said I didn't know anything about sports."

175

"Did so! You said you've never seen a football game before."

Kenny realized what Father James was doing and grinned.

"If you had been listening closely, I said I had never sat in the stands to watch a football game, and that is God's truth."

"Then what do you mean?"

"My parents did not approve of football, but they did not mind that I got a scholarship to college because I was one of the best linebackers in the state."

Emmy punched him in the side. "I don't believe you."

"Look it up online."

"I will when we get home."

"There's Tony." Kenny pointed.

The game started with the Bears kicking off.

"So if you played linebacker, can you tell me what kind of coverages the Bears use?" Emmy asked.

"You mean like zone or man-to-man?"

"I can tell that. I've been watching him play since he was a sophomore at Roosevelt High. I mean can you tell if they're in a two-deep zone, or if the strong safety is taking the deep zone to allow the cornerback to come up to cover the run? Stuff like that."

"I remember the basic defenses we played, but things are more sophisticated and complicated now."

"Tony has been the starting middle linebacker since he was a rookie. He's responsible for calling the defenses, and making adjustments."

"And here I thought he just ran around and bumped into people," Father James said as he grinned.

The Bears fell behind early and lost by eleven points.

"I'm never taking you to another game. You're bad luck." Emmy poked Father James in the side on the way back to the Odyssey.

"Yeah, it was my fault that Maynard sucks as a quarterback and the offensive line couldn't block the Cardinals, and I don't mean the ones from Arizona. I'm talking about those old guys with the pointy hats."

"Aren't you afraid God will punish you for making fun of

176

your church?" Emmy held onto his arm as they walked through the crowd.

"No, I'm sure God has a sense of humor and doesn't follow the NFL."

They got back to SoHam, and Kenny pulled up to the rectory of St. John's church.

"We're going over to Tony's later for a birthday party. Taylor Beckett will be four in a couple of days. Wanna come with?" Emmy asked as Father James got out.

"Thanks, Emmy, but I'll be busy. I have to make sure that young priest didn't offend my parishioners, or steal the offering money. Thanks for taking me to the game, Kenny. If I had known beer costs so much, I would have stolen the offering money myself and brought it with me."

"You're a goof. I better pray for you." Emmy grinned and waved goodbye.

When Kenny, Emmy and the kids got to Tony and Sloane's house later that evening, John and Kristen were there with their kids. Derrick and Amber arrived a few minutes later.

Emmy walked through the kitchen and into the family room. She stood in front of Tony with her hands on her hips. "I can't believe you guys lost to the Packers. What kind of way is that to end your home career?"

Tony sat on the couch with Taylor Beckett and Coby draped over him. He shrugged. "What can I say? We played the best we could with the people we had available."

"So you're blaming it on injuries, huh? All teams have injured players this late in the season." She sat next to Tony and held two-year-old Coby on her lap.

Tony pulled a football from under the pillow next to him. "I brought this for you." He handed it to Emmy. "It's the one I intercepted. Could be my last interception ever."

"Could be at that," Emmy said. "Now that they're pulling you off the field in third down and long situations."

"The defensive backs can cover better than me now. I'm getting old."

"You're not old, Daddy," Taylor defended his father.

177

"He's getting old for a football player," Emmy said.

Tony responded by getting up, grabbing Emmy, putting her on his shoulder and marching out into the hallway.

"Watch this, kids." He waited until all the kids were ready, grabbed Emmy around her waist and put her head close to the nine-foot high ceiling.

"I thought you weren't going to do this anymore since I'm no longer a kid."

"Consider this one final time for old times sake."

Heather pointed to Emmy. "Uncle Tony, are you going to leave Mommy on the ceiling?"

"Do you think I should?" he asked.

"You better not!" Isabella poked Tony in the thigh.

"Okay, I'll let her down."

Emmy frowned as Tony slowly lowered her to the floor. She waited for a second and then punched Tony's arm.

"Ow! That hurt." Tony grinned as he rubbed his arm.

"Good! I meant for it to hurt."

Isabella shook her head and said, "Mommy, you told us it wasn't nice to hit people."

"It's okay, Isa. She didn't hurt me." Tony picked her up.

"Hang me from the ceiling!" Heather jumped up and down.

"Me, too!" Ben wanted in on the action.

Tony shook his head. "I'm sorry, but I can't do that anymore. I'm getting too old and might hurt my back."

"Thanks for taking the time to listen to our demos, Kenny." Jeremiah Tolla handed Kenny a CD Monday morning.

"No problem. Let's go downstairs." Kenny led Jeremiah to the studio. "Have a seat." He pointed to one of the recliners.

Jeremiah checked out the control room for a few seconds and then sat down.

"Does your band have a name?"

"We're using BearFace for now. Mia came up with it. She calls me that sometimes because of my beard." He bunched his bushy beard together with one hand.

Kenny sat at the console, and they listened to the tracks.

178

"Where did you record this?"

"My computer using an older version of Pro Tools."

"You did a good job."

"Thanks."

"Your bass player needs to tighten up. The drummer is steady and not very flashy. I like how he knows how not to play."

"How about the vocals?" Jeremiah asked.

"How many layers are there? It's all you, right?"

"Four." Jeremiah explained how he tried to harmonize with his lead voice.

"Not bad. I'm not sure I get could Mr. Kesson to sign you guys, but maybe in a couple of years. You need to work on a few things. What goals to you have for the band?"

"I would like to put out an independent CD. We're never going to be big time, but we do like to play."

"Would you like some help?"

Jeremiah smiled. "Yeah! For sure. Would you be willing to find someone to help us produce a better recording?"

"I was thinking I would help you guys if that's all right."

"Yes!" Jeremiah pumped his fist. "When? I know you guys are busy with your own project."

"We're taking a break around the holidays. Would your band be available the first couple weeks of January? That's probably the only time I would have."

"Tell us when to be here, and I'll make sure we're ready to work."

"Let's iron out some details, and be ready to go in January."

"Right! You need to be paid."

Kenny waved a hand. "That's not what I meant. I will help you guys out, but I'm not going to charge you anything. I'll see what I can do to help get your project manufactured if you want. I have some connections."

Jeremiah stood and shook Kenny's hand. "You have no idea how much this means to me."

"Hey! I remember what it was like to try to break into the business. It's not easy."

Chapter Nineteen

"What do you think of the place?" Liz asked her parents after showing them the house.

"All you did before you moved in was paint your bedroom, right?" Liz's father asked.

"That was it. We know we will eventually need to replace the carpet in the living room and family room, but it should last a few more years. Come and sit down. How was your trip?"

Liz sat with her parents in the family room.

"Not too bad. The van is loaded to the max and the trailer is full," Dusty Kimmerle answered.

"Dany has so much stuff," Liz said and then laughed.

"I don't know how she expects to fit it all in an apartment." Karen Kimmerle glanced around the family room. "I like this light peach color. It goes well with your brown couch and chair."

"How soon do you expect everyone back?" Dusty asked.

"They should be here soon," Liz said.

"Lizzie, why are you grinning? Is there something you're not telling us?" Karen asked.

"I kinda wanted Dany to tell you, but since she's not here, I will."

"Tell us what? Are you expecting again?"

Liz waved a hand. "Nothing like that."

"Derby, will you tell us what's going on?" Dusty rubbed Derby's head. Derby wagged her tail while holding a chew toy in her mouth.

"You might not need to help Dany find an apartment after all," Liz said and grinned again.

"Has she found one already? I thought she was going to wait until your father and I could help her."

"She didn't exactly find an apartment," Liz said.

"What do you mean?"

"A place to live kinda found Dany." They heard the front door open and got up to look.

Natalie and Grayson ran through the entryway and into the kitchen where they collided with their grandmother.

180

"Slow down! What's the big hurry?" Karen Kimmerle hugged the kids. "You almost knocked me over."

"Sorry, Grandma," Natalie said and then looked up at Liz. "Mom! We played in the woods at Emmy's house, and I didn't get scared. Grayson didn't like it at first, but Kevin played fireman with him. It was so much fun. Can we build some woods here?" Natalie bounced on her feet and clapped her hands.

"I don't think we have enough room for some woods here, sweetie," Liz answered. "Would you play in your rooms for me? I need to talk to Grandma, and it's almost bath time."

Natalie and Grayson scampered away jabbering about the woods. Tyler shook hands with his father-in-law. Dany hugged her mother.

"Liz was telling us something about an apartment. Did you find one, Dany?" Karen asked.

"I found a place to live, but it's not an apartment. Come and sit down, and I'll explain."

Again the Kimmerles sat in the family room.

Dany sat with Liz on the love-seat, faced their parents on the couch and asked, "Do you remember Emmy and Kenny from the church?"

"Of course they do, Dany."

Dany grabbed Liz's hands. "Stay still and let me tell the story."

"We remember them," Karen said.

"Okay, they live in this gigantic home, and a little ways from the house is a ranch-style house. It's where they lived while the big house was built. Anyway, right now it's empty because the band moved their office out to the Steward Music building. Emmy knew I was looking for an apartment, so she talked to Kenny, and they agreed to let me live there. Isn't that great?"

Mom and Dad Kimmerle looked at each other, then at Dany and Liz, and then back at each other.

"That sounds wonderful, Dany, but can you afford to rent a house? It sounds expensive."

"Mom! That's the best part. Emmy said I could rent it for five hundred a month, and no utilities."

"It doesn't have utilities?"

Dany rolled her eyes. "No, Mom. They pay the utilities. I just have to pay for my phone and cable. The gas and electric are covered."

"How big is this house? How old is it? Is it safe to live by the woods?" Karen expressed her concern by wringing her hands together.

"Mom, they live in a very exclusive gated community. Dany will be very safe there," Liz said.

"I would like to see this place before I make a decision." Dusty stood up. "That's if I have have any say in where my youngest child will live."

"Of course you do, Daddy," Dany said.

"You mean right now?" Liz asked.

"Why not?"

"It's dark outside now. You won't be able to see much. Let's wait until morning," Liz suggested. "The kids and I are on Christmas break. We can take a ride out there, and you can see for yourself how secure it is."

Mom and Dad Kimmerle agreed to wait until the morning. A few minutes later Tyler carried his in-laws' luggage into the house, up the stairs and into the guest bedroom where Dany had been staying.

"The basement okay with you?" Tyler asked.

"It's fine," Dany answered.

Natalie stood in the doorway, heard the conversation and insisted, "No, Daddy! Dany has to stay in my room. She wants to. She can't sleep in the basement. It's... it's too scary. You will be scared, Dany. You better sleep in my room." Natalie grabbed Dany's hand and pulled her into her bedroom.

"It's okay, Tyler. I can sleep with Natty."

"Okay, but you have to go to sleep. You can't stay up all night playing with your dolls."

Dany looked up at Tyler, grinned and said, "We won't stay up all night."

"I meant Natty," Tyler muttered while walking away.

Liz called Emmy after feeding the kids breakfast.

182

"Come over anytime. Kenny's working at the studio, but I can show your parents around."

"Thanks, Emmy. I'll watch the kids for you," Liz offered.

"No need. Sofia's here. She can watch all the kids."

Liz drove their Ford Flex, and her father sat in the front passenger seat.

"Where is this subdivision? Is it much farther," Karen asked from behind Liz.

"Not much farther. In fact." Liz turned onto Springdale Lane. "We are almost there." She stopped by the security station, and the guard recognized Liz. He opened the gate and waved as she drove by.

"Is there always someone on duty?" Dusty asked.

"I'm pretty sure there is." Liz let two cars pass before turning left onto Emmy's driveway. "Tony and Sloane Bertucci live in that house."

Dusty glanced at the large house at the top of a hill. "Is this the only entrance?"

"This road is like a horseshoe, Dad. There is another gate at the other end, but no guard. Emmy said you need either the right code, or a remote; like a garage door opener to get in from that direction. You can always get out that way, but not in." Liz made the turn and drove past the opened wrought iron gate.

"Is this another street?" Karen asked. "I don't see any houses."

Dany grinned. "Just wait, Mom. You'll see a house."

As Liz came around the last bend in the driveway, she stopped the Flex.

"Can you see a house now, Mom?" Dany pointed.

"My goodness! That is quite a large home."

Liz pulled up to the garage, parked, and Emmy and the girls walked out from the garage service door.

"Good morning. How was your trip, Dr. Kimmerle?" Emmy tended to be rather formal with Liz and Dany's parents.

Dusty Kimmerle answered for his wife because she appeared to have lost the ability to speak. "The trip was uneventful," he said while hugging Emmy.

Heather and Isabella started talking with Natalie.

"Can we go back inside, Mommy? It's too cold."

"Yes, take Natty and Grayson with you, and behave for Sofia." Emmy watched the kids scamper inside. "Would you like to see the guesthouse first, or come inside?"

"I'd like to see the guesthouse if it's not too much trouble, Emmy," Dusty said.

"I'll drive." Liz and Dany got back in the car.

Karen Kimmerle stared up at the house and then at Emmy. "How far away is this other house?"

Emmy pointed to the south. "It's far enough that it's easier to drive than walk. At least in this kind of weather."

Emmy got in the middle with Karen since Dany had moved to the third row. Karen stared at Emmy for a moment. *I would have never guessed you lived in such a beautiful home. You don't act like you have any money.*

"I see you have left most of the property in a natural state," Dusty said.

Emmy pointed out the window. "We did some landscaping along the driveway and this section, but most of the acreage is still wooded."

Liz pulled onto the ranch house driveway and parked.

"Mom, don't you love the porch? It makes this place look like it's been here forever," Dany said.

Dusty climbed the three wooden steps and slapped one of the wooden roof supports. "It's really rustic."

"Wait till you see the inside." Dany raced past Liz to the front door. She punched in a code and the door unlocked.

"You don't need a key?" Dusty asked Emmy.

"You can use a key or the keypad. The back door needs a key to open it."

"Oh, I love the high ceiling in here." Karen looked skyward. "That skylight makes this so bright and sunny."

"Kenny had that put in last year. It wasn't part of the original design."

"How many bedrooms?" Dusty asked.

"Can I give them the tour, Emmy?"

184

"Sure, Dany. I'll talk to Liz."

Dany showed her parents the three bedrooms and two baths.

"Very nice. The master bedroom is just spacious enough without being too large," Karen said.

Dusty opened the door to a hall closet. "Where are the furnace and water heater?"

"In the utility room. There's a washer and dryer, a laundry tub and a counter with cabinets on the wall. The back deck is new. Fairly new. Two car garage with an opener."

"It seems perfect, Dany. Are you sure you want a place this big?" Karen asked. "You will have more to clean."

"I won't mind that." Dany stared up at her father. "Daddy, what do you think?"

He looked at Emmy. "How much is the rent?"

"If it was up to me, we wouldn't charge anything. Would five hundred a month be too much?" Emmy asked.

Dusty laughed and then shook his head. "You could charge that much per week, and it wouldn't be enough."

"We used to rent the place to Lindsey and Cam from church, and we didn't charge much then either. Dany needs a place to live, and we need someone living in the house. She wouldn't have to shovel snow, or mow the yard. We have guys who do that. We pay the utilities."

"Dany, I think you've found your new home," Dusty said. "Can she sign a lease?"

"Kenny had Derrick draw one up. He's Kristen's brother, and an attorney. It's back at the house. We can go back there. I'll make some coffee, and you can check out the big house if you want."

"How soon can I move in, Emmy?" Dany asked.

"Today if you want," Emmy said as she shrugged. "Kenny can probably get a truck and some guys tomorrow, but today might be too late."

"We could unload the van and the trailer, Dany." Liz sat on one of the chairs left in the great room. "Can Dany use the furniture in here?"

185

Emmy nodded. "Sure, unless you don't like it."

"I like these chairs. They're big and comfortable."

They drove back to the main house. Emmy brought out the lease and a copy. She and Dany signed it, and Emmy gave her the keys, the garage door opener and a remote to open the security gates.

"This will be so great having you live with us. Close to us, I mean. I hope you like it, and if you do, you can live there as long as you want," Emmy said and then hugged Dany.

That afternoon Dusty returned to the guesthouse with Tyler. Emmy and Sofia had kept Natalie and Grayson with them to allow Dany, Liz and Karen a chance to thoroughly check out and clean the guesthouse. The men unloaded the van, which was all boxes, and the trailer, which contained Dany's bedroom set. Dany and Mom Kimmerle started emptying the boxes while Liz unpacked the suitcases. Emmy dropped by to offer her assistance.

"You don't need to help, Em. We got this," Dany assured her.

"Do you have any questions about the place?"

Karen did. "Does this kitchen table stay here?"

"It can. We didn't need it at the big house, so we left it here. We can move it out if you don't like it, Dany."

"I like it."

They finished all the unpacking, and Dusty dropped Tyler off at the church and drove the van and trailer back to Tyler and Liz's house.

Karen, Liz, Emmy and Dany sat at the kitchen table drinking coffee and discussing what Dany still needed.

"You need more stuff for the kitchen if you plan to ever cook," Karen said while admiring the cabinets. "I love how the cabinets match the rustic appearance of the house."

"They may look homemade, but they were actually custom-built," Emmy said.

Dany got up and put her empty cup in the sink. "I will cook occasionally, but not every day."

"You can have the TV from the basement, Dany. It still works, and we never watch it," Liz offered.

"Are you planning to use one of the other bedrooms as a guest bedroom?" Emmy asked.

"I probably should. I might have family or friends crash sometime, but I'd like to use the bedroom next to the hall bath as an office. I'd like a computer desk and a bookcase."

Liz wrote down everything Dany might need.

"We could go shopping tomorrow, Dany. If you want our help." Karen put her empty coffee cup in the sink.

"I would appreciate that. I wouldn't have a clue about how much to pay for a bedroom set."

Liz chuckled, "You should take Emmy with you. She knows how to find real bargains."

"Who do I call to set up the Internet, and should I get a landline, or just use my cell phone?" Dany asked.

"I'll help you set up the Comcast stuff. They're a pain in the butt to deal with, but I know how to handle them. You could bundle your phone in with TV and Internet at a cheap rate for a year, then they try to double the price."

"What about furniture?" Dany asked.

"I know the perfect place to go. Turk Brothers. They have good quality new stuff, but they also have used pieces." Emmy stood up and pushed in her chair. "That's where I found this table and chairs. Only paid two hundred for the set. It would have been over a thousand brand new."

"Do you know the Turk brothers?" Liz asked.

"Oh, no! There aren't any of the brothers still alive, but I know one of the sons who runs the place now. I'll make sure you get a fair deal."

Chapter Twenty

"Good morning, Emmy. Thank you for calling. I'm sorry to hear your mother is not doing well." Franklin Turk smiled as he adjusted his trademark red suspenders. "How may I assist you today?"

"These are my friends, Mr. Turk. This is Dr. Kimmerle. Ooops! I mean Dr. Lindower and her two daughters. Liz and Dany. I forgot you are called Dr. Lindower," Emmy said.

"It's all right. I use Dr. Lindower at the office to avoid confusion," Mrs. Kimmerle explained. "You should call me Karen."

"Liz is our pastor's wife, and Dany just moved into our guesthouse. We're looking for a few things." Emmy handed him a list.

Mr. Turk put on his wire-rimmed reading glasses and read the list. "Hmmm."

Liz and Dany spotted a bookcase and walked over to check it out. "I wonder if he always wears suspenders and that red bow-tie?" Dany asked looking over her shoulder.

"I think he looks dapper." Liz spotted the price tag. "This is too much, Dany."

Mr. Turk handed the list back to Emmy. "I have a couple of bedroom sets that you might like. There are plenty of end tables and lamps. I would have to talk to Ms. Kimmerle and learn more about her need in a computer desk."

"Can we see the bedroom sets first, please?"

"Certainly," he said. "I will meet you on the third floor." He paused and then chuckled. "I assume you will take the stairs, but perhaps Dr. Lindower would like to take the elevator with me."

"See you up there," Emmy grinned. She joined Liz and Dany.

"I like this bookcase, but it's too expensive," Dany told Emmy.

Emmy checked the price. "Don't worry. I'll see if Mr. Turk will bargain with me. Come on. We have to take the stairs to the third floor."

Liz watched Mr. Turk and her mother get into an old-fashioned elevator. "Why are we taking the stairs?"

"Because they are gorgeous. Come on, I'll show you." Emmy led Liz and Dany to the side of the showroom floor. "Aren't these stairs absolutely beautiful? This is real mahogany."

Liz ran a hand over the polished wood.

"How old is this place?" Dany asked.

"The original Turk brothers started this business back in the twenties or thirties. It's been in this building ever since then." Emmy dashed up the stairs while Liz and Dany followed at a more sedate pace.

Emmy got to the third floor, leaned over the railing and laughed. "Hurry up, you guys." She waited, and then they joined Mr. Turk and Mrs. Kimmerle.

"See anything you like, Dany?" Liz asked.

Dany wandered back and forth through the bedroom sets until she spotted one she liked more than the others. "This one."

"Ah! You have a good eye," Mr. Turk smiled. "This is a Blasingame set from the late fifties. We bought this in an estate sale two weeks ago. It is in almost perfect condition, and should last a lifetime."

"Dany will need a decent mattress," Emmy said.

Fifteen minutes later Emmy had closed the deal with Mr. Turk.

"Should we look at the computer work stations?" he asked.

Mr. Turk led everyone down to the second floor. Dany explained what she would like and Mr. Turk found something that fit her needs. They returned to the first floor, and Mr. Turk totaled up the purchases.

"When would you like it delivered?" he asked Dany.

"As soon as possible," Emmy answered for her.

"I could have it delivered later this afternoon. Would that be soon enough, Ms. Colasanti?" He smiled and adjusted his suspenders.

"That would be perfect, Mr. Turk," Emmy smiled and then pointed. "Oh, Dany likes that bookcase over there, but it's a little pricey."

189

"How much are you willing to pay, Emmy?"

After a little haggling, Mr. Turk shook Emmy's hand. "Was it your mother or father who taught you how to negotiate?"

"It was Grandma Isabel," Emmy answered.

"I should have known," he said. "Isabel was always a shrewd customer."

Mrs. Kimmerle paid the bill after a short discussion with Emmy.

"I will not let you pay for this. Isn't it enough you are letting Dany rent your house for a pittance?"

"But..."

"No arguing with me, young lady."

Emmy conceded defeat. She texted Kenny to let him know she wouldn't be needing a truck or any guys to help with the furniture.

He texted back. "Did you let Mr. Turk make a little profit?"

Later that afternoon, a Turk Furniture truck pulled up to the guesthouse. They unloaded the pieces, and Emmy persuaded them to set up the furniture exactly where Dany wanted them. They even put the computer desk together.

As the two guys were leaving, Emmy made sure no one could see and then handed the older man a hundred dollar bill.

"Ms. Colasanti, you know Uncle Franklin doesn't allow tipping." He tried to hand the money back.

Emmy stuffed in it his shirt pocket. "And you know I always tip you guys, anyway. Split the money between you and don't tell your uncle."

"Thank you, Emmy."

"You're welcome. Merry Christmas."

"Who wants to go with me to see Dany?" Emmy asked after breakfast the next morning.

"I want to go!" Heather squealed.

"Me, too!" Isabella responded.

"Kevin Michael, do you want to go?"

He scrambled down from his chair. "No, I'm going to play with my firetrucks."

190

"I'll stay with Kevin if you and the girls want to go for a walk. It's so beautiful outside." Sofia stared out the window. "I love fresh snow and sunshine."

"Okay, girls, you need to wash your hands and faces." Emmy cleared the breakfast nook table. "And then put on your coats, mittens and hats. It's still cold even though the sun is shining. Wear your snow boots because we're gonna walk."

When they got close to the guesthouse, Heather and Isabella raced ahead of Emmy. They bounded up the steps, across the porch and knocked on the door.

Dany opened it after a few seconds. "What a pleasant surprise. Did you come to see me?" Dany saw Emmy approaching as the girls scampered into the house.

"We don't have school because it's almost Christmas," Heather said.

Dany held the door open as Emmy wiped her feet on the welcome mat.

"Good morning, Emmy."

"Did we come at a bad time?" Emmy looked at the girls and then at their boots. "Heather Rose and Isabella Marie! You are tracking snow into Dany's house."

The girls glanced at the floor.

"Sorry, Dany," Isabella said.

"It's all right. Let me get some paper towels and wipe it up." Dany walked into the kitchen and grabbed the towels.

"Let them wipe it up, Dany. They know better than to forget to wipe their feet." Emmy handed the towels to Heather.

"Come on in, and have a seat," Dany motioned.

Heather and Isabella wiped up the melting snow.

"Do you have a garbage can, Dany? We're sorry for making a mess," Heather apologized.

"It's by the end of the countertop."

The girls tossed the towels away, and then came back and sat by Dany on the couch.

"Are you finished with school, Dany?" Heather asked. "Mommy graduated from college, and now it's Daddy's turn to go."

191

"I might go back one of these days if I want to become a doctor," Dany answered and then looked at Emmy.

"Kenny's got a bug up... he wants to get a degree, so he starting taking online courses," Emmy explained.

"Daddy might have to live at the college, but he can come home on Sundays." Isabella looked around the room. "Where is the Christmas tree? When Jana was here, she put up a tree in that corner." Isabella pointed.

"That is the perfect spot for a tree, Isa, but I don't have one. I need to go to the store and buy one."

"We don't go to the store to buy a tree," Heather said. "We go to Uncle Tony's, and Daddy and Uncle Tony and Peter go out to the woods and chop down a tree." She motioned as though she was chopping down a tree.

Isabella held her hands out wide. "We have a super, gigantic tree in the family room. It touches the ceiling."

Heather nodded. "You should ask Uncle Tony to find you one. He has a whole forest of Christmas trees."

Dany looked at Emmy. "I don't want to bother him. He's busy with football."

"Nonsense!" Emmy laughed. "He loves to play Paul Bunyon. I'll call him later, and tell him you need a tree. Do you have a stand?"

"I did pack a tree stand and the white cloth that goes under it. I think I know which tub it's in."

After visiting with Dany for over an hour, the girls and Emmy headed home.

"I'll call you later. We'll find a tree," Emmy promised.

After dinner Tony and Peter led Emmy and Dany through the woods in search of the perfect tree.

"How tall a tree do you want?" Peter asked Dany. "Scout! Go find a bunny."

Scout disappeared in the trees.

"You know the great room has a cathedral ceiling, Tony," Emmy reminded him. "We just have to be able to fit the tree through the front door."

Tony led them to the same area where Emmy and Kenny

192

found their tree. "How about that one?" Tony pointed. "Or that one. It's not quite as tall."

"I'll take it, Mr. Bunyon," Dany said.

Scout returned and jumped up on Dany.

"Scout! Bad girl. Get down," Peter scolded.

Dany got on her knees and let Scout lick her face. "It's all right. I play with Derby all the time. Maybe I should bring Derby over so she and Scout can play together."

Tony chopped down the ten-foot-tall tree, and he and Peter carried it through the woods and back to the house.

"How are we supposed to get it home?" Emmy poked Tony's arm.

"Fine, brat. I'll tie it to the top of the van," Tony said and then rolled his eyes.

"Will you help set it up?"

"You're pushing your luck, but I'll do it for Dany." Tony pulled Emmy's stocking cap down to cover her eyes.

Emmy pushed the cap up and stuck out her tongue. "Creep!"

Tony and Peter carried the tree into the guesthouse. Emmy cleaned up the snow they dragged in, and Dany showed Tony where to set it up.

"Does it look straight?" Tony looked at it with his head tilted.

"Yeah, just like it came from Pisa," Emmy said.

Dany laughed.

"How about now?"

"That's better," Dany said. "Thank you for all your help, Tony."

"You... are most welcome." Tony smiled at Dany and then tugged on Emmy's hair. "Come on, Peter. Our work here is finished."

"Hi-Yo, Silver! Away!" Emmy pushed Tony toward the door.

"Thanks again," Dany said as she closed the door behind Tony and Peter. She looked at Emmy and began to laugh. "What's up with you guys?"

193

"What do you mean?" Emmy opened the plastic tub and discovered Christmas decorations. "Do you want me to help decorate it?"

"Liz told me you and Tony dated in high school. Now you guys act more like brother and sister."

"I suppose we do." Emmy pulled out a box of homemade-looking ornaments. "Did you make these?"

"Lizzie and I did over the years. So what about you guys dating?"

"Kristen introduced us. She tried so hard to keep us together, but it wasn't meant to be. He's too big for one thing." *I wonder if you know about Tony proposing.*

"I suppose I am concerned about how tall Darian is," Dany admitted while inspecting the ornaments.

"I can understand that, but it really shouldn't matter if you two are meant to be together," Emmy said.

"We've only gone out twice." Dany picked up another decoration. "I made this when I was six."

"Has he kissed you?" Emmy asked.

"Not yet," Dany answered.

"Don't worry about it. It took Kenny years before he kissed me." Emmy leaned down and pulled out a string of lights.

Dany stared at Emmy.

Emmy straightened up and saw the look on Dany's face. "What? He was only ten when we met."

"I can see why Liz thinks you are so adorable." Dany hugged Emmy and they giggled.

Kenny drove the Odyssey to church on Sunday morning. He dropped Emmy and the kids off at the front entrance and parked behind the building. He made his way to the music suite and saw Chase in his office.

"Merry Christmas, Chase."

Chase glanced up, saw Kenny and waved him into the office. "Hi, Kenny, and Merry Christmas to you. Pastor Jeremiah asked if the worship band could sing some Christmas songs to open the service."

"Good thing we anticipated that and practiced some tunes," Kenny said.

"Have you seen the platform?" Chase smiled.

"Not yet, but I can guess how it might look. Mia is very talented when it comes to creating a visual effect."

"The whole platform has been turned into... well, you'll see soon enough. There's just enough room for us to play, but the drums are totally covered. Robby won't be able to see us."

"That's all right. I've seen him close his eyes at times when we play."

Chase closed his laptop and stood up. "I heard that Heather and Isabella are singing a duet."

"They've been singing it almost non-stop for the last two weeks."

"I remember when Anna and Jada were young enough to be in the program. Seems like only last year, but Jada is already fourteen and in high school."

"Dad is always telling me how time speeds up as he gets older." Kenny turned and saw some of the other members of the worship team enter the music suite. "I'm beginning to understand it."

"Yeah, me too," Chase sighed.

Emmy escorted the kids to Noah's Ark, the children's worship center, and listened to the organized chaos as Jeremiah and Mia Tolla helped the Sunday School teachers keep their pupils organized.

"Mommy, are you going to watch the program?" Heather asked.

"Of course, sweetie. I want to hear you and Isa sing your song."

"Come on, Heather." Isabella tugged on her sister's arm. "We have to sit with Miss Lenore."

"I'll see you later," Emmy spotted Kristen with Grace and Zachary.

"Hi, Emmy. Did you hear that my parents and Mama are coming to see the program?" Kristen watched as her children scampered away.

"That's great," Emmy said. "Too bad Tony can't be here."

"Next year he won't be playing football. He won't have any excuse not to be here every Sunday."

"Is John here?"

"Yes, he took Mama to mass last night. I'll try to save some seats for you guys." Kristen waved to one of the other mothers and left.

Emmy grabbed Kevin as he chased one of the other kids. "No running. Let me look at you." She inspected his clothes and tried to comb his unruly hair. "Make sure you sing loud so I can hear you."

"Okay, but I might forget the motions."

"Just watch Mia and the other kids."

Pastor Tyler opened the special service as the worship team took their places.

Liz nudged Emmy. "This looks like a real manger."

"And it kinda smells like one, too," Emmy said and then held her nose.

Chase led the congregation through some Christmas songs. The ushers collected the offering, and Pastor Tyler turned the service over to Jeremiah and Mia. Emmy and Kenny hurried to the seats Kristen had managed to save for them.

Halfway through the program. Heather and Isabella sang "Hark! The Herald Angels Sing."

Mama Bertucci turned in her seat and patted Emmy's knee. "They sounded like angels, dear. You must be very proud of them."

"Thank you, Mama. We are."

The program concluded with all the children singing two songs written especially for the program by Jeremiah and Mia.

Kenny shook hands with John Randolph afterward. "Do you still miss playing for the Bears?"

"I did at the beginning of the season, but not so much now. I'm busier now than ever, and I don't miss the feeling of being banged up at the end of the season."

One of the ladies sitting behind Emmy tapped her on her shoulder. "Were those your twins who sang that song?"

196

"Yes," Emmy saw Heather and Isabella running toward her.

"Mommy, did you like our program?" Isabella asked.

"Yes, but you aren't supposed to run in the sanctuary."

The older lady leaned over to talk to the girls. "You sang very well. You must have inherited your parents' talent."

Isabella shyly thanked the lady, but Heather grinned. "We're gonna make CDs like Mommy and Daddy when we get older."

"I'll look forward to hearing them."

Kristen touched Emmy's arm. "Do you guys have plans for this afternoon?"

"We're going home for lunch, but then I want to take the kids to see Mom. What are you guys doing?"

"I invited everyone to our house for a late lunch. Mom and Dad are coming and so are Derrick and Amber. Mama and Sloane are bringing their army over, too."

"Sounds like you'll have a full house," Emmy said.

"You're welcome to join us."

"Thanks, Krissy, but I need to see Mom."

"I understand. Let me know how the visit goes."

Emmy cautioned Kevin and the girls later that afternoon as they rode the elevator to the second floor at Sunrise Garden. "I want you to be on your best behavior. No running around and no yelling."

"Is Grandma sick?" Heather asked.

"She has an illness," Kenny answered.

"I hope she doesn't throw up," Kevin said.

"It's not that kind of illness." Emmy looked at Kenny for help just as the elevator door opened.

Kevin dashed out of the elevator and ran down the long hallway.

"Kevin Michael! Get back here right now," Emmy scolded.

"I know which door is Grandma's," he said and pointed.

"You need to wait for us," Kenny said calmly.

Emmy opened the door and entered followed by the kids and then Kenny.

"Hi, Mom. We thought we'd stop by to see you. Merry Christmas, by the way." Emmy walked over to her mother who sat in her chair and stared at the TV.

"I didn't know today was Christmas. I didn't have time to go shopping." Patricia stared at Emmy and then noticed everyone else. "You girls look so pretty in your dresses. Did you dress up for Christmas?"

Isabella walked up to her grandmother. "We dressed up because today was our program at church. Heather and I sang a song."

"Is today Sunday?" Patricia asked. "I can't remember."

"Yes, Mom, and in two days it will be Christmas. The kids brought presents for you. Would you like to open them?"

"Is it my birthday?"

Emmy sighed. "Yes, Mom."

Heather walked up and handed Patricia a bag decorated with Christmas colors and snowflakes. "These are for you, Grandma."

Patricia opened the gifts with help from the girls, but didn't show any interest in the new clothes.

"I need to watch my show. It starts soon." Patricia stared at the TV.

"Would you like to hear our song, Grandma?" Heather asked. "We can sing it without music."

Patricia glanced at the girls and then at Kevin and Kenny. "I want to watch my show, so sing fast."

The girls looked up at Emmy.

"You can sing your song just like you practiced." She sat on the couch and Kevin climbed onto her lap.

The girls sang their song and expected a response from their grandmother. Patricia stared at them for a moment.

"Did you like their song, Mom?"

"I want to watch my show now."

Kenny rose from the rocking chair in the corner. "Maybe we should go, Em."

"Okay." Emmy bit her lip. "Get down, sweetie," she told Kevin, but he clung to her and didn't move. Emmy stood up and

198

Kenny took Kevin from her.

"We're gonna go so you can watch your show, Mom." Emmy patted her mother's hand. "Kids, tell your grandmother goodbye."

Heather and Isabella wished Grandma a Merry Christmas, but she didn't respond.

"I'll talk to you later, Mom." Emmy held hands with the girls.

"Thanks for coming to see me, Emily. Sorry, you missed your father." Patricia turned her attention to the TV.

Heather let go of Emmy's hand and looked up at her parents. "Grandma didn't throw up. Are you sure she's sick?"

"She's sick in a different way, sweetie. It's not her belly that's sick."

"My belly gets sick if I eat too much candy," Isabella said.

Kevin scrambled down from Kenny and ran to the elevator.

"Stay by the door," Kenny said.

"Did Grandma like our song?" Heather asked. "She didn't clap or anything."

"I think she liked it, but she's getting older and probably forgot to clap," Emmy explained.

"Daddy." Isabella grabbed his hand as the elevator door opened.

"Yes, baby?"

"Are you going to start forgetting things because you're getting old, too?"

Emmy giggled and Kenny frowned at her.

Chapter Twenty-One

"How much have we missed?" Emmy rushed into the family room at Tony's house and plopped down on the floor.

"You haven't missed too much. The first quarter just ended, and the Bears are ahead 10-3," Mama said. "Are you going to sit on the floor? You can sit by me." Mama patted the couch.

"I thought Sloane might be sitting there. I'm all right on the floor." Emmy lay on her stomach, put her feet in the air and moved them back and forth.

Mama shook her head but then grinned. *I've seen you watch a game like that ever since I first met you.*

Sloane came back into the room and sat beside Mama. "Do you need anything to drink, Emmy?"

"I'm good. If I get thirsty, I'll grab a water." Emmy answered without moving her from the TV. "Where are the kids?"

"Dotty and Noemi are upstairs having a party with their dolls. Peter and the boys are watching the game in the basement. Peter understands this is Tony's final game, but I'm not sure the other ones do."

The Bears upped their lead to seventeen points in the second quarter, but they surrendered a touchdown with less than a minute to go.

"Come on, you guys! You know the Lions don't have a rushing attack. Ninowski has to pass every down," Emmy whined after the Bears slot-coverage back slipped to allow the score.

"I'm going to check on the kids," Sloane said.

Emmy jumped up. "Can I get you anything, Mama? Are you thirsty?"

"I'm okay, thanks."

Emmy walked into the kitchen and helped herself to a cold bottle of water. She saw some freshly-baked chocolate chip cookies on the counter and grabbed three. "Did you just make these?" She sat next to Mama and offered her a cookie.

"I thought you might want some."

"Thank you for the holiday cookies. The kids loved them."

"Did you eat them all, or did you share?" Mama asked.

"I set aside one container for Kenny and myself, but the kids ate the other one. I explained how you've been making holiday cookies ever since your kids were little."

"You might have to take over that tradition one of these days, sweetie." Mama put an arm around Emmy and squeezed. "You are still too skinny."

Emmy laughed and squeezed back. "You have been telling me that since my senior year at Roosevelt. Wow! That was over fifteen years ago. Unbelievable! Has it really been that long?"

"I remember the day Tony brought you home. It was snowing, and you were outside having fun." Mama smiled, but then she looked serious.

"Are you thinking about Heather?" Emmy whispered.

"Yes, I still miss her. Dotty is starting to look more like Heather. She has Heather's eyes and nose and a round face. I just hope she doesn't end up as tall as Heather."

Emmy grinned. "Somehow I can't picture Dotty being six-feet-tall."

Mama closed her eyes for a few seconds. "I was watching Peter and Dotty and the younger kids playing in the snow on Christmas. It made me feel so good to watch them having fun."

"Did you hear from Marco and Nancy?" Emmy wondered about Tony's older brother. "Tony said they didn't make it here."

"He Skyped from Florida. Nancy's parents live in Tampa. The boys wanted to go down there," Mama explained. "The older boys. Dwight is still at school because he's on the football team."

"The boys must be all grown up by now," Emmy said.

"Travis is still at Johns Hopkins. He wants to be a doctor, and I believe Bryan is studying to be a school administrator like his mother. He's at Loyola."

"I saw some Notre Dame games this year. Can you believe they're undefeated and playing for the national championship? Is Tony going to the game?"

"He is taking Marco with him."

"I heard the announcers call Dwight's name in one of the games, but it was because he got called for holding. He looks huge on TV."

"He's bigger than Tony and still growing."

Sloane returned in time for the second half. Emmy returned to the floor to watch the game.

Midway through the quarter the Lions scored to cut the deficit to three.

"You guys better get your act together," Emmy frowned at the TV. "Don't go all conservative on offense."

The Bears added two field goals by Brad Ellington to increase the lead to nine, and Emmy relaxed a little.

"At least the Lions have to score twice to take the lead."

"The defense needs to stop them," Sloane said and then closed her eyes for a moment.

The Lions quarterback used short passes to move his team down the field, and the Lions scored with just under six minutes left. The Bears' lead dwindled to two points.

"Did you see that, Mama?" Emmy asked. "One more block and he would have scored."

"I saw that. The Detroit player had the angle."

Maynard hit Brandon Shariff on the sideline for a nineteen-yard gain. Two running plays gained five yards and the Bears faced a third-and-five.

"Come on, Maynard. Spread the Lions out and hit Lymore on a crossing pattern over the middle."

Maynard faked a hand-off to Dante Setta, and the Lions linebackers bit on the fake. Lymore, the tight end blocked and then made his move.

"Hit him!" Emmy yelled. "He's wide open."

Maynard spotted his tight end, but the ball was tipped at the line of scrimmage and the Bears had to punt the ball away.

Emmy made fists, closed her eyes and prayed. *Please, Lord. Tony only has a few minutes left in his career. Don't let him get hurt, and it sure would be nice if the Bears win.*

"You okay, Emmy?" Sloane asked.

"Yep, I was saying a prayer."

The Lions took over with four and a half minutes left.

"They've got all their timeouts, but they'll probably save them if the Bears get the ball. Keep the receivers in bounds."

Ninowski surveyed the defense from the shotgun position. He tried to hit Kelvin Jackson over the middle, but the tall receiver dropped the ball. A short pass in the flat gained five yards.

"Come on, Tony! One more stop. You guys have to double-team Jackson. Don't let him beat you." Emmy closed her eyes, but opened them in time to see the play.

Ninowski took the snap and looked for his favorite receiver, but the Bears double covered Jackson. Ninowski avoided the rush and moved to his left. He waited as long as he could before checking down to another receiver. The pass sailed out of bounds, and the Lions chose to punt.

"The Bears need a couple of first downs." Emmy crossed her fingers. "Mama, I can barely stand to watch," Emmy said from her position on the floor. She buried her head in a pillow. "My heart is beating a hundred miles an hour."

"The Bears will win, Emmy. I just know it," Mama said. *You are still like a child in so many ways, sweetie.*

The Lions punter kicked the ball down the middle of the field, and the Bears took over on their forty after a fair catch.

Emmy checked the time remaining. "Three minutes and change. Come on you guys. Get a first down."

A running play gained four yards and the Lions called their first timeout. A second down running play gained two more yards, and the Lions used their second timeout.

Emmy scooted closer to the TV as Bears broke the huddle. "Count the guys in the box," Emmy said.

The Bears snapped the ball and Maynard turned his back to the line-of-scrimmage.

"No!" Emmy screamed as two Lions defenders broke through the line. They tackled Dante Setta for a huge loss.

"Look!" Emmy jumped to her feet, hopped up and down while pointing at the TV. "Maynard kept the ball. He can't run as fast as Mama, but he fooled them. He's got a first down. No!" Emmy slumped her shoulders. "How can you run out of bounds? What a bonehead play. You just saved the Lions a timeout."

"But they have a first down, Emmy," Sloane said.

"Yes, but there's still 2:42 to go and the Lions have a

203

timeout and there's the two-minute-warning. The Lions still have time. Oh, what a stupid move, Maynard."

A running play up the middle was stuffed for no gain and the Lions called their final timeout.

"That play only used four seconds." Emmy bit her lip. She picked up the pillow and held it almost like a football.

Maynard surveyed the defense on second down. He backed away from the line-of-scrimmage and motioned to his receivers.

"He's calling an audible," Emmy said. "See how the Lions are committing to stopping the run. I bet Maynard fakes the ball to Setta and hits Shariff on a slant pattern."

"Is that what they will do, Emmy?" Mama asked.

"It's what I would call."

Maynard moved Setta from one side to the other. Seven Lions crowded the line of scrimmage.

"They're going to blitz everybody," Emmy said while squeezing the pillow to her chest. "It's a total jailhouse blitz!"

Maynard got the play off just in time and raised up to fire a pass to Shariff, but he held onto the ball. Somehow he saw the three Lion linebackers drop back into pass coverage and handed it to Setta. Setta broke a tackle and spun around another defender before being gang tackled by five Lion defenders.

Emmy jumped up and down. "What a move! He got another first down."

The clock stopped with two minutes to go.

"Can they run out the clock now, Emmy?" Sloane asked.

"All Maynard has to do is kneel down. The Lions can't stop the clock anymore."

Maynard took a knee three times, and the Bears won.

Emmy pulled Mama up from the couch and hugged her. "They won! They won!"

"I don't know why you are so excited, Emmy. I knew they would win all along," Mama said while clutching her rosary beads.

Emmy turned back to the TV and listened to the announcers talking about this being Tony's final game. One of the cameras picked up Tony as he removed his helmet, said a prayer and then made the same signal that he had been doing throughout

204

his entire career. He touched his nose, then his mouth and then both ears.

"He's all right, Mama," Sloane said.

Mama watched as Emmy slid to her knees and covered her eyes.

"Are you all right, sweetie?" Mama moved behind Emmy and put her hands on Emmy's shoulders.

Emmy sniffled. "I've been watching him play for fifteen... No! Seventeen years! I saw him play as a sophomore. That's over half of my life and now it's over."

"It's okay. He's had a good career. I'm glad he decided to retire. I won't have to worry about him getting hurt anymore."

Emmy stood up and faced Mama. "He's always wanted to play football. He told me he would carry his football with him all the time when he was a kid."

Mama smiled. "That's right. He did."

Sloane heard a commotion in the basement and left to check on the boys. Emmy and Mama headed to the kitchen. Emmy put her water bottle in the recycling bin.

"I'll be right back, Emmy. Don't leave," Mama said.

"I'll stay for a little bit, but I need to get home."

Mama walked into her part of the house. She opened the closet in her bedroom and pulled down a cardboard shoebox. She sat on the bed, removed the lid and began looking through some old photographs. She found the one she wanted a minute later.

"Emmy, would you come here, please?" Mama said and then stared at the photo.

"What is it, Mama?" Emmy skipped into the room.

Mama patted the spot on the bed next to her. "Sit by me, sweetie. I want to show you something."

Emmy sat next to Mama Bertucci.

Mama put her arm around Emmy's shoulders. "You're still too skinny."

Emmy took the photo from Mama and stared at it for a few seconds. "You still have this photo?"

"Why would I get rid of it?" Mama brushed away a tear.

"I remember the first time you showed this to me. I was

205

seventeen, I think." Emmy looked at the photo again. "Number fifty-two," she whispered. She peered closely at the little boy in the photo. "He's wearing number fifty-two and holding a football." Her heart began to race even faster. She gazed intently at the little girl in the photo. She concentrated on the rag doll in the girl's small hand. "Doll Kitty," she whispered. "It's my Doll Kitty." She turned to face Mama as tears filled her eyes. "This is my favorite picture of me and Tony."

"Yes, baby, I know. It's my favorite, too." Mama held Emmy close as they both cried.

"Thank you for watching the kids on such short notice." Emmy smiled at Sofia and Niles on New Year's Eve.

"It's all right, Emmy." Sofia hung her coat up in the mudroom and then covered it with Niles' long coat. She and Niles sat on the bench and removed their shoes.

"Didn't you guys have any plans?" Emmy asked. "I feel guilty about spoiling your New Year's Eve."

Sofia put her hands on Emmy's shoulders and looked down into her eyes. "Will you stop apologizing. Niles and I are homebodies. We wouldn't have gone out at all tonight, but we love taking care of the kids."

"Where are they?" Niles asked.

Emmy smiled while staring into his green eyes. "They are upstairs. Kristen dropped off Zach and Gracie earlier. I told them if they behaved they could stay up until ten. Feel free to send them to bed earlier if they give you any trouble." Emmy led them into the kitchen. "You know where everything is, and Kenny and I should be home by twelve thirty. He doesn't want to stay out too late because we have such a long drive home. He's a total dork."

"I heard that, Emmy. Are we really going to drive to Tony's?" Kenny walked into the kitchen. "It's across the road."

"It's cold out." Emmy frowned at Kenny.

"You guys have fun, and don't worry about us. Maybe one of these days I'll need a babysitter for my kids," Sofia said.

Emmy spun around to face Sofia. "Are you expecting?"

Niles put his hands on Sofia's shoulders.

Sofia patted his hands. "Not yet, but we are trying now."

Kenny grabbed his keys as Emmy told the kids good night. She walked into the garage and saw Kenny sitting in his Civic. She put her hands on her hips and stared at him. He lowered the driver's window.

"What?"

"Why are we taking this car? You do realize there is fresh snow on the driveway, right?"

"I am aware of that," Kenny answered.

"If we get stuck in Tony's driveway, I'm going to make you carry me." She got in the car.

Kenny made it most of the way up the hill of Tony's long driveway before the car came to a stop. He tried a couple of times to get the car moving.

"Sorry, Em. I guess we should have taken your BMW," he said as he shrugged.

"Ya think!" She got out of the car and slammed the door. "Sorry."

Kenny turned off the car and got out. "Do you want me to carry you?"

"Can you give me a piggyback ride?" Emmy asked.

"I'll try." He carried her on his back up the hill and into the open garage bay.

"You can set me down now, Kenny," Emmy said as she kissed his check. "You need a shave."

They walked into the house, hung up their coats, removed their shoes and met Mama and Sloane in the kitchen.

"Kenny wanted to drive his car, so we're stuck in the driveway." Emmy stole one of the freshly-baked cookies and quickly ate it.

Mama smiled and handed the plate of cookies to Kenny. "Would you take these out to the family room, please? Do you need the guys to help get your car unstuck?"

"Maybe later." Kenny sniffed the chocolate chip cookies as he walked out of the kitchen.

"Did you mention the party to Diane and Brady?" Sloane asked. "Or did you forget because you're upset with her?"

"I told her, but Lily has a cold, and Diane didn't want to take her anywhere."

"They could have gotten a babysitter." Sloane's smile hid her true feelings.

"What can I say." Emmy shrugged.

Emmy waited until Kenny and Sloane disappeared around the corner and reached into her small purse. "I brought your photo back. Thanks, for letting me take it home. I scanned it into my computer. Now we can make copies if you need any."

"Thank you, Emmy." Mama patted Emmy's shoulder. "I should have made copies a long time ago. Did you let Kenny see it?"

Emmy bit her lip. "No, I didn't want to."

"It's only a photo, sweetie."

"Yes, but there are a lot of memories attached to it."

"I'll put this back before anyone sees it." Mama took the photo and went into her part of the house.

Tony walked into the kitchen, picked Emmy up and deposited her on the island. "I hear you caused Kenny to get stuck."

"I did not!" She pointed to Kenny as the rest of the group entered the room. "It was his choice to drive the Civic." She grinned at Tony. "Since you are now officially retired from football, are you finally going to get a real job?"

"I have a real job. Two actually. I work construction and landscaping." He made a face. "When are you going to get a real job?"

"I have a very real job, you creep. I'm a mother." She poked Tony in the chest. "And why didn't you clear your driveway?"

Tony shrugged. "The kids like to go sledding down the hill. We did that all afternoon."

"Do you realize there is a road at the bottom the of driveway?" She put her hands on his shoulders and jumped down. "Do you want them to get run over?"

"The driveway curves, and Peter stood at the bottom to make sure they stopped in time, brat." Tony grinned.

"That sounds like fun. Can we go sledding tonight?" She looked around the room. "How about taking the snowmobiles out for a ride?"

"Can't go snowmobiling," Tony said. "My machine is in the shop."

Derrick Keasling put his arm around Amber's waist, smiled and asked, "Do you remember going to Windsor Hill?"

"Do you mean the time when Becky was here?" Tony asked.

Sloane nudged Tony in the ribs. "Did you have to bring that up?"

"What? It was a long time ago."

"Who else wants to go sledding?" Emmy raised her hand and looked around.

"It's too cold, Emmy," Kristen said and shook her head.

Emmy's eyes sparkled. "Oh, come on, you guys. It will be fun." She looked around but no one else raised a hand.

Finally, Amber slowly raised a hand.

"Yes! Amber wants to go sledding." Emmy moved closer and high-fived Amber. "Who else?"

Derrick smiled at his wife. "Really? You want to go sledding? I would have thought you would consider that as being too immature."

"We didn't have much snow in southern Arizona. Dad used to take us skiing, but never sledding. Let's do it, Emmy."

"Are you coming, Krissy? You used to like to have fun." Emmy grabbed Kenny's hand and pulled him toward the back door.

John looked down at Kristen. "Come on. Remember that game in Denver? We played in a blizzard, and everyone thought it was so much fun. We joked about making the game go overtime so we could keep playing."

"Yes, I remember watching with Emmy, and it was fun," Kristen said but then sighed. "But I was inside."

Emmy refused to be deterred, and soon all four couples bundled up, put on boots, gloves, and hats and marched outside.

Tony grabbed the sleds. "Show us how it's done, brat."

Emmy sat on the plastic disc. "Give me a push to get started."

"Gladly!" Tony pushed her in the back and added a bit of a twist.

Emmy spun slowly at first but then with more speed as she zoomed down the steep driveway.

"You okay, Em?" Kenny hollered after hearing a thud.

"I'm fine. That was a blast! I wanna do it again." She carried the disc back up the hill.

Eventually all the ladies rode one of the sleds down the hill.

Kenny chuckled. "This is sure a lot easier than that day at Windsor park. Over there we had to carry the sleds up the hill every time. Now we just let the wives carry them up while we stand here and freeze."

Twenty minutes later Emmy tugged on Tony's arm. "Kenny won't go down the hill with me. Will you?"

"As long as you promise not to crash."

Tony got behind Emmy on the longer sled.

"Hold on tight, Tony."

Tony wrapped his arms around Emmy. John and Derrick gave them a push. Emmy screamed as they flew down the hill.

"Em, look out for that..."

It wasn't in time. Emmy hit a snow bank, and they tumbled off of the sled.

"You okay, brat?" Tony asked as they finally stopped.

"I don't think anything's broken. But will you get off of me, creep?"

Tony tried to get up, but Emmy held his arm.

"Thank you for letting me have some fun, Tony."

"It's okay, Em," he said. He grinned and then rubbed some snow on her nose and cheeks.

"Stop that, you creep!" she hollered.

Tony smiled at her. "Why? You used to like it."

They stared into each other's eyes for a moment.

Emmy bit her lip and then whispered, "I still like it. That's why you need to stop."

Chapter Twenty-Two

Kenny opened the basement door to let Jeremiah and the guys in. "Come on in, guys. The studio is that way."

The three guys followed Kenny.

"Emmy said it was all right to use the garage service door and come on in," Jeremiah mentioned.

"Not a problem," Kenny said.

Jeremiah took off his coat. "Guys, this is Kenny Colwell."

"I think we know that, Jeremiah." the taller one laughed as he shook hands with Kenny. "A pleasure to meet you."

"I should introduce these guys," Jeremiah said. "That yahoo is Cecil Hardin. He plays bass and tries to sing."

"Pleased to meet you, Cecil."

"And this is our drummer Warren Dewar. He's been living in the Upper Peninsula. That's why he looks like a bear," Jeremiah joked.

Kenny's hand was swallowed by Warren's enormous paw. "Is that where the band's name came from?"

"Kinda, but since we all have bushy beards, you could say we all look like we have the face of a bear," Warren smiled.

"New Zealand?" Kenny asked.

"Grew up on South Island. Wellington. Right on the Cook Strait."

"I've been there. I love the islands," Kenny said.

They took fifteen minutes to get to know each other a bit.

"Should we get started?" Kenny asked. "I'd like to start with the song 'Brothers' if that's all right."

"Why that one?" Cecil asked.

"I like the arrangement. I don't want to change it at all," Kenny answered. "Plus, I know it better than some of the others. I want to record you guys live as much as possible. I know we'll have to add guitar tracks and vocals, but otherwise, I'd like to capture your live sound."

"We only have two weeks, guys," Jeremiah reminded the guys. "And we have lots of work to do."

Pastor Tyler opened the Monday morning staff meeting with prayer. The staff spent fifteen minutes praying before Tyler closed the prayer.

He looked around the conference table. "Before we get started Chase would like to say something."

Chase nodded. He glanced at the guys around the table. "I'm sure you guys have heard this before, so it won't be a big surprise, but Yvonne and I have accepted positions back at my home church in Toledo."

Darren Eaton smiled. "It's been the worst kept secret since... I don't know what."

"I want to thank everyone of you. It's been my pleasure to work with some outstanding ministers over the years. Yvonne and I have seen the church grow from a couple of hundred to a couple of thousand."

"I do believe you've had an important role in that growth," Pastor Herb Ausland said softly.

"Thank you, Pastor Herb." Chase turned to look at Jeremiah Tolla and Jonah Galves. "You guys might already know this, but Pastor Herb hired me for this position. He probably never imagined Yvonne and I would be here this long. I've got more seniority, if you want to call it that, than anyone here except for Reed and Mrs. Millner."

"Is it true they built the building around her?" Darren asked while grinning at Chase.

"I tell that to everyone," Chase admitted. "She is one of the original members."

"Do you know when your last Sunday will be?" Tyler asked.

"I'd like to start my new position on February eleventh. If that's okay. I could leave sooner if you want."

Reed Shafer, the head of the buildings and grounds department, chuckled. "We've put up with you for twenty-odd years. I'm sure we can survive another month."

"Were they really odd years?" Darren teased.

"The stories I could tell," Reed said with a smile.

Pastor Tyler checked his notes. "We need to talk to Pearl

212

Barnoski, so she and her hospitality team can organize a potluck that Sunday."

"You don't need to do anything special for us," Chase said.

Darren grinned. "It's not for you guys. We just love to eat."

The seven men sitting at the conference table spent a few minutes sharing memories of working with Chase Hillman; most of the stories were humorous. Chase took the ribbing in stride.

"I'm sure we could tell stories about Chase for most of the day, but we need to get serious for a moment," Tyler said.

The men quieted down.

"With Chase leaving, we have two positions to fill. When the church hired me as the senior pastor, they didn't replace the youth pastor. You know what I mean," Tyler chuckled. "Darren and Jody have been filling in, but he has other responsibilities. I'm going to suggest we search for two people, or couples. Obviously, we will need a new worship pastor."

Chase raised a hand.

"Yes, Chase."

"Might I make a suggestion. The technology has fallen under my umbrella for all these years. Mostly because I supposedly knew more about it than anyone else. Now that Jonah is here, I think he should assume most of the responsibility for all the tech stuff. Church and school. He has a large staff of volunteers to help with the recreation programs, but there aren't nearly as many tech savvy people in the church."

"Are you willing to take on that responsibility?" Tyler looked at Pastor Jonah.

"Yes. Yes, I would be willing," Jonah replied.

"Good. That might make the search for a worship leader a bit easier."

"We definitely need a full-time youth pastor," Darren sighed. "It's too much for Jody and I. Tyler and Liz have helped out when they could, but that just takes time away from his main purpose."

"I agree," Pastor Herb nodded. "The church has been without a youth minister for fourteen months. I'm afraid if we don't hire one, the youth group will regress."

"That's true," Darren glanced around the room. "Jody keeps the attendance records and has noticed a decrease in the teen service."

"Do you have any candidates in mind, Tyler?" Jeremiah asked.

"I do know of a couple looking for a new position."

"Anyone we might know?" Darren asked.

"Jake and Maddy Boyter. Maddy and Liz roomed together at Olivet for a year. I met Jake because of Maddy. He's about my age, but he graduated from Mount Vernon Nazarene University in Ohio."

Chase shook a finger. "I'm not sure we should hire someone from MVNU. Cougars and Tigers don't get along well together," he joked.

Tyler spend several minutes talking about Jake and Maddy.

"They sound like a possibility," Pastor Ausland said. "We should probably ask for a resume to present to the board."

"What about someone to replace Chase?" Jonah asked.

Darren kept a straight face as he said, "We could step outside and ask the next person we see."

"True, but they might be over-qualified," Jeremiah added.

"Do we even need to replace him?" Reed asked.

Chase folded his arms over his chest while he listened to the men talk about him as if he were already gone.

"We could save a bundle of money. We need to update the red cones we use in the parking lot," Jonah suggested.

"Someone suggested we replace the toilet paper holders in the restrooms," Reed added. "That's probably more of a priority than a new worship pastor."

Tyler grinned. "Okay, I think we've had our fun with Chase. Let's get serious."

"We really do need more red cones," Jonah mentioned.

"I'll take care of that tomorrow." Reed wrote it in his notes.

"Do you have any suggestions, Chase?" Pastor Herb asked.

"Back in the old days when I was a kid," he waited for a response, but no one laughed. "Most churches used a member of the congregation to lead the singing. Over the years the position

214

evolved and became more complicated."

"So true," Reed nodded. "When we first came to this church, there wasn't a band. There was a piano player and sometimes a guitar player. A couple of singers, but that was about it. Chase is responsible for the growth of our worship team. I'd hate to see it take a step backward."

"Thanks, Reed. I have a radical idea."

Tyler chuckled and asked, "And what might that be?"

"It could take several months to find someone willing to come here and work with you guys," Chase said. "But what if we could find someone already on the worship team to take over for an interim period?"

"Like who?" Darren asked.

"If not for the fact they travel quite a bit, I would suggest Kenny and Emmy. Emmy already leads the service whenever she's here, but there is another very capable couple on the team."

"Robby and Regina," Tyler said.

"Bingo! You got it," Chase pointed a finger at Tyler. "They are very talented. They don't travel. Regina already helps pick out the music."

"What about Heidi and Ross Knapp?" Jeremiah stroked his beard.

"Heidi is willing to be on the team, but doesn't have the time for more than that," Chase answered. "I don't think Ross would ever take on a leadership role. He is contented to play his guitar and remain in the background."

"Should we ask Robby and Regina about taking the position temporarily?" Pastor Herb glanced around the room.

"Now that the rumor about us leaving is no longer classified, I can approach them about the open position," Chase answered.

"Will there be any resentment from the team if Robby and Regina are suddenly in charge?" Darren asked.

"I don't think so." Chase rubbed his jaw. "Everyone kinda leaves their ego at the door. They see Kenny being a regular guy, and that kinda keeps them in check."

"Let's move on," Tyler checked his tablet. "I love being

215

paperless. I'll get in touch with Jake and Maddy, and Chase will talk to Robby and Regina."

They spent another hour together before Pastor Herb closed the meeting with a prayer.

By the time Jeremiah and the guys walked out of the studio at five, they had two tracks finished except for polishing the vocals.

"Same time tomorrow?" Jeremiah asked on the way out.

"I'll be here," Kenny answered. "This is so much fun compared to a Fridays At Five project."

Dany Kimmerle left the offices of the Hampshire Medical Group shortly after five. She checked her cell phone and saw a text from Emmy inviting her over for dinner that evening. She decided to call back instead of texting.

"Hi, Emmy, I'm just leaving work, and I got your text. I'd love to come for dinner. What time are you thinking?"

"Hang on a sec, Dany." Emmy put a hand over the phone and turned to face the kids. "Will you be quiet so I can talk on the phone. I don't care who's been playing with that thing the longest. Either share, or I will take it away. Now scoot!" Emmy sighed and put the phone to her ear. "Sorry about that. The kids have been driving me nuts this afternoon. Today was the first day back at school. We'll probably eat around six. I'm not making anything special. Just a pot of spaghetti, a salad and garlic bread."

"Sounds yummy. Should I bring anything?"

"No need. Come on over whenever you're ready. I'll leave the service door unlocked."

Dany made it home, showered, changed clothes and walked to Emmy and Kenny's. She entered the garage and walked to the stairs leading into the mudroom. She removed her coat, boots, mittens and stocking cap and then knocked on the kitchen door.

"If that's Tony, go away. If it's Dany, come on in," Emmy hollered from inside.

"It's me." Dany opened the door and stepped inside. "Were you expecting Tony and Sloane?"

"No, he's in Miami with Marco. Notre Dame is playing for the championship tonight. Tony played for Notre Dame. Sloane called a few minutes ago wanting to know if I could spare a box of mostaccioli. I told her yes. I was going to get after Tony for being too lazy to go grocery shopping, but then I remembered he was gone."

"Isn't he working for Bertucci and Keasling now?" Dany walked over to the stove. "Can I help with anything?"

They both heard a thud and then a loud wail from somewhere in the house.

Emmy pointed in the direction of the sound with her head. "Could you find the source of that, and make sure the kids are not killing each other, please?"

Dany grinned, "I can handle that. It's what I went to college for." She traced the source to the living room. "Kevin, what's the matter? Are you hurt?"

"Heather hit me with my firetruck because I took it away from her."

"Where did the truck hit you?"

"Right here!" Kevin pointed to his forehead.

Dany examined the area. "I do see the beginning of a bump, but you're not bleeding." She noticed a red firetruck on the floor. "Is that the firetruck that hit you?"

"Yes," he stammered.

"I better make sure it's all right." She inspected the plastic toy. "I don't see any damage to the firetruck. Are you feeling better now?"

"I feel better, Dany." He reached out for her.

Dany hugged him.

"Am I 'posed to call you Aunt Dany? I heard Natty call you that."

"That's because I really am her aunt, but you can call me that if you want."

Kevin tilted his head as he stared at Dany. "Are you an old person like Aunt Diane and Aunt Kristen? I thought you were just a big kid."

"I'm twenty-two. Does that make me an old person?"

217

He nodded. "It sounds pretty old."

Kenny walked into the room. "What happened, Kev. Did I hear you crying?"

"I'm all better now, Daddy." Kevin rubbed his forehead. "I got a bump. Did you know Dany is old? She's not a big kid like Peter or Carson."

"I didn't realize that," Kenny said. "Maybe you should play in your room until dinner is ready, okay?"

Emmy hollered from the kitchen, "Dinner is ready. Can you get the girls, Kenny?"

Kenny left to round up the twins while Dany held Kevin's hand and led him into the kitchen.

"We usually eat in the breakfast nook, Dany. I hope that's all right."

"Fine with me." Dany watched as Heather and Isabella burst into the room, scampered over to the breakfast table and took their seats without realizing they had company.

Isabella noticed Dany first, jumped down from her chair and dashed over to her. "Dany! I didn't know you were here. Are you going to eat with us?"

"I am. Your mother invited me."

"You have to sit next to me and Heather. We have to tell you what happened at school. Do you know that Miss Liz is our teacher?"

"Yes. Did Liz have to get after one of the students?" Dany took a seat between Isabella and Heather after Isa switched places.

"She put Dominick in timeout because he threw a fit," Isabella explained.

Heather nodded in agreement. "He lay on the floor and kicked his legs and yelled. He said a bad word, too."

"Okay, girls. Let's quiet down so we can eat. Does anyone want to say the prayer?"

The girls grinned at Dany and raised their hands together.

"How about if you both say the prayer." Emmy sat next to Kevin and shook her head at him because he tried to grab a piece of garlic bread. "They're still hot."

The twins said the prayer almost in perfect unison.

"Anyone home? The door was open." Peter opened the mudroom door. "Mom needs some pasta."

"In the pantry on the right. Top shelf," Emmy said.

"I'll get if for you, Peter." Kenny got up.

"He can reach it," Emmy said. "He's almost as tall as me now."

Peter flipped on the light and used the step-stool. "Found it." He turned off the light and closed the pantry door. "Thanks. Are you going to watch the game, Auntie Em?"

"That's tonight isn't it?"

"Yeah! The Irish are playing Alabama for the National Championship," Peter reminded her. "Papa Tony and Uncle Marco are at the game. I hope they win."

"Me, too, Peter."

"Thanks for the pasta."

"You're welcome, Peter. Be careful crossing the road."

"I will. I'll close the door."

"He's growing up so fast," Emmy said.

Emmy and Kenny tried to get the girls to stop talking to Dany and eat without much success.

"If you don't clean your plates, you can't have your something special for dessert," Emmy tried once more.

"We don't need something special tonight, Mom. We want to show Dany our room again," Heather said.

"If you are finished with dinner, you need to wash your hands and faces, brush your teeth and put on your pajamas."

"But, Daddy!" Heather sighed and rolled her eyes. "It's too early for bed. We're not babies. We're big girls now."

"You don't have to go to bed yet, but you have school tomorrow," Kenny said.

Emmy looked at the microwave for the time. "You can stay up until eight, but then it's time to get in bed, and I don't want you pestering Dany anymore. I want to talk to her now."

Heather and Isabella reluctantly left the breakfast nook and walked slowly upstairs.

"Are you finished, Kev?" Kenny checked his plate and then the floor underneath Kevin's chair. "Good job! You ate most of your food tonight."

"All done. I want something special." Kevin pushed his plate toward Emmy and managed to spill his glass of water."

"I'll get it, Em. I'll take him upstairs and check on the girls, so you and Dany can actually visit."

"Something special!" Kevin reminded his father.

"How about an apple?"

"No, something special."

"Okay, one cookie, but that's it."

Kevin grinned, got down from his chair, moved his little step-stool up to the counter, managed to reach the cookie jar and picked out his something special.

"I'm going to find a better place for that," Emmy said while shaking her head. "He's big enough now to reach the countertop."

Dany smiled. "My mother would hide the cookie jar in the cabinet above the fridge. I would make Larry climb up and steal cookies for me."

"Do you drink coffee?" Emmy asked.

"Once in a while in the morning."

"Would you like some tea? I have a bunch of different herbal teas."

"Tea would be all right."

Emmy brewed some Lemon Zinger, and she and Dany went into the family room to relax. Emmy turned on the TV, but the game hadn't started.

"How was your first day of work?"

"Not too bad. I actually worked a couple of half days last week."

"My first job after I graduated from high school was with Coventry Shield Healthcare." Emmy sat on her feet. "I was only seventeen, so I mostly worked with filing things away and finding patient files. Pretty boring, but it was a job."

Dany moved her feet under her since it appeared Emmy wouldn't mind. "That's what I did last week. Today I worked at the front desk for a few hours, and then I worked in the file room."

"Do you ever work with your parents, or did you in the past?" Emmy asked.

"They used to take me to the office if they couldn't find anyone to watch me, but in high school I would work a few hours a week. They had a room for the kids, so I was mostly babysitting."

They finished a second cup of tea and then Dany checked the time.

"I should go so you can get the kids to bed."

"They won't go to sleep unless you say goodnight."

Emmy and Dany went upstairs. Emmy peeked into Kevin's room first. "He's out cold, but I can hear the girls reading."

"Mom, we can hear you. Is Dany still here?" Heather asked.

Dany walked into the girls' bedroom followed by Emmy.

"Will you read a book with us?" Isabella pleaded."

Dany glanced at Emmy.

"Only one story and then it's lights out." Emmy held up one finger.

Dany read a Junie B. Jones book, and though the girls begged for another one, Emmy held fast. "One book means one book. Now say your prayers and don't drag them out like you try to sometimes. Jesus knows if you are doing that just to avoid going to bed."

Dany watched as the girls knelt by a bed, held hands and said their prayers. *Ah, that is so adorable.*

Emmy kissed them and tucked then in. "Go to sleep. You have school in the morning." Emmy turned off the light and Dany noticed the ceiling glowed like a princess's castle.

"How did you do that?" Dany asked in the hallway after Emmy closed the door.

"Sofia did it for us. Isn't it precious?"

"Yes, and I loved the way they held hands to say their prayers."

"They fuss and fight like all kids, but they are very close. Even though Diane is only two and a half years older than me, we were never close as kids. It's a lot better now."

Dany walked down the stairs behind Emmy. *I would have thought your sister was maybe ten years older.* "Thanks for dinner, Emmy. Maybe one day I'll learn how to cook something other than

221

canned soup and invite you over for lunch."

"You're just like Kristen. She hated to cook when she got married. She used to burn instant oatmeal when we lived together."

"You guys lived together? At college?" Dany asked.

"No, after Krissy graduated, we shared a house. I'll tell you about it someday." Emmy looked out the kitchen window. "Do you want a ride home? It's snowing like crazy."

"Thanks, but I won't get lost. I love the snow."

Emmy followed Dany to the garage and waved as Dany dashed through the snow. *I can see a lot of Liz in you, but in some ways, you remind me of myself.*

She returned to the family room and saw Kenny watching the game. "Any score?" She plopped into her recliner.

"You're not gonna like this, but Alabama is up by fourteen already."

"They can come back," Emmy felt confident.

By the end of the first half, the Irish trailed by twenty-eight points. They traded scores with Alabama in the second half, but were never really in the game.

"Tony must be so disappointed," Emmy said.

"I'm sure he is, but he does have two Super Bowls rings."

"If he hasn't lost them. I've never seen him wear them like some former jocks do."

Kenny turned off the TV. "He has other priorities, Em."

Chapter Twenty-Three

Heather and Isabella crept stealthily into their parent's room and climbed onto the bed without a sound. They moved between Kenny and Emmy and pretended to be asleep. Kenny knew they were there, but played along.

"Emmy, are you awake?"

"No, don't bother me. I'm not in the mood." She tried to pull the comforter over her head.

"Emmy." Kenny drew out her name.

"I said no." Emmy felt something close to her so she swatted at it.

Heather and Isabella began to giggle. Emmy cautiously peeked out from under the thick white comforter.

"Mommy, do you remember what day this is?" Heather asked.

"It's Sunday, so I get to sleep late," Emmy stretched her arms out.

"I think it might be an even more special day, Em," Kenny grinned.

Emmy turned onto her side and raised her head. "Is it Christmas again?"

Isabella giggled. Heather shook her head.

"Not Christmas, huh? Then it must be the Fourth of July."

"Mom!" Heather drew out the name and rolled her eyes. The Fourth of July is in the summer. It's still winter."

"It is? Then maybe we should build a snowman later."

"Daddy, is Mommy old now? Is she forgetting things like Grandma?" Isabella asked.

"I know what special day this is!" Emmy sat up and grabbed the girls. "It's my precious little darlings' birthday."

"Mom! We're not little anymore. We're seven now." Heather screamed as Emmy and Kenny began to tickle her.

"We need to get up and get ready for church," Kenny said. "I hear there's going to be a party later."

"Is it a surprise birthday party?" Isabella asked.

223

Chase and Yvonne met Robby and Regina Collins in the music suite after the service. They sat at one of the round tables.

"I think the congregation was more surprised this morning than the worship team was on Thursday," Robby smiled.

"Did I hear a few cheers?" Chase asked.

"I think that was Emmy clapping," Yvonne teased.

Regina chuckled, but then glanced at the clock on the wall. "What time is the party?"

"Emmy told me one. This won't take long," Yvonne assured Regina.

"When I submitted my resignation, I made a suggestion to Tyler about a possible replacement." Chase looked at Robby and then Regina very deliberately.

Robby noticed the look and waved a hand. "Hang on there! Are you saying you think Regina should replace you?"

Chase shook his head.

"Good, because I could never do that," Regina said and then sighed.

"I suggested the two of you as a team."

"Get out!" Robby slammed a hand on the table. "You can't be serious."

"Oh, but I'm very serious." Chase noticed the tattoo of a cross on the dark skin of Robby's forearm.

Regina's dreadlocks moved back and forth as she shook her head. "I could never lead worship. You should ask Emmy and Kenny. They're the pros."

"That's why I can't ask them. Not that I think this position would be beneath them. That didn't come out exactly right." Chase looked to Yvonne for help.

"I think what my husband is trying to say is that it's not a matter of talent as to who leads worship," Yvonne said and then put a hand to her mouth.

"Thanks, dear. I think you just made it worse," Chase said but then started to grin.

Robby and Regina saw Yvonne's expression and began to laugh, too.

"I get what you're trying to say," Robby held Regina's

hand. "It's not a matter of Kenny and Emmy being capable of taking over the responsibility, but they won't always be available. Regina and I are here every Sunday."

"It's more than that," Chase said. "There are other people here every week, but they don't have your ability to lead worship. You are ignoring the obvious."

"What might that be?" Robby wondered.

"Regina picks out the music with help from Heidi. Robby, you keep the band in line. You organize the rehearsals and keep us on track. You guys are already leading the worship team. You just aren't making the big bucks like I am," Chase said with a grin.

Yvonne rolled her eyes.

Robby waved his enormous right hand. "Hold it, Chase. Let's say we decide to do this, and this is not saying we will, but if." He looked at the ceiling. "If we decide to do this, I want it understood we are accepting this as a temporary assignment on a voluntary basis."

"You would receive compensation," Yvonne said.

"Do you get paid for running the tech team?" Robby asked.

"Well, no, but..."

"Case closed. How soon do you need an answer, Chase?" Robby asked.

"Our last Sunday is February tenth."

"We should know in a week."

"Does Emmy know about this?" Regina stood up.

Chase nodded. "She suggested you guys as soon as I approached her. She won't have any trouble working with you. If you're lucky, she won't hassle you as much as she does me."

"This could evolve into a permanent position," Yvonne said as she hugged Regina.

"If that happens, we will accept some compensation." Robby rubbed his fingers together. "Hey! I just thought of something. Who is going to take over the tech team?"

"I've been training Gabby Morrissey. She's actually gone solo twice. Some of the young adults who worked as techies for the teen group are older now. They are filling positions that once would have been filled by older adults."

225

"Yvonne is tactfully trying to say the young people are better equipped to handle the evolving technology. Everything is digital now."

"Robby, I need to run out to the car. I didn't bring the gifts in for the girls." Regina held out a hand and Robby dug the keys out of his pocket.

"So you guys ignored Emmy's policy, too."

"Of course! I want to watch those adorable girls open presents. They aren't spoiled like some kids. They get a kick out opening a present even if it turns out to be clothes." Regina laughed and shook her dreadlocks.

"Emmy, would you like some help?" Liz grabbed one of the helium-filled balloons before it escaped to the high ceiling in the all-purpose room at church. "What time does the party start."

"I told everyone one o'clock, but some people didn't bother going home after church."

Kenny and Tony walked into the area with two stepladders. "Where do you want the banner, Em?"

"Could you hang it up on that wall, please?" Emmy pointed. "And then set up a table for gifts."

"I thought you told everyone not to bring a gift." Tony smiled.

Emmy put her hands on her hips and asked, "Did you and Sloane bring presents?"

"Of course," he answered. "Since when have I ever listened to you?"

"You're a creep."

"And yet we're still friends. Go figure." Tony moved his ladder into position.

Later, Andy Walker turned off his digital video-recorder as the twins opened the last of their gifts. "They are so adorable. I recorded most of it, Emmy."

"Thank you, Andy. I should be mad at you for buying such expensive presents. They don't need tablets. They're only seven."

"They know how to use computers. The tablets are more portable, and I made sure they won't be able to defeat the security

226

measures Charles programmed."

Emmy turned to Charles La Rosse. "Thank you for being here. I know you were on vacation."

Charles used his good arm to hug Emmy. "I was not on vacation. I was in Tennessee visiting my mother. I should thank you for giving me the perfect excuse to leave."

Andy slapped his lifelong friend on the back. "Charles is taking me to McBride's for dinner. They have the best burgers and tater tots in the area."

"And I assume they have blue cheese." Emmy pinched her nose. "I still can't stand the smell."

"Do you think anyone will mind that you give most of the presents to charity?" Andy whispered.

"I warned them that if they ignored my request for no gifts, there would be a good chance their present would be donated. The girls have tons of stuff. Kenny makes them get rid of stuff they don't need or play with anymore. We would need two extra bedrooms if he didn't."

"Are the girls down for the night?" Kenny asked as Emmy walked up behind him.

"They are in bed but not asleep." She stood behind his recliner and ran her fingers through his hair. "Are you keeping it this long so it covers your funny ears?"

"I can't help it if my ears stick out. Now what did you want to show me?" He closed his textbook, set it on the end table and stood up.

Emmy picked up the heavy book. "Is this the one that cost two hundred bucks?"

"It would have if I hadn't found a used one."

"You're so cheap," Emmy teased.

"I prefer to think of myself as frugal unlike some people in this house who buy expensive cars just because they like the color."

"If you're trying to make me feel guilty, it isn't working, and you still can't drive my BMW. You are stuck with your sensible, old, unreliable car." She used air quotes. "Come down to

227

the studio with me. I want you to listen to some tracks I recorded."

Kenny sat in one of the comfortable leather recliners as Emmy turned on the gear, booted up the computers and cued her demo tracks.

"These are guide vocals, so don't listen to anything other than the lyrics, okay?"

"I won't criticize the vocals." *I haven't heard you go flat or sharp since you were a kid.*

"I don't have titles for all of them, but a rough idea." She handed him the handwritten lyrics. "Hold your response until the end."

Kenny read the lyrics as he listened to the demos. Emmy watched him without letting him see her looking. He glanced at Emmy once in a while. *Holy smoke, Em! These are really personal.*

Emmy stopped the last track, turned her chair around and looked at Kenny. "Well, what do you think?"

"Is this really how you feel?"

"It was how I felt at the time. Are they too personal? Should I throw them in my desk and lock them away?"

"Don't do that. We know how personal the lyrics are, but we aren't the only people to ever go through stuff like this, Em."

"You think people will relate to the lyrics, huh?" She took the lyrics sheets away. "They won't just listen to the music?"

"Definitely," he said. "Do you have more songs?"

"I have a few more."

"Enough for a new CD?"

"Probably."

"Let's start recording them right away." He stood up, pulled her out of her chair and held her close.

"Are you forgetting about your real job? You guys are in the middle of your own project," she reminded him.

"We're almost finished."

Emmy laughed. "I know better than that. You guys could take another year to finish it."

"Not a year, but I see your point. I'll talk to the guys and see what I can do."

Dr. Bartolo Bergman pushed up his wire-rimmed glasses as he walked into the conference room. He glanced up from his notes. "Good, you're here." He sat across the table from Diane and Emmy.

"Are we going to have to move her across the street?" Diane asked.

Dr. Bergman tugged on his ear. "Across the street? I don't understand."

"Sorry. The memory care facility at Sunrise Garden is across the street from where she lives now," Diane explained.

"Ah, I see." He read his notes for a moment. "Yes, I recommend she be moved within the month. She needs more care than they can provide in the assisted living facility." He spent several minutes going over his evaluation. "Other than her mind, she is in excellent health for a woman of her age. How old is she?" He checked his notes.

"She's seventy," Emmy answered.

"Seventy? For some reason I thought she was eighty." He read his notes again.

"Does that mean she's not in good health?" Diane asked.

Dr. Bergman removed his glasses to clean them. "Her blood pressure is high, but under control with medication. Her heart is strong for her age. She is showing some reduction in muscle memory, but overall she could live for another ten years. You never can tell with these patients."

"Grandma lived to a hundred, and she was in better shape than Mom until the last few months," Emmy mentioned.

"Isabel was a remarkable woman. It did not surprise me that she lived that long. Unfortunately, her daughters have not fared as well. I don't know your aunt, but I know she suffers from a more advanced stage of Alzheimer's."

Diane smiled. "Mom and Aunt Betty could be roommates and not realize they're sisters. How weird is that?"

"That's not funny, Diane." Emmy crossed her arms over her chest and frowned.

"I understand you are concerned about your mother's security." Dr. Bergman replaced his glasses and looked at Diane.

"Yeah, last week I came to see her, and she wasn't in her apartment. I checked the bingo room and the other places she goes, but she wasn't there. I told one of the care partners, and we eventually found her on the third floor at the far end of the building. She couldn't remember where her apartment was. She didn't know what floor she was on."

"The memory care facility will be more secure. She won't be able to leave her floor," Dr. Bergman assured them.

"That's good because she can still get around pretty good," Diane said. "I hope we don't have to lock her in a room."

Late Friday morning, Kenny removed his headphones, set down his guitar and smiled at Jeremiah and the guys. "I think we're finished. Let's take a break and spend the afternoon listening. We've got a rough mix, but we will do a final mix as soon as I can free up the time."

After lunch Kenny listened to the tracks for the as yet untitled BearFace album. He made notes about the mix.

"Do you have any suggestions for a title?" Jeremiah asked. "Mia has been working on the artwork without a title." He showed Kenny the artwork on his laptop.

"That looks really good as is. Some bands release their first CD without a title. You could consider that."

Jeremiah looked at Cecil and Warren. "What do you guys think?"

Warren stood up and filled the room. He twirled a drumstick in his beefy paw. "I'm happy with that."

Cecil ran a hand through his bushy beard. "I can't think of a better title, and I like the pictures Mia took. Somehow she made me look more handsome than you guys. Course, that don't take much," he guffawed.

"For the time being, let's not go with a different title," Jeremiah said. "It's not like there's going to be thousands of copies of the CD."

Chapter Twenty-Four

"How much!?" Emmy hollered into the phone.

"About eleven hundred dollars," Kenny repeated.

"That's crazy! You are not spending that much money on that car. It's not worth it. You spent that just two months ago."

"Yes, but the car could last another ten years," Kenny said.

Emmy shook her head even though he couldn't see it. "I know that car is your baby, but you have to face the facts. It's time to trade it in. Something that won't break down and leave you stranded. What if I needed to use the car to take the kids somewhere, and it crapped out on me, huh? What would I do?"

"Em, you never use my car anymore."

"Yes! Because it's so old and unreliable."

He shook his head. "You have a BMW in the garage."

"And you have a Honda Odyssey. What's your point?"

"We use the Odyssey when we all need to go somewhere. I use my Civic the rest of the time."

"Don't you want something reliable?"

"The Civic is reliable. It just needs some work." Kenny glanced at the owner of SoHam Auto Service and then turned away. "Do you know how much new cars cost?"

"Yes, they're expensive. If you had to replace your car, what would you buy?"

He shrugged. "Probably another Civic. I like Hondas."

"Kenny, I know how much you love that car, but it's time to sever the cord. I'm sure you could find a new Civic you like."

"But..."

"No buts. Come home, and we'll talk. We can go online and look at cars."

Kenny waved goodbye to the man behind the counter. *I bet you're going to be sorry if I buy a new car. You smile every time I come in here because you know the repairs are getting expensive.* He drove home and parked the Civic in the garage. He closed the door and stared at the car for a moment. *Emmy may be right, but that doesn't make it easy to say goodbye.* He walked inside and hung up his coat.

"Em, where are you?"

"In the den," she hollered.

He walked into the den and looked over her shoulder. "You're researching cars, huh?"

"Yes, and I found a Civic you might like."

"Is it red?" he laughed.

"No, it's blue. Aren't you sick of red cars?"

"Not really, but I would consider another color."

Emmy grabbed their checkbook from the desk. "Good because we're going to look at one. Where's the title to your car?"

Kenny found the title and followed Emmy out to the kitchen. "Are we taking the Civic?"

She grabbed her purse and walked into the mudroom. "Yes, and it won't be coming home, so if there's anything in it you want, better get it out." She put on her coat. "Grab both sets of keys."

Kenny drove to D'Antoni Honda and parked out front.

"When did this change?" Emmy asked. "It wasn't D'Antoni before."

"Mr. D'Antoni bought it a couple of years ago after the previous owner passed away," Kenny explained. "Do you remember Marc?"

"Sorta," she saw a blue Civic parked by the front doors.

"That's the son, and he's running this place for his father."

She grabbed his arm. "How about this one?"

"It's a coupe, Em. I want a sedan."

"Do you at least like the color?" She rolled her eyes.

"It's not red," he said, but then grinned.

She pulled him through the door. "You're such a dork."

They entered the modern steel and glass showroom holding hands. Emmy looked left and Kenny looked right. They tried to tug each other in opposite directions, but only succeeded in bumping into each other.

"Will you watch where you're going?" Emmy pushed Kenny. "There's a Civic over there."

A man laughed a few feet in front of them. "Am I finally going to have a chance to sell you a car?" Allan D'Antoni asked.

"Mr. D'Antoni! What are you doing here? I mean, it's a

232

surprise to see you here and not the other place," Kenny said and then shook the offered hand.

"I stop over here once or twice a week. Hello, Emmy. It's good to see you again. Is there anything I can help you with?"

"Kenny needs a new car, and he wants another Civic. He wants a red one, but I'm sick of red Civics. I like that blue color." She pointed to the coupe.

"Are you dealing with any particular salesman?"

"Not really. The one Dad always bought his Hondas from retired a couple of years ago," Kenny said. He looked around the showroom and a new Odyssey captured his attention.

"Hey, guys. How are you?" Marc D'Antoni approached with an outstretched hand.

"Hi, Marc. Good to see you." Kenny shook hands.

Emmy smiled as Marc shook her hand.

"Kenny needs a new Civic according to Emmy," Mr. D'Antoni said.

"We might have a few stashed around here somewhere. Have you talked to anyone?" Marc asked.

Kenny explained the circumstances.

"I have just the right person for you to talk to. Let me see if I can find him." Marc looked around. "If you guys would have a seat, or look around if you'd like, I'll send him right over."

"Thanks, Marc." Kenny tugged on Emmy's arm. "I want to look at this Odyssey."

Mr. D'Antoni waved to a customer. "Who do you have in mind?" he whispered to his son.

"Vernon Heintz has been struggling since he transferred over here. He could use a boost in confidence, and I'm pretty certain Kenny wouldn't be here unless he was ready to buy."

Mr. D'Antoni slapped his son on the back. "Good choice. He had no trouble selling trucks for me."

Marc introduced Kenny and Emmy to Mr. Heintz.

"How can I help you?"

Emmy explained what Kenny was looking for.

"So a Civic EX-L in any color other than red, huh?"

"I wouldn't want black, or silver. No gray ones, either."

233

Kenny noticed some of the other colors on vehicles in the large showroom.

"We like that blue color." Emmy grinned as she pointed to the coupe again.

"We should have that in a sedan. Let's have a seat, and I'll check the computer."

Kenny sat down with Mr. Heintz.

"I want to check out that car over there," Emmy said.

"Go ahead, Em."

She walked over to a lighter blue Civic sedan, opened the door and looked inside.

Mr. D'Antoni walked over to Emmy. "Are you looking for a car, Emmy?"

"Not really. I've got a BMW X3."

"Nice car."

"I like it, but this one's kinda cool looking. It's a Civic, right?"

"It is, but it's the Civic Si. It's a sports version. Do you know how to drive a stick?"

"Oh, yeah. A friend taught me how to drive one. He had a '93 Camaro Z28 with a six-speed and an eight cylinder engine."

"And he let you drive it?" Mr. D'Antoni chuckled. "He must have been a good friend."

"He is. I want to show this one to Kenny."

Mr. D'Antoni checked his watch. "Let Marc know if you guys need anything. I have to run."

Emmy walked over to Kenny. "Where did the salesman go?"

"He left to grab the keys for a car. I want to drive one first."

She tugged on his arm. "Come and look at this one. It's an Si and it looks sharp."

Kenny followed Emmy. "What do you think?" Emmy sat in the car.

"Em, it's a stick shift. I want an automatic."

"You should drive it. It's their sporty version. You might like it." She looked up at him.

Kenny shook his head. "Not for me, Em. There's Mr.

234

Heintz. Do you wanna go with us?"

She shook her head. "I know how a regular Civic will drive. Boring!" She faked a yawn.

"Suit yourself." Kenny left and joined Mr. Heintz for a test drive.

"What do you drive now?" Mr. Heintz opened the driver's door of the new Civic.

Kenny pointed to his '99 Civic. "That, or an Odyssey."

Mr. Heintz took a few minutes to point out the features of the new car before Kenny drove off the lot.

Emmy ran through the gears as she sat in the car for a few more minutes.

Marc D'Antoni walked by and saw her in the car. "Are you interested in a car, too?"

"I tried to talk Kenny into driving this one, but he's not interested. He's still a dork."

Marc laughed. "Would you like to drive an Si? It's a manual."

"Do you have one I could drive?" Emmy scooted out of the car.

"I think we've got three or four out back. Let me drop off this folder, and I'll show you."

"I don't want to bother you. You're the boss."

"That's right! I can do whatever I want," he said. "Let's have some fun. I don't often get to drive the cars, but it's slow today."

"What do you think of the new Civics?" Mr. Heintz asked Kenny as they took a ride.

"Certainly better than my '93. That was my first Civic," he explained. "I bet it still gets great gas mileage."

Mr. Heintz assured him it did. "Turn right up there and we can take it through some winding roads."

"I grabbed the keys for one of the cars, Emmy." Marc jingled the keys. "They all drive the same." He walked out back with her and opened the doors to a Si coupe in the same light blue color as the one in the showroom. He started it up and checked the gas gauge. "Ready to take it for a spin?"

235

"You bet!"

She surprised Marc with her ability to drive the sporty car.

"Who taught you to rev match like that?"

"A friend of mine taught me on his Z28." She floored the Si.

Kenny glanced at the Civic Si as it passed him going down the road where he had just been.

"Someone is flying a little low," Mr. Heintz said.

"I'm afraid I might know who," Kenny said with a sigh.

"I think that was Kenny putzing along," Emmy told Marc. "He is always telling me I drive too fast."

"This car is cool. You don't have to be breaking the sound barrier to have fun driving it." Marc grabbed the dashboard as Emmy cornered without slowing down.

She checked her speed. "I see. I'm only doing fifty, fifty-five. I thought I was going a lot faster. This is way more cool than Kenny's old car."

"It's a lot more fun to drive than a normal Civic." Marc didn't flinch as Emmy took another corner at speed.

Back in the showroom Mr. Heintz motioned for Kenny to have a seat. "What did you think?"

"I liked it. I need to trade in my older Civic."

Mr. Heintz took Kenny's keys and had the used car sales manager appraise it.

Emmy returned, and sat beside Kenny. "Did you see me?"

"I saw a blur fly past. Was that you?"

She nodded and giggled. "You should drive it. It's a lot more fun than a regular Civic."

"I agree. It would be more fun, but I'd rather have an automatic and get better gas mileage." He glanced over his shoulder and saw Mr. Heintz talking to Marc D'Antoni. "If you like it so much, Em, then you buy it. You could trade in your BMW."

I might just do that. You have a second car to use when you don't have the kids. Why can't I?

Mr. Heintz returned. "It is an older Civic, and it needs some work. We could wholesale it, but we couldn't sell it here."

"I understand. I would keep it, but..."

"No way! We're not putting any more money into it," Emmy insisted. "I don't care if it's only worth ten dollars as a trade-in. You're not keeping it."

Mr. Heintz slid a piece of paper over to Kenny. "This is what I can do for you."

Kenny checked the numbers. "Will you take a check?"

Mr. Heintz inhaled deeply and then let his breath out rather slowly. "We will take your check."

"Where do I sign?" Kenny shook his hand.

Mr. Heintz showed Kenny where to sign and then stood up.

Emmy looked at the light blue sedan in the showroom. *Shoot! I don't need a car, but that was such a blast to drive.* She shook her head. *No, I'm not buying a car.* She kicked the corner of the metal desk, and then looked back at the car again. *Why not? The BMW doesn't get very good mileage.* She bit her lip and made up her mind. "Before you leave, Mr. Heintz," she said. "How much would that Civic Si over there cost?"

He froze in place, looked at her, and then at Kenny. Kenny stared at Emmy and then shifted his gaze to Mr. Heintz. Then he looked at the car and then back at Emmy.

"You sure, Em?" Kenny asked.

"I've never bought anything on a whim like this, but I want it."

Kenny tilted his head and watched her eyes. "Okay."

"Should I ask the boss?" Mr. Heintz stood up straight.

"Yes, please."

Mr. Heintz hurried over to Marc. He pointed to the Si and then back at Emmy.

Marc laughed and said, "I'll give you a number. Give me a minute."

Mr. Heintz returned to his desk. "Mr. D'Antoni is going to check."

Five minutes later, Marc walked over with the numbers. He handed the paper to Mr. Heintz who lifted his eyebrows as he looked at the figure. He passed the paper over to Kenny, but Emmy grabbed it first.

237

"Em, let me see." Kenny spent some time checking the figures. "It looks like we are buying two cars today."

Emmy hugged him. "I promise I'll sell it if I get too many tickets."

Kenny and Emmy signed the contracts, handed over a check and left to grab some lunch. They returned ninety minutes later to take possessions of their new cars.

"I'll race you home," Emmy said.

"No way, Em. Remember what you promised?"

"Fine! Spoil sport."

Marc D'Antoni shook hands once more. "I don't suppose I'll see you for ten years or so."

"You never know, Marc. I might decide to trade this one in a lot sooner," Kenny said.

Mr. Heintz shook hands with Kenny and Emmy. "Let me know if any of your friends need a car. I'll treat them well."

"I'll do that, Mr. Heintz. Thanks for everything."

Marc walked up to Mr. Heintz after Kenny and Emmy drove away. "Nice job! You sold two cars in less than an hour."

Mr. Heintz shook his head. "I've been in this business a lot of years. You knew he was going to buy a car today from someone. Thank you for giving me the opportunity. I needed it."

"Nonsense! You've been under a lot of pressure. Take the rest of the day off, and visit your wife. Tell her I said hello."

"Thanks, boss, but she doesn't remember me anymore. I might as well stay here. I can run up to Sunrise Garden this evening."

Diane called Emmy Friday morning. "You are coming with me to Sunrise Garden, right?"

"Do I have to? You're the one in charge of making the decisions," Emmy whined.

"She's your mother, too. You are coming," Diane insisted.

"Fine, but I'll drive."

Emmy picked up Diane thirty minutes later. Diane got in the car without really noticing it.

"What do you think?" Emmy asked as she pulled out onto

238

Springdale Lane.

"About what?"

"The car." Emmy sighed.

"Is this Kenny's new car? Why are you driving it?" Diane glanced around the interior, noticing the red stitching and then spotted the shift lever. "Why did he buy a car with a manual transmission?"

"It's not Kenny's car. This is mine." Emmy floored it pulling away from a stop sign.

"Did you trade in your BMW for this? Tell me you didn't." Diane looked over her shoulder into the rear seat. "You can't fit the kids back there."

"I didn't get rid of my BMW. I still have it, but now I don't have to drive it if I'm by myself," Emmy explained.

"This is like a sports car, and will you slow down." Diane put a hand on the dashboard as Emmy took a turn too fast. "Thank you."

"It handles better than Kenny's new car."

"Maybe so but I like sitting up higher so I can see better." Diane watched as Emmy shifted through the gears. "Where did you learn to drive a manual transmission?"

"Rory taught me."

Diane thought about it. "He let you drive his old Camaro?"

"Don't get all upset, but, yeah, I learned how to drive his stick before I had a license. He let me drive around Raynor Park. This one is a lot easier to shift, but you have to rev the engine to get the best performance."

"When did you become a gearhead? I've never seen you drive a car without an automatic transmission before. Why on earth would you buy this?"

"Duh! Because it's more fun." Emmy roared past a red Civic. "See?"

"Just make sure you watch your speed. You might not be able to charm the cops the way you did when you were younger."

"I know how to avoid getting pulled over for speeding. You know the BMW actually is faster if I really get on it, and I haven't gotten any tickets. This car will be a lot better on gas mileage."

"Not as good as Kenny's Civic, I bet."

"His car is too boring. I would never buy one like his," Emmy said.

"Whatever. We have to convince Mom that it's in her best interest to move out of the apartment."

"Will she even know the difference?" Emmy asked. "Have you been inside the memory care facility?"

"Not yet, but that's why we're meeting there today."

"Are we going to see Mom?"

"I hadn't planned to. Do you want to stop and see her?"

Emmy shook her head as she parked the car. "No, it hurts to see her like this."

Diane and Emmy met with the director of the memory care facility. They toured the building and Diane signed the paperwork.

"How soon will they move her?" Emmy looked across the road to the large brick building where Mom currently resided.

"Next week." Diane waited for Emmy to unlock the car. "Are you going to let me in?"

"Sorry," Emmy unlocked the car and they got in. Emmy turned on the car and started to back up, but stopped. She turned it off and bit her lip. "Do you think Mom will live as long as Aunt Betty has? Aunt Betty has been sick forever."

"Who knows, Em? Other than losing her mind, Mom is as healthy as any other person her age. Maybe in better health. She could live to be a hundred like Grandma."

"I don't know if I can deal with that."

"Em, it's out of our control. I know you pray for Mom every day. That's about all you can do at this point."

"You could pray for her, too," Emmy whispered.

Diane chuckled and then patted Emmy's hand. "I'll leave the praying and church stuff in your hands."

"And I'll keep praying for you, too."

Chapter Twenty-Five

"Does anyone want more coffee?" Emmy carried the ceramic coffee pot as she walked around the basement lounge area.

"I'll take some more, Emmy." Bobby O'Connor held up his cup.

"Don't give him anymore, Emmy," Quinten Matthews grinned. "It will stunt his growth, and he's a shrimp already."

Bobby pointed in the direction of Quinten's stomach. "Are you going to blame that expanding area on coffee?"

"In case you have forgotten, I sit at my keyboards to play. I don't dance around the stage like some people." Quinten grinned at Emmy and held a hand over his cup. "Thanks, but I'm good."

"I sit at the drum kit to play. I don't move all over the place," Bobby said and then tossed a drumstick at Quinten.

"Knock it off, Bobby," Quinten said.

"Miles, you okay? You haven't said more than two words." Emmy tugged on his ponytail. *You're always quiet, but you seem nervous today.*

"I'm fine." He drained his tomato juice. "I'm a little nervous about recording. I don't want to make any mistakes."

"Everyone makes mistakes, Miles. I was too young to know enough to be nervous the first time I recorded with Kenny. You'll do all right. The other guys might act like it's no big deal to record, but they haven't been in the studio all that much. Other than Christian, I mean. He's been working a lot out in LA." Emmy checked the time. "I should call Micah. Christian flew in yesterday and was crashing with Micah. They used to room together before Christian moved to the coast."

"I didn't know that." Miles watched Bobby goofing off by pretending to do a drum solo. "You missed a beat."

"Speak of the devils," Bobby chuckled as he pointed with a drumstick. "Look who finally decided to make an appearance."

Christian Becton and Micah Hurst didn't pause in their conversation as they entered the basement.

"How's Holly-weird treating you?" Bobby asked.

Christian walked over to shake hands with the guys while

Micah removed his purple beret and knee-length, gray coat.

"I haven't been to Hollywood. I'm living in Hawthorne in an apartment about the size of a bathroom and working as much as I can."

"In the studio?" Quinten asked.

"As much as I can get, but I'm working in a restaurant part-time. Gotta do what you can to pay the rent."

Emmy patted Christian's arm. "We're glad you joined us. I want you to meet Miles. He's going to play bass."

Christian smiled and shook hands with Miles. "Good to meet you. Micah said you're playing with the worship band."

"I am," Miles answered.

"Anyone heard from Jared since he moved to Georgia?" Micah carefully placed his coat and beret on the back of a chair and walked over to the group.

"I get emails from him occasionally," Quinten said. "He's teaching a bunch of rowdy fifth graders."

Bobby twirled a drumstick. "Hey, Micah, are you sure you can play a regular guitar? They've got more strings than a bass."

"I'll figure it out, punk." Micah grabbed Bobby's arm. "What is this? When did you get a tattoo?"

"A few months ago." Bobby tried to pull away, but Micah tightened his grip. "It's a cross."

"Duh! Even on your skinny arm, I can see that." Micah released Bobby's arm. "Where's Kenny?"

Emmy pointed to the control room. "In there with Will Consoli. They're getting everything ready."

"I didn't know Will would be here," Micah said. "Is he going to hang around with us? I know Fridays At Five are recording, too."

"Kenny is going to steal him as much as the band will allow."

Kenny walked out of the control room. "Are you guys ready? Hey, Christian, good to see ya. I heard you played lead guitar for Steve Pelini at the Whiskey."

"Yeah! That was a cool gig," Christian shook hands with Kenny. "Good to be back in this beautiful weather."

"Yeah, rub it in. At least we don't have to worry about earthquakes." Micah laughed.

Will joined everyone in the lounge.

"Hey, Mr. Consoli, does the band know you're over here with us?" Bobby grinned. "You are going to stay, right?"

Will rubbed his graying mustache. "We worked out a deal. Kenny and I can help you guys two days a week for a month or two. You better not screw up, Bobby, or else I'll erase all your drum tracks and use a machine."

All the guys laughed except for Bobby. He wasn't sure if Will was serious or not.

"Who will be here the rest of the time?" Quinten finished his third donut.

"Will is going to let Bruce Sutherland work the other three days," Emmy replied as she brushed some powdered sugar from Quinten's chin. "Bruce knows this setup, and he does all right with that other band, so I trust him to do a great job for us." Emmy grinned at Kenny.

"Then we better get to work. Time is money out in LA." Christian led the way into the studio.

"SoHam is more laid back," Emmy said with a grin.

"Why do I have to move? I like this place. Put that back!" Patricia watched the movers carry out her couch.

"You will like the new place, Mom. Your apartment will be just like this one." *For the most part. You won't be able to leave your floor without a code, and you might not understand that.* Diane took her mother's hand. "Let's go downstairs and see if any of your friends are around. They might want to say goodbye though you won't remember if they do or not."

"Your father won't know where I am." Patricia jumped back as one of the movers walked by with an armful of boxes.

"How long will it take?" Diane asked the man in charge.

"We should have the new apartment set up in an hour, Mrs. Robertson," he answered.

"I'll take Mom downstairs, and get her out of the way. She's getting agitated watching you guys."

243

"We will take good care of her stuff."

"Thank you," Diane said. *She won't know, but thanks.*

Ninety minutes later Diane sat on the couch and faced her mother. "Do you like your new place?"

Patricia looked around. "Does my TV still work? I want to watch my shows later."

"Yes, your TV and phone are just the same as before," Diane explained. "I bought you something." Diane pulled it from the closet.

Patricia looked at it. "What do I do with that?"

Diane moved it back and forth across the carpet. "It's a Bissell Sweeper. You use it to keep the carpet clean. See? You don't have to plug it in or turn it on."

Patricia watched and then smiled. "I haven't had one of those since your father and I first got married. Let me try."

"Here you go, Mom." *This is supposed to keep you busy. I hope it works.*

"You can go now. I have work to do. I have to make sure dinner is ready for your father." Patricia shooed Diane out.

Don't wait for him to come home before you eat, Mom. Dad's been gone for almost five years. "Call me if you need anything," Diane said. "My number's on the fridge if you remember how to use the phone.

"Sorry, if I kept you waiting," Kenny said as he dashed into the control room and removed his coat and hat. "We got busy with a track, and I lost track of time."

"No problem." Jeremiah leaned back in a chair in front of the mixing console. "I got here early. Emmy was still working with her band. You just missed them and Bruce."

"Now that I'm here, you will have my undivided attention." Kenny booted up the system, and Jeremiah followed each step in the process.

"Let's start with track one," Kenny said. "Are you still pleased with the track order? It can always be changed."

Jeremiah nodded. "I'm happy with it, and Mia already has the artwork finished. I don't want to ask her to change it now."

"Then let's get to work. I want to be finished by Friday night."

An hour later Emmy walked into the control room and stood behind Kenny. She rubbed his shoulder muscles. "Are you guys hungry? The kids and I ate soup and sandwiches for dinner. I could make more sandwiches."

Kenny paused the track. "Come to remember, I haven't eaten anything since around two. I'll take a couple sandwiches, Em. Whatever kind you got is all right. Except tuna. Did Sofia leave? I need to pay her."

"I took care of it before she left." She kissed the top of his head and then turned to Jeremiah. "You hungry?"

"I won't turn down a sandwich, and I'll take whatever you make for Kenny. I'm not picky." He patted his stomach.

"The girls are in their room pretending it's a recording studio. They're making Kevin be the engineer, or whatever it's called." She waved a hand as she left. "Be right back."

"Could we add a bit more kick to the chorus?" Jeremiah asked as they resumed working.

"Yes, and I want to bi-amp this guitar track. It's a little thin." Kenny took a few minutes to make the adjustments. "That sounds better. Let's move on to track three."

Emmy brought sandwiches, chips and cold beverages a few minutes later.

"How long are you going to work?"

"I promised Mia I would stop no later than midnight," Jeremiah answered.

"Good! I need someone to cuddle with." Emmy grinned as she left the room.

Kenny repeated the same routine on Thursday. He worked in Steward Music Group's Studio Four during the day with the guys from Fridays At Five, drove like Emmy to get home to work on the BearFace CD with Jeremiah and struggled up to bed just after midnight.

"Are you guys almost finished?" Emmy scooted over to her side of the bed. "Put your arm around me. I'm cold."

245

Kenny slipped into bed and cuddled against her. "Two tracks to finish tomorrow, and then one final listen."

"Oooh! Your feet are freezing. Don't let them touch me."

"You could wear flannel pajamas." Kenny moved his feet away but scooted closer. "Do you still have any pj's with feet?"

"No, I threw them all away when we got married, but I might buy some new ones."

"We could always turn the furnace up higher than sixty-five," he suggested.

"Our gas bill is already more than the rest of the city put together." Emmy exaggerated a bit.

"This house was built to be green and efficient. Our gas bill isn't much higher than at my parents' house, and we have the guesthouse." He moved her hair so he could kiss and nibble on her ear. "Speaking of the guesthouse, have you talked to Dany lately? I haven't seen her other than on Sundays."

Emmy turned to face Kenny and kissed him for a moment. "She came over for dinner tonight, but you were busy, so I didn't bother you."

"Does she still like living there, here, whatever?"

"She loves the guesthouse. She bought a few things to decorate it."

"Are we going to do what we did when Cam and Lindsey lived there?"

"If you mean putting her rent into an account and then giving it back, then yes. I would like to do that. Do you mind?"

"Not at all," he said and then kissed her throat. "I thought you wanted her to live here forever. Did you change your mind?"

"No, but she might want to get married someday. She told me she wants five kids."

"Would you kick her out if she gets married?"

Emmy grinned as Kenny moved a hand. "She could still live in the guesthouse. Cam and Lindsey did."

Kenny kissed Emmy until he needed to stop for a breath. "Cam told me Lindsey wants to either remodel their kitchen, or find a bigger house."

"They could add a second story like that house on Canton

246

Lane down from the church. That would double their room. They like the neighborhood and it's close to church and school." Emmy wrapped her arms around Kenny and kissed him back.

"Do you think they will ever leave Jamie McGee Junior High? They could teach at the church's school." Kenny let his hands warm up on Emmy's belly.

"They won't do that. The church can't offer the same salary."

"Is Dany still dating Darian?" Kenny's hands were now warm.

"Yes, and she let it slip that he kissed her. You should have heard the girls. They giggled and made kissing noises." Emmy moved his hands again. "Dany said they're not getting serious, but she does like him."

"Do we need to start worrying about them? They're seven now."

"We still have a few years before they reach puberty."

Kenny kissed her neck. "I remember one seven-year-old who showed an interest in boys."

"I was only interested in one boy and that was because he liked to play football." Emmy's eyes sparkled. "I might have to throw a flag for illegal use of hands."

"Did Dany talk about her job?" His hands continued to flirt with a holding call.

"She likes her job. She gets to do a lot more than I did at Coventry. Of course, Dany is older and already has a master's degree."

Kenny grinned. "Are we going to keep talking all night, or are you..."

"Shut up and kiss me. I have to get up early."

By nine o'clock Friday night, Kenny finished the mix on the final track. He removed his headphones and leaned back. "Let's take a break and then listen to the whole CD. I'll see if Em is busy. She has a good ear."

Emmy joined them in the control room after getting the kids in bed. "What's up? Are you finished?"

247

Kenny put an arm around Emmy's waist. "Did the girls fuss about going to bed?"

"They want to stay up later on Friday nights because they don't have to get up on Saturday morning. What do you think?"

"They could stay up until ten, but no later than that." He smiled at her and thought about last night. "Do you have time to listen?"

"Yes, but can I make suggestions, or is it too late for that?"

"You can offer constructive comments, but I'll probably ignore you," Kenny teased.

They listened to the full CD twice.

"Well? What do you think, Em?"

Emmy put a finger to her mouth and tilted her head. "Could I hear the second song again? What's it called?"

"'Brothers,'" Jeremiah answered.

Kenny played the track again.

"Stop it right there!" Emmy pointed at the board.

Kenny paused it.

"What are you saying, singing? I can't make out that word."

"The line is 'we always hurt each other and I've had enough,'" Jeremiah said. "I know I mumble it. Should we fix it?"

Emmy shook her head. "Nope! People don't care about the words in a rock song. They only care how it sounds." She stood up. "Sounds like a hit CD. I might even buy a copy if you promise to autograph it for me. Of course, I could always download it and not have to buy the physical CD." She laughed. "I'm going upstairs. See you on Sunday, Jeremiah."

Chapter Twenty-Six

"Mom! Someone needs to talk to you. They said it's important." Ten-year-old Carson shouted from the family room Saturday morning.

"You don't need to yell." Diane took the phone from him, and he resumed his video game. "This is Diane Robertson."

"I'm sorry to bother you this early, but I'm sorry to inform you that Betty Rochon passed away last night. Are you Diane Colasanti? Do I have the right number?"

"Yes, I'm remarried now. If you check Aunt Betty's file, it has specific instructions about which funeral home to call."

"Yes, ma'am. We've called them. Betty passed away sometime before midnight, but we didn't want to call that late."

"That's quite all right. Did Betty have any personal items? I know we got rid of most everything after Uncle Clifford died."

"Nothing to speak of. Her clothes."

"Give them to Goodwill, or some charity group. If you find anything else, please put it aside. I'll stop by tomorrow or Monday."

"Thank you, and I'm sorry for your loss," the voice on the other end said monotonously.

Diane hung up and waited for some tears. They didn't materialize.

"Who was that?" Brady asked.

"The nursing home in Florida. Betty passed away last night," Diane answered.

Brady held out his arms. "I'm sorry."

Diane let him hug her. "I don't mean to sound hard, but it's for the best. She couldn't function anymore. She couldn't get out of bed. She had to wear a diaper. Ugh! I hope that never happens to me. Please don't keep me alive using machines."

"Do you need to fly down there?"

"I really should."

Brady rubbed his forehead. "I'll call and get Dad's plane ready for tomorrow. Unless you want to go today. Do you?"

"Tomorrow will be soon enough. I should call Emmy."

"Are you going to call her, or should you tell her in person?" Brady wondered.

"I'd tell her in person if it was Mom."

"I should hope so."

Diane dialed Emmy's landline.

Emmy answered on the fourth ring. "What is it, Diane? The kids are running around and causing chaos as usual. I'm watching Ben and Taylor in addition to my bunch."

"Can you hear me, Em? It's important."

"Hang on a sec." Emmy put the phone on the kitchen counter and whistled. The kids froze in place.

Kevin covered his ears. "Mom! That hurts my ears."

"I need to talk to Aunt Diane, so you guys scram." Emmy pointed toward the stairs and the kids sprinted away. "Okay, what's up?"

"I just got a call from the nursing home. Aunt Betty passed away last night. I'm going to fly down to Florida." Diane paused then asked, "Em, are you all right? Are you crying?"

Emmy sniffled and wiped her nose with her sleeve. "Yes."

"Oh, Emmy. I'm sorry. I didn't know you would take it so hard. We've known Betty would go soon."

"Doesn't make it any easier. I know she didn't know any of us anymore, but she was still our aunt."

"Do you want me to come over? I can if you want."

"No, I'll be okay. Is she going to be cremated like Uncle Clifford?"

"Yes. She's already at the funeral home. I'm going to call them next. I'll fly down tomorrow and take care of whatever. She never had any kids, so Mom is her only living relative, and since I'm in charge of Mom's stuff, I get to take care of Betty's too."

"Do you want me to go with you?"

"No need. There won't be any service like with Clifford. I'll take care of everything. You won't have to miss church, or the Super Bowl. I know how much that means to you."

"I could watch the Super Bowl in Florida."

"Don't worry. I'll handle it."

"Do you ever wonder if we'll turn out like Mom and Aunt

250

Betty?" Emmy asked and then bit her lip.

"Can't control the future, but if I ever get that bad, you have to promise to shoot me."

"I can't do that. Only God can take a life," Emmy replied.

Diane rolled her eyes. "I'm kidding, you goof. I'll have Brady do it."

"Not funny, Diane."

"I'll talk to you later. Gotta go."

Diane looked in her address book and called the funeral home. She went over the necessary details and assured them they would be paid the next day.

"Everything has been prepaid," the funeral director said.

"Do I need to sign any papers?"

He checked the file. "No, everything is in order. Should we proceed as planned?"

"Yes, and I will be there tomorrow around noon."

Emmy called Diane back a few minutes later. "Why didn't Aunt Betty want a memorial service? I think we should do something? We had a beautiful service for Grandma Isabel. We could do something for Betty and Clifford."

"Isabel had a lot of friends who would have been upset if we didn't. Betty has been sick for a long time, Em. She didn't have any friends left. That sounds harsh, but it's the reality of the situation. Why should we have a service when you and I would be the only people there?"

"I suppose you're right." Emmy sighed and said, "I'm glad we have kids. Someone should be left to attend our funerals."

Diane shook her head. "You're sick, Em. I'll talk to you later."

"You could come to church tonight, since you won't be here tomorrow. You haven't been to church for a while."

"I went last month, and I'm not coming tonight. Brady and I are having dinner with some client from the government."

Later that evening Emmy glanced out at the sanctuary from her position on the platform. "Liz, why are we even here? There can't be more than fifty people out there. It feels like a waste of time."

251

"Some of these people might have to work on Sundays," Liz said.

"Maybe, but some of them come on Saturday just to free up their Sundays. They could be here in the morning."

"You can't say anything, but I think the board is going to consider dropping the Saturday night service."

"I don't mean to be so negative, but I hope they do."

Brady drove Diane to the SoHam airport on Sunday morning. He grabbed her travel bag from the backseat. "Do you need anything else?"

"I'm fine, Brady. You don't need to worry about me. I'll take care of whatever needs done and fly home tomorrow. Please thank your father for letting me use his jet."

"This is why he keeps it around."

"When are they leaving on vacation?"

"Wednesday, but they don't need the jet. They're flying to London, but taking the train the rest of the time. Dad wants to see everything he can because he isn't sure if he will ever leave the country again. Things are getting crazy over there."

Diane kissed Brady and walked over to the waiting Gulfstream III. She waved goodbye and stepped inside.

"Are you nervous, Regina?" Emmy asked as they walked out onto the platform of Crest Ridge United Nazarene for the second service.

"Not nearly as nervous as for the first service. I survived that, so how bad can this one be?" She shrugged as she laughed.

"You'll be fine. I remember the first time Chase made me lead the service. I about... fainted."

"You were going to say something else, weren't you?" Regina laughed.

"Yeah, but I shouldn't talk about it in church."

"If you ladies are ready, may we start the service?" Chase asked.

Emmy made a face at him. "We're ready if you are."

The worship team finished their part of the service and left the platform.

252

Emmy grinned at Regina. "You are a natural. You should take the position if they offer you a big raise from what they pay Chase."

"I heard that, Emmy," Chase said.

Regina fanned her face with her hand. "Lord a'mighty! I thought I would pass out. How do you do this all the time, Emmy?"

"She is finely attuned to the leading of the Holy Spirit," Chase said. "That, plus the fact she is too crazy to be scared."

"Don't listen to Chase. He's only partly right." Emmy grinned and walked into the ladies' room behind Regina.

The Gulfstream III landed in Tampa, and Diane was met by a Cadillac Escalade.

"How was your flight, Mrs. Robertson? Uneventful, I hope." The driver opened the door for her. "I'm Rosco Sandchek."

"Thank you for picking me up, Rosco. I could get used to traveling like this," Diane said. "Did my husband, or my father-in-law set this up?"

"I know Brady and Bennett, but I used to work for their father. I'm retired now, but I pick up some spending money on the side. I love to drive. Please, don't tell my wife. She thinks I'm playing golf all the time."

"I won't rat you out, Rosco." Diane noticed a small bulge under the otherwise-perfectly-tailored black suit.

"Would you like to check in at the hotel first?"

"Yes, please."

Rosco drove to the Marriott Lakeland Resort, parked, grabbed Diane's small travel bag and escorted her inside.

"I believe I have a reservation. I'm Diane Robertson."

The clerk snapped to attention. "Yes, Mrs. Robertson. If you would please sign here, I'll have someone take your luggage."

Diane signed and was handed a key card.

"You are in the Ambassador Suite on the fifth floor. There is an elevator right there. If you need anything at all, please dial four, and you will be connected directly to the concierge."

"I suppose Mr. Robertson upgraded me to a suite, huh?" She looked at Rosco, who nodded almost imperceptibly.

"I will escort Mrs. Robertson to her suite," Rosco said.

"Yes, sir," the clerk nodded.

Rosco escorted Diane to the suite, opened the door for her and out-of-habit entered first. Diane followed. She smiled as Rosco checked every room.

"I will be nearby. This is my card with my cell number. Call me if you want to go anywhere. I am at your service."

"Something tells me that it would be an insult to offer you a tip." Diane put a finger to her mouth. "Exactly what did you do for Mr. Robertson? May I ask?" *You're not a huge man, so you don't look like a typical bodyguard, but yet you move with the grace and agility of a much younger man.*

Rosco smiled. "I worked as his head of security. I often accompanied him on his travels. In fact Teresa and I are planning a vacation. We are leaving on Wednesday."

"Is Teresa your wife?"

"She is," Rosco beamed.

"Why is it I've never met you, or even heard your name?"

"That's because I'm very, very good at what I do."

Diane stared into his eyes. "Am I this protected all the time? Is Emmy?"

"No, ma'am, but sometimes you might be accompanied by an extremely capable couple. For instance when your sister travels there might be someone providing a bit of extra security."

"But if I mention this to anyone, you would have to kill me, right?" Diane grinned.

"That would be defeating the purpose. Call me when you are ready to travel, please." Rosco left and made sure the door closed securely.

Diane looked around the luxurious suite and walked out onto the balcony. *Emmy would freak if she knew about Rosco. This is one instance where it is better if I keep a secret from her.*

Later, Rosco drove Diane to the funeral home and escorted her inside.

"I'll wait in the hall, Mrs. Robertson."

"Rosco, would you please call me Diane? I'd feel better."

"Yes, Mrs. Diane."

Thirty minutes later Diane walked out into the bright sunshine carrying a silver-colored urn.

"I'm taking Betty home," she said as Rosco opened the door. "I'm going to spread her ashes over Grandma Isabel's grave."

"Is that legal?" Rosco stared at the urn.

"Don't know. Don't care."

Rosco grinned and showed off his gleaming white teeth. "I like your style, Mrs. Diane."

"I'll settle for that," Diane said as she laughed.

"Thank you for the ride, Rosco. I hope you and your wife enjoy your vacation," Diane said Monday morning as Rosco drove her to the airport.

"I'm looking forward to an enjoyable trip," he answered.

By that you mean an uneventful trip, I presume. Diane boarded the Gulfstream and returned home. Brady was waiting at the SoHam airport for her.

"Did you have a good trip, Diane?"

"I did. Your father saw to that. Do you know Rosco Sandchek?"

"Name doesn't ring a bell. Why?"

"You sure?"

Brady didn't bat an eye.

"Don't you dare lie to me." Diane stood her ground.

Brady glanced around. "He uses different names. Rosco whatever is a new one."

"He looks like a regular guy, but then I suppose he is supposed to. It wouldn't make sense if he looked like some big wrestler dude."

"It helps."

They got in the car, and Brady headed home.

Diane looked out the window before holding out the urn to get Brady's attention and blurting out. "I want to be cremated."

Brady nearly drove off the road.

"Not now, silly. When I die. I want to be cremated and scattered somewhere. I don't know where, but I'll let you know."

"Before you go, right?"

255

"Yes."

Brady shook his head. "No way! I want to be buried next to you."

"What difference does it make? You'll probably die before me."

"Why are we talking about this?"

"Because of Betty. What if I end up like her. I want to make sure everything is planned out, and paid for, ahead of time."

"Could we discuss this at a later date? Say, in thirty years?"

"Fine! I'll add it to my will or something."

Diane dropped the kids off at school Tuesday and stopped at Emmy's house on the way back to Bristol Ridge. She walked into the house and saw Emmy in the kitchen.

"You need to come with me," Diane insisted.

"Where? Why? I'm going downstairs to work on my CD. I can't leave." Emmy backed up as Diane tried to grab her.

"We're going to Rose Hill."

"The cemetery? Why?" Emmy checked the calendar. "This isn't the day Daddy died. Why are we going there today?"

"You'll see. This won't take long, but you're coming with me."

"All right, but you owe me."

Emmy got in Diane's van and noticed the silver urn on the seat. "What's this?"

"Who."

"What?"

"You should ask 'who is this?'"

Emmy stared at the urn. "Is this who I think it is?" She tried to hand the urn to Diane. "You take it."

"I can't hold it and drive. You have to hold Aunt Betty. Now buckle up and hush."

Emmy held the urn away from her body with both hands while staring at it. "What are we supposed to do with Aunt Betty?"

"You'll see."

Emmy held onto the urn until they arrived at Rose Hill. "You can hold her now." Emmy thrust the urn at Diane as soon as

256

she put the van into park.

Diane wasn't expecting that move and Aunt Betty fell to the floor of the van.

"Emmy!"

"Diane!"

They screamed at each other without looking down.

"Did it open? Is Aunt Betty scattered in your van?" Emmy bit her lip.

"I hope not." Diane continued to stare directly at Emmy.

"Should we look?" Emmy asked.

"Yes," Diane said.

"You look first," Emmy insisted.

"We'll look together on the count of three."

"You count."

Diane counted but they continued to stare at each other.

"One of us is going to have to look sooner or later," Diane said.

Emmy shook her head. "I can be more stubborn than you. Always could." She crossed her arms over her chest.

"Fine! I'll look." Diane slowly looked to the floor and then sighed. "It's okay. Betty is still inside."

Diane picked up the urn, and they got out of the van.

"Where are we going?" Emmy bit her lip as she glanced around.

Diane rolled her eyes. "I thought we would scatter Betty on the first grave we come to."

Emmy looked around and realized where they were. "Oh, you want to scatter her by Grandma," Emmy said nonchalantly as they kept walking. Then she froze and put a hand to her mouth. "You really want to scatter Aunt Betty on top of Grandma!?"

"Sure! Why not?"

"Is that legal? Will we be arrested if we get caught?"

"Don't know, but if we make it quick, we won't get caught."

Emmy's concerned expression slowly turned into a grin. "Let's do it. She's already cremated, and I don't want that urn thing in my house."

They hurried to Grandma Isabel's grave.

"Hurry, Diane! Open it before someone sees us." Emmy danced around while looking for someone watching them.

Diane sighed. "Will you hold still. You look like you have to pee."

"Open it."

"I'm trying, but it's like stuck. Help me."

Emmy pulled on the top and was just able to jump back as the top flew over her head and part of Aunt Betty escaped.

"Crap!" Emmy swore.

"Double crap!" Diane swore back.

"Should we say something?" Emmy picked up the top and handed it to Diane.

"You hold it. I'll... I'll spread Betty around."

"Sorry, Grandma," Emmy said.

Diane carefully spread Aunt Betty over the grave. "Okay, it's done. Let's get the heck out of here."

They ran back to the van, which attracted the attention of several people gathered for an early morning graveside service. Diane jumped into the van and started it.

"Let me in!" Emmy pounded on the passenger glass.

"Sorry, Em." Diane unlocked the door.

"Let's go home. I need to shower because I think I have some of Aunt Betty in my hair."

Chapter Twenty-Seven

"Emmy, why are you crying? Don't you like the songs we chose?" Regina Collins tried to dry Emmy's tears.

Emmy sniffled and then looked up at Robby and Regina. "I'm sorry for bawling like a baby, but this is the last rehearsal we'll ever have with Chase and Yvonne. I'm going to miss them. They've always been here with me."

"Oh, honey! We're all going to miss them." Regina smothered Emmy to her chest.

"Are we ready to go over these songs?" Chase walked into the music suite.

"Give us a moment, please," Regina said over her shoulder.

Chase stopped walking and looked at Emmy. *Should I pretend this is just another rehearsal? Or should I get this over with now?* He decided by opening his arms and reaching out.

"I'm sorry, Chase. I tried not to cry, but you know me." Emmy allowed Chase to hug her.

"Yes, I most certainly do."

The rest of the team gathered around. Robby touched Chase on the shoulder and Regina put an arm around Yvonne.

"You can speak for all of us, Robby," Cam said.

Chase let go of Emmy, but she stayed at his side.

"Some of us have only known you for a short time while others have known you for many years, but I think we all feel the same. We're really going to miss you. We'll miss your dedication. Your professionalism. Your deep spirituality."

"Your ability to deal with Emmy every week," Bobby O'Connor teased.

"That is a real gift from God," Chase said.

"I'm not a diva."

The guys responded by coughing.

Chase waited until everyone stopped. "Yvonne and I deeply appreciate the opportunity we've had over the years. We've seen this church grow, and then shrink, and then grow way beyond our wildest hopes. It's been a pleasure to work with a great bunch of singers and musicians."

Emmy frowned. "Singers are musicians, too."

"Some are better than others," Steve Van Zant said to Emmy. He thought about some of the other singers from years past. "Some are definitely more talented than others."

"We are fortunate to have this facility and the gear. We're going back to the stone age in Toledo," Chase said. "But that's where God wants us."

"Let's form a circle around Chase and Yvonne and lay hands on them and pray," Robby suggested. "I'll start and if you feel led, go ahead and pray out loud, and then I'll close."

Chase smiled at Yvonne. *I believe we're leaving the worship team in very capable hands.*

The team prayed for ten minutes.

"All right! Now that we have that out of the way, let's go over the songs for Sunday," Chase said in his business-like voice.

Emmy grinned at him. "You may get away with acting like this is no big deal tonight, but I bet you cry on Sunday."

Chase shook his head. "Never happen, Emmy. I don't get emotional."

Chase tried bravely but lost the bet as the team sang their final song under his leadership. He made the mistake of looking at Emmy who was bawling like a baby.

Kenny nudged Steve Van Zant. "Looks like Emmy was right."

Steve stopped playing. "I've known Chase for twenty years at least. I've never seen him lose it before."

Emmy signaled the band to keep playing. Regina and Liz kept singing the chorus to *How Great Is Our God* as Emmy walked over to Chase.

"Looks like you won the bet, Emmy." Chase tried to keep playing.

"I know. I cheated. I made sure you saw me crying. I'm a real stinker." Emmy took his hands and pulled him to the center of the platform.

The entire congregation stood to their feet. Even Birdie Tibbets, who was close to a hundred years old, managed to stand with a little help. Pastor Tyler dashed onto the platform and hugged Chase. Emmy motioned for Yvonne, who was sitting in the second row instead of her usual place in the tech booth balcony, to come up to the platform. When Yvonne shook her head, Emmy ran down the steps and pulled Yvonne back to the platform with her.

"You shouldn't make me do this," Yvonne pleaded.

"Too bad," Emmy said as she grinned.

Pastor Tyler waved his hands and tried to get the congregation to stop clapping but without any luck.

"Should I whistle?" Emmy asked Tyler.

He shook his head. "I've heard you whistle. You might scare everyone." Tyler finally managed to get everyone to sit down. "We will have plenty of chances to thank Chase and Yvonne later."

That was as far as he got.

Doris Smith rose to her feet. "I would like to say something if I may."

Tyler nodded. "You may."

"Ron and I have been members of this church from the beginning..." She began.

Liz grabbed her wireless mic and hurried down the steps and over to the spot where Ron and Doris always sat.

"You should use this, Auntie Dorie, so everyone can hear you." Liz handed Doris the mic.

"I don't know how to use this, honey." She looked at the microphone as if it were alive and might attack her.

Liz grinned and said, "You hold it up and talk into it. It won't bite you."

"Thank you, sweetie." Doris tried to remember where she left off but couldn't, so she started again.

Doris stopped and one of the other ladies stood up. Darren reacted to the situation by taking the microphone from Doris and rushing it over to Naomi.

Tyler smiled on the platform.

Emmy moved closer to him. "Is your mic on?"

"I turned it off for now. Why?" Tyler answered.

"I bet you don't get to preach today."

261

Tyler whispered to Emmy, "I'm going to preach even if it's only for fifteen minutes."

Fifteen minutes later, Emmy looked up at Tyler again. "Fifteen minutes, huh? Remember there is a potluck today. You might have a riot on your hands if you preach too long."

"Five minutes maybe."

Darren looked around. "Anyone else like to say something about Chase and Yvonne?"

Emmy moved closer to Kenny. "Should I say something? Tyler still wants to preach."

"Your call, Em."

She closed her eyes for a second as she bit her lip. She moved back to stand next to Chase and Yvonne and looked up at Bruce Sutherland in the tech booth. He immediately unmuted her mic. "If it's all right with Pastor Tyler, I would like to say something."

Tyler chuckled. "Go ahead, Emmy."

"I'll be brief, but I need to say something. When I first accepted Jesus as my savior, I came back to this church. I talked to Lynette and Paul and this became my church home. My family. Lynette convinced me to try out for the worship team, so I did. I was so scared, but Chase made me feel like I belonged. He even encouraged me. He didn't tell me I couldn't dance around." She paused and looked up at Tyler. "Do I have to stop dancing now?"

You are something else, Emmy. Tyler put a hand to his face to keep from laughing and then shook his head. "You may do whatever the Holy Spirit tells you."

"Thank you. I will. I have been so blessed during my years working with Chase. I will probably cry later, but for now, I won't. I just want to say thank you for all your support over the years, and for putting up with me when I do something stupid."

"When have you ever done anything stupid, Emmy?" Chase whispered. "Goofy maybe, but never stupid."

"That's all I have to say."

The worship team left the platform and Pastor Darren took over. By the time the offering was collected, Tyler had ten minutes left. He prayed like he did every week, and then looked at his

262

tablet and sighed. "I think I'll save this for next week." He talked about Chase for a time and thanked him for the opportunity to work together. "It's been a custom of this church to present a parting gift to staff members. Jim, do you have something to say?"

Jim Rosek walked onto the platform. "All righty then." He smiled and glanced at the screens behind him. "I need Chase and Yvonne to come up here." He waved at them. "Come on! People are getting hungry." He waited a moment. "In the past, we've given away vans and stuff. We even named the building for someone. When the board met to decide what to give Chase and Yvonne, we struggled. What can I say?" He smiled and shrugged his wide shoulders. "You have two fairly new vehicles and two daughters who are driving, or learning how to drive, so a new car didn't seem appropriate." He waited until the laughter subsided. "We don't have any other buildings to name other than the old garage, and we might have to replace that pretty soon." He pointed. "I'm not sure who first suggested this, but the board decided this would be appropriate." He looked up at the screens again. A picture of a house appeared. "We know you are selling your place here in SoHam, or you've already sold it, I guess. But you needed a place in Toledo, and I think this is the one you liked. Am I right?" He looked at Chase, who nodded. "Good! We didn't make a mistake. Anyone who has ever served on the board here knows that being a preacher is not the way to get rich. Worship leaders won't ever get rich either."

Liz walked out onto the platform with a large bouquet of red roses. She stood next to Tyler and noticed Emmy and Kenny ducking out of the sanctuary. *You stinker! Get back in here so I can get after you.*

Jim Rosek continued, "We learned from Heidi Knapp, who is your real estate agent, by the way, that this house was at the very upper limits of your budget, but you guys loved it. Well, now, I live in a decent enough house and it's paid for. I don't owe the bank a dime. Of course, we all know about real estate taxes here in Illinois, but anyway." He waited again. "I can't tell you who, but someone made a unanimous, I mean anonymous donation to provide a large down payment for the house."

263

Liz nudged Tyler. "You know who, right?"

He nodded.

Liz mouthed the names Emmy and Kenny.

Tyler nodded again.

"Wait til I see her again." Liz smiled.

Liz walked over to Yvonne and handed her the roses.

The congregation rose to their feet again. This time Tyler was able to get them to stop after a minute. "Let me pray, so you can go eat. There are photos in the large gym and tons of food." Tyler prayed and then dismissed everyone.

Liz hurried out of the sanctuary and searched for Emmy. She finally found her with the kids in Noah's Ark. "You are a real stinker!" Liz hurried over and hugged Emmy with all her might.

Dany laughed as she tapped Liz on the shoulder. "Liz! You have to let go. Emmy is turning blue."

Liz released Emmy.

Emmy took a deep breath. "Why am I a stinker?"

"You know why," Liz grinned and picked up little Scarlett.

Emmy bit her lip.

"You and Kenny are so generous. You are charging Dany a fraction of what you should, and now this."

"Please don't say anything," Emmy pleaded. *Boy! Are you and Tyler going to be surprised when you get your mortgage statement.*

"I won't tell a soul and neither will Dany."

"Tell anyone what?" Dany asked.

"Exactly!" Liz hugged Emmy again. "Let's go eat. I want to see the old photos of Chase and Yvonne. I've heard rumors he once had hair down to his shoulders."

The church board met the following evening. They moved through the reports and Tyler brought up old business.

He looked at the notes on his tablet. "I'm not sure if this is old or new business, but we need to discuss the Saturday night service."

"The attendance has dropped to practically nothing," one board member said. "There were fifty-four people last Saturday."

Another one replied, "There are some people who work on Sunday. Where will they go? We don't want to chase them away."

The discussion continued for fifteen minutes until Tyler sensed the board had reached a decision. "Do we have a motion?"

Jim Rosek made the motion and William Griffith seconded it.

"Any more discussion," Tyler waited. "All in favor of discontinuing the Saturday service raise your hand."

Everyone raised a hand.

"All opposed, raise a hand."

Not a hand was raised.

Tyler chuckled. "I'll never get over how you agree to disagree. You talk about stuff and have differing opinions, but when you vote, you all come together. It's amazing."

After more discussion, the new times for the Sunday services were voted on and approved.

"Let's get through the rest of the agenda as quickly as we can, so we have time to interview Jake and Maddy."

Ten minutes later, Tyler left the conference room to get Jake and Maddy Boyter. He introduced them and gave a short summary about them.

"I'll let Jake tell you more, and Maddy can share her testimony, also. Then I'll open it up to questions."

"Thank you, Pastor Tyler. I'm Jake Boyter and this is Madalyn, or Maddy, as most people call her. I graduated from Mount Vernon Nazarene University..."

"I'm Maddy, and I grew up in Kankakee. I graduated from Olivet..."

Jake and Maddy shared their stories and shared their passion for the youth of the church. Then the board asked questions for fifteen minutes.

"Are you really twenty-five?" Lenore Toth grinned. "If not for your mustache, I would think you were still a teenager."

"I get that a lot," Jake said with an infectious smile. "I use it to my advantage with the teens."

"Any more questions?" Tyler looked at the board members. "If not I want to thank Jake and Maddy for their time. They are crashing with us tonight so they don't have to drive back to Merionville this late at night."

Jake and Maddy left the room. Tyler gave each board member a chance to share their thoughts. Everyone expressed positive opinions about the twenty-five-year-old couple.

"Do you have any other candidates in mind?" Roger Goldman, the chairperson for the finance action team, asked.

"Not really," Tyler said as he chuckled.

Roger smiled. "Good, because I really like this couple. We know what happens when we hire young couples."

"We need to do something before we lose the youth we have," Dylan Michaelis mentioned. "Dahlia told me some of the kids have stopped coming because we don't have a youth pastor. No offense to Tyler and Darren, but they have other duties. Jonah has tried to fill in, but... We need a youth pastor."

The board quickly reached a decision.

"Should we put together a compensation package?" Tyler asked and then looked at Roger. "Are you ready to discuss that?"

Roger nodded. "I have spoken to Ron Smith, who by the way has expressed a desire to be relieved of his duties as church treasurer. He suggested we ask May Burns, who has been the assistant for several years, to take over. Anyway, this is what Ron and I suggest."

"That's quite a lot less than we paid Chase," Bob Cartwright mentioned a moment later.

"It's in line with other youth pastors with the same experience," Roger explained.

The board passed a motion to offer the position to Jake.

"I will pass along this offer... tonight, since they will be at our house," Tyler said.

The meeting adjourned and Roger Goldman, Dylan Michaelis, William Griffith and Jim Rosek stayed behind.

"We are in sound shape financially. The church has no mortgage. The school is close to paying for itself. We have the housing available now that Tyler and Liz have a place."

"Are we going to search for a new worship pastor?" Jim asked.

"Not at the moment. Chase suggested we give Robby and Regina a chance first. I think she did a wonderful job the Sunday before last," Roger mentioned.

"I agree," William said. "We already have people on the worship team who can take over for the present time. The youth situation is more critical."

Tyler returned home and presented the offer to Jake and Maddy.

"That is a generous offer. We will pray about it and let you know as soon as we know."

Jake called Tyler the next evening.

"Have you reached a decision already?" Tyler chuckled.

"We have. We would like to accept the position."

"That's great. Do you want to see the house first?"

"I don't think that will be necessary. From what you described, it sounds a lot better than our cramped apartment in Merionville."

"It's a great place for a couple without kids. Once our kids came along, the house shrunk."

"I think this is the right position for us even if there wasn't a house," Jake added.

"The board will want to know how soon you can be here," Tyler said.

Jake adjusted his glasses and looked to Maddy for an answer. She smiled and held up two fingers.

Jake nodded. "I would like to give our current church a two-week notice. They've known we would be leaving for three months, but I still have to give them an official notice."

"Sounds fair." Tyler checked the calendar in the church office. "We start our new schedule on the first Sunday in March. That would be the third. We could make that your first Sunday. You could move in anytime before then."

"I'll talk to Maddy, but that sounds like a good idea."

"Welcome to Crest Ridge United Nazarene, Jake."

Chapter Twenty-Eight

"Regina, are you okay? Why are you pacing in the bathroom?" Emmy walked into the ladies' room before the start of the first service.

Regina held a white handkerchief in front of her face as she shook her head. "I can't do this, Emmy. I just can't. You have to take over. You need to be in charge of the worship team. I think I'm going to be sick."

Emmy walked up to Regina and held her hands to make her stop pacing. "You won't puke on me, will you? This is a new dress."

"I'll try not to." Regina closed her eyes. "I thought I could do this, but I can't. It's one thing to fill-in for a Sunday, but this is different."

Emmy squeezed Regina's hands. "I remember the first time I had to lead worship. Have I told you this story before?"

"I don't know. Maybe."

"Doesn't matter. I'll tell you again. I hadn't been with the worship team very long, but for some reason Chase thought I could lead the worship service. I memorized this verse in Philippians."

"I know which one you mean."

"Let's take a few minutes to pray together," Emmy suggested.

They held hands and both of them prayed out loud.

"Do you feel better now?" Emmy asked.

"I'm still as nervous as a long-tailed cat in a room full of rocking chairs." Regina waved a hand in front of her face.

Emmy stared at her. "Where did you hear that? My mother-in-law uses that expression."

"It's an old saying that I probably first heard from my grandmother. Thank you for praying with me. I'm still scared, but I know I'll make it through because I won't be relying on my strength but His."

"Good! And thank you for not throwing up on my new dress," Emmy said as she grinned.

Pastor Tyler dismissed the congregation after the second

268

service and Emmy walked over to Regina. "See! You made it through both services, and you didn't puke. You didn't throw up, did you?"

Regina's dreadlocks shook as she laughed. "No, I didn't, but I came close."

"You have to remember to rely on His strength and not your own. That's sometimes hard to do. We think it's us doing stuff and forget that we couldn't even breathe without His help."

"I'll try to remember, Emmy."

"Hey! Are you and Robby going to that service at Olivet tonight?"

"Yes, we're riding on the bus. Are you going?"

"We hadn't planned on it, but Liz told me it's usually really good. She used to go when she was still at Olivet."

"You should go. I think there might be a few seats left on the bus if you don't want to drive," Regina said. "They have a huge chorus and a band from the college. It's pretty amazing."

"I'll talk to Kenny. Who's in charge of the bus?"

"Pastor Darren, I think. You should talk to him before you leave," Regina suggested.

"Maybe we'll see you this evening." Emmy weaved her way through the crowd and spotted Darren talking with some teens. She walked up behind him and waited until he finished his conversation.

He turned suddenly and almost ran over her. "Hi, Emmy. Did you need to talk to me?"

"If Kenny and I wanted to ride the bus, is there still room?"

"There is! We added a second bus and still have about a dozen seats left. Should I pencil you in for two seats?"

She held up a finger. "Hold on a second. I see Kenny. I'll ask him and get right back to you." She scurried over to Kenny and asked him. He nodded his head. She dashed back toward Darren and held up two fingers. "We'll take two seats. How much are they?"

Darren grinned. "For you they're twenty bucks, but Kenny can ride for free."

"You're teasing me."

269

"The church is paying for the buses, and the service is free, but they take up an offering."

Emmy edged forward to avoid some teenage boys and bumped against Darren. He put his hands on her shoulders to steady her.

"Sorry, Darren." She looked up and bit her tongue.

"No problem. The buses are leaving at four thirty. The service starts at six." He looked into her eyes and let go of her. "Let me know if you're running late."

"Thanks, Darren. We'll be here on time."

Later, Emmy walked into the auditorium at Centennial Chapel in front of Liz and Dany. She stopped suddenly and Liz bumped into her.

"This place is awesome." Emmy glanced around.

"Haven't you ever been here before?" Liz asked.

"No, never."

Dany waved at some friends. "Not even for a concert?"

Emmy shook her heard. "I bet the acoustics are amazing. I'd love to hear someone play here someday."

Dany grinned, "I meant haven't you ever played a show here."

"Who me?" Emmy shook her head. "They probably have big stars playing here."

"You should have your manager, or whoever does your booking, arrange for you to do a show here. You'd sell out the place for sure," Dany suggested.

"Why did Kenny stay home?" Liz wondered.

"He claimed he wasn't feeling well, but I think it might have been a case of him not wanting to be recognized. He thinks it causes a disturbance if people recognize him."

"I can't imagine what it would be like to not be able to go somewhere because people might mob you." Dany waved at some more people she knew. "Save me a seat. I have to talk to my friends."

Emmy followed Liz toward the front where most of the other people from church were sitting. They saved a seat for Dany, who joined them a few minutes later. Dr. Schofield opened the

270

service and everyone stood.

"Wow! I've never seen that many people in a choir," Emmy grinned.

The music continued for over twenty minutes.

"They were really good," Emmy whispered to Liz. "Maybe we should start a choir."

The service ended and Emmy checked the time. "That was a fast two hours."

Liz agreed. "Dr. Schofield is an amazing speaker."

Dany rolled her eyes. "You two are carrying on like your church is full of old people who frown all the time. Your services are just as good. Tyler is getting better all the time. You just don't have a big choir."

"Emmy, you can't compare this service to any other church. You have to remember that this is a service for all the churches on the Chicago Central District," Liz said.

"I guess I'm not used to coming to these Nazarene district meetings."

After visiting for nearly an hour, Darren and Tyler loaded the buses, and they drove back to the church.

"See you guys later," Dany hugged Liz and Tyler. "I hitched a ride with Emmy."

Thursday night Robby walked out of Chase's old office in the music suite and had everyone take a seat. He waited a moment for everyone to settle down. "I hear I have a mutiny on my hands. Would someone like to talk for the whole group, or do we need to hold a debate?"

"You can talk for the team, Steve. You've been kind of neutral through this, but you have heard both sides," Cam Frees said.

Steve Van Zant had been part of the worship team longer than anyone in the room. Though normally a quiet man, he did occasionally express his opinion. When he spoke, people tended to listen. He rose from his seat and straightened up slowly.

"There has been some grumbling about the schedule. Some people would like to go back to having one team scheduled for the

271

entire week. Now that we are eliminating the Saturday service, that really means playing for two services on Sunday and rehearsing on Thursdays."

"What do you think we should do?" Robby asked.

He stroked his chin. "I rather like the idea of only playing on the weeks I'm scheduled and having the freedom to sit in the congregation and listen the other Sundays."

The team spent ten minutes discussing their options.

Robby waved to quiet the group. "Regina and I have been looking at the people on our list. We have enough people to form three teams if we get a couple of volunteers to play an extra Sunday. I'd love to expand that to four teams."

Emmy raised her hand. "Have you thought about using the teen band?" She looked around the room. "We have a new youth pastor coming, and Liz told me he has experience leading worship. I think he might be able to get the teen band back in shape within a month or so."

"I like that idea," Regina said. "That would be a perfect way to involve the teens in the service. They need to feel they are just as important as anyone else."

Several minutes later Robby sensed the discussion had come to an end. "Should we take a vote? Everyone who would like to switch back to having one team scheduled for the week, please raise a hand." He looked around the room and started to count the hands, but then stopped. "Let me make this easier. Anyone who wants to keep the current schedule raise a hand." He waited a few seconds and then smiled. No one had raised a hand. "I'm flexible. Regina and I will work on a schedule and have it ready by Sunday. You can look it over then, and if we need to make changes, we'll try to accommodate everyone. For now, we need to split up and get ready for this weekend."

"I have a question," Emmy stood up. "Will we sing different songs for each service? We might need to sing some hymns for the first service."

"I will look into that, Emmy. That's a good point. The older members still like to sing hymns."

Most of the worship team arrived early Sunday morning. They migrated to the music suite to check the new division of teams and the schedule for the coming months.

"Do you think we'll be on the same team?" Emmy asked Kenny.

"Don't you want us to be on the same team?"

"It would make it easier."

They walked into the music suite and saw many of the team members crowded up close to the cork message board where announcements and different news items would be pinned. Eventually, they were able to see the new posting.

"We can make some changes if needed, but this is what Heidi, Regina and I thought would offer three strong teams," Robby announced.

Emmy stared at the list of the new teams.

<u>Team A</u>
Regina Collins – vocals
Heidi Knapp – vocals
Cam Frees – keyboards & vocals
Ross Knapp – electric guitar
Steve Van Zant – electric guitar
Larry Kimmerle – acoustic guitar
Jackson Brewster – bass guitar
Robby Collins – drums

<u>Team B</u>
Emmy Colasanti-Colwell – vocals
Liz Hammond – vocals
Adam Vicini – keyboards & vocals
Kenny Colwell – guitar
Boyd Goldman – electric guitar
Micah Hurst – acoustic guitar
Ross Knapp – bass & guitar*
Bobby O'Connor – drums
Robby Collins – drums*

Team C

Regina Collins – vocals
Robby Collins – vocals
Quinten Matthews - keyboards
Perry Johnstone – electric guitar
Freddie Bender – electric guitar
Marshall Bender – acoustic guitar
Miles Goossens – bass guitar
Skip Mason – drums

*backups

Emmy double checked the list and then turned to Robby. "I didn't know you could sing."

He grinned. "Regina and I often sang together at our old church. I haven't needed to sing here because they are so many talented singers on the team."

"Do we need to listen to you. We need to make sure you can sing on key," Emmy teased. "We don't want someone who sounds like Louis Armstrong."

"What? You don't like Louis Armstrong," Robby feigned shock.

Heidi smiled. "I've heard Robby sing, and I can assure you he would pass the audition."

"Does he sound like Barry White?" Emmy grinned.

Regina's whole body shook with laughter. "Honey, he only uses his Barry White voice when we're alone. The rest of the time he sounds like Luther Vandross."

"We'll see about that." Emmy poked Robby's arm. "I want to hear you do Barry White. He's so sexy."

Robby smiled down at Emmy. "Can't get enough of your love, babe," he sang in his sexiest voice.

Emmy put a hand to her cheek. "Oh, Robby, you are making me weak in the knees."

He laughed and put his arm around Regina.

"Maybe he sounds more like Richard Pryor." Regina laughed.

Chapter Twenty-Nine

Emmy turned on the Mr. Coffee machine and grabbed a cup from the wooden mug-tree on the counter. She opened the fridge and pulled out a half-gallon orange juice container. She opened it and sniffed. "Oh, yuck! How old is this?" She checked the date. She set the orange juice in the sink just as her cell phone chirped. She checked the caller ID.

"Barry, this better be good news for you to be calling this early. No one else is awake yet."

"And good morning to you, too," Barry said.

"Morning. What's up?"

"I wanted to introduce you to someone special."

"Did Linda have the baby? Are you at St. Bart's?"

"Yes to both questions."

"Give me all the details." Emmy sat down on a barstool. "Is Linda okay. Is the baby all right?"

"Are you going to let me talk?"

"Sorry, go ahead."

"Her name is Zooey Michelle. She arrived at 5:28. She weighs exactly eight pounds and is twenty inches long."

"Does she have hair?"

"Lots of dark hair. She's all red and wrinkled..."

"All babies are, you goof."

Barry glanced over his shoulder. "She has a good set of lungs."

"I can tell. Who picked out the name?" Emmy wondered. She got up, poured herself a cup of coffee and dumped the orange juice down the drain. Then she sat back down. "Was it Linda?"

"Yes," he answered softly.

"It's a pretty name. I like it."

Barry walked out of the hospital room into the hallway. "Maybe I shouldn't tell you, but I will. You just can't let Linda know I told you, okay?"

"What is the big secret?" Emmy asked and then giggled.

"Promise you won't tell?"

"Swear!" Emmy crossed her heart with her pinky finger.

"Once we knew we were having a girl, I picked out a name, but Linda threw a fit. She threatened to leave me."

"Wow! That's serious. What name did you want?"

"I wanted to name her Emmy Michelle," Barry said and then paused. He waited a few seconds for a response. "Em, you still there?"

"You were really going to name her Emmy?"

"Yeah, it's a pretty name."

"Thank you, Barry. I can understand why Linda would get mad at you."

"I can't. Emmy is a pretty name, and it's not like you're the only Emmy in the world. Linda has a cousin named Emmy. I can think of a bunch of people named Emmy."

"Did you tell Linda you were naming the baby after me? Please tell me you didn't."

"I might have been talking about you at the time. I can't remember for sure," he said.

"You are such a nerd. No wonder she got pissed at you."

Barry shrugged. "I didn't think it would be a big deal, but she was mad at me for a week. She made me sleep on the couch."

"Oh, poor baby," Emmy teased. "How do you spell her name?"

"M-i-c..."

"K-e-y! No! You goof! How are you going to spell Zooey. I've seen it a couple of ways."

"Two Os. Like a zoo with animals and stuff."

"I should put you in the zoo with your ancestors."

"You mean the gorillas and apes?"

"No, the baboons because you are a baboon."

"Are they the ones with the funny butts?" Barry asked.

"What? I don't know."

"I think those might be orangutans."

"Whatever!" Emmy rolled her eyes. She took a sip of coffee. "Can I ask you something personal?"

"You can ask, but I might not answer."

"Such a nerd. Why did you guys wait so long to have another baby? Hattie must be five by now."

276

"She's five and Fender is nine. Oh, he wants everyone to call him Isaac now. He told us the kids at school tease him about his name."

"Ya think!"

"Are you still going to call him Fig?"

"No, I haven't called him that for a long time. I like Isaac. No one teases a kid named Isaac. So why the long wait?"

"Uh, we didn't plan to wait this long, but Linda suffered two miscarriages."

Emmy clapped a hand to her mouth. "Oh, Barry! I'm so sorry. I didn't know. When did this happen?"

"A couple of years ago. We probably won't have any more babies. Linda is having plumbing trouble."

"You are such a nerd," she said and rolled her eyes again. "I won't come up to the hospital because that might upset Linda, but I want to see Zooey soon."

"I'll bring her around, or maybe you can come to the house sometime with the girls. Hattie would love to see them again."

"I know. I should stay in touch better, but we get so busy. I'm sorry about the miscarriages, but I'm so thrilled for you now."

"Thanks, Emmy. I should call Linda's parents."

Emmy finished her coffee, read her Bible and devotional book before anyone else got up. She checked the time.

"Shoot! I better get Kenny up, or we're going to be late." She rushed upstairs and lay down next to him. "Are you awake?"

"Kinda. Why?"

"It's getting late. We need to get the kids up and get ready." She cuddled next to him.

"What time is it?"

"Almost seven."

He turned on his side to face her. "Are you forgetting something?"

"What?"

"The new schedule."

She put a hand to her mouth. "I totally forgot about that. We don't have to be there until Sunday School. We aren't on the schedule for today. It's like a free Sunday."

"I kinda like the idea of only playing every three weeks."

"That means we don't have to get up as early." She moved even closer. "What should we do with the extra time?"

"Mommy, my tummy hurts," Kevin whined from the doorway. "I think I need some ice cream to make it feel better."

Kenny grinned. "So much for free time. Do you want me to get up?"

"I'm already up. I'll take care of it." She kissed his cheek and then got down from the bed. "Let's see if we can find something more suitable for breakfast than ice cream. How about oatmeal with blueberries."

"Ice cream! Daddy let me have ice cream last week."

Emmy turned and stared at Kenny.

He shrugged. "We were out of instant oatmeal."

"Come with me, Kev. How about blueberry pancakes?" Emmy closed the door to the bedroom.

Kevin dashed down the stairs ahead of Emmy. "Can I have a scoop of ice cream on my pancakes?"

Emmy shook her head. "No ice cream for breakfast." *I'm gonna have to get after your father.*

Before the Sunday School class started, Emmy talked to Kristen and Sloane. "Kenny let Kevin have ice cream for breakfast."

Tony overheard Emmy as he walked behind her. "Is there something wrong with that?"

Sloane frowned. "Ice cream is not a breakfast food. Some people say breakfast is the most important meal of the day."

"Then why do people eat it in the morning? They should eat breakfast for dinner." He took a seat in the back.

Don Williams, their teacher, walked in and set his briefcase down next to the podium at the front. "Good morning, everyone. Since the church is starting a new schedule today, I took the liberty of rearranging the classroom. Please try it out for today, and then let me know what you think."

Emmy raised her hand.

"Yes, Emmy. You don't have to raise your hand to speak."

"I wasn't sure because this feels like we're really in school."

Everyone laughed which embarrassed Emmy.

"I assure you that is not the case. You may feel free to speak at any time," he said as he smiled.

"Thank you, but now I can't remember what I wanted to ask."

"Did it have anything to do with ice cream for breakfast?" Tony asked.

Emmy turned in her seat. "No, and stop trying to embarrass me."

"If you remember what you wanted to ask, feel free to ask." Mr. Williams smiled and then turned to write on the whiteboard.

Emmy waved a hand. "I remember now."

Mr. Williams turned back. "Yes, Emmy."

"I know Mason plays bass for the teen band on Wednesday nights and according to what I've heard, he's pretty good."

"He practices all the time," Mr. Williams said.

"The worship team is looking for another bass player, and I wanted to know if Mason would be interested."

"You would have to ask him, but I think he would be delighted to be asked."

Emmy grinned. "I'll talk to him, and I won't interrupt anymore."

"There has been a slight adjustment in the order of service today," Robby told the worship team before the start of the second service. "Pastor Tyler would like to introduce Jake and Maddy to everyone at the beginning of the service instead of right after the announcements and offering. This way they can get to the Cross Fire center. The teens are meeting in there today."

Regina added, "If you have checked online, you would see that we have replaced the hymns we did for the first service with two contemporary songs."

"That's good because I'm not real familiar with some of the songs in this new Nazarene hymnal," Heidi Knapp replied. "Do you plan to only do the hymns in the first service?"

Regina looked at Robby before answering. "That's the plan as of now. It could change if more of the older folks start coming to the second service.

"Don't forget to keep checking online for the service orders and songs. And I would like to thank those of you who have volunteered to play more than one Sunday. I did have a chance to talk to Jake about the teen band taking charge of one Sunday a month. He did say it might take a few weeks, but he was very open to the idea."

"How about Pastor Tyler?" Ross Knapp wondered.

"He is totally in favor of that. Once the teen band has practiced enough."

Regina checked the time. "Let's pray before we go out."

Tyler opened the second service with a prayer and then brought Jake and Maddy to the platform. "Some of you have already met Jake and Maddy Boyter, but for the rest of you, I would like to introduce Jake and Maddy." Tyler chuckled. "They have joined the team as our youth pastors. Well, I guess technically Jake is the youth pastor, but like Liz and myself, they are a team. They have agreed to hang around after the service so you can talk to them. Also, the teens are meeting in the Cross Fire Youth Center this morning. Any teens who might be in here, and would like to join the other teens, you are dismissed."

Emmy nudged Kenny. "Have you talked to them yet?"

"Not really. You?"

"No, I guess we'll meet them sooner or later."

Kenny grinned, "Maybe when the girls are teenagers."

Diane called Emmy on Monday morning.

Emmy set her coffee cup down and answered. "What's up?"

"Can you go with me this morning? I want to stop and see Mom for a few minutes."

"As long as I'm back by ten. We're working, you know."

"We won't stay long. Have you been to see her lately?"

Emmy bit her lip. "I've only been there twice, and she got on my case for missing school."

Diane sighed. "Tell me. I've been going once a week, but it's getting harder to deal with her. One of the caregivers said Mom tried to get off of the floor and threw a fit when she couldn't."

280

"I'll go with you, but let's not stay very long, okay?"

"If we time it right, she'll be eating breakfast in the dining area."

"I found out there's a dining area on each floor. Is that for security reasons?" Emmy asked.

"Probably. Are the kids ready?"

Emmy checked. "They just have to put on their coats. We'll be ready when you get here."

They dropped the kids off for school, and then Diane drove to Sunrise Garden. They found their mother eating breakfast.

"Hi, Mom, how are you today?"

Patricia looked at the girls and smiled. "My, don't you girls look so pretty." Patricia turned to the lady sitting next to her. "These are my daughters. That's Diane and the little one is Emily. Don't they look pretty?"

The other lady smiled without speaking.

"They are both grown up now."

Emmy looked up at Diane.

"Today must be one of the good days, so let's not blow it," Diane whispered and then moved behind Patricia. "What are you having for breakfast?"

"I ordered eggs and bacon, but they brought me oatmeal, too. Do I have to eat it if I don't want to?"

"You don't have to eat anything you don't want to," Diane assured her.

"I don't want to pay for oatmeal that I didn't order. Will you tell the waitress to take it off the check? Otherwise, I won't leave a tip."

"I'll take care of it, Mom." Diane looked at Emmy, who happened to be looking at some of the other residents. "Em, are you going to talk to Mom?"

"Hi, Mom, you look good. Did you get your hair done?"

Patricia patted her hair. "I went to the beauty parlor yesterday, or maybe the day before. Do you like?"

"Yes, it looks great."

Patricia looked at Emmy for a moment without speaking. "Did you get rid of your ponytail? Didn't you have a ponytail the

281

last time I saw you?"

"No, I got a new hairstyle a while ago." Emmy turned in a circle. "This is much easier to take care of."

"It makes you look more mature." Patricia turned to the lady beside her again. "Emily has graduated, and she is going to go to college." Patricia smiled and nodded her head emphatically. "She has always been so smart."

The other lady smiled and nodded to match Patricia.

Diane and Emmy stayed a few more minutes.

"We have to go now, Mom. I'll see you soon," Diane said.

Emmy kissed the top of her mother's head. "I love you, Mom."

Patricia smiled and tapped her lady friend on the arm. "Did I tell you those are my daughters. Aren't they pretty?"

The lady friend smiled and nodded.

Diane punched in the code to leave the floor and almost ran into a man walking around the corner.

"Mr. Heintz! What are you doing here?"

Diane nudged Emmy in the ribs. *Geez, Em! Why do you think he's here?*

"Hello, Uh, I'm here to see my wife. Emmy, right?"

"Yes, and this is my sister Diane. Our mother is here. She's only been here since the end of February. Has your wife been here long?"

Holy smoke, Em! Try not to sound so cheerful.

"It's been a year now. I should go. Nice to see you again." Mr. Heintz scurried through the doors.

"Who was that, and why did you have to sound so cheerful? People don't come here because it's a five-star hotel."

"Sorry, but I didn't know what to say. That's Mr. Heintz from D'Antoni Honda. He's the salesman Kenny and I bought our cars from."

"Did you know about his wife?"

"No, but now I understand why he seemed so sad."

Chapter Thirty

"Are you sure the guys aren't mad at you for taking the morning off?" Kenny opened the door to the steel and glass Walker Management building.

"Thank you, Kenny." *You've been opening doors for me a lot lately.* Emmy smiled at Kenny. "They aren't mad, and if you weren't busy recording yourself, you would realize we haven't been starting until noon."

"Why don't you start earlier?" Kenny asked as the automatic doors slid open.

"The guys like to use the mornings to get personal stuff done. It gives me a chance for some alone time," Emmy explained.

"Good morning, Mr. Colwell. Hi, Emmy!" Genna Santos greeted them with a smile.

"Morning, Genna. Are we the last to arrive?" Kenny asked. *Why do you insist on calling me that?*

"Actually you are the first ones here other than Andy and Charles," Genna replied.

Emmy smiled as she looked at Genna's abdomen. "How much longer?"

"Six more weeks if Dr. Walsh is right about the due date." Genna patted her belly.

"Have you and your boyfriend picked out a name yet?"

"We keep going back and forth. We probably won't decide until she is born. Should I inform my mother you guys are on your way up?"

Gladys Santos worked as Andy Walker's executive secretary.

"No need. I'm sure she knows we're here." Kenny pushed the button for the elevator. He looked at Emmy as the door silently closed. "Why do you always bring up Genna's boyfriend?"

"I'm trying to encourage her to get married. She's almost thirty and they have two kids already. I think people should get married to raise a family. Am I being too pushy?"

"I guess not." The door opened and they approached Mrs. Santos' desk.

283

She waved and pointed in the direction of the conference room without a break in her phone conversation.

"Good to see you, Mrs. Santos," Emmy said with a smile.

Kenny led Emmy down the hall and into the large conference room. Emmy noticed a large TV on the wall.

"Is that new?"

Andy Walker turned around. "Yes, we use it for conference calls and to display information." He put an arm around Emmy and hugged her. "You're early."

"We didn't want you to accuse us of being late."

Charles La Rosse walked over and hugged Emmy. "How are you? I haven't seen you for two months."

"That's because you went back to Germany. Are you going to stay in the states for a while now?"

"I plan to be here through the end of the summer, but I might be traveling. There's this new band I want to hear," he teased.

Over the next twenty minutes everyone else drifted into the conference room. Emmy spent a few minutes talking to her manager, Nelson Grapella, about his new baby boy.

"He's growing like a weed."

"Are you guys going to call him Nikolai or just Nick?"

"Belinda insists we call him Nikolai because it sounds exotic or something. She claims Nick is too plain."

"At least you won't have any trouble remembering his birthday," Emmy grinned.

"As long as I can remember the number twelve. Twelve-twelve-twelve."

"Can we get this meeting started?" Andy took his seat at the head of the table. "Ty is passing out the itinerary for the tour."

Emmy smiled as Ty Dalicandro handed her a copy. "Have you been keeping out of trouble?"

He nodded. "I've been working with Jennifer Sinclaire. Been too busy to get into trouble. She and Ryan said to say hi."

"Is she pregnant yet?" Emmy asked.

Kenny frowned at her.

"What? Can't I ask if one of my friends is expecting?"

284

Emmy looked up at Ty again.

"To the best of my knowledge, she is not pregnant. I'm not speaking as her doctor, but I think she or Ryan would have mentioned it at some point."

"May I continue, Emmy?" Andy tapped a pencil on the table.

"I'll be quiet." Emmy zipped her mouth closed.

"Okay, the band wanted this tour to be a bit different since they aren't touring to support a new album. Are we still on schedule for a November release?" Andy asked.

"I think we're ahead of schedule, and we're still thinking it will be a double-disc release," Kenny glanced at his band mates. They nodded in agreement.

"Good. Back to the tour. All shows are on Friday and Saturday with the exception of the SoHam Fourth of July show which is a Thursday. The guys at Prater-Saylor managed to fill the schedule mainly with smaller cities. Some of which I've never heard of. Where is Missoula, Montana?" He pointed his pencil at Emmy. "Don't you dare say it's in Montana."

Kenny explained, "Missoula is in the western part of the state. It's the home of the University of Montana, and we played there in '09. We probably stopped there on that first super long tour back in '97."

"Thank you for that... piece of information," Andy smirked and turned to Charles. "Does anyone live in Montana? I thought it was all buffaloes and cowboys."

Charles grinned and added, "And rich movie stars."

"Anyway, I think most of these cities are college towns which doesn't make a whole lot of sense because no one goes to college in the summer, but that's besides the point. Since we are flying to all these shows, we need a place to land, and according to Steve Prater, there are no airports anywhere in North Dakota. So they couldn't schedule a show in that state. It is a state, right?" He looked at Emmy. "I'm joking. I can name all forty-five states and some of the capitals."

"We may have to take a bus to Fargo some year," Kenny said.

Jeff laughed. "We've been there! We played at North Dakota State University in '97. I remember because we kept blowing the power."

"We played two shows in North Dakota in '09 and one in South Dakota," Kenny added.

Andy frowned at Kenny. "Thanks for that bit of info." He turned to Charles. "Are there two states named Dakota?"

Charles shrugged. "How would I know? I live in Germany."

"Are we set on the rest of the gigs?" Dave Persching asked.

"I'll double check, but I think we have contracts with all the promoters," Andy replied.

The meeting delved into the logistics of the tour for the next half hour.

"Are you sure you want Emmy to open every night? Won't you guys get tired of having her around?" Andy kept a straight face.

"Doesn't matter. We usually ignore the opening acts," P.J. said nonchalantly. "After all! We are superstars, right?"

"I just hope we sell a few tickets. We haven't toured for ages. People have probably forgotten we even exist," Dave said.

Emmy grinned. "Might just be that the people come out to see me. They might not even hang around for your show."

"Oh, really. And exactly how many people listened to you sing the last time?" Andy asked.

Emmy held up three fingers. "Three! I sang for the kids at breakfast yesterday, and they wanted an encore," Emmy replied.

Charles patted her shoulder. "We're going to have to book you into larger venues, Emmy."

By the time the members of Fridays At Five left the meeting, they were pumped and excited about playing in front of audiences. They headed next door to the Steward Music Group studios with renewed energy. Emmy returned home and waited for her band to arrive.

"Hey, Emmy. How did the meeting go?" Bobby O'Connor arrived with his bag of drumsticks. "Did they decide to make us the headliner?"

286

Emmy laughed. "No, but they didn't kick us off the tour."

"Do we still get to fly everywhere?"

Emmy nodded.

"Sweet," he turned it into a four syllable word. "Hey! Are we still going to be recording the days we're not gone?"

"I would like to finish this project sometime this year. Kenny's CD is supposed to come out in November." Emmy waved as the other guys walked into the basement.

"Is Kenny going to be here today?" Quinten asked.

"Not today." Emmy shook her head. "The guys decided to work since they were already next door. They've got studio four booked solid for three more months, so they can record whenever they want."

Micah removed his long coat and beret and tossed them on the couch. "Who's going to record us? No Kenny and I assume no Will."

Emmy pressed a finger to her chest. "I can record everything. I know how."

"Maybe you should produce this yourself, Emmy. It's great having Kenny here, but he has his own project to finish," Christian said.

Bobby nodded. "Yeah, too bad it didn't work out with Jeremiah. He's a great guy and all, but..." Bobby shrugged.

"Were we able to salvage any of the tracks he recorded?" Quinten asked.

"I've saved it all, but I don't know how much we'll be able to use. Too bad. The kids love him as their pastor."

Jeremiah walked into the control room of studio four as the Fridays At Five guys took a break to listen to their latest track.

"Hi, guys. I hate to interrupt, but I got a delivery this morning." He held up several CDs.

Kenny jumped up from one of the chairs at the control board. "Let me see."

Jeremiah handed him a copy.

"Cool!" Kenny inspected the artwork. "I'm glad you included a photo of the band. You guys really look like bears."

Jeff grabbed one of the CDs from Jeremiah. "Do we have

287

anything around here that can play a CD?"

The guys shrugged and began looking around the room.

"Will that play CDs?" Dave pointed to one of racks against the wall.

The guys tried to find a slot for a CD without any luck.

"What about that?" P.J. pointed.

"I think that's something to do with the headphones," Adam replied.

Jeff handed the CD back to Jeremiah. "Do you have any eight-track cartridges? I'm sure we have an eight-track player in here somewhere."

Jeremiah looked at each of the guys.

"Give me that thing." Will Consoli grabbed one from Jeremiah. He ripped it open and tossed the wrapping at Jeff. "These guys wouldn't know how to play a cassette if their lives depended on it."

Jeremiah grinned. "I've heard of eight-tracks, but I don't think I've ever seen one."

"My father still has a few at home. He's even got an old Wollensak recorder that still works," Kenny mentioned.

Will began playing the BearFace CD.

"Turn it up," Jeff said. "I want to hear the bass rumble."

Adam inspected the liner notes. "Hey, Kenny, did you get paid for producing this?"

Kenny nodded. "The guys gave me gift certificates for Darby's."

"Awesome!" Andy Walker walked into the room. "That doesn't sound like Fridays At Five." He waited for a reaction. "It sounds a whole lot better. If that's a new band, I want to sign them to a long-term management contract."

Jeremiah handed Andy a CD. "You can have that one, Mr. Walker."

"Why, thank you very much, Pastor Tolla."

"I think he's trying to say he wants you to call him Andy like everyone else does," Dave said.

"You are supposed to call me Mr. Walker!" Andy pointed at Dave before taking a seat on the couch.

The guys listened to the entire CD.

"I love it," P.J. clapped while sitting on a barstool and leaning against the wall.

"I like it, but who did that guitar solo in track three?" Jeff asked. "It sounds like a kid just learning how to play. I don't think the guitar was in tune."

Kenny laughed. "Go ahead and make fun. That's the only solo I added. The only thing I played other than that childish solo was rhythm guitar. All the lead parts are Jeremiah."

"Hey, Jeremiah, if your band ever breaks up, maybe you would consider joining Fridays. We've been looking for someone with real talent." Jeff slapped Kenny on the back.

"How many copies do you have?" Andy asked.

"I've got a thousand copies. Minus these. I'm going to give some away and try to sell the rest on our website."

"It sounds pretty good. Maybe when you guys record again, we can find you a real producer," Jeff teased.

Jeremiah left, and the guys looked at each other.

"Should we help him out?" Dave opened his laptop.

Adam nodded. "I thought it sounded pretty amazing. I'll buy a copy."

"Me, too," P.J. added.

Dave found the BearFace site and opened the store. "No t-shirts. Just the CD. Andy, do you think there's enough money in the corporate account to order a hundred CDs?"

"How much are they?"

"Ten bucks each." Dave looked at the guys.

"We can't order too many. He needs some to sell to his fans."

Dave typed on his laptop for a bit. "There! Done!"

"Where are you having them shipped?" Adam asked.

"To our office next door."

"Hey! You're not cluttering up my building with CDs. I already have a room full of unsold Fridays At Five CDs," Andy joked.

"Maybe we can give them away," Kenny said.

Andy shook his head. "Already tried that."

289

"Would you like to eat your cake first, or open your presents?" Emmy asked Kevin Michael.

"Cake first," he answered immediately.

Emmy brought the cake over to the table in the breakfast nook. "You boys sit in your chairs, and I will light the candles. You can sing to Kev, and then he can blow them out."

Kevin had insisted no girls be invited to his fifth birthday party. Carson, Caden, Zachary and the Bertucci boys—all four of them—grabbed seats around the table. Emmy helped Coby into his booster seat. *You're getting too big for a high chair.* Emmy sighed. *No more babies to spoil.*

"You have to sing before blowing out the candles," Emmy explained to Taylor Beckett and Ben. She lit the five candles and the boys sang. Kevin blew out the candles, but to his surprise, they reignited. He blew them out again, but once more they ignited.

"Mom! Did you buy stupid candles?" Kevin asked.

"They're not stupid. You shouldn't use that word. It's not nice," Emmy scolded.

Carson, who was now eleven and the oldest, smiled. "These are the candles that never go out, right, Aunt Emmy?"

"Yes, I thought it would be fun, but Kevin is just frustrated." Emmy removed the candles and sliced the cake.

"Can we have ice cream, too?" Kevin asked.

"Yes, I have chocolate or vanilla to match the cake."

Emmy made sure all the boys received the flavors they wanted. She left the room to let the boys eat. She returned ten minutes later.

"Cody! Did you eat any of your cake? Your face is covered." She heard Kevin and Ben laughing. "What is so funny?"

"We put cake on Coby's face."

"That wasn't very nice. You should say you're sorry," Emmy wet a washcloth to wipe Coby's face and hands.

"Coby liked it, Auntie Em," Peter said. "He was laughing the whole time."

"I guess it's not a big deal. I remember one of my birthdays when your papa smeared cake all over my face," Emmy smiled. "I kinda liked it, too."

290

"Mommy, Kevin says he won't sing 'Happy Birthday' to Lily," Heather whined on the way to Brady and Diane's house after school on Monday. "Tell him he has to sing."

Emmy looked in the rearview mirror. "Kevin, don't you want to sing for your cousin? She's one today."

"I'll sing if I can play my tambourine," Kevin said.

"It's a rather short song. Maybe you can play your tambourine for me later," Emmy suggested.

"Is Daddy coming to the party?" Isabella wondered.

"He will be there. He's coming from the studio."

"Are Grandma and Grandpa Robertson going to be here?" Heather asked.

Emmy tilted her head as she pulled up to Brady's garage. "Kinda. They're still on vacation in Europe, but they will be there on the computer."

"They're going to Skype us, right?" Isabella asked.

Emmy parked and helped Kevin get down from his car seat. "Yes. Computers can be very useful at times."

"Does Lily know how to walk yet?" Kevin asked.

"Not quite, but she can pull herself up and move around using the furniture. Try not to knock her over."

Kevin heard another van pull into the driveway. He waved and ran toward the van as soon as it stopped. "Ben and Taylor are here!" He looked back at Emmy and then pointed to the van as Tony jumped out.

"Kevin Michael! You should never run toward a moving vehicle," Tony scolded but then picked him up and held him upside down.

"I waited until you stopped, Uncle Tony," Kevin insisted.

Soon all the kids from Bristol Ridge were there. Even Bennett and Marissa Robertson stopped by along with Spencer and Abigail. Brady wandered from room to room taking photos with his latest digital camera.

Emmy looked up at Abigail. "You're almost through with high school. Just a couple of months to go. Are you excited?'

"I'll be more excited in the fall. I'm going to Stanford," Abigail said as she grinned.

291

"You're not going to attend North Park?" Emmy sounded disappointed.

"I need to get away." Abigail sighed. "Mother is driving me totally insane."

"I love your hair. It frames your face so nicely." Emmy complimented Abigail. *Too bad you and Spencer have inherited your grandfather's long nose, but you're still as tall and slender as a supermodel.*

Spencer Robertson held out his hands as he walked toward Lily. "How is my little sweetheart today? I hear this is a special day for you."

Lily held up her hands, took a step toward Spencer and promptly fell on her butt. Spencer picked her up as she giggled.

"The bee is going to get you, Lily." Spencer buzzed and poked her in the arm with a finger.

Lily continued to giggle.

Diane walked up to Bennett. "Lily loves to see Spencer."

"He really loves his little cousin." Bennett nodded.

At five o'clock Brady gathered everyone into the family room. He connected his laptop to the huge TV and within a minute, everyone could see and talk to Bill and Mona. Diane sat on the floor with Lily. Lily squealed and pointed to her grandparents. Grandpa and Grandma stayed at the party for an hour even though it was after midnight in France.

Carson and Caden sat on the floor in front of the TV to help Lily open her gifts. She squealed every time she ripped the wrapping paper. Carson placed one of the bows on top of Lily's head.

Emmy held Coby Bertucci against her hip while standing next to Tony. "Lily is more excited about the pretty paper than the actual gift." Coby squirmed in her arms so she set him down.

"I think you're right," Tony agreed. "Hey, I'm sorry about getting after Kevin earlier."

"Better not be. I would get after your kids if I saw them doing something wrong. He loved being held upside down." Emmy noticed Grace sitting on Kristen's lap on the couch. "Did Kristen look a lot like Gracie does? Gracie certainly has Kristen's golden hair. I love those curls."

"From the pictures I've seen, Grace looks almost like Kristen did." Tony snapped his fingers at Ben and Taylor. The boys stopped wrestling and sat up.

"Where's John?" Emmy asked.

Tony chuckled. "Still at work."

"How did you manage to get off for the party?" Emmy nudged him in the side.

"Because I'm not a workaholic like John. He's been working twelve hours a day."

"Don't you feel guilty that he's working and you're having fun?" Emmy grinned.

"Not a bit. John actually has a title. He's the project coordinator. I'm just one of the owners, remember?" Tony joked.

Emmy elbowed him. "So are Derrick and Kristen. Aren't they?"

"And Marco," Tony reminded her.

"Why?"

"If you're asking why Uncle Daniel isn't the owner anymore, it has something to do with taxes. You should ask Derrick if you really want to be nosy," Tony said as he tugged on Emmy's hair.

"I'm not being nosy. Just curious. Does Mama get any income from the company?"

"Not anymore. She gets a Social Security check, and she has the money from selling her house and some investments," Tony divulged. *She's not rich like you and Kenny.*

"Why didn't she come with you guys?"

"You are full of questions today." Tony grabbed Emmy's hand so she couldn't hit him. "She said she would feel out of place. She's home making dinner."

"No one would mind her being here."

"We know that, but Mama can be funny like that at times."

"What's the story with Two Bears?" Emmy wondered. "I heard Sloane talking to Kristen about the company."

"Two Bears Landscaping has officially been sold to the Quezada brothers," Tony answered. "It is their company as of last

293

Monday. They've already added more customers."

"Are they going to change the name?" Emmy grinned.

"Why would they want to change a perfectly good name?"

"Yeah, right," Emmy harrumphed. "How much did you sell it for? If I may ask."

"You may not, but I'll tell you because I know you'll keep bugging me until I do, brat. We sold it for ten grand."

"Get out!" Emmy poked him in the side. "The truck and trailer alone are worth four times that. Maybe more."

"I suppose you would have sold it for full price." Tony rubbed his side.

Emmy grinned. "Nope! I would have sold it for a dollar and a bunch of shiny beads and buffalo blankets." She laughed and then walked away.

Diane set Lily in her high chair and removed her dress. "You can be as messy as you want."

Emmy lit the candle on Lily's personal cake, and Heather and Isabella led everyone in singing. Diane helped blow out the candle. Kristen and Sloane cut the large sheet cake into pieces as the kids jostled for positions in line.

"Lily, you can use your hands to eat the cake," Emmy put a bit of frosting on Lily's nose.

Brady took several shots as Lily grabbed a handful of cake and tried to stuff it in her mouth. The cake ended up all over her face.

Diane smiled at Emmy. "Remind you of anyone?"

"Who?"

"You, you goof. You know that picture from one of your birthday's?"

"Kinda," Emmy answered.

"There aren't a lot of photos of us as little kids, but I have that one somewhere in the house. It was in with Grandma Isabel's property. She must have taken the original picture."

"Probably," Emmy sighed. "I don't remember Mom or Dad ever taking pictures of anything." She picked up a slice of cake and walked over to Tony. "Hey, do you remember what you did to me on my twentieth birthday?"

"Did I kiss you? If I did, I'm sorry," he said.

"You might have, but I'm thinking of something else."

"That was the birthday you got that sexy nightgown, right?"

"How can you remember that? Barry bought it. It was almost transparent, but that's not it either."

Tony rubbed his jaw. "Nothing else stands out."

"You and Derrick smeared cake all over my face. Don't you remember?"

He chuckled, "Oh, that. You got kinda mad and vowed to get revenge."

"Today's the day, creep!" Emmy tried to smash the cake in Tony's face, but he grabbed her hand and the cake ended up on Emmy's face. "You creep!"

"How does it taste, brat?"

"Pretty good, actually." She removed some of the cake with her hand. This time Tony didn't resist as she smeared it on his face.

Tyler Hammond walked into the lobby of the Crest Ridge Federal bank, waited in line for a time, and then presented his mortgage statement to the person behind the desk. "I need to talk to someone about this."

The employee glanced at the paper and asked a couple of questions. Tyler answered, and the employee directed him to one of the cubicles. Tyler walked over to the cubicle and the lady motioned for him to have a seat.

"How may I help you today, Pastor Hammond?" Katherine Cordell asked.

"Mrs. Cordell, something is wrong with my mortgage account. Could you help? I need to make my payment. I don't want it to be late." He told her how much his payment should be.

Mrs. Cordell pulled up the account on her computer. She studied it for a moment. Tyler listened as her fingernails clicked on the keyboard.

"Apparently, you don't owe the bank a payment," she said as she smiled.

"Are you saying the bank sold my mortgage to some other

company? Who do I pay now?" Tyler asked a bit impatiently.

"That's not what I mean at all."

"I don't understand," Tyler said.

"How can I put this?" She tapped her fingernail to her chin. "Your mortgage has been paid. You don't have to make another payment." She waved a hand in the air. "Poof. Gone. Erased. No more house payments other than taxes and insurance. You should receive the deed in the mail."

Tyler clenched his jaw for a moment. "Are you certain? Can you check again? There might have been a mistake. Someone must have paid for the wrong house."

Mrs. Cordell smiled while shaking her head. "No mistake, Pastor Tyler." She handed him back his statement. "Anything else I can help you with today?"

"Who? How?"

"I'm sorry, but I can't divulge that information," she said and kept smiling. *You will have to figure it out on your own.*

Tyler took his statement and slowly rose from his chair. "Thanks, Mrs. Cordell."

He drove to the church, walked into Liz's classroom and interrupted the class. He whispered into her ear.

"Are you sure?"

"According to Mrs. Cordell, it's been paid. Paid in full. She couldn't, or wouldn't give me any more information."

They both looked at Heather and Isabella who were reading a book together.

"I'll find out the truth," Liz whispered.

Chapter Thirty-One

Reed Shafer unlocked the door to the storage closet in the hallway outside of the sanctuary. "Yesterday we set up every padded chair we have. We better be ready. I think we might need every other chair we have," he mentioned to some of the men on duty as ushers. "We haven't used these metal folding chairs for a few years, but we might need them today."

"We should roll these racks out. I agree with Reed. I think we'll need more chairs." Jess Zawaski nodded to his brother Joe.

Reed watched as the brothers easily rolled out the steel racks heavily laden with chairs.

"Where should we put these, Mr. Shafer?" Joe asked.

"Let's move them into the sanctuary against the far wall in back. We might not need them for this service, but I have a strong hunch we will for the second one."

Jess and Joe rolled the racks into place and then adjusted their ties and smoothed out their black suits.

Robby and Regina helped Worship Team B rehearse the songs for the Easter services in the music suite.

"Do you want to lead worship, Regina?" Emmy asked. "I know it's not your turn, but you and Robby are kinda the worship leaders even if you aren't ministers."

"What do you think, Emmy? Will people expect us to lead the team because it's Easter?"

Liz Hammond entered the music suite, walked over to Emmy and Regina, coughed and then spoke in a hoarse voice. "I don't think I can sing today. I can barely talk."

Regina patted Liz on the shoulder. "You won't have to. I'll cover for you."

"Thanks, Regina," Liz said and then coughed several times.

"That settles it, Regina. You and Robby should lead the service, and I'll sing harmony with you," Emmy said.

Robby led the service and sang a solo on two verses of their second song. Emmy couldn't see an empty seat in the sanctuary. After the service she heard Roger Goldman talking to Tyler.

"The counters added their totals. Care to venture a guess?"

"Did we hit a thousand?" Tyler asked.

Roger smiled. "Counting everyone in both buildings, the total came to 1103. That could be a record for the early service. I'm pretty sure we will top that for the second service."

"I should talk to Reed. Where will we put everyone? I saw some people standing and others sat in the coffee shop."

Roger placed a hand on Tyler's shoulder. "I'll talk to Reed, Pastor. You have more important things requiring your attention."

"Thanks, I appreciate it. What are we going to do next year?" Tyler asked.

Instead of having Sunday School classes on Easter, the church traditionally did an Easter brunch. The hospitality committee planned to feed five hundred and probably surpassed that because they ran out of everything other than pancakes.

Reed Shafer and the Zawaski brothers located two hundred old, metal chairs in the garage. They hosed them down, cleaned and dried them as best they could and set them up in the gym. Reed found Jonah Galves, and Jonah set up the gym so people could watch and hear the service on the two large TVs.

"This will have to do for this year," Jonah said to Reed.

"Who is going to sit in here?" Reed asked.

Jess raised his hand. "Joe and I will talk to some of our friends. We won't mind sitting in here."

Reed smiled and placed a hand on Jess and Joe. "You guys are terrific. Thank you."

Tyler and Liz didn't leave the church until close to one o'clock. Tyler started the Flex, sat back and sighed. "I'm exhausted. Roger told me there were over 1300 people at the second service, and I think I shook hands with all of them."

"Jonah stayed in the gym, and he said there were close to 200 people in there," Liz mentioned.

"If the church keeps growing, we are going to have to do something. I don't want to even think about having three services on Sunday." Tyler turned off of Canton Lane and pulled into their driveway a minute later.

"What about Saturday night?" Liz asked.

"Been there. Done that. Don't wanna go back."

298

Liz made a pot of spaghetti for lunch using a recipe from Emmy, who got the recipe from Mama Bertucci. After lunch Grayson went down for his nap. Natalie played in her room with her dolls and Tyler fell asleep in the family room watching basketball.

"Derby, I need some time for myself. Will you be a good doggie and stay with Tyler?" Liz rubbed Derby's ears and, as a bribe, gave her a new rawhide bone. She went upstairs to her bathroom and opened a drawer in the vanity. She pulled out three home pregnancy test kits. *It might be too early to tell, but I'm late and I think there's a strong possibility I might be pregnant again.* She read the instructions, used all three kits and waited.

Liz quietly walked down the stairs so she wouldn't disturb the kids. She touched Tyler's arm and he woke with a start.

He yawned and tried to clear his head. "I fell asleep."

"Yes, you did. I have something to tell you," Liz said. "I'm pregnant."

Tyler stared at her for a few seconds. "Oh, no," he sighed.

Liz tapped his arm with a bit more force. "I thought you'd be happy. We've been trying for another baby."

Tyler pulled Liz onto his lap. "I am happy. It's just there's so much going on. The church is keeping me busier than ever. We might be getting more foster kids. The mortgage is on my mind."

"Don't worry about the house. I'll find out what happened. I have a pretty good idea already."

"Is it a boy or a girl?" Tyler asked.

"Yes," Liz nodded.

"Duh, I guess it's too early to tell, right?"

"You are so smart." Liz kissed him and Derby barked.

"Did you have a chance to check Facebook today?" Kristen called Emmy after dinner.

"I haven't had time to even check my email for a couple days. I haven't looked at Facebook since last week." Emmy placed the leftovers in the fridge. "Why? What's up?"

"Should I tell you, or do you want to find out for yourself?"

"Tell me, Krissy. Did something bad happen?"

299

"Maddy had the baby early this morning." Kristen typed a comment on Maddy's Facebook page and hit the like button.

"She did! What did they have? I should know, but I can't remember."

"They had a boy, and his name is Lucas Caden." Kristen rattled off the other details.

"Too bad he wasn't born yesterday," Emmy said.

"Why would you want him to be born on April Fool's Day?" Kristen asked.

"Yesterday was Caden's birthday," Emmy explained. "I wonder how they're going to spell Caden?"

"C-A-D-E-N." Kristen spelled it for Emmy. "I've never seen it spelled differently."

"Why didn't Christopher call me? Did he call you?" Emmy sat on one of the barstools by the kitchen island.

"No, I'm looking at Facebook."

"He should have called us. He's had plenty of time. It's been over twelve hours," Emmy complained.

"Maybe Maddy didn't want him calling ex-girlfriends."

"I'm not an ex-girlfriend," Emmy said indignantly. "You were his girlfriend. Not me."

"I was never technically his girlfriend. We dated a few times, but the relationship was never serious," Kristen reminded Emmy. "You are the one who had a big crush on him."

"I did not!"

"Don't lie to me. You were interested in him from the time you met."

"Fine! So I thought he was hot," Emmy admitted. "He still looks like a California surfer dude."

"Have you seen them at church lately?" Kristen continued to check Facebook.

"I saw Christopher sitting with Randy and Vanessa in the second service last Sunday, but I didn't see Maddy," Emmy answered. "Do you think Randy and Vanessa will ever have another kid? Stephen is a year older than Kevin Michael."

"Don't know, but if they've waited this long, maybe they don't want anymore. I need to let you go. I have to help Zach with homework. I don't remember ever having as much as he gets."

"Heather and Isa don't have much homework, and they are in the same class," Emmy said. "Maybe Zach goofs around too much at school."

"Yeah, maybe. Talk to you soon." Kristen ended the call. *Are you rubbing it in my face because your girls are so smart. I know Zach isn't the brightest student, but he is not slow.*

"Good morning, Emmy. Do you know what day this is?" Kenny leaned over her from his edge of the bed.

"It's Friday, and there better be a very good reason for you to wake me up so early." Emmy rolled over and answered without opening her eyes.

Kenny moved closer and put a hand on her hip. "It's someone's anniversary. Can you guess who?"

She moved onto her back and opened her eyes. "You remembered."

"Have I ever forgotten our anniversary?" He leaned over and kissed her cheek. "I haven't brushed my teeth."

"I can tell. What time is it?"

"Nine thirty. Give or take."

"Where are the kids? Did you take them to school? I need to get up."

"Sofia took them to school. You can stay in bed if you want," Kenny said and then grinned.

She grinned back. "You mean if you want." She jumped out of bed. "I need to get dressed, and you need to go to work. It will still be our anniversary later."

Kenny returned home from the studio earlier than usual that afternoon. Emmy and her band finished about the same time, and she came upstairs. They met in the kitchen.

"Good. You're home early." She opened the fridge. "I need to fix something for dinner. What would you like?"

"I would like to take my wife out for our anniversary. Where would you like to go? Anywhere at all?" He hung up his keys and set his wallet on the shelf.

Emmy closed the fridge and grinned. "Darby's. I want to go

301

to Darby's and have a chili cheese dog and root beer."

"We can always go to Darby's. Pick somewhere special. Anywhere in the world?"

"Anywhere, huh?" Emmy put a finger to her mouth. "Take me to Paris. Remember that place on the Champs-Elysees?" Emmy Americanized the name of the famous French avenue. "I want to go there if I can't go to Darby's."

"Maybe I shouldn't have said anywhere in the world. How about anywhere within an hour's drive."

"Party pooper," she teased. "We haven't been to Ciao Bella for a while."

"Excellent choice, my dear," he said and then bowed.

"Why even ask where I want to go if you've already made the reservations?"

"How did you know?"

"How long have I known you?"

"Well, we met..."

"It was a rhetorical question, dear. What time do we need to be there?"

Kenny sat down on a barstool. "Mr. Sabatino reserved a special table for us at seven thirty."

"When you say special, I hope that doesn't mean a table in the middle of the restaurant."

"No, I'm sure he meant one of those little private booths in the new addition," Kenny explained.

"Did you ask about the specials?"

"No, but I did mention it was our anniversary and asked for a bottle of champagne," Kenny said.

"Oooh! Are you planning on getting me drunk and taking advantage of me?"

"Now there's a thought."

"Mommy, I'm hungry," Kevin walked into the kitchen. "Can I have some cookies?"

"I will fix your dinner in a minute," she said and then looked up at Kenny. "Did you get a babysitter? Sofia and Niles aren't available tonight."

"I called Dany, and she agreed to watch the kids."

302

Heather and Isabella ran into the kitchen just in time to hear about Dany. "Is Dany coming over? Where are you and Daddy going?"

"Daddy is taking me to Ciao Bella for dinner, and maybe a movie after that." Emmy looked over her shoulder. "We haven't been to a movie in like forever."

"I took the kids to see..."

"I want to see a movie made for adults. Not a cartoon about cars or penguins."

"An adult movie?" Kenny raised his eyebrows.

"You're a dork."

Emmy fixed dinner for the kids and then ran upstairs to get ready. Kenny let Dany in and then changed clothes.

"Dany, can we watch a movie? Mommy and Daddy are going to the movies." Heather pleaded with her eyes.

"Okay, but you still have to be in bed by..." Dany glanced at Emmy. "... nine thirty."

"Let's watch *The Princess and the Frog*," Isabella suggested.

"I want to watch *Cars*," Kevin said.

"You can watch *Cars* on my computer and the girls can watch their movie on the TV," Emmy decided.

Kenny drove slowly though the Hill district of SoHam looking for a place to park.

"There's one, Kenny!" Emmy shouted as a car pulled out of a space. "And we'll only be a mile from the restaurant."

"We're four blocks away, Em. It is a Friday night." Kenny slipped his Civic into the space. "See how easy it is to park."

"Do you really think we'd ever bring the Odyssey down here?"

"Not at night." He straightened out the car by moving back and forth.

"You finished?" Emmy stared at him. "Can I get out now?"

"I'm done." He turned off the car.

They walked over to Ciao Bella, up the steps and entered the crowded restaurant. Kenny walked up to the front desk and the hostess recognized him. She turned and looked at Mr. Sabatino. He

303

smiled and quickly approached Kenny.

"It is so good to see you again. Your table is ready, and the special champagne you ordered is on ice."

"Thank you, Mr. Sabatino."

He proudly led Kenny and Emmy through the filled-to-capacity restaurant. Emmy noticed a few stares from other patrons. Mr. Sabatino held the chair for Emmy. "Melissa will be with you in a moment. If you need anything, please don't hesitate."

"Thank you, Mr. Sabatino." Emmy smiled.

An hour later Emmy set her fork on her plate. "I can't believe I ate the whole thing."

"I'm so proud of you, Em. You ate all of your spinach and cheese ravioli and your tiramasu," Kenny smiled and wiped his mouth with the red cloth napkin. "Do you want more champagne?"

"No way. I am so stuffed. I may not eat for a month."

Melissa dropped off the check, and a minute later, Florentina Sabatino stopped by to chat.

"Everything was so scrumptious, Mrs. Sabatino. I don't know how you do it," Emmy gushed.

"Did you recognize Melissa?" Mrs. Sabatino asked.

Emmy inhaled, "No! Tell me that's not little Melissa."

"She is eighteen already. She's my oldest grand-baby."

"I can't believe it," Kenny said. "I remember when she was a baby. We are getting old, Em."

"You might be, Kenny, but Emmy certainly is not." Mrs. Sabatino put her hands on Emmy's shoulders. "I remember when your grandparents would bring you here and all you would eat was spaghetti. I would make you a special dessert to take home."

"I remember. Diane and I would share it. That was the best chocolate cake ever."

"Come back and see us soon. If you want to bring the kids, call ahead and I will make a cake for them."

"Thank you, Mrs. Sabatino. We will."

Kenny paid the check and left a generous tip. They saw Mr. Sabatino on the way out.

"Did you enjoy your ravioli, Mrs. Colwell?"

Emmy put her hands on her hips, looked up at him and her

eyes sparkled. "Mr. Sabatino! My name is Emmy."

He laughed and his whole body shook. "Ah, my child, I remember you telling me the very exact thing and standing the same way when you would come here with your grandparents. I remember it as if it were yesterday."

Tyler brought the monthly board meeting to order. They approved the reports and discussed old business for thirty minutes. They filled in the church calendar for the next three months.

"It is getting more and more difficult to fit everything on the schedule," Tyler noted. "We need eight Saturdays a month."

"Not if that means we have eight Mondays," Jim Rosek said. "I hate Mondays."

Eventually, they came to the last item on the agenda.

"I saved this for last because I feel it is the most important." Tyler paused, put his hands out and then chuckled. "We are running out of space. I realize Sunday was Easter, and that is not typical of our regular Sunday attendance. However!" He held up a finger. "Our average attendance is climbing at the rate of fifteen percent a year. It won't be long until a regular Sunday crowd will be like Easter Sunday's."

Lenore Toth, the school's head administrator, mentioned, "We need more classroom space for next year. We might have to move some of the classrooms into the sanctuary."

The board discussed the situation for several minutes.

"I sense we have a consensus regarding the buildings," Tyler looked around the room. "I have talked to Carl Tomanek. He agreed to take a look at our buildings and make a recommendation. He could certainly design a new sanctuary and even a new educational building."

"Do we have any idea what he might charge?" Roger Goldman asked.

"He offered to look at our buildings for free, but I'm sure we would need to pay for architectural designs."

Roger looked around the table. "We are in a great position financially. We have no real debt. Our budget payments to the District are current. I talked to May Burns. She would like to make a few changes in our method of accounting and budgeting, but that can be worked out with the finance action team."

"How long would it take to replace the sanctuary?" Tanya Paduchik, the local Nazarene Missions International president, and one of the youngest members of the board, asked.

William Griffith, the buildings and grounds action team chairman, offered his opinion. "I would estimate it would be two years, possibly longer, before a new sanctuary building could be built and ready for occupancy."

"If we don't keep moving forward, we will stagnate and decline. We don't want that to happen, do we?" Tyler asked.

"Wouldn't it be easier and less expensive to add another service?" Pearl Barnoski asked.

Tyler shook his head. *Oh, no. I hope no one suggests a Saturday night service.*

Roger Goldman came to Tyler's rescue. "I am not in favor of trying the Saturday night service again, and I think adding a third service on Sunday would place too great a stress on Pastor Tyler and the staff. We already have the land, and while we need to keep enough space for the recreation program, we could put the existing acres to better use."

Thank you, Roger. Tyler sighed.

"Should we look into buying the rest of the cornfield?" Jim Rosek asked.

"That would add thirty more acres to our property. We might never need to use it, but we don't want to pass it up if the owner wants to sell more acres," William suggested.

The board passed a motion to have Carl Tomanek take a look at the existing buildings and draw up plans to replace the sanctuary and add on to the educational unit.

"I have one question," Jim Rosek laughed. "If we add on to the education wing, will that addition still be called Behren Hall?"

"We could name it the Rosek Addition," Roger teased.

"All righty then. Forget I asked." Jim laughed and his whole body shook.

Chapter Thirty-Two

"Mama, are you all right? You look pale," Sloane asked when she saw her mother-in-law sitting on the edge of her bed in her wing of the house Sunday afternoon.

"I'm okay. Just a bit tired," Mama waved a hand, but then put her other hand to her chest.

"I'm going to call Tony. He's mowing the yard." Sloane dialed his cell phone, but heard it ring in the kitchen. "Shoot! He never takes it with him," Sloane rolled her eyes. "Peter!" She stepped into the hall and shouted. "Peter! Would you come here, please?"

Peter ran from the kitchen, down the hall and into Mama's room. "What is it?"

"Peter, would you run outside and ask your father to stop mowing and come in here. Mama doesn't feel good."

Peter looked at his grandmother. "I'll fly like the wind, Mama." He dashed out of the room and out a side door. He heard the large commercial mower in the back and sprinted for it while waving his arms.

Tony moved in time with the music on his iPod and didn't hear Peter hollering. He changed direction and saw Peter waving a few feet away. He shut down the blades, lowered the throttle and pulled out one earbud. "What's wrong, Peter?"

"Mom needs you because Mama doesn't feel good. You need to come with me." Peter made sure Tony was following as he ran back to the house.

Tony shut down the mower, leaped to the ground and sprinted for the deck on the back of the house. He ripped open the sliding door and stepped inside. "Where are you, Sloane?"

"They're in Mama's room." Peter pointed as he stepped inside.

Tony dashed through the kitchen and into his mother's area. "What's wrong?"

"It's nothing," Mama insisted.

"It is not nothing," Sloane argued. "She doesn't look well, and she is having trouble breathing."

307

"Are you having a heart attack?" Tony's eyes widened.

Sloane shook her head. "I don't think so, but you need to take her to the ER."

"Okay." Tony picked up his mother as easily as if lifting a small child. "Peter! Get my wallet and the keys to the van. They are by the back door. I need them right away."

Peter grabbed the keys and wallet and followed Tony out to the garage. Peter even opened the garage door by pressing the right button.

Tony held Mama up with one hand and opened the door with his other one. He buckled her in and then looked at Peter.

"Here you go, Papa," Peter said.

Tony took the keys and stuffed the wallet in his pocket.

Sloane handed him his cell phone. "Take this and call me as soon as you get to St. Bart's."

Tony got in the van, started it up and was soon on his way.

"Don't drive like Emmy," Mama said. "I want to get there in one piece."

Peter stood next to his mother. "Will Mama be okay?"

"I sure hope so, son."

John Randolph called five minutes later. "Hi, Sloane, can I talk to Tony? I tried his cell, but he didn't answer."

"Sorry, John, but right now he's on his way to St. Bart's."

"St. Bart's! Did one of the kids fall and get hurt?"

"No, it's Mama. She was complaining about not feeling good."

"Mama was complaining?"

Sloane shook her head. "No, she never complains. I saw her sitting on her bed..." Sloane explained the situation.

"I better tell Kristen." John hung up and told his wife.

Kristen immediately her mother and explained.

"Maria never complains. She must really be sick. Come and get me and take me to the hospital. I'll call your uncles."

Karla Keasling called her older brothers, Carmen and Vincent Lombardi and told them Maria was going to the hospital. Carmen agreed to rush to St. Bart's, but Vincent was in Florida.

Tony reached St. Bart's in near record time. He pulled into

308

the ER and Mama was taken inside. Kristen and Karla arrived a few minutes later.

"Where is she?" Karla looked around the modern ER facility.

"They took her in there," Tony pointed.

Karla boldly marched into the examining room.

"Mom! You can't just walk in there." Kristen tried to stop her mother.

"Let them try and stop me!"

No one dared.

"Maria, what is going on?" Karla rushed to the side of the bed and looked at the machine next to Mama.

"I'm all right," Mama insisted. "I had trouble getting my breath."

The nurse walked in at that moment. "Dr. Lawless will be here in a minute, Mrs. Bertucci. He will take a look at you and don't be surprised if he admits you. Your blood pressure is high and your heart is racing. We want to make sure you are all right before we let you go home."

"I'm all right. I feel a lot better now," Mama said.

"Good! But just in case, I think I'll keep you here until the doctor can see you," the nurse smiled.

Dr. Lawless came in three minutes later. He quickly and efficiently examined Mama.

"And you are?" he asked Karla.

"Her sister. I'm Karla Keasling."

Dr. Lawless told the nurse which tests he wanted and then looked at Karla. "Bertucci and Keasling. I'm going to take a stab in the dark, but are you related to the construction company people?"

"Yes," Karla answered.

"They built this ER, you know."

Kristen sat beside Tony and held his hand. "She will be all right. I just know it."

"She never gets sick."

Carmen Lombardi arrived a few minutes later. He spotted Tony and Kristen. "What happened?"

Tony explained.

309

"Vincent had a heart attack a few years back," Uncle Carmen mentioned.

"I don't think it's her heart," Kristen said. She suddenly put a hand to her chest.

"You okay, Krissy?" Tony asked.

"Has anyone called Emmy?"

Tony shrugged. "Don't know."

"Shoot! She will freak when she hears about this. I better call her."

"Maybe Sloane called her," Tony said.

"I'll try her cell." Kristen walked out of the room.

Tony followed.

Emmy answered on the fourth ring. "Hey, Krissy, I had to find my phone. Kevin had it. What's up?"

Kristen twisted her long blonde hair. "I'm at St. Bart's in the ER."

"Oh, no! Did one of the kids get hurt?" Emmy assumed it had to be one of the kids.

Kristen looked at Tony for support.

"Just tell her."

"The kids are okay. Tony brought Mama in because she wasn't feeling well."

"No way! Mama never gets sick. What's going on?" Emmy asked and then bit her lip.

"Yeah, I know, but she's in one of the examining rooms now. Mom is with her. Uncle Carmen just got here."

"Shoot! This is serious. Are you telling me everything, Kristen?" Emmy frowned. "You better not be holding anything back."

"She is getting older," Kristen whispered.

"I'm hanging up now. I will be there in five minutes."

"Emmy, you can't... Are you there?" Kristen sighed and looked at Tony. "She hung up. She's on her way. I hope she doesn't have an accident. You know how she drives."

"I know," Tony said and then rubbed his jaw.

"Kenny! Kenny!" Emmy hollered.

"What is it, Em. Who was on the phone?" Kenny sat in his

310

recliner in the family room watching TV while reading a book.

"Kristen! I'm going to St. Bart's."

"Did one of the kids get hurt?"

"No, it's Mama." Emmy grabbed her purse and the keys to her Civic Si. *Let's see how fast you can really go.*

"Mama? Mama Bertucci?" Kenny dropped his book and tried to sit up. "But she's never sick."

Emmy arrived at St. Bart's without getting arrested for speeding, or causing an accident. She pulled into the valet lot and threw her key fob at the attendant.

"Hi, Mrs. Colasanti. I mean Emmy. Everything okay?"

"It better be." She dashed into the ER. She looked left and then right. She saw Tony talking to Uncle Carmen. She dodged one of the caregivers pushing an old man in a wheelchair. She slid around a row of seats and bumped into Tony. "Where is she?"

Tony grabbed her shoulders.

"Where is she, Tony?" Emmy bit her lip as tears filled her eyes.

Kristen walked over. "She's in there somewhere, Em. Mom is with her. I talked to one of the nurses, and she said the doctor is going to admit her. They're waiting for a room."

"What happened? Is she okay?"

"Give me your handkerchief." Kristen held out a hand.

Tony handed her his handkerchief. "It's clean."

Kristen wiped Emmy's tears away. "She's all right. The doctor wants to keep her here for observation."

"Don't give me that crap! They don't admit people for observation unless they have a good reason." Emmy crossed her arms over her chest.

"She was having trouble breathing and had some chest pain."

Karla appeared and saw Kristen and Tony. She walked over and stood beside Carmen. "They're taking Maria up to the fifth floor in the new wing. We should be able to see her in a half hour. Of course in hospital time that probably means three hours. They are so slow around here."

Emmy talked to Tony and Kristen for a few minutes before

311

calling Kenny.

"So what is going on? Is Mama all right?" Kenny asked.

Emmy explained everything she knew. "They ran an EKG and some other stuff. I'm going to stay here for a while. Will you be okay with the kids?"

"I do know how to take care of my children, Em."

"Sorry, but don't give them ice cream for dinner. There are leftovers in the fridge."

"Can I have ice cream for dinner?" Kenny teased.

Emmy rolled her eyes.

Before the hospital staff moved Mama upstairs, Tony's cell phone buzzed.

"Hey, Marco. Don't get too excited. She's doing better."

"What happened?" Marco asked. "I talked to Mama yesterday, and she sounded normal."

"Not sure. Might be stress related," Tony said and then shrugged. "I'll call you back when I know more. They're going to keep her overnight just to be safe. I gotta go. Kristen is waving at me."

Tony walked over to Kristen and Emmy.

"We can see her now," Kristen said. "Room 51024. Mom and Carmen went upstairs already."

"That didn't take long."

Emmy grinned. "Aunt Karla and Uncle Carmen kinda helped things move quicker than normal."

Tony smiled. "I can see why the hospital would not want Aunt Karla getting upset."

"I'll join you in a bit. I want to see if the chapel is still there," Emmy said.

"See you upstairs, Em." Kristen headed toward the elevators with Tony following.

"Do you know where to go?" Tony asked.

"Maybe. Hit the button for the fifth floor," Kristen said.

The door opened. Kristen checked a sign and pulled Tony's to the right. "It's this way." They entered the room and saw Karla fluffing the pillows for Mama while Uncle Carmen sat in the recliner in the corner.

312

"Is that better, Maria?" Karla adjusted the blanket.

"Yes, thank you, Karla. I don't like wearing this gown."

Karla covered Mama better. "I know. We'll get you a proper nightgown later."

Tony walked to the opposite side of the bed as Mama held up a hand. "You don't need to worry, son. I'll be all right."

"I know, Mama."

Karla moved back to allow Kristen to get closer. Kristen sat on the edge of the bed and held Mama's other hand.

"You didn't have to rush over here, dear."

"I drove Mom."

"All this fuss just because I couldn't catch my breath," Mama sighed.

"I may not be a doctor, but I'm pretty sure breathing is rather important," Kristen said. "Oh, Emmy is here."

"Where?" Mama looked around.

"She's downstairs in the chapel," Tony answered.

"You shouldn't have bothered her with this."

"Mama, can you imagine how she would feel if we didn't tell her? You are like a second mother to her. You always have been," Kristen said as she rubbed Mama's hand.

A couple of minutes later Karla heard a light knock on the door. She opened it and saw Emmy waiting. "Come in, Emmy. You don't have to wait outside."

"I didn't want to intrude on a family visit."

"Don't be silly! You are family." Karla pulled her inside.

Kristen stood up and waved for Emmy to come closer. "Sit here so you can talk to Mama."

Emmy bit her lip. She saw Carmen and nodded. He smiled at her.

Mama patted the spot on the bed where Kristen had been sitting. "Thank you for saying a prayer for me."

Emmy sat on the bed and Mama squeezed Emmy's small hand. Kristen put an arm around Emmy's shoulders.

"Are you okay?" Emmy whispered.

Tony handed Kristen his handkerchief. "It's still clean."

Kristen frowned at him but then used the handkerchief to

313

wipe Emmy's cheeks. *You can't hide your emotions at all, Em.*

"I feel much better now. Must be your prayers working," Mama said while managing a weak smile.

A few minutes later Carmen stood up. "I need to get home before I fall asleep. Call me if anything changes, Karla. Otherwise, I will check with you tomorrow."

Tony shook hands with his still intimidating uncle. "Thanks for coming, Uncle Carmen."

"I'll see you later." He put a hand on Mama's shoulder. "Get some rest."

"Have you ever tried to get any rest in a hospital? Can't be done," Karla said. "Would you give me a ride home, Carmen. I think Kristen is going to stay for a while."

"No problem."

"I will call you later, Maria." Karla turned to Kristen. "Check to see what she can eat and order her some food. Don't stay too long. She needs to get some sleep."

Tony took Carmen's place in the recliner while Kristen and Emmy moved the other chairs close to the bed.

Later, Kristen looked at the tray of hospital food. "You should try to eat something, Mama. There's soup and Jello. Some mashed potatoes, and I think this might be meatloaf."

"Let Tony eat it. I'm not hungry."

Tony waved a hand. "I'll pass."

"Emmy, it's almost eight. How long are you staying?" Kristen asked an hour later.

"All night. I already called Kenny to let him know."

"You don't have to spend the night, sweetie. I feel much better," Mama said.

"I'm not leaving," Emmy repeated.

Tony laughed. "We might as well go, Kristen. You know how stubborn Emmy can be."

"Will you be okay, if Tony and I go home?" Kristen felt Mama's forehead. "You don't feel warm."

"I should go home with you," Mama tried to sit up.

"Oh, no you don't," Kristen said while waving a finger. "You have to stay here."

"I'll call you if anything changes, but I don't think it will," Emmy whispered to Kristen in the hallway as Tony talked to his mother.

Tony walked out of the room. "Ready to go?"

"We drove separately, remember?" Kristen reminded him.

"Right. You don't have to spend the night, Em." Tony tried once more.

"I know, but I will. I can sleep in that recliner."

"Call me." Kristen put a hand to her ear as she and Tony left.

Emmy watched until they were around the corner and went back into the room.

"Would you move this tray away, please, dear. The smell is making me sick."

"Of course, Mama." Emmy sniffed the tray. *This would make me sick.* She set the tray on the other side of the room. "Would you like to watch TV?"

"You can turn it on if you want, but I'm not interested," Mama said and then closed her eyes.

Emmy turned it on just for background. She sat next to the bed. "You should try to get some rest before the nurse comes back. They always seem to need to take your blood pressure or something right when you fall asleep."

"It doesn't matter. I doubt if I will get any sleep. I can't sleep in a strange bed anymore."

Emmy looked at the recliner. "I should be able to sleep in that."

Emmy watched TV for a time, but then turned it off.

Mama opened her eyes. "You can watch it, dear. I'm not asleep."

"There's nothing on that interests me," Emmy said. "I'd rather talk to you."

"What would you like to talk about?"

"Would it upset you if I asked about Tony's father?"

"Not at all, sweetie. What would you like to know?" Mama replied.

"You've told me about how you met at church, and I kinda

315

know the story of how he died, but what was it like when you were young and married. I know you worked for the company until Heather was born, right?"

"I did. For the most part."

Emmy waited for more, but Mama closed her eyes.

"You were married in 1963, right?" Emmy asked.

"I was nineteen. Daddy thought I was too young, but my mother reminded him of how old she was when they married."

Emmy grinned. "Did you ever kiss another man?"

"Of course not! I loved Peter and would have never thought of kissing someone else." Mama let a smile creep over her face. "You knew that already. You just wanted to tease me."

"I'm bad, huh?" Emmy said and then giggled.

"You can be so funny."

"My parents got married in '59, but Diane wasn't born until '78. Mom has never said why they waited so long to have her, but Diane did some snooping. Somehow she learned that Mom had three miscarriages before Diane arrived. Grandma Isabel confirmed it." Emmy noticed a sad look on Mama's face. "Should I talk about something else?"

"No, sweetie, it's all right."

"You and Tony's father waited several years to have kids, too."

Mama squeezed Emmy's hand.

"What is it, Mama? Are you okay?"

"Could I have a drink of water, please?"

Emmy opened the bottle of water from the tray. "Here's a straw."

Mama took several sips of the water before handing it back to Emmy. She rested her head on the pillows and closed her eyes again. "We were going to name her Dorothy Rose," Mama said softly.

Emmy started to ask who Mama meant, but stopped.

"It was in 1968, and in those days, you never knew if you were having a boy or a girl. I knew in my heart we were having a girl. We never picked out a boy's name, but I lost her."

Emmy held Mama's hand as she let her own tears cascade

316

down her face.

"We didn't try again for a few years. You can't tell Karla or Kristen, but I used birth control. I was quite the rebel because no good Catholic woman used birth control," Mama admitted.

Emmy stifled a giggle. "Sorry, Mama, but I can't picture you as a rebellious Catholic."

Mama opened her eyes. "In some ways, you remind me of myself. You always have."

"You could have never been as wild as me," Emmy said and then bit her lip.

"You were never as rebellious as you pretend." Mama squeezed Emmy's hand. "Later, Peter and I decided to try again. It took three years, but I finally got pregnant. I know how God blessed you with your miracle babies. We thought of our children as miracles, too. Heather came along and then Marco. We wanted one more, so we had Tony. After that we didn't try to have another baby, but we didn't do anything to prevent it either."

Emmy did giggle this time. "Mama! You had sex?"

"Shush, child! You'll embarrass me."

Emmy put a hand to her mouth and gasped.

"What is it, dear?"

"I just realized something. You're going to think I'm stupid."

"Never, sweetie."

"We named Heather for Heather. Duh! But I didn't know until now that Heather Rose meant something different to you. We named her for more than Heather, right? We used the same middle name you were going to use." Emmy let her tears flow again as Mama pulled her head to her chest and rubbed Emmy's back.

"Just let it out, sweetie."

Emmy sobbed for a moment and then suddenly sat up. "Tony has never mentioned anything about this."

"I told Heather, but I've never told the boys," Mama said.

"When did you tell Heather?" Emmy asked.

"She was in college. I don't remember the exact year."

"Did you tell Heather about the name you picked out?"

"Yes, and when Heather found out she was having a girl,

317

she told me she was going to name her Dorothy Rose. I was so pleased."

"But Dotty's middle name is Jane," Emmy realized.

"Alex insisted on Jane. It didn't matter to me."

"Is that why Dotty is your favorite?"

"I don't have a favorite grandchild," Mama said.

"Yes, you do, but it's all right. I won't tell anyone. It will be our secret. Does Kristen or Karla know about your miscarriage?"

"Karla was only ten at the time, so we never told her. My parents and Peter's parents knew, of course."

"So Kristen doesn't know either, huh?"

Mama shook her head.

"Heather knows she was named for your Heather. I've showed her pictures, and I think she and Isa kinda understand that Heather was Peter and Dotty's mother."

"Dotty looks a lot like Heather."

"Does that make you sad?" Emmy asked.

"Once in a while. Sometimes Dotty will do something that reminds me of Heather, but I know I will see her and Peter again someday. That gives me the strength to carry on."

"Just make sure that day is a long way off."

Emmy stretched her arms over her head and opened her eyes. She glanced at Mama and then at the clock. *It's six already. I must have slept through the nurse's visits.* She got up and tiptoed out of the room. She found a bathroom, used it and was headed back to Mama's room when she saw Father James.

"Emmy! What are you doing here? Are the kids okay?" he asked.

Emmy explained her reason. "Let me see if she's awake. You could bless her or whatever you priest guys do nowadays."

"That will cost you, Emmy."

Emmy saw one of the nurses in the room taking Mama's vital signs again. She waited in the hallway with her half-brother.

"You may go in now, Father," the nurse said as she left.

Emmy entered first. "Mama, I need to introduce you to my brother." She motioned for him to enter.

318

"Good morning, Father James. You didn't need to come up here." Mama waved a hand. "I'm all right. I shouldn't be here."

"I visit all my parishioners who are in need," Father James said with a smile. "How are you feeling, Maria."

Emmy stared at Father James and then Mama Bertucci. Then she slapped her forehead. "How silly of me. You already know each other because St. John's is your parish and Mama goes there now."

"Duh!" Father James teased Emmy. "You just now realized that? I thought you were supposed to be the smart one."

"You never told me, you stinker." Emmy poked him in the side. "Mama! Father James has been at St. John's for over a year. Why haven't you said anything?" Emmy put her hand to her mouth. "Oh, my God! You knew he was my brother before I did. He looks so much like Daddy, you must have figured it out. Why didn't you tell me?"

Father James put a hand on Emmy's shoulder. "I made her promise not to tell. She approached me one day after mass and remarked on my resemblance to our father. I told her the story and asked her not to tell you until I could. She agreed."

"Mama, isn't it super!? I have a big brother," Emmy squealed. "A real one! I still think of Tony as a brother, but James is a blood brother."

"I'm happy for you, dear."

Karla arrived at eight and convinced Emmy to go home. The doctor saw Mama later that morning and discharged her. Karla took her home and Mama walked into the kitchen.

"Mama! Mama!" Taylor Beckett squealed. "Coby and I made you get well cards because you had to spend the night in hospital because your tummy hurt. We missed you this much." He and Coby spread their arms as wide as they could.

"I missed you even more," Mama hugged them both."

Tyler, Liz, the kids and Derby left SoHam Friday afternoon of that same week for a weekend vacation back home in Michigan.

"Are we going to tell everyone, or should we wait?" Tyler asked.

Liz tried to get comfortable with Derby on her lap. "I don't want to wait."

Derby licked Liz's face.

"Yuck! You need to stop that Derby, and I should warn you. Mom has a house full of cats who do not like dogs," Liz said and then rubbed noses with Derby.

"Everyone out. We're here," Tyler announced later.

Derby soon learned to keep a safe distance from the nine cats. Tyler's parents came over that evening after dinner.

"We have news for everyone," Tyler said and then looked at Liz.

"We are expecting again!" Liz exclaimed.

"I knew it!" Liz's mother smiled. "I'm a doctor. I can tell these things."

"Oh, Mom," Liz said and then sighed. "I'm barely pregnant. You can't tell."

Jim Hammond grinned. "That means I will have four grandchildren." He held up his hand with fingers extended.

Derby barked and jumped into the air.

"Excuse me, Derby. I didn't mean to leave you out." Jim laughed.

Chapter Thirty-Three

Emmy spotted Liz and Tyler in the hallway outside of their Sunday School room and dashed over. "Liz! Is it true? Are you pregnant?" Emmy spun Liz around to face her. "Are you? You don't look pregnant."

"I am." Liz nodded. "We thought about waiting, but decided to announce it today before the word got out." Liz looked at her sister who stood next to her and Tyler.

"I wasn't going to say anything," Dany stated.

Emmy bounced on her toes. "We got here early. Just as the first service ended, and people were talking about it. How pregnant are you?"

Liz smiled. "If you're asking how far along I am."

"That's what I meant. I know you're either pregnant or you're not."

"Probably seven weeks. I found out on Easter Sunday and told Tyler."

"How did he take the news?"

Dany laughed. "He said 'Oh, no!'"

"Did you really?" Emmy looked up at Pastor Tyler.

"She caught me off guard. I had been napping, and it just surprised me. I'm thrilled to have another baby."

"Let's go inside, and I'll give you all the details," Liz suggested.

Don Williams had been at the early service, so he knew about the news. "Liz, would you like to pass along your status to the people who might not have heard?"

"Thank you. I promise not to take up much time."

"Take all the time you need." Emmy grinned at Mr. Williams.

"For those of you who don't know, Tyler and I are expecting. I'm seven weeks along, and my due date is late November. Mom did an ultrasound when we were in Michigan. I might have said December before."

"I heard something about blueberries," Emmy said.

Tyler grinned. "The baby is about the size of a blueberry is

321

what I told the first service."

"I love blueberries," Emmy sighed.

"So we've heard," Liz laughed.

"I wish I could have another blueberry. I miss having one around."

"Do you mean you miss having a baby around?" Liz asked.

"Yes, what did I say?" Emmy asked.

Tyler smiled. "You said you wanted another blueberry."

"You knew what I meant." She waved as Kenny entered the classroom. "Liz is having a blueberry, and I want one, too."

"Okay." Kenny sat next to his wife and looked at Tyler.

"We're expecting," Tyler explained. "And I mentioned the baby is about the size of a blueberry right now."

"Ah, I understand." Kenny turned to Emmy. "You can have blueberries for breakfast every day if you desire."

Emmy blushed and poked Kenny in the ribs.

"I'm talking about real blueberries," Kenny shook his head.

Kristen walked in and sat down. "Why is everyone laughing. What did I miss?"

"I want another blueberry," Emmy said and then bit her lip.

Tyler sat behind his desk in his church office on Monday morning going over the financial report for the month of April. The phone rang, and he reached for it without checking to see who might be calling.

"Yes, this is Tyler Hammond."

"Hi, I'm Imogene Virtanen from Lutheran Child Services."

"How are you? How can I be of help?" Tyler asked. *Do I really want to know?*

Imogene quickly related the reason for her call.

"Three of them, huh?"

"Yes, two boys, who are not twins, but they are each five. And their darling little sister Avery, who is eighteen months."

"How soon will they arrive?" Tyler couldn't bear to say no.

"Three o'clock. We really need to move them today. Will anyone be home?"

Tyler looked at the clock to his right. "I will make sure I

322

am home, Mrs. Virtanen."

"Thank you so much," Imogene gushed. "Not many foster parents will take in three children at a time. Especially boys who have issues."

"We are willing to do what is necessary." *I wonder what she meant by issues.*

Tyler walked into the education unit and found Liz in her classroom eating her lunch. "Guess what?"

Liz tried to figure out the look on Tyler's face. "I give up."

"We have three kids coming this afternoon."

"Really?"

Tyler explained the situation.

"So they might not have anything but what they're wearing, huh?"

"Probably."

"Five-year-old boys. I'll make some calls. There are mothers with boys who might have some clothes we could borrow. Some of Natty's clothes might fit the little girl."

Tyler thought about bringing Grayson home with him from the day care enter at the church, but decided to let Liz bring him home after school. It turned out to be a wise decision.

Imogene arrived a few minutes before three with the three children.

"This is Dillan. He's the oldest. That is Liam and this is Avery," Imogene handed Avery to Tyler. "I just changed her at the office, but you might want to check again. She smells a little ripe."

"Do they have any other clothes?" Tyler held Avery away from his body.

"Sorry, but we had to get them out." Imogene got back in her car and raced away.

"Let's go in the house, boys." Tyler looked into Avery's blue eyes. She smiled and his heart melted. *Who would ever give up someone so precious?* He watched as Dillan threw a rock at Liam. *Lord, give me strength and wisdom.*

Liz returned home at four with Natalie and Grayson. "Tyler, there is a bag of clothes in the Prius. Some of the women dropped off clothes. I have diapers and a few toys."

Dillan and Liam stampeded down the stairs and ran into the kitchen. "Are you our new mom?" Dillan asked.

"Yes, I'm Liz. What is your name?"

"I'm Dillan. I'm the oldest. Want to see how fast I can run?" He sprinted out of the room.

Derby barked and chased him.

"I'm Liam. I'm five, and I can run fast, too."

Tyler walked in holding Avery. "She won't let me put her down. If I do she follows me. She doesn't cry, but she follows me."

Liz picked up Avery. "Such pretty blue eyes, and I love your blonde hair. It's so fine."

Avery looked at Liz for a moment, but then twisted around and reached out for Tyler.

"I think she likes you better." Liz handed Avery to Tyler and caught a glimpse of the boys chasing Natalie and Derby. "We are going to have our hands full, huh?"

Tyler chuckled as Avery smiled at him and said "Dada."

Kenny and Emmy knocked on Tyler's door on Friday evening after dinner.

"Is that someone screaming?" Emmy looked at Kenny.

"Sounds like it. Maybe we should come back later," Kenny answered.

Liz opened the door. "Oh, hi, guys. Come on in. That sound is Dillan throwing a fit. Don't let it scare you."

Kenny and Emmy stepped inside and saw Dillan on the floor kicking at the air.

Dillan looked up at them and stopped yelling. He jumped up and ran to Kenny. "Do you have toys in that bag?"

"I might have a few toys, but I only give them to children who make good decisions," Kenny answered. "Have you been making good decisions?"

Dillan nodded.

Liz waved a finger at him. "We don't lie in this house."

Dillan looked up at Kenny. "Sorry, I will behave now."

Tyler walked in carrying Avery.

Emmy set her bag of clothes down and walked over to

324

Tyler. "Hi, Avery. I like your pretty new dress?"

Avery looked at Emmy, then her dress and then back at Tyler without saying a word.

"My God, Tyler! She looks like an angel. Those blue eyes are just gorgeous, and I love this blonde hair. It's so soft."

"Avery, will you let Emmy hold you?" Tyler asked softly.

Avery looked at Emmy, but then snuggled against Tyler.

"She loves Tyler," Liz said. "She prefers him over me any day."

Liam ran into the room followed by Derby. "Who are you?"

"I'm Kenny and this is Emmy. We brought you some clothes."

"Any toys?"

Kenny grinned. "They are definitely boys."

Natalie and Grayson walked into the room.

"Are Heather and Isa here?" Natalie looked around.

"I'm sorry, Natty, but they are at home with Sofia," Emmy explained.

Dillan ran over to Grayson and accidentally knocked him down.

"Dillan, please be careful. Grayson isn't as big as you or Liam," Tyler rebuked him.

"Sorry, Grayson." Dillan helped Grayson to his feet and then ran after Derby.

"Do they ever slow down?" Kenny asked.

Tyler chuckled. "Never. It's like they're on a sugar high twenty-four hours a day."

"Hi, Avery," Natalie smiled at the little girl.

Tyler set Avery down and she walked over to Natalie and Grayson.

"Avery likes Natty and Grayson because they are gentle with her. Her brothers don't know how to play with her," Liz said.

Kenny and Emmy stayed long enough to help put the kids to bed.

"Anyone want something to drink?" Liz asked.

"Sure, I'll take a beer," Emmy teased. "Oh, I forgot. Water

325

will be fine, or maybe a Coke."

Liz made a face at Emmy. "We have tea, but no pop."

"Oh, I forgot. You couldn't drink alcohol even if we were Presbyterians. You're expecting another blueberry," Emmy said and then giggled. "Water is okay."

Liz brought the water to the wooden table and chairs situated between the kitchen and the open family room.

"I really like this open floor plan," Emmy said. "My kitchen is kinda closed off from the rest of the house."

Kenny checked out the deck through the patio door. "We could always knock down that wall between the kitchen and the living room. We might use the living room more if we did."

"I thought that was a load-bearing wall." Emmy opened her water."

Kenny shrugged. "You might be right."

"So how are things going now that your family has doubled in size?" Emmy grinned.

Liz looked at Tyler. He sighed.

"Oh, that doesn't sound good. Anything you can share?" Emmy asked.

Liz started to say something, but Tyler interrupted.

"Sorry, go ahead, Liz."

"As you could see, Avery is the sweetest little thing. She never fusses. Unless you take her food away. All the kids will eat everything in sight if you let them. They eat until they get sick. We have to break them of that habit," Liz said.

"I caught Liam eating some of Derby's dry food," Tyler stated.

Liz stared at him. "You didn't tell me about that."

"He didn't get sick, so I figured you didn't need to know."

"Gee, thanks." Liz sat next to Tyler. "We could sit in the family room. The couch and love seat are more comfortable," Liz suggested.

"Sounds good to me, but you guys can have the love seat." Emmy got up and headed for the couch. "You can snuggle together that way."

They made themselves comfortable.

326

Emmy looked at the peach-colored walls. *I might have changed that color, but it's not bad.*

Tyler talked about the boys for a moment. "We didn't realize what a difference there could be. Grayson is so easy going. He's calm and doesn't fuss. Dillan and Liam are an entirely new species to us."

"Has Dany seen them?" Kenny asked.

"She came over on Tuesday, and watched the boys," Liz said. "She has dealt with kids with special needs before, but even she struggled with the boys. We might have to seek special help. We aren't equipped to handle them. You heard Dillan when you got here."

"Does he do that a lot?" Emmy snuggled closer to Kenny.

"Depends on what you consider a lot. Would five times a day be a lot?"

"Really?" Emmy asked.

"Close to it," Tyler said and then shrugged. "He throws his fits, and then a minute later will be back to normal."

"Could it be a medical condition?" Kenny wondered. "Could he be epileptic or something?"

"It's not that. The people at the foster care agency think it's because of the parents mistreating them. You won't say anything, will you?" Liz braided her long hair.

"Of course not," Emmy assured her.

"We have no idea how long we will have them, but it could be several months," Tyler said.

Liz continued to braid her hair. "We could have them for years."

A week later, Emmy walked down to the mailbox in the afternoon and sorted through the junk mail on the way back to the house. She found an envelope from North Park College.

This is probably Kenny's grades. She stared at the envelope. *Should I go ahead and open it, or should I wait and let him?* She decided to wait.

"I'm home!" Kenny announced as he entered the kitchen two hours later.

Emmy closed the oven door and straightened up. "You have mail."

"Email?"

"No, the old-fashioned kind. It's on the island."

The twins rushed into the kitchen.

"Mommy's making meat loaf and cheesy potatoes," Heather informed him.

"Did you work hard today, Daddy?" Isabella asked.

"I did work hard, but we got a lot accomplished." He set his keys on the island.

Emmy picked them up and hung them in their regular spot. "I finished early and had a taste for meat loaf."

Kevin crawled into the room pushing a firetruck. "I'm hungry."

"Dinner will be ready in twenty minutes. Are you gonna open your mail?"

"Should I?"

"If you don't, I will." Emmy tried to grab the letter, but Kenny snatched it away. "Daddy got his report card from school today," Emmy told the kids.

"Did you get good grades, Daddy?" Isabella asked. "Or do you need to improve on your subjects?"

Kenny opened the letter, but turned his back so Emmy couldn't see.

"What did you get?" Emmy reached around and tried to grab the letter.

Kenny turned around and smiled. "I got an A in each class."

"Good job, Daddy!" Heather exclaimed. "You need a treat, and Isa and I will eat a treat, too."

"No treats until after dinner," Emmy said. "You may have treats if you eat everything on your plate." She kissed Kenny. "I always knew you were smart. After all you did marry me."

He kissed her back and said, "I suppose that was one of my better decisions."

Dylan Michaelis put an arm around Cora and squeezed.

328

"Three down and one more to go."

They watched with pride as Eli received his bachelor degree in education from North Park College.

"And he already has a position at Jamie McGee Junior High for the fall," Mr. Michaelis continued. "It takes some graduates a year or more to find employment."

"It has been worth all the sacrifices to get the children through college," Mrs. Michaelis said.

"Kenny and Emmy have made it easier."

"Now we face the biggest challenge," Mrs. Michaelis glanced at her younger daughter. "Dahlia is satisfied with a B average. She doesn't have the same drive for perfection."

Mr. Michaelis scratched an ear. "It's difficult to believe she will be sixteen in less than two months. She will be wanting to start dating."

"Dylan, I hate to burst your bubble, but Dahlia has been on several dates already."

He stared at Cora and then at Dahlia. "Why didn't I know about this?"

"Because they were supposed to be group dates, and I didn't want to upset you."

"How will I ever survive until she is married?" Mr. Michaelis sighed.

Chapter Thirty-Four

"We have less than a month to get things together," Kenny said as he walked onto the stage in the band's warehouse. Frankie Hanna handed Kenny one of his Fender Telecasters. "Thanks, Frankie."

"No problem, boss," Frankie said.

The band hired Kenny's cousin Frankie Hanna as their first roadie, and he still worked for the band eighteen years later. In the early days, he did everything. He helped set up the gear. He drove the van. He mixed their sound and even did the lights. Now he worked as Kenny's guitar tech and had two assistants to help him.

Kenny played the chords to one of the band's early songs and then his fingers flew over the fretboard as he played a solo. "I'm ready."

The guys studied the set list they prepared for today's rehearsal. For this tour the band chose sixty songs from their catalog; including some never played live before.

"Ready?" Dave checked the guys, and then he counted off the first song.

They played the first song ever released by the band. A track called "Too Bad" they could play in their sleep. They quickly ran through the first five songs before getting stuck on the bridge of "Last Hard Town." A song from the *Transition* CD they had not played since first recording it back in 1997.

"Do we play the bridge twice?" Jeff asked. "And is that B-sharp necessary?"

"I didn't play it," Adam Vicini said. Adam had replaced Jeremy Lenhart on keyboards when Jeremy decided to take time off to care for his daughter, Jennifer, who suffered from lymphoblastic leukemia.

"We know," Kenny smiled at P.J.

P.J. hit the B-sharp on his guitar. "I played the B-sharp because I knew Kenny would. It doesn't fit but that was on purpose, I imagine."

Paul Joseph had been added to Fridays At Five as the second guitarist. The guys had known Paul from his time as the

330

leader of The Notable Exceptions. Another local SoHam band.

"Hey, Will, could you play that track for us?" Kenny spoke into his microphone.

"Give me a second to find it." Will Consoli pulled up the song on the computer back in the mixing booth. The guys listened to the track.

"I haven't heard that in fifteen years," Jeff said. He tried to play along. "I wouldn't play it like that now."

"Does that mean you finally know how to play the bass?" Dave teased.

"At least I don't just beat on a drum kit like some people I know," Jeff teased back.

The guys knew Dave could play guitar and keyboards as well as the drums.

"Let's try it again," Kenny said.

By the end of the rehearsal, the band managed to get through half of the songs on their list.

"Let's knock off for today, and try to get through the other half tomorrow," Kenny suggested.

"Yeah, I need to stop before my fingers start bleeding," P.J. looked at his right hand. "I need to build up my callouses. I've been slacking off."

"Should I leave everything on?" Will asked through the monitors.

"Yes, please. Emmy should be here anytime," Kenny answered.

Since the band used digital equipment now, using the same mixer didn't create a hassle for the mixing engineer. Will saved the Fridays At Five settings, and could easily return the board to the correct mixes.

The other guys left, but Kenny waited on stage for Emmy and her band. She arrived ten minutes later, and the rest of her band followed shortly.

"How did your rehearsal go?" She kissed Kenny. "You smell sweaty, and you look like a frump."

"We've been working hard all day," he replied and then grinned. "You, on the other hand, smell as good as a blueberry."

"Hush! Someone might hear you."

"So what? They won't know what I mean." Kenny kissed her again.

Bobby O'Connor walked past them twirling a drumstick. "Are you guys going to stop that? You're a bad influence on me."

"Look who's talking," Emmy said and then stuck out her tongue at him.

Bobby's marriage to Maria DeGott of the Katie Hollins Band lasted only five months.

"I've learned my lesson, Emmy. I'm not dating anyone who doesn't go to church."

"Better late than never," Emmy said.

Nelson Grapella had hired a brand new road crew for this tour. Emmy didn't have to rely on the "Fridays." The name affectionately given to the crew from Kenny's band. He and the other bosses would have their hands full training the new guys.

The stage used for rehearsals in the band's warehouse stretched over eighty feet wide and forty feet deep. It easily held the gear for both bands. Thirty minutes after arriving, Emmy's front of house mixer Tobias Wouters announced that everything was ready.

Emmy turned to look at Bobby. "Count it off."

He did, and Emmy's band roared through their set without even pausing between songs. Emmy used the extended solos to sip on tea sweetened with honey.

Bobby ended the rehearsal with an impromptu, extended drum solo.

"Hey! You should really do that to end the show," Micah Hurst suggested.

"Really?" Bobby asked though he knew Micah was teasing.

"We could fit in in somewhere, Bobby," Emmy suggested. "We aren't playing in churches, so we can rock the joint as they say."

"As who says, Emmy?" Christian Becton tilted his head as he stared at her. "I've never heard that expression before. Have any of you guys ever heard that?"

The guys shook their heads.

"Never heard it, huh?" Emmy made a face at the guys. "Are you trying to tell me I'm getting old?"

Other than Nelson Grapella and some of the men on the crew, Emmy was older than the guys, if only by a couple of years or so.

"You? Getting old?" Bobby said. "Never happen, Em. You still don't look a day over eighteen."

"Are you sure you don't mean she doesn't act a day over eighteen?" Micah teased.

"If you guys weren't so good, I would fire the lot of you and hire the teens from church, but I will not be goaded into making rash decisions."

Bobby walked out from behind his drums. "If you're talking about the guys from The Only Hope Band, I hate to break this to you, Em, but they are all old guys now."

Quinten hit a minor chord on his keyboard. "I hate to break it to you, Bobby, but those guys are about the same age as us. You might be a year or two younger, but we are all about the same age."

Emmy glanced at Miles Goossens. "What year were you born?"

"In November of 1987," he answered.

Emmy looked at all the other guys. She knew approximately how old they were. "Miles, you are hereby declared the youngest member of the team. Bobby, you have lost your title as the youngest member of the band, so shut up."

"Woo! Hear that, Bobby?" Quinten laughed.

"I might not be the youngest anymore, but I am still young at heart." He grabbed a microphone began to croon the old standard by that name.

"Stick to the drums, Bobby. You're no Frank Sinatra," Micah teased.

Brady and Bennett Robertson opened a box delivered by a special courier at the offices of Carson & Caden on Tuesday morning. They pulled out several documents. Brady began to read.

"Did we get the contract?" Bennett asked. "I can't stay all

morning. I have a school to run."

Brady looked up from the legal document. "We might have to put in a few more hours if we are to live up to this contract."

Bennett's eyes lit up. "For real?"

Brady nodded. "For once in your life you won't have to live on your teacher's salary. You will be making real money."

"I'm an administrator." Bennett puffed out his chest. "I make twice as much as my teachers. I'm making close to twenty thousand a year," he said and then laughed.

"This contract will earn you more than you've earned in all your years as an administrator, little brother." Brady high-fived him.

"Do you think Dad had anything to do with our company getting the contract?" Bennett asked.

"Does it matter?"

Bennett put a finger to his chin. "Not really."

Bill and Mona Robertson landed in New York City, and boarded his Gulfstream III for the flight back to SoHam.

Brady met his father and stepmother at the airport. "Are you pleased to be home?"

Bill shook hands with Brady. "I thoroughly enjoyed the trip, but I will be happy to sleep in my own bed tonight." He looked at Brady's car. "Is that new?"

Brady nodded. "I splurged. That's a Mercedes E-Class. It's an E550 4Matic Sedan. Four-wheel drive. Twin turbos. Terrible gas mileage."

The male flight attendant loaded the luggage into the trunk. "You're all set, sir."

"Thank you. There is an envelope on the table for you."

"Thank you, sir." He smiled and bowed to Mrs. Robertson.

"Where did you find him?" Mona asked. "He always appears from nowhere as if by magic whenever I needed something. It's spooky in a way."

"He works for a man who works for me," Mr. Robertson replied mysteriously.

Brady glanced in the mirror as he drove back to Bristol

334

Ridge. "In case you haven't heard, Carson & Caden was awarded the contract."

"That's great news. I'm thrilled for you and Bennett."

"Dad, did you by any chance pull some strings?"

Mr. Robertson shook his head. "I thought about it, but I decided to stay out of it. Your company earned that contract without any influence from me."

Brady smiled. "Bennett will be thrilled to hear that."

"Brady, do you know when Abigail's graduation ceremony is scheduled? We came back a few days early in order to attend."

"You have time. It's scheduled for May 31 in the morning. It will be held indoors at the Barclay Country Club. You won't have to worry about the weather."

"Thank you, Brady." Mona grinned at Bill. "No, you can't play golf during the ceremony."

"I wouldn't think of it," he said. "I will wait until she receives her diploma."

"Is Abby still planning to attend Stanford?" Mona asked.

Brady chuckled. "Yes, and it infuriates Marissa to no end. Her mother is still insisting she attend Wellesley College, but I don't think Abby is going to budge."

"Good for her." Mr. Robertson nodded. "Marissa can be very insistent."

Mona smiled. "Before we left on our vacation, Abby confided to me that she would rather attend Paul Frank Junior College than give in to her mother."

Brady laughed. "Can you picture the look on Marissa's mother's face if Abby attended a junior college? It would be the scandal of the century."

"You better not let Grandmother Abigail Hartley hear you say that. She may be old, but she would wallop you with her fan," Mona warned.

Diane drove next door in the morning to talk to Mona and Bill. She parked the car, got out and looked around. *I'm getting paranoid. I'm looking for spies everywhere.* She rang the bell and Mona opened the eight-foot tall door a moment later.

"Come in, Diane. Are you alone?" Mona peered around Diane. "Oh, the boys must be in school, but where is my little Lily?"

"I'm sorry, but she has a runny nose. I think she might be catching a cold." Diane stepped inside the huge foyer. "I hate to bother you because you're probably exhausted from your trip, but is Mr. Robertson here?"

Mr. Robertson heard Diane and walked out of the front parlor into the foyer. "Did I hear my name?" He hugged Diane.

"Do you have a moment to talk to me? If you're busy I could come back later," Diane said nervously.

"I always have time for you, Diane." He smiled and then looked at Mona. "Would you make some tea for us, please."

Mona excused herself. "The tea will be ready in the kitchen whenever you are finished."

Bill and Diane walked into the parlor.

Diane glanced around. *I can see why Emmy thinks this place reminds her of Tara from that movie.*

"Let's sit on the couch," Mr. Robertson suggested.

Diane sat on the couch and looked at the floor to ceiling brick fireplace. I could stand in there and not bump my head.

"What is on your mind, Diane?"

"This might not be any of my business, but do you know a man named Rosco Sandchek?"

"Ah," Mr. Robertson sighed.

"I know that's not his real name now, and I know he works for you."

"Yes, he does. He uses several names."

"Do you know his real name?" Diane interrupted.

"Yes, dear. I have known him for most of my life. We attended school together in SoHam. We graduated from Roosevelt High together."

"You did?"

"Does it surprise you that I went to school?" he asked and then shrugged.

"For some reason I always picture you as an adult. I can't think of you as a child."

336

"I actually had parents at one time."

"I'm sorry. Now I feel like Emmy."

"Are you wondering why... Rosco... stayed close in Florida?"

"Yes. He mentioned going on your trip and that sometimes people are watching me and Emmy. Are we in danger?"

"Yes, and no. Let me explain. You have not been threatened or anything like that. Neither has Emmy, but several years ago a man tried to kidnap her."

"She has never mentioned anything like that," Diane insisted.

"She wouldn't because she doesn't know. The man never came close to her, and he was later shot and killed here in SoHam."

Diane stared at Mr. Robertson for a time without speaking. "Oh, my God! You're talking about Todd Delaney, right?"

"Yes. He.. well, let me say I'm not sorry he is no longer around. I knew his father. He went to school with... Rosco... and myself."

"I could search the records at Roosevelt. They have yearbooks going back over a hundred years."

"You could, but you wouldn't know his name, and he doesn't look anything like he did back then."

"Why not?"

"He was involved in an accident and needed surgery."

"So you don't want me to search for him, huh?"

"It would be best if you didn't pursue that, Diane."

"So has Rosco always been around?"

Mr. Robertson waved a hand. "For the most part. His first wife died in the accident, so he took several years off to grieve. He returned and came back to work. Later he met... what name did he use for his wife?"

"Teresa," Diane answered.

Mr. Robertson sighed. "That was his first wife's name. He shouldn't use that."

"Should I worry about the safety of my children? What about Emmy's kids?"

337

"They are as safe as possible in this crazy world."

"Are we watched all the time?"

"No, dear. Only intermittently here in SoHam. More often if you travel away from here. Then you might be accompianed by a couple who are working for Rosco."

Diane closed her eyes. "I can't picture anyone who might have been watching me or the boys."

"Then they are doing a good job."

Diane shook her head. "We can't tell Emmy about this. She would freak out."

"She might not be as understanding as you."

"Is there more to the Delaney story? Are you withholding information?" Diane asked.

He nodded.

Diane stared at him for a moment. "Okay, I understand."

"Would you like some tea now, Diane?"

"Yes, please."

Chapter Thirty-Five

"All right, children. It's time to clean up," Liz instructed her students. "Place all your trash in the bag."

Emmy and Kristen walked among the students carrying trash bags.

"We never got to have a party on the last day of school," Emmy complained.

"That's because you attended public school," Kristen reminded her. "Are you finished with your juice, Miranda?"

Miranda took one last drink and then placed her empty cup in the bag Kristen held open.

"I think we probably had twice as many kids in my first grade class," Emmy said while picking up a half-full cup of punch.

"Did you love your teacher the way these kids love Miss Liz?" Kristen asked.

"Not a chance," Emmy said and then laughed. "All I really remember about her is her name. Miss Rosenbach. I can barely remember what she looked like. I do kinda remember her as being rather fat, though."

"I can't remember the name of my first grade teacher or my kindergarten teacher," Kristen said as she picked up some trash left on the table by the students. "Can you remember anything about kindergarten?"

Emmy paused for a moment. "All I remember is that we moved a couple of times. I don't remember which school I ended up at."

"I thought you went to school with Kenny at his grandfather's school."

"That was later. I started at Robert T. Colwell in second grade. I remember my second and third grade teachers. Mrs. Prater and then Mrs. Saylor."

Kristen straightened up. "Those names sound familiar for some reason."

"Their husbands started the Prater-Saylor Agency. They book our tours." Emmy wiped off the table.

"We have five minutes left." Liz checked the clock.

"Should we sing a song? Who would like to choose a song?"

Many of the kids raised a hand.

"Guillermo, what song would you like to sing?" Liz asked the diminutive Hispanic child.

"Victory in Jesus!" he answered in Spanish.

"I think we all know that one. Would you like to start us, Heather and Isabella?"

Emmy and Kristen stood at the back of the classroom and listened.

"Are you crying, Em?" Kristen put an arm around her best friend.

"I can't help it. I cry all the time now. If I didn't know it was impossible, I would think I'm pregnant."

"Maybe your tubes came untied," Kristen grinned.

"You're so funny."

Emmy and Kristen watched Miss Liz hug each child. Heather and Isabella waited in line with Noemi, Zachary and Caden.

Liz got on her knees and hugged the twins tightly. "I will miss you both so much next year. You are the bestest students ever."

"We love you, Miss Liz," Isabella said.

Heather held on tight and cried.

"I better go find John and Gracie," Kristen said. "See you later, Em."

"See you. Call me," Emmy bit her lip when she saw Noemi crying. She picked her up and held her close. "What's wrong, sweetie? Why are you so sad?" Emmy carried her to Liz.

"Why are you crying, Noemi?" Liz asked.

"I'm sad because I thought you would always be my teacher."

"Oh, baby. I'm sorry, but you will have a new teacher next year."

"But Mrs. Tindall teaches her kids every year," Noemi sobbed.

"That's because she home schools them," Liz said. "They don't go to a regular school."

340

Noemi stopped crying and thought about it for a moment. "Then I want to go to a home school. You can teach me, and all the other kids from the neighborhood."

Liz replied, "We will have to think about that someday."

"Do you want me to take you to the doctor?" Emmy called Diane the next morning. "I can if you want."

"Thanks, Em, but that won't be necessary. Brady's home this morning. He will drive me," Diane answered.

"Are you sure? Shouldn't he be at work? I heard about the contract." Emmy tried again. "It's no problem."

"Emmy, you just want to take me so you'll know what we're having. Are you afraid I won't tell you?" Diane laughed.

"I can't wait to know. Please let me drive you," Emmy pleaded.

Diane moved the phone to her side and looked at Brady, who was drinking coffee and reading the *Wall Street Journal*. "Would you mind if Em takes me this morning? She's going to have a stroke until she knows what we're having."

"Actually, I was going to suggest you get a ride. I need to meet with the company officers this morning."

"I didn't know you had a meeting today."

Brady took another sip of coffee and then set his cup down. "It is a last-minute meeting to discuss technical details about the patent." He continued to explain in great detail.

"I didn't understand a word of that, but it sounds important." Diane brought the phone back up to her ear. "Brady says you can take me, but you have to drive like an old grandmother. Think you can manage that?"

Emmy grinned though Diane couldn't see. "I will. Promise. How soon should I be there?"

"My appointment is at ten, so be here by nine thirty," Diane answered. "And crossing your fingers doesn't count, Emmy."

"Where are the kids?" Emmy asked as soon as Diane let her in.

"They're over at Bill and Mona's." Diane grabbed her purse. "I'm ready to go."

341

Emmy drove slower than usual, but still over the speed limit, and got Diane to her appointment without incident.

"See! I can drive the speed limit if I have to." Emmy parked her Civic and turned it off.

"Ten miles over the limit is still speeding, and won't you hurt the car by driving in third gear all the time?"

"I love to hear the engine rev," Emmy shrugged. "It's a VTEC engine."

"What does that mean? Are you becoming a gearhead now like Rory?"

"No, but he did teach me a few things about cars."

Diane stared at Emmy.

Emmy saw Diane's look. "What? They weren't all in the back seat," Emmy said and then giggled.

Diane rolled her eyes. "You are never going to grow up, are you?"

"Not if I can help it," Emmy said as she grinned.

Diane didn't have to wait long before the technician took her back to a room. Emmy followed, grinning all the way.

"I should have driven myself," Diane sighed and shook her head.

"This might feel a little cool." The technician applied a gel to Diane's belly. "Aha!" she said a minute later.

"Is it a boy?" Emmy asked.

"He's definitely a boy," the technician said.

Emmy clapped her hands. "Good job, Diane. I think Brady wanted a boy this time."

"Thank God it's a boy because Brady was going to keep knocking me up until he got a son." Diane looked at the technician and then Emmy. "I'm kidding. I'm pretty sure this will be my last baby."

"You don't have to drive like a grandma now, Emmy." Diane held the ultrasound of her baby in her hand as she dialed Brady's cell phone.

"Do you know?" Brady asked without saying hello.

"It's a boy," Diane said. "We need a name for the next generation of Robertson men. Do we have to choose a name that

342

begins with B?"

"No, why would you think that?" Brady wondered.

"Brady, Bennett, Bill," Diane rattled off the names.

"William actually starts with a W, but no one calls Dad that. Spencer starts with an S. We can pick any letter you want," Brady's voice expressed his joy. "Except maybe Q or X. I can't think of any good Z names, either."

"Go back to work. I'll see you later." Diane laughed.

Emmy gunned the car and shifted into fourth.

Mona opened the door for Diane and Emmy. "I can tell by the look on Emmy's face that the ultrasound was a success," Mona said. "Bill is in the parlor. Let's tell him together."

They entered the parlor, and Diane saw Lily sitting on Grandpa's lap while he read her a book.

"We are learning about different colors today," Grandpa said. "What color is this Lily?"

"Blue," she said and then giggled.

"All colors are blue today. What did the doctor say?"

Mona sat on one side of Mr. Robertson and Diane sat on the other. Emmy plopped down in a recliner facing them.

Diane held up the ultrasound. "This is what your grandson looks like right now."

For the first time she could remember, Emmy saw tears in her godfather's eyes.

Chapter Thirty-Six

"Mommy, do we get to wear our princess dresses today?" Heather looked at the three dresses hanging up in Emmy's closet.

"Not today, sweetie. Tonight is just practicing for tomorrow," Emmy explained. "Tomorrow we will get to wear our pretty new dresses."

Isabella giggled. "Tomorrow Mary is going to wear her princess dress, and she's going to kiss Jonah."

Emmy smiled at the girls. "She might even kiss him today."

"Is Mary going to move away?" Heather asked.

"Not that I know of. Why would you think that, Heather?"

Heather shrugged. "Because she has to live with Jonah now. They might move away."

"I'm pretty sure Mary and Jonah are going to live in his apartment until they find a house."

"Are you going to buy them a house?" Isabella asked. "You and Daddy should build them a house like Dany's house."

"We might just do that, Isa." Emmy smoothed out her bridesmaid dress.

"Do I get to go to the practice?" Kevin asked while he and the girls ate an early dinner.

"Mary said you could come, but you have to promise to sit down and behave. No running around. Agreed?" Emmy walked around the kitchen island... again.

"Yes, Mommy, I will behave," he promised.

"Em, how soon are we leaving?" Kenny asked.

Emmy wrung her hands together as she checked the time. "Mary wants to start the rehearsal at six thirty. We need to leave around six." Emmy checked the time again and bit her lip. "Do I look all right?"

Kenny's eyes opened wide. "You're wearing jeans and a top. You look normal."

"Should I change? Maybe I should wear a dress. What do you think?"

Kenny put his hands on Emmy's shoulders to stop her from pacing. "You look perfect. Stop worrying. Everything will be fine." *Geez, Em, how will you ever handle the girls getting married?*

"I should change." Emmy turned and tried to walk away, but Kenny grabbed a belt loop. "Do I really look okay?"

He kissed the top of her head. "I would marry you all over."

She turned to face him and wrapped her arms around his waist. The kids squealed as they watched their parents kissing. Emmy broke off the kiss and scooted away.

"I'm going to wear a dress."

Kenny looked at the kids and shrugged.

Later, Kenny stopped the van in front of the Crest Ridge United Nazarene church. "All ashore who's going ashore."

Emmy shook her head. *Such a dork.*

"Daddy, you are so funny." Isabella laughed.

"Come on, Isa!" Heather hollered. "We have to see Mary."

"Don't run," Emmy said but then watched as the girls held hands and sprinted to the front doors.

"Whoa! Where are you going in such a hurry?" Eli Michaelis opened the door for the twins.

"Eli! We have to see Mary!" Heather insisted. "She's practicing getting married, and we have to help. Don't you know anything?" Heather rolled her eyes. "Come on, Isa."

Eli watched as the girls scampered away.

"Hi, Emmy," Eli held the door open for Emmy and Kevin.

"Thank you, Eli. Which way did they go?"

"Down the hallway. High-five?"

Kevin Michael high-fived Eli. "I have to behave tonight, or Mommy will spank my butt!"

"If you see the girls again, please tell them to come to the sanctuary."

"Will do, Emmy."

Emmy walked into the sanctuary and saw Mary and Dahlia talking to their mother Cora, Paula Kratzsky and Pastor Tyler.

"We walk in God's house, Kevin Michael."

"Yes, Mommy."

Emmy walked to the front. Dahlia picked up Kevin.

345

"Mommy says I have to behave."

"Is that so?" Dahlia set him down and he scampered over to a chair and sat down. "What did you do to him, Emmy?"

"I didn't beat him. I told he needed to behave, or I might have to spank his butt."

"Do you remember the last time you spanked him?"

"No, usually the threat is enough to get my point across." Emmy looked up at Dahlia. "Are you taller than Mary now?"

"By about an inch and it infuriates her to be the shortest one in the family," Dahlia said and then grinned.

They heard people talking and looked to the back of the sanctuary as Jonah entered with his family. His parents and three brothers walked in.

"Excuse us! Excuse us!" Heather edged past Jonah. She and Isabella dashed to the front of the sanctuary. "Mary! We've been looking all over for you."

"Can we see your ring again?" Isabella asked.

"Girls! You know better than to run in the sanctuary," Kenny scolded.

"Sorry, Daddy, but we had to see Mary."

Jonah led his family to the front. He kissed Mary and smiled at her mother.

A few minutes later Tyler asked Mary, "Is everyone here?"

Mary mentally checked off her list. Paula checked off her printed list and nodded.

"Should we get started?" Tyler chuckled as he watched Emmy biting her lip and wringing her hands.

"I should introduce everyone, Pastor Tyler," Mary said. "Not everyone knows my cousins."

"Go right ahead." Tyler kept watching Emmy.

"I want to thank everyone for coming tonight. I'm Mary Michaelis," she grinned.

"Good! For a second I thought I was at the wrong church," Darian teased.

"I want to introduce my bridesmaids first. Is that okay, Jonah?"

"Whatever you want, Mary," he said.

346

"Well, Dahlia is my maid-of-honor because she's my favorite sister."

"You will pay, Mary." Dahlia laughed.

"These are my cousins." Mary stood beside them. "This is Amelia. This is Jenny, and this little one on the end is Stephanie, but everyone calls her Stevie because she's acts more like a boy than a girl." Mary stepped back to avoid getting hit by Stevie.

Dahlia pointed at Emmy. "Aren't you forgetting someone?"

"Oh, I figured everyone knew Emmy, but just in case. This is Emmy Colasanti-Colwell, and that's Kenny, and this is Heather and Isabella, and over there sitting like a good boy is Kevin Michael." Mary opened her arms and Kevin jumped down and ran to her side.

"How about us?" Darian held out his hands. "Don't we count?"

"Right! We needed two extra guys, so Jonah asked my goofy brothers. That's Darian and this is Eli. They're my favorite brothers." Mary wrinkled her nose.

"My turn?" Jonah asked.

Mary nodded because her parents and Jonah's parents met for dinner about a month previously.

"These are my parents Jesse and Elmira. Otherwise known as Dad and Mom." Jonah paused until his brothers stopped laughing at him.

"These shrimps are my brothers." Though Jonah at five eight was not exactly tall, he did tower over his brothers by a couple of inches. "Eduardo is the oldest, then Alfredo and then Philip. I'm the youngest."

"He was an accident," Eduardo teased.

"I'm Pastor Tyler, by the way."

Mary pulled Paula over to the group. "You have to listen to Paula because she's coordinating everything. Thank you, Paula, and Emmy." Mary grinned at Emmy.

Paula took over. Within fifteen minutes she organized the men and began practicing with the ladies.

"Emmy! Are you ever going to learn how to walk slow? This is not a race. There is no prize at the end."

347

Dahlia grinned and whispered to Amelia. "I thought Jonah was the prize."

"For Mary, but not for Emmy. She already has her prize," Amelia stared at Kenny. *I've never met a celebrity before.*

Regina Collins rehearsed her songs, and Sofia arrived and sat in the back.

Twenty minutes later Paula waved her hands in the air. "I've done all I can do."

"Let's go eat!" Jonah announced. "Does everyone know how to get to Kerry Lynn's Pizza and Pasta?"

"We will follow you, Jonah," Mrs. Galves said.

"Mommy, do we have to go home?" Heather pleaded.

"That was our deal. You agreed to come to the rehearsal and then go home with Sofia. Mommy and Daddy will be out way past your bedtime."

Heather pouted a little but didn't ask again.

"We'll try not to be out super late," Emmy said.

"Don't worry, Emmy. I'll get them to bed and read my book. You guys can stay out as late as you want." Sofia gathered the kids and left in the Odyssey.

Mary and Jonah used the same room for their rehearsal dinner as Kenny and Emmy.

Emmy saw Liz walk in and ran over to talk to her. "Who's watching the kids?"

"Dany volunteered to watch them both nights," Liz said. "She thought it would be good experience. Where are yours? Tyler told me they were at the rehearsal."

"Sofia took them back to the house," Emmy answered. "Kenny and I can party all night. Within reason I suppose." Emmy glanced down at Liz's stomach. "How is the little blueberry doing?"

"I think I can see a baby bump already," Liz patted her stomach.

Emmy put a hand to Liz's belly. "Maybe you're having twins and one baby was hiding behind the other during the ultrasound."

Liz shook her head. "Not happening, Em."

348

The mothers of the bride and groom made sure everything was ready and asked pastor Tyler to pray. He prayed and Emmy looked up at Kenny.

"You promised you would wait in line, Em. Let Mary and her family go first."

"I'll wait, but if my belly starts rumbling like a volcano..."

"Go ahead, Em." Kenny waved and then sat next to Tyler. "How are things going with the kids?"

"Getting better, but the boys are still a handful. Avery is a piece of cake. I hope Grayson doesn't turn out like that."

"He won't. He's had the benefit of you guys for parents."

Emmy and Liz got in line behind Mary and Dahlia and the cousins. "Can you eat pizza?" Emmy asked.

"Mom gave me a list of foods to avoid, but pizza wasn't on the list. Did you have to follow a special diet?" Liz wondered.

"Not really. I ate pretty much what I wanted. Once in a while I would tell Kenny I had a craving for something goofy. Once I begged him to get me a corn dog with honey on it."

"Yuck! That doesn't sound very appetizing."

"Trust me it wasn't, but I ate it anyway."

"Have you met Jonah's family before, or Mary's cousins?" Liz asked.

"No, why? Have you?" Emmy looked over her shoulder at the Galves brothers.

"They are sneaking glances at you, and I caught Mary's cousins staring at Kenny and giggling."

"Why would they do that?" Emmy asked.

"Seriously? You're asking why?" Liz pushed Emmy forward in the line.

"Oh, get out. Are you serious?"

"You and Kenny are celebrities to them. Trust me I know. Sometimes I watch new people at church just to see their reactions when they see you guys."

"Stop it. People should realize we aren't any different than anyone else." She stacked three slices of pizza on her plate.

Liz shook her head. *Yeah, anyone can just pay for another family's mortgage.*

Ten minutes later Kenny stood up. "I think we should grab our pizza before the Michaelis brothers get back in line. They can pack it away like Tony and John."

"I think you're right. They're pretty good basketball players, too," Tyler added.

After everyone devoured their fill of pizza, Jonah and Mary passed out gifts to the wedding party.

"We want to thank everyone in advance for helping make this weekend special for us." Jonah tried to be serious while his brothers were trying to get him to crack up by making jokes.

Kenny watched the Galves brothers for a time. Then he leaned closer to Tyler. "Do you know anything about Jonah's family that you can share?"

"Jonah was very open about his family from the beginning. He wasn't raised in a church-going family. In fact, he's still the only one who attends church. He worked full-time while going to Wheaton College." He paused for a moment. "I suppose it's all right to mention this since everyone will know tomorrow, but Jonah said there was quite a battle over whether or not to have alcohol at the reception."

"I can see where that might be an issue." Kenny scratched his ear. "Mary grew up in a home where alcohol was prohibited. I think Em told me Mary's never had a drink."

"Jonah wanted the reception to be alcohol free, but his family balked at that plan. They reached a compromise."

Kenny nodded. "Emmy told me they decided to have an open bar before the meal and after that if people wanted something else, they had to pay for it. The Lincoln Hotel probably makes a ton of money from the sale of drinks."

Tyler chuckled. "We'll see how it goes. We might have two totally opposite crowds."

"Yeah, on one side will be the sober crowd, and on the other side will be the rowdies," Kenny said.

"Mother! For the last time. I am going to Stanford," Abigail said slowly for emphasis. "I wouldn't go to Wellesley if it was the only college on the planet."

350

Spencer laughed. "You won't consider Wellesley because there are no men there."

"I'm attending Stanford because of the opportunities it offers," Abigail insisted.

"Like I said," Spencer teased some more. "Men!"

"Please stop bickering," Marissa pleaded. She dramatically put a hand to her forehead. "I'm getting a migraine."

Bennett entered the living room. "How soon do we need to leave?"

Abigail rolled her eyes. "Father! You are the headmaster. Don't you know what time graduation starts?"

Bennett ran a hand through his thinning hair and then chuckled. "I guess they won't start without me, huh?"

"Will you at least wear the new dress I purchased?" Marissa glanced at the peach-colored satin dress on the couch and then back at Abigail in her jeans and t-shirt. "Your grandmother will be thrilled if you dress like a lady."

"Yes, Mother, I will wear the dress." Abigail turned to her father. "Are you going to kiss all the young ladies as they receive their diploma?"

"Of course not!" Bennett stammered. "Why would I do that?"

"You wouldn't, of course. You will shake hands, right?"

Bennett nodded and fell into Abigail's trap.

"Then please don't embarrass me by treating me any differently."

"But..."

Abigail waved a finger at her father.

"Have it your way, Abby," Bennett sighed.

Spencer laughed. "She always does."

Priscilla DeHaven, the principal of The Barclay Academy, continually pushed her glasses up her long nose while reading off the names of the graduates. Bennett Robertson shook hands and handed the graduates their real diplomas. Unlike some schools, The Barclay Academy passed out the real thing at the ceremony.

Bennett smiled as he heard the name Abigail Hartley Robertson. Abby walked across the platform smiled at Mrs.

351

DeHaven and approached her father. He handed her the diploma and offered his hand.

"Oh, Daddy," Abby sighed and then hugged her father.

Principal DeHaven paused for a few seconds and then read the next name.

"Heather and Isabella, you get in here this instant!" Emmy hollered from the bathroom in the twins bedroom. "You have to take baths and let me wash your hair."

"But, Mom! We aren't finished playing," Heather replied indignantly from the playroom.

"If you want to be in Mary's wedding, you are finished playing."

"Come on, Heather. We want to wear our princess dresses." Isabella ran into the bedroom. "We're ready for baths, Mommy."

Emmy, Heather and Isabella needed to be at the church by noon. The guys were luckier. Since they weren't part of the wedding party, they could show up a minute before the wedding if they chose. Emmy parked her BMW in the back of the church.

"Come on, girls. We can use the back door."

Paula chose the music suite as the area for the ladies to use to get ready. The recent addition of a private restroom allowed that choice.

Heather and Isabella spotted Mary and dashed over to her.

"Mary, when are you going to put on your princess bride dress?" Heather asked.

"Not until later. I have to finish getting my hair done and putting on my makeup. I wouldn't want my princess dress to get dirty, would I?"

"Mommy doesn't wear makeup. She says she wants to look natural," Heather watched as Mary's hairdresser fixed her hair.

"Will you girls stop pestering Mary. She has enough on her mind without you guys hanging around," Emmy shooed the twins away. "Is there anything I can do, Mary?"

"Nothing at the moment. Unless you want to calm Ma down. She's upset about the reception."

"The alcohol thing?" Emmy asked.

352

"Yes. I shouldn't say anything, but Mrs. Galves might have started drinking a little too early."

"Where are they?"

Mary shrugged. "Don't know at the moment."

"I'll look around."

Emmy searched the building and found Mrs. Galves in the Coffee Club off of the foyer. Emmy sat down across a table from her. "Hi, Mrs. Galves, how are you?"

She stared at Emmy. "I'm fine! I don't know why everyone is making a big deal out of a little bit of Scotch."

"Would you like some coffee? I can make you some," Emmy offered.

"Sure, I could use some."

Emmy made the coffee and sat down with Mrs. Galves again. "This is a pretty important day for Jonah and Mary. Wouldn't you agree?"

"I know it is, and I'm not going to spoil it for them. I just needed something to calm my nerves."

"I met your other sons last night, but are they married? I didn't hear anyone talk about wives." Emmy spoke in a calm voice.

Mrs. Galves took a sip of the hot coffee. "They're all married. The wives will be here today along with my grandkids. I have six of them. Would you like to see some pictures?"

"Sure! I have three kids. My girls are in the wedding party."

"I saw them last night. They look adorable."

Emmy and Mrs. Galves talked for fifteen minutes, and by the end of their conversation, Emmy knew quite a bit about the Galves family history.

"Mary worked as our nanny for several years. She's really good with kids. My kids adore her."

Mrs. Galves looked around. "Do you happen to know the time?"

"It's almost one. I need to get dressed."

"Would you tell Mary I'm sorry, and let her know I won't take another drink until tonight," Mrs. Galves promised.

"I'll let her know."

"Thanks, and I know you and your husband are famous and all, but you seem really nice. You're like a regular person."

"Thank you, Mrs. Galves." Emmy headed back to the music suite. She found Heather and Isabella sitting at a table, wearing their princess dresses and reading books.

Isabella saw Emmy first. "Mommy, we're ready. That lady fixed our hair. Do you like it?"

"You both look so adorable," Emmy said.

At one forty-five Paula and her assistants escorted the female part of the wedding party to the room normally used during church services for mothers with small noisy children.

"I remember this room so well," Emmy looked around She glanced out at the crowd. "The place is packed, Mary. Did you invite all these people?"

"Jonah has a large family."

"It's two o'clock, and the men will be taking their places in a couple of minutes. We need to line up and take one last look at each other." Paula quickly organized the ladies and smiled at Heather and Isabella. "You look like princesses." She signaled for the mothers to be seated and did a final check of the bridesmaids. "Emmy, you still look so young. You have to tell me your secret."

"The kids keep me young," Emmy said.

"Ha! My kids aged me." Paula laughed.

Mary tapped Emmy on the shoulder. "Before we get started I want to thank you for everything."

"I would hug you, but I don't want to mess up your dress."

Mary grinned and asked, "Are you going to cry?"

Emmy shook her head. "No, I'm gonna focus on the clock on the back wall and not pay any attention to the ceremony."

"Why is it I don't believe that?" Mary hugged Emmy.

"Mary! Stop that. You will wrinkle your dress." Paula rushed over and inspected Mary again. "You still look perfect."

Tyler led the men onto the platform, and Paula scooted the ladies into position.

"Try not to trip going up the steps," Dahlia said.

Heather and Isabella led the way. Though they were older than most flower girls, Mary wanted them to be a part of her special day. The other bridesmaids followed, and then Cora Michaelis stood. The rest of the crowd rose to their feet.

"It's time, Da," Mary held onto her father and they walked slowly down the aisle. Mary smiled and would have waved to some of the people had she not been carrying her flowers. She got close to the front and looked at Dahlia, who was smiling. Then Mary glanced at Emmy. *You might be able to keep staring at the clock for a little bit, but I know you too well.*

Tyler stepped forward and the ceremony began...

"You may now kiss your bride," Tyler said. He glanced at Liz who pointed with her eyes toward Emmy. Tyler glanced over at Emmy and chuckled as the tears poured down her face.

"Mommy! Mommy! Mary's kissing Jonah," Heather said loud enough for the people in the front to hear.

Soon, Tyler introduced Mr. and Mrs. Jonah and Mary Galves to the crowd. Mary and Jonah scurried down the aisle. Emmy and the girls waited their turn.

"Mommy, are you sad, or are you crying because you're happy?" Isabella grabbed Emmy's hand.

"I'm so happy, Isa."

Eli joined Emmy. "I think it's our turn, Emmy."

"You can go back down the aisle, girls, but don't run, please." Emmy watched as the girls walked at a moderate pace until they reached the halfway point. Then she heard them giggle and watched as they raced out of the sanctuary.

"Didn't Mary look beautiful?" Eli commented.

Emmy looked up at him and grinned. "You guys act so tough and all, but I saw you both crying." She poked him in the arm. "I was doing fine until I saw you guys losing it. That made me lose it."

"You won't tell anyone, will you, Emmy?" Eli implored.

"No, but it will cost you."

Paula paced back and forth inside the Lincoln Hotel. They should be here by now. Where could they be?" She looked out the door and spotted the large, white limousine.

"All right, everyone. I want the wedding party over here. The DJ will introduce everyone in the same order."

Emmy smiled and looked up at Eli. "Are you a good dancer? We will have to dance together."

"I'm not real smooth, but I've been practicing with Dahlia."

"Where have you been?" Paula fussed over Mary and Jonah.

"We took a little detour and visited my grandmother," Mary said.

Paula looked around. "Where is she? Isn't she coming to the reception?"

Mary shook her head. "We stopped at Rose Hill."

"Oh, sweetie, I'm so sorry." Paula, the most professional wedding planner in the city, nearly broke down in tears, but she controlled her emotions. "Emmy, send the girls in."

"It's time for you to go," Emmy said. "Remember to walk slowly." She watched with motherly pride as the girls carried their white baskets and walked all the way to the front without running.

"Em! Em! We have to go. They already introduced us," Eli nudged her.

"Oh, sorry, I wasn't listening."

The rest of the wedding party marched into the room, and then the DJ announced Jonah and Mary. The crowd rose and gave the new couple a standing ovation.

Kenny heard a loud whistle and looked at Emmy. She shook her head and mouthed, "Wasn't me."

Shortly after eight, the DJ announced the first dance for the bride and groom.

"Are you ready, Mary?" Jonah took her hand and led her onto the dance floor.

"I know you've danced a lot in your younger days, but I'm nervous," she whispered.

"Just follow my lead, and it will be over before you know it."

The next dance was for the bride and her father.

"Da, you don't have to be nervous. I don't care if you just stand there with me. This is the happiest day of my life," Mary said as she smiled and tried hard not to cry.

"I haven't danced since your mother and I got married."

"We did practice, and you did fine."

"I'll just hold you and try not to mash your feet." He looked down and then back up into her eyes. "I remember your first pair of shoes. You were so little and look at you now. You're all grown up."

"Oh, Da. I still feel like your little girl at times."

Jonah danced with his mother, and then the DJ wanted the entire wedding party on the dance floor.

"Come on, Eli. This is your chance to wow me with your dance moves." Emmy pulled him onto the dance floor as the DJ played an uptempo dance track.

"Emmy, look!" Eli pointed after a couple of minutes.

Emmy smiled at Heather and Isabella dancing with many of the kids from Bristol Ridge. "The crowd is going to have a blast watching the kids."

A few minutes later Tony walked up to Emmy. "Wanna dance? Sloane and I are taking all the kids home to our house, remember?"

"I remember. You guys are so brave. Letting the kids have a sleepover. Thank you." Emmy remembered the first time she danced with Tony and how he surprised her with his gracefulness. "I noticed Sloane hasn't been dancing."

"No, she doesn't like to dance. She grew up a Nazarene."

"Right, I forgot."

The song ended and Tony smiled. "Thanks for the dance, brat."

"You're welcome, creep."

Emmy joined Kenny at the table with Tyler and Liz. "Are you going to dance with me, Kenny?"

"I will if they play a slow song." Kenny shook his head because the DJ announced he was going to slow down the pace. "Did you bribe him, Em?"

"Nope! Just a happy coincidence."

Kenny held her close for five minutes while they danced. They returned to the table.

"Have you guys ever danced together?" Emmy asked Tyler and Liz. "I probably asked you before."

"We did ballroom dancing at school, but that's it. I really don't mind people dancing, but as a Nazarene pastor I feel I need to set an example."

"You have to follow the church manual, right?" Emmy grinned.

"I don't want anyone to be able to say I don't practice what I preach," he said and then chuckled.

"What if Liz and I wanted to dance together?"

Tyler looked at Liz and shrugged. "Her choice."

Liz watched the dance floor and bobbed her head in time with the music. "I'm tempted, but I'm expecting. I can always use that as my excuse."

"When Kristen and I were younger, we would dance together at receptions and other dances. I suppose we're too old now." Emmy eyed the younger crowd having fun.

"I saw John and Kristen dancing before," Kenny said.

"I like how the DJ has the speakers set up. We can talk and carry on a conversation without having to shout," Tyler said.

Emmy put a hand to her ear. "What did you say?"

Kenny shook his head.

Isabella came over to the table and sat down. "I'm tired, Mommy." Isabella lay her head on her arm.

Heather rushed over a moment later. "Mommy, did you see us dancing? I danced with Carson and Peter! They're boys."

"I saw you. Did you have fun?"

"It was fun, but boys don't know how to dance. They just wave their arms around and act silly like this." Heather demonstrated what she meant.

"That does look silly." Kenny grinned. He leaned closer to Emmy and asked, "Do I dance like that?"

"Not anymore, sweetie. You're much better now," Emmy said and then patted his arm.

Tony and Sloane gathered up all the kids shortly after nine thirty.

"We wanted to have them in bed by ten, but it might be a little later," Sloane said rather apologetically.

Emmy looked at Heather and Isabella. "I think most of

them will fall asleep on the ride home. Thanks for driving two vans."

"No problem, Emmy. Actually, it's a good excuse for us to leave early. I'm not much of a party person anymore. Not that I ever was."

"If you want, you could drop the girls off at our house. Sofia is there with Kevin Michael."

"No, Mommy, we want to have a sleepover with Dotty and Noemi," Heather said.

"Okay, but you can't stay up real late. We have church in the morning."

The anticipated battle over alcohol never manifested itself. Very few of the guests from the Michaelis side drank at all, and even the Galves family limited their consumption.

"Are you ready to go, Liz?" Tyler noted it was ten o'clock.

"Ready whenever you are," she replied. "See you guys in the morning."

Emmy noticed Mary and Jonah getting ready to leave an hour later.

"We have to say goodbye, Kenny," Emmy insisted.

Mary saw her coming and opened her arms. "We're going to leave, Em. Thanks so much."

"You're welcome, Mary. I'll talk to you when you get back."

On the way home, Kenny thought about something. "Em?"

"What, Kenny?" she yawned.

"You didn't ask Mary where they are spending their wedding night. Why? You used to always need to know details like that."

"Oh, Kenny, I'm much more mature now. That's something that should remain private."

"If you say so." He stared at her.

Emmy turned to look out the passenger window. *And I already knew. I set it up for them, but I can't tell you. It is good that your parents are out of town though. Mary might feel self conscious about staying in the carriage house otherwise.*

359

Kenny and Emmy made it to church on time the next morning, but they let the kids stay home and sleep. Sofia stayed with them. Worship Team B was scheduled to play.

"How late did you guys stay?" Liz joined Emmy in the music suite.

"We left around eleven because Mary and Jonah were leaving. Wasn't it a beautiful wedding?" Emmy sighed.

"It was, and that hotel is amazing. You guys had your reception there, right?"

"Yes, but we never would have if Kristen hadn't booked it for me. I thought it was way too expensive."

Darian and Dany went out for lunch after church. Darian talked about the reception and how much he wished Dany had been there.

"It must have cost a fortune. Could your parents afford it? They're teachers and teachers don't make a ton of money."

"It wasn't bad. Kenny and Emmy paid for most of it," Darian confessed. "Oh, shoot! I wasn't supposed to let that out."

"I won't tell anyone other than Liz and Tyler," Dany whispered. "Are they going on a honeymoon?"

Darian grinned. "I certainly can't tell you they're going to Hawaii for two weeks."

"Who wants to go to Aunt Dany's house?" Tyler asked.

"I do," Liam answered.

"We need to get in the car, and you need to behave," Tyler said. "Otherwise, we will come right back home."

"Does she live in the woods?" Dillan asked as he stared out the window. "Are there bears and elephants?"

"She kinda lives in a forest," Liz explained. "But there aren't any wild animals."

"Can we play in the woods?" Liam stared out the other side of the car. "Can we, please?"

"We'll see," Tyler answered.

"But he said please. We want to play in the woods," Dillan insisted.

"Just because you asked politely does not mean you get everything you want," Liz said. "We'll see how you behave and make a decision based on that."

The boys sat restlessly on the couch while Tyler, Liz and Dany talked.

Dany talked about her lunch conversation. "Darian spilled it accidentally. He also said Mary and Jonah are going to Hawaii for their honeymoon."

"I can understand the Hawaii part," Liz said. "We used the timeshare for our honeymoon, and Kenny and Emmy stayed at Mr. Robertson's ranch at the same time. That's probably where Jonah and Mary are staying, but it must have cost a considerable amount to pay for the reception and probably the hotel rooms."

"Can we play outside?" Dillan asked again.

"No! Sit there and don't move," Tyler ordered.

"I told you about the mortgage, and we can't think of anyone other than Kenny and Emmy who could, or would, have done that," Liz whispered to Dany. "Mr. Robertson could have easily, but he wouldn't have a reason."

"It was probably them. You should ask them. They won't lie to your face."

"Who wants to go for a walk?" Tyler stood up.

Dillan and Liam shot a hand up immediately.

"Let's walk over to Kenny's house and see if they're home," Tyler suggested. "You could push Grayson and Avery in the stroller."

"I'll go with to show you the way," Dany said to the boys. "The woods can be scary."

When they came within sight of the main house, Dillan and Liam took off running. Tyler jogged after them. Kenny and Emmy heard the boys coming, saw Tyler and waved.

Dillan ran up to Emmy and pointed. "Do you live there?"

"Yes, we do."

"Is your house haunted? Aren't you afraid to live in the woods? Have you ever seen a monster?" Dillan rattled on and on.

"As far as I know, the house isn't haunted, but the woods are rather frightening. Peter once got lost, and everyone had to go looking for him."

Liz and Dany arrived with the stroller and Natalie. Heather

361

and Isabella jabbered with Natalie and then took her over to the playhouse.

"We are having a wedding and reception. You can play with us," Isabella explained.

Heather pulled Dany along. "We need you to be the preacher."

Kevin decided to play with Dillan and Liam which left the girls without a groom. They recruited Grayson, who was still intimidated by the older boys. Tyler ordered Dillan and Liam to stay in the yard, and then the adults sat on the deck around one of the circular glass patio tables.

"That was quite a reception," Liz said. "It was very generous of you guys to pay for it."

Kenny looked at Emmy. Emmy bit her lip and stared at Liz.

"Darian mentioned it to Dany," Tyler said.

"We love Mary like family. We wanted to help out." Emmy smiled at the girls and Grayson pretending to hold a wedding ceremony.

"I understand, and that brings up something else," Tyler said and then looked at Liz.

"Did you pay off our house?" Liz asked bluntly.

"Liz, please don't be mad at us," Emmy answered without thinking.

Kenny shook his head. "So much for anonymity."

"You guys are way too generous. You do so much for the church. You helped fund the school. You pay off mortgages. You can't keep giving away your money!" Liz waved her hands around.

Kenny looked at Emmy. "I don't want to sound egotistical or pompous, but we kinda have to give away some money."

Tyler looked at Kenny for a few seconds. "Taxes, huh?"

Kenny nodded.

"My parents are doctors and Grandma Lindower has plenty of money," Liz mentioned.

Kenny and Emmy squirmed in their deck chairs. Tyler studied them for a moment.

"Liz, I think we are talking Kia and Ferrari here."

"I don't get it." Liz started braiding her hair.

362

"We don't have a clue as to how much you earn, do we?" Tyler chuckled.

Kenny shook his head. Emmy bit her lip.

"We don't want to pry. Let's talk about something else," Tyler suggested.

"Sometimes I feel guilty because God has blessed us with so much," Emmy confessed. "I think about Matthew 19 and how that rich young ruler guy valued his possessions more than loving Jesus, and I never want to be like that. I would give everything away if God told me to." Emmy's voice cracked with emotion. "I would live in that playhouse if I had to."

"You shouldn't feel guilty, Emmy." Liz saw Dillan trying to climb a tree and motioned to Tyler.

"Dillan! Stay out of the trees, please. Thank you." Tyler watched until Dillan moved away from the tree.

"So, we shouldn't worry about you and money?" Liz asked.

Kenny answered, "Our money is invested wisely. We are rather conservative about investing."

"But you drive Civics and you clip coupons and buy clothes on sale," Liz mentioned.

"They also live in a dream house," Tyler said.

"When new people come to the church and see you without knowing who you are, they would never believe this." Liz waved her hands at the house and yard. "You guys are just so normal."

"Kenny isn't normal. He's a dork," Emmy teased.

"You know what I mean," Liz said to Emmy and then looked at Kenny. "I don't think you're a dork."

"Please don't think we don't appreciate what you did. Buying the house really stretched our budget to the limit," Tyler admitted.

"Yes, but you guys did it with the idea of using the house for the foster kids. I could never do that." Emmy pointed toward the boys.

"Dillan! Liam! Do not throw rocks."

Dillan ran over to Tyler. "We saw an animal in the woods. A big one!"

"Okay, but please don't throw rocks."

Dillan scampered back to Liam and Kevin.

"You are using your house to do what God wants you to. We don't have the same call, so we decided to make things a little easier for you," Kenny said.

"Some people toss money at the church and don't do anything more. You guys are so involved in the church, and very few people are aware of your generosity."

"We don't want to draw attention to ourselves," Emmy said.

"Other than when you dance around on the platform," Tyler said and then chuckled.

Emmy made a face at Tyler. "I don't dance nearly as much as I used to. But I can't just stand there and do nothing. I've been to churches where the singers look like they just swallowed a dill pickle and it's stuck in their throats."

"Now you're supposed to say you may now kiss the bride," Heather said to Dany and Grayson. Grayson looked at his aunt and made a face. The twins giggled.

Chapter Thirty-Seven

"I want to try one more thing," Kenny sat behind the mixing console at Steward Music Group's Studio Four. He adjusted two tracks of keyboards and played "The Last Crusade" again. "What do you think?" he asked Jeff and Adam.

"Could you play it again, please?" Adam requested.

Will Consoli repeated the section.

"I like it. It adds just a bit more texture," Adam said.

"Sounds good to me," Jeff said and then checked the time. "Are we done? If so, I'm outta here. I'm taking tomorrow off to go fishing. I need to forget about music for a day."

"We're finished." Kenny stood up and high-fived the guys. "Some days I thought we would never finish this project."

Kenny and the band finished the recording of *Dangerous Circumstances*. The double CD project would be mixed by Kenny and Will between tour dates, mastered, manufactured and ready for the planned November release.

"I don't want to see the inside of a recording studio for two years," Jeff said. "This project has given me more gray hairs than stressing out over the kids ever did."

"I need a break, too." Adam smiled and looked at Kenny. "Now you can help Emmy with her CD."

"True, but she said something the other day about pushing her CD back until the spring. She heard the girls singing a Christmas song and mentioned she might like to record some Christmas songs."

"The girls were singing Christmas songs in June?" Will chuckled.

"They sing them all year."

"We aren't rehearsing tomorrow, are we?" Jeff asked.

"We're as ready as we're ever gonna be. The tech guys have worked out all the kinks. Right, Will?" Kenny nodded.

"The trucks are getting loaded tomorrow, and the drivers will leave early in the morning."

"Have you thought about flying to the gigs, Will?" Jeff asked.

Will shook his head. "I appreciate the offer, but I'd rather ride the bus. The highway relaxes me. I get uptight on a plane."

"Is everyone on the plane?" Andy Walker asked Jana Cordell early in the afternoon on Friday.

Jana checked her list against that of her assistant's. "Everyone is aboard. All the wives, nannies and children are seated and ready to go. Teresa is staying home because Tommy and Taylor have baseball games."

The flight crew ran through their final checks, received clearance to depart and the 737 taxied down the runway heading for Madison, Wisconsin. The cities on this tour were close enough together to allow the ground transportation to make the hops between cities in less than eight hours. By using Mr. Robertson's jet, the band and families could spend less time traveling. They would stay overnight in hotels in one city on Friday night and fly back to SoHam after the Saturday shows.

"Mommy, can we go swimming when we get to the hotel?" Heather asked.

"You will have to ask Sofia. I will be busy with your father," Emmy answered.

Isabella stared out the window. "Can we watch you sing tonight?"

"You can tonight, but tomorrow you need to go to bed at your regular time. It's important to get enough sleep so you aren't tired for Sunday School and church."

"We don't want to miss church because Pastor Jeremiah and Miss Mia are going to teach us new songs," Heather explained.

Emmy looked across the aisle at Kenny. "Have you listened to the teen band lately? Are they ready to be put on the schedule?"

"Robby and I checked out their rehearsal on Tuesday. I think they're ready. The two new singers are gaining confidence and they sound good together. Jake will lead on some songs, but I think he'd like to see the teens take charge. They need experience."

"Isn't Susan Lemmert one of the singers?"

Kenny nodded. "And David Belanger is the other one. That's Dan's son." Kenny referred to Daniel Belanger who mixed

366

the monitors for Fridays At Five.

"How old is David now?" Emmy remember him as a child.

"He's sixteen and Susan is fourteen. Remind you of anyone?" Kenny grinned.

"No way! Susie Lemmert can't be fourteen already. That's not possible. Didn't I change her diapers?"

"You are getting older, Em. Susan sings and she plays the piano. She's really talented like this other fourteen-year-old girl I remember."

Emmy stuck out her tongue at Kenny just as Andy Walker happened to walk by.

"What are you doing, Emmy? Do I have to separate you two?"

"Kenny told me I was getting old." Emmy made a face at him.

"I did not say you were getting old. I said older. There's a big difference," Kenny offered in his defense.

"Yeah, I'm not getting involved in that scene." Andy laughed and continued to the back of the plane to talk to Ralph Glissman. Ralph, the longtime tour manager for the band would be retiring at the close of the summer tour. He wanted to spend more time with his grandkids. Ty Dalicandro would be promoted to fill that spot.

"I don't think you're getting old, Mommy," Isabella said. "You're not old like Grandma or Me-maw."

Kenny snickered.

"Thank you, Isa."

People bought every available ticket for the show in Madison and also for the next night in Omaha, Nebraska. In fact, the entire tour sold out within hours of the tickets going on sale. The plane landed at the expanded SoHam airport in the middle of the night. Kenny carried the kids out to the van without them waking up. He and Emmy caught a few hours of sleep before getting up for church.

Emmy leaned back in her seat on the way to church and yawned. "I have an idea."

"What, Em?"

"I know you guys scheduled the shows on Friday and Saturday because that makes sense, but since you are going to sell out no matter what, how about Thursday and Friday instead. That would give us Saturday to be home. The kids wouldn't be so tired for church on Sunday."

"The kids?"

"Fine! I wouldn't be so tired on Sunday morning. Wake me up when we get there."

Two weeks into the summer tour brought the entourage to Tampa, Florida. Emmy emailed Rory Porter to make sure he received his tickets and backstage passes. He replied that he had them in his possession.

As soon as Emmy had the kids settled in the hotel, she called Rory. "We're here!"

"What time did you arrive? How was the flight?" He sounded chipper.

"We haven't been here too long. Maybe an hour. It's great being able to fly like this. I don't have to worry about the kids disturbing other passengers. How have you been? Are you working lots of hours?"

"I've been putting in sixty a week on average, but I don't mind. I took today off," he informed her.

"Did you eat already? The kids and Sofia ate on the plane, but Kenny and I haven't had lunch yet. You should come to the hotel, and we can do lunch," Emmy said.

"Are you sure it's all right?"

"Of course it is. We're staying at the Marriott Tuscany because it's real close to the venue. We have a suite and the kids are heading down to the pool with Kenny and Sofia. They think we're on vacation."

"I'd love to see you and the kids. Kenny, too," Rory admitted.

"Then come on over. We can do lunch and catch up. You could stay here until we leave for the show. I have to be there at five for my soundcheck, but we would have a few hours together."

"Okay, you've twisted my arm hard enough. I'll be there in

thirty minutes," Rory said as he checked his watch.

"Bring a suit if you want to use the pool. Oh, we're in 4210. I guess it would help to know our room number," she said and then giggled. "I'm registered as Olivia Porter, by the way."

Rory knocked on the door twenty-nine minutes later.

Emmy opened it and waved him in while she talked on her cell phone. He glanced around the open area and Emmy motioned for him to sit on the couch.

"Okay, I'll talk to you tomorrow, Diane. I gotta run."

"Is Rory there?"

"He just got here. I haven't even had a chance to say hi."

"Say hi for me, and don't do anything you shouldn't," Diane cautioned.

"I won't." Emmy ended the call, tossed her cell phone on the table, ran over to the couch and jumped onto his legs. "Did you miss me?" She hugged him.

He patted her back. "I have missed you. I didn't think you would have missed me this much."

She moved and sat next to him with her bare feet on the couch, her arms wrapped around her legs and her chin resting on her knees. "I think about you a lot. I kinda worry because you're all all alone down here."

"Are you trying to tactfully ask if I have a girlfriend?" he asked.

"Oh, stop grinning like that. I should just ask you. We are good friends."

He nodded.

"Does that mean you have a girlfriend, or are you saying we are good friends?" She poked him in the side.

"We are good friends, and I... don't have a girlfriend."

"Please tell me you have dated someone. You aren't neglecting your social life and turning into a workaholic, are you?"

"Not exactly. I've been out a few times, but nothing serious. I had dinner with the lady in the apartment down the hall, but she drove me nuts taking about her ex-this-and-that."

"The kids have been talking about seeing you. The girls made cards for you. Kevin will show you all his new cars."

369

"Is he still fascinated by firetrucks and diggers and stuff?"

Emmy sighed. "He tried to fill his suitcase with them, and got upset when I made him pack clothes. Are you thirsty? Hungry?"

"Yes, to both," he said.

"Let's go down to the pool, so you can see Kenny and Sofia and the kids. Then we can see about food. I can't imagine having to do this without Sofia along. Even the other wives have nannies to help watch the kids even though they don't have to work like I do."

"You guys are so spoiled. Can you imagine our mothers hiring someone to help watch us. Mom basically left us to fend for ourselves as soon as she could. She had to work."

They headed downstairs and outside. Emmy shielded her eyes from the sun and looked for Kenny.

"They're over there, Em." Rory pointed.

She scurried over to where Kenny was sitting on the edge of the shallow pool. She knelt behind him and kissed his ear. "Rory is here."

Kenny turned to look. "Hey, Rory. How have you been?"

"Good." He saw Sofia and waved.

Heather and Isabella heard his voice and squealed. They scrambled out of the pool and wrapped their arms around his legs.

"Girls, you're getting Rory all wet," Emmy scolded.

"It's all right, Emmy. I'm wearing sandals and shorts. It doesn't matter if I get wet."

Kevin climbed out of the pool, walked up to Rory, held up a toy and then handed it to Rory. "I got a new boat, and it floats."

"I see. It looks super." Rory examined the plastic toy and then handed it back.

"Rory is hungry, and so am I. Did you eat anything?" Emmy asked Kenny.

"I grabbed a sandwich. Just enough to tide me over until we get to the venue."

"Would you mind if Rory and I grab something?"

"No, go ahead. Sofia and I'll watch the kids. There's a cafe over there, or you could eat inside," Kenny suggested.

"Your choice, Rory."

370

"I don't mind eating outside. The humidity isn't bad today."

"We'll be over there. Do you have your key card?"

Kenny patted his pocket. "Got it right here. You can use yours to charge everything to the room."

I know. I've done some traveling. "Don't let the kids stay in the sun too long."

"I made sure I used a lot of sunscreen. We'll be okay. You and Rory can catch up. We need to be ready to leave by four thirty."

Emmy and Rory found a table with an umbrella and a breeze. They ordered salads and sweet tea from the college-age blonde waitress.

"Tell me everything you've done down here," Emmy grinned.

"Remember the old van I used to haul my stuff down here?"

"Yeah, did it make it?"

"It did surprisingly enough. I sold it and bought a 2013 Honda CR-V."

"Get out! You bough a CR-V. Why?"

"It's more practical."

"I can't believe it. Rory Porter is getting old," she teased. "Kenny bought a new Civic and so did I. I bought a Civic Si just for fun."

"Did you get rid of your BMW?"

"No, I still have it. We are crazy because we have four vehicles at home."

"At least you have that huge garage."

"What else is new?"

"Not a lot. I would offer to let you see the apartment, but you don't have a lot of time, and it's nothing special. Just a place to crash. I did buy some furniture, but I work so many hours. I'm not there a lot."

"Maybe one of these days you could buy a condo," Emmy took another sip of her tea. "This is really sweet."

"How's the tour going?"

"Great! Every place we've been has sold out. My new band

371

is really good. We're more like a rock band now. Musically, I mean. We don't trash hotel rooms or anything like that," she added and then grinned.

"What about groupies?" He raised his eyebrows.

She bit her lip. "Are you offering to be mine?"

"You know better, Em."

"Why haven't you been dating more often?"

He stared at her for a moment. "You want the truth?"

"Of course," she nodded.

"I have this horrible habit of comparing every woman I meet to you, and none of them stack up."

"Oh, Rory. You make it sound like I'm something special, and I'm not."

He laughed. "You don't even realize how special you are."

They finished their lunch and went back to the pool.

"We were just taking them upstairs, Emmy." Kenny dried Kevin's arms and checked for sunburn.

"Rory, you can come upstairs with us," Emmy invited him.

"I will because that will give me a chance to see these adorable little girls. You must be about five now, right?"

"Oh, Uncle Rory, you are so silly. We're seven now and we're going to be in second grade." Heather rolled her eyes and grabbed his hand.

"But Miss Liz won't be our teacher next year. We will have a new teacher." Isabella grabbed his other hand.

They went back upstairs and Sofia went to her room to get ready for later. Emmy made the girls take a quick shower.

Kenny sat on the couch with Rory and they talked about his job and Florida.

"I'm used to the heat, but sometimes the humidity gets to me," Rory said.

"I don't think I could live here all year round," Kenny said.

"I do kinda miss the different seasons," Rory admitted.

Heather and Isabella finished getting dressed, ran out of the bedroom and joined Rory on the couch.

"Are you going to watch Mommy and Daddy tonight?" Heather asked.

"I am going to the show."

"We want to be singers when we grow up," Heather said.

"Kenny, would you give Kevin his bath and get him ready, please?"

"Okay. Kevin, come with me." Kenny got up and headed to the bathroom.

"His clothes are on his bed," Emmy said.

"Mommy, can we watch the show with Rory?" Isabella asked.

"Maybe for a little while, but you can't watch the whole show. You will have to come back to the hotel with Sofia."

Heather grinned at Rory. "We sit behind the speakers and watch. Sometimes we even get to help Frankie."

"Mommy, are we going to eat with all the other kids?"

"Don't you want to?"

"Yes, can Uncle Rory eat with us?" Isabella asked.

"He might want to eat with me and Daddy," Emmy replied.

"Aw, that's okay."

Rory rode over to the venue with Kenny and Emmy. Emmy secured an all access pass for him and took him upstairs to the stage. She reintroduced him to her band and introduced him to Miles Goossens.

Bobby walked over and grinned. "Well, if it isn't Tim Burine. How are you? Are you ready to sit in with us tonight?"

Rory grinned. "I'm not sure. I haven't been practicing, so my wrist is out of shape."

"The girls would get a kick out of seeing you onstage. You should do the soundcheck at least," Emmy said.

"Sure, why not? Do you have a tambourine handy?"

Bobby tossed one to him.

"It's a left-handed model, but if you turn it over, it works all right," Bobby teased.

Emmy shook her head. "You are such a funny guy, Bobby. Do you label your sticks for the right and left hand?"

"Duh! They wouldn't work right if I held them in the wrong hand now, would they?"

"We're ready for your soundcheck, Emmy," Tobias

Wouters announced over the PA.

Emmy finished twenty minutes later.

"Will you play with us, Rory?" Emmy asked.

"Sure," he said. "It will be fun to surprise the girls."

"Let's see if the kids are here. We can grab a bite to eat if you're hungry."

Emmy took Rory back downstairs and they saw Sofia with the kids.

"Where's Kenny?" Rory looked around.

"Oh, he's busy doing interviews and greeting fans and stuff with the guys. We might not see him, or we might see him for a little bit," she said and then shrugged. "Just depends."

The kids saw Emmy and Rory and raced toward them.

"Can we eat now? We're hungry?" Heather asked.

"Okay." Emmy looked around, saw Jana Cordell and waved. "Jana, where is catering?"

"Hi, Emmy. It's actually around that corner and the first door on the left." She pointed.

"Thanks."

Jana waved to the kids.

Emmy made sure everyone was wearing their passes and entered the catering area. Rory checked the buffet table.

"Wow! You've got a lot of choices. It's almost like a restaurant."

He helped Emmy fill plates for the kids and they found seats. Rory waited for Emmy to pray and they ate. Kenny did pop in for a moment.

"I have to grab a plate and run. One of the radio stations ran a contest, and we have to meet the winner."

"Did you do your soundcheck already?" Rory asked.

"Yeah, we did ours right after Emmy's. See you later." He kissed Emmy and hugged the kids. "I'll kiss you goodnight when I get back to the hotel, but you better be asleep."

"Bye, Daddy. Sing good, and listen to Frankie," Kevin said.

They finished eating, and Rory checked the time. "What time does your set start, Em?"

"Eight, so we have about an hour to kill. We play for forty-

374

five minutes and Kenny goes on at nine. They'll probably play until eleven and as soon as they finish their last encore, they are brought to the hotel. Saturdays are a little different because we would all go to the airport together to fly home."

"What do you usually do until your set?"

"I check email. Play with the kids. I usually wait until the last minute to get changed. I meet the guys in the green room. They are almost never green. We pray and then we start. It's kinda fun because the guys go out and start playing, and then I run out there like I'm some kind of star. Sometimes I wish I could wear old jeans, a t-shirt and go on with the guys."

Rory hung out with Emmy, Sofia and the kids until Emmy needed to use her dressing room to change. He joined the band in the green room.

"You're still going to play, right?" Emmy asked as she entered the room.

"Are you sure I won't screw anything up?"

"You won't. Are you nervous?"

"A little, but I want to see the girls' faces when I go out there."

"They will get a kick out of it."

Rory stayed out of sight of the audience with the kids and Sofia until Emmy introduced him. He wore a borrowed sport coat and walked stiffly on stage. Miles handed him a tambourine, and Rory bowed. Not to the crowd but to Miles. Since Miles had never seen the Tim Burine character before, he didn't know what to expect. As before, Rory stood ramrod straight and tapped the tambourine against his leg. Sofia moved the kids to a position where they could see him.

Kevin noticed Rory and pointed. "Sofia, look! It's Uncle Rory."

Heather and Isabella put their hands to their mouth in surprise. Rory played on two songs and then made his exit. He never spoke, never changed his facial expression. It was as if he were a mechanical man.

"Uncle Rory! You know how to play a tambourine." Kevin ran to him and wrapped his arms around Rory's legs.

375

"Did I surprise you?"

The girls nodded, but didn't speak.

Emmy and the guys finished their set and ran off stage. Emmy rushed to her dressing room and changed into comfortable clothes before joining Rory, Sofia and the kids.

"Mommy, did you see Uncle Rory? He played a tambourine." Kevin was more amazed by Rory being on stage than the talents of all the other real musicians.

"Can we listen to Daddy for two songs?" Heather begged.

"Okay. Two songs, but then it's back to the hotel, and you have to go to sleep for Sofia."

The kids watched as Daddy's band opened their show.

"It's time." Emmy kissed the kids and Rory hugged them. Sofia took them downstairs and they were escorted to a black SUV and driven to the hotel. Sofia didn't notice the SUV following them, or the one in front.

"They still sound so amazing," Rory shouted into Emmy's ear.

"I still love watching and hearing them play."

Before the show ended Emmy took Rory downstairs.

"It was so good to see you, Emmy." He looked into her eyes and saw them sparkle.

She hugged him and whispered with her head against his chest, "You should come up for a visit sometime. We have extra rooms, so you could stay with us."

"I'll try to make it back soon." He kissed the top of her head. "I better go, Em. You take care."

"I will. Do you want a ride to the hotel to get your car?"

Rory shook his head. "Naw, it's only a couple of blocks. I can walk. See ya, Em."

Chapter Thirty-Eight

Emmy waited for the beep. "Hi, Liz, I wanted to remind you about Thursday. I added your names..."

"Hi, Emmy. Sorry I didn't get to the phone in time." Liz was breathing hard. "I was chasing Dillan and Liam around the yard with Derby. I'm trying to wear them out, so they'll sleep all night. What's up?"

"Nothing much. I called about Thursday. You guys are still planning to come, right?" Emmy could hear the boys hollering in the background.

"Yes, but it will just be the four of us. Six counting Dany and Darian. The boys and Avery will be spending the day with their parents. I hate to say this, but I'm glad. The boys wear me out."

"You need to be careful, Liz. You don't want to hurt the baby," Emmy cautioned.

Liz yawned. "I need some sleep."

"You could borrow Sofia if that would help," Emmy offered.

"I might take you up on that. What time does the concert start?"

"Let me look at the schedule. Hang on a sec."

Liz looked out the window and saw Dillan and Liam chasing Derby around the backyard. *Poor Derby. The boys wear you out, too.*

Emmy returned to the phone. "I've got it. The gates are supposed to open at two, but they're usually late. The girls are excited because Pastor Jeremiah will be playing."

"What's the name of his band? I should know, but I can't remember."

"BearFace," Emmy answered. "Because all the guys have beards and... you know. They kinda look rugged like that guy in the TV show from a long time ago. Anyway, Jeremiah is supposed to go on at three. The Katie Hollins Band at four. Have you ever heard of Jennifer Sinclaire?"

"I've heard of her, but I've never seen her in person." Liz

377

sighed because Dillan pulled Derby's tail.

"I've known Jennifer for ten years. She married Ryan Lederer who was in my band. They live in Knoxville. She's going to be here. I can't remember the last time we saw each other. She is scheduled for five thirty. I'm at seven, and Kenny goes on at eight thirty. The times will vary a little, but Ralph is in charge, and he runs a tight ship. The crew is the best in the business when it comes to changing the stage."

"I'm not sure what time we'll get there. Natty might like to see Pastor Jeremiah play. Where do we pick up our tickets?"

"I'll bring the tickets and a parking pass to church tomorrow. That will get you guys in the lot behind the stadium. You can park there, and there's a gate labeled stage or something like that. You give them your name, and they will let you in and give you your access passes. You will be able to wander wherever you want."

"Will there be a lot of trucks?" Liz asked. "Grayson might like to see the trucks."

"By the time you get there, the trucks and crew buses will most likely have been moved to the far south of the complex. There's not a lot of room right behind the stadium, so the trucks unload and the drivers move them out," Emmy explained. "The band buses usually stay there though. I know Jennifer travels in a bus, and I think Katie Hollins does now, too. Have you ever seen the inside of one of those tour buses?"

"No," Liz said.

"They are kinda cool. I might be able to sneak you onto Jennifer's."

"We'll see. So we park in back and use that gate to get in, right?"

"Yeah. You can call my cell, and I'll make sure I'm close. The girls like to watch the street performers. There are usually guys on stilts, jugglers, clowns and people like that. It's almost like a circus."

"I'll see you tomorrow, Emmy. I gotta go before Derby attacks the boys. They're chasing her and throwing rocks at her."

378

The recent expansion of SoHam Memorial Stadium doubled the seating capacity to just over 20,000. The once horseshoe-shaped stadium now completely encircled the football field and running track. The promoters sold 5,000 tickets for reserved seating on the field to make up for the unusable seats behind and to the sides of the stage. An additional 15,000 general admission tickets filled the rest of the area.

Buses and large semis with the FAF logo on the trailers began arriving early Wednesday morning. Though the show wasn't until Thursday, the crews worked feverishly to build the stage and get everything set up. A hundred men from SoHam Site Services erected fences, set up tents and porta-potties and closed off entrances to the stadium. Since the vast majority of the crews lived in SoHam, they would have almost a full day and a half to be home. Around noon another truck pulled in behind the stadium followed by a tour bus. This truck carried the gear belonging to Emmy's band. Six-foot-high letters emblazoned her name on both sides of the trailers. Her crew rode on the bus.

The crews finished shortly before two. Ralph Glissman and his staff inspected the eight-foot-high stage, which covered the entire endzone and everything else from one side of the complex to the other. Ralph communicated with his men and some officers from the SoHam police and fire departments. He voiced his approval, and the crews headed for home. The security teams took over and would patrol the complex until the last bus and truck departed sometime in the early hours of Friday morning.

Kenny parked the van in the spot reserved for him only a few feet away from the backstage exit under the south stands. Andy Walker and Nelson Grapella walked over to help get the kids out.

"Hi, Uncle Andy! I brought two diggers." Kevin Michael held up his toys.

"Wow! Can I see those?"

Kevin handed the toys to Andy. "You can play with them for a minute, but then I need them back."

"I'm going to be rather busy now, Kevin. I'll let you play

379

with them, but thank you for letting me hold them."

Emmy grabbed Kevin's hand before he could run away. Sofia stood with the girls. Jana Cordell and Ty Dalicandro approached with the all access passes. Jana and Emmy put one on each of the kids. These person-specific passes contained a tracker chip which allowed the security office to track their movements. Rosco Sandchek watched from a distance and nodded to the three men assigned to provide visual surveillance on the children, before he melted into the background.

"Are the other guys here?" Kenny asked.

"On their way," Andy replied. "Jana has the agenda for the day. I tried to avoid some of this, but you know how it goes."

Jana handed Kenny a printout of his pre-concert schedule.

He quickly scanned it. "All right! I have thirty minutes to eat, and fifteen minutes to get dressed."

"Your sarcasm is duly noted." Andy gestured as more of the guys arrived.

Emmy checked her phone for the time. "Kenny, will you keep Kevin with you. I promised Liz I would meet her at the gate. They should be here soon."

"Come on, Kev. Let's see if we can find Frankie."

Emmy waved to Tyler, Liz and the kids, ran up to the security gate and mentioned their names. "These people are on my list." She told the guards who checked to verify.

"Thank you, Ms. Colasanti." The guard handed Emmy five passes and waved for Tyler's group to enter.

"You guys made it. I was worried. Jeremiah's band is getting ready to play. Where's Dany and Darian?"

"They decided to sit out front. I think Dany was a little nervous about being back here. I don't know why."

"If she changes her mind, let me know. I will get passes for them."

Heather and Isabella talked with Natalie and Tyler carried Grayson on his shoulders.

"We have to hurry because Pastor Jeremiah is going to sing real soon," Heather said.

On the way to the backstage entrance, Tyler saw Kenny

and Kevin. "I'm going to take Grayson with me. I don't think he's interested in listening. We'll see you later."

Emmy, Liz, Sofia and the three girls made it onto the side of the stage behind a black wall of fabric that covered the front and sides of the nearly forty-feet-tall scaffolding. Emmy looked up to the top of the structure which supported the speakers and the trusses for the lights.

"Will it be loud here, Mom?" Natalie asked Liz.

Liz looked at Emmy and shrugged.

Emmy squatted to talk to Natalie. "If you could see through this material, you would see a whole bunch of speakers hanging in the air. They are all pointed away from us. It will be kinda loud, but not too bad. A bit louder than the worship band at church." *Quite a bit louder.* Emmy grinned.

Isabella took Natalie's hand. "We are used to it. Sometimes we cover our ears like this." Heather and Isabella covered their ears with their hands, made funny faces and danced around as if in pain.

Natalie giggled.

"Okay, girls, the PA announcer just introduced Pastor Jeremiah. See? He's walking out from right over there."

Heather, Isabella and Natalie squealed and waved both hands at Jeremiah. He smiled and waved back. Midway through the BearFace set, Emmy felt a tap on her shoulder and spun around.

"We thought we might find you here. Kenny told us about BearFace." Ryan Lederer and Jennifer Sinclaire looked down at the girls.

"Wait a minute," Jennifer drawled. "You can't possibly be Heather and Isabella because you are too big. Heather and Isabella are still babies."

"We're not babies," Heather said while Isabella moved closer to Emmy. "We're seven and we're going to be in second grade." Heather looked at Ryan and Jennifer without a clue as to who they might be. "This is Miss Liz. She taught us in first grade, and this is Sofia. She's our nanny."

Emmy put her hands on Isabella's shoulders. "It's so good

to see you guys. When did you get here?"

Ryan answered, "We pulled in around nine this morning. We drove in from Raleigh. Unloaded some gear, and then ate breakfast."

"Ryan Lederer, you sound just like a redneck," Emmy teased as she looked up at him. "I see you've put on a few pounds."

Jennifer patted Ryan's belly. "He picked up an accent real quick, and he loves my mashed potatoes and fried chicken. He has even learned to eat grits."

"Do you guys have time to grab a bite?" Emmy asked. *I love your new hairstyle. I keep mine short now, too.*

"We'll take the time. My band headed to the catering tent a few minutes ago. If we're lucky, there might be some fried chicken left."

Emmy talked to Jennifer as they walked down the back steps of the stage, under the new concrete stands and onto the parking lot to the catering tent. Liz held Natalie's hand as they followed. Heather and Isabella walked on either side of Ryan.

"Mommy said you used to be in her band, but then you got married and joined her band," Heather said while pointing at Jennifer.

"That's true, and my father used to work with your daddy's band and your mother's band, too."

"Do you have any kids?" Heather asked.

Ryan smiled. "Not yet, but we might one of these days."

Heather kept chattering all the way to the catering tent. Isabella lost her shyness and asked Ryan a few questions.

Emmy entered the catering tent and glanced around. She heard a chuckle to her left.

"Well, if it isn't the diva in person," Jimmy Sinclaire grinned as he set down his heaping plate of food. He walked over and hugged Emmy. "How you been?"

"Jimmy! Let go of her," Jennifer said. "I'm sorry, Emmy, but when he found out we were comin' up here, he insisted on tagging along."

"It's okay," Emmy grinned. "You still remember that gag we pulled on you, huh?"

382

"I remember. You pretended to be Jennifer's friend and didn't let on about who you really were. I didn't have a clue until you ran out on that stage and started singing."

Emmy turned to Liz. "This is Jimmy Sinclaire. Jennifer's brother. Are you married yet?" Emmy turned back to Jimmy.

"Been hitched for five years and got two little ones at home."

Emmy glanced at the table where Jennifer's band sat and waved.

"You probably don't remember their names, but these are still the same guys. For some reason they like hanging out together and driving all over the country with me."

Emmy, Liz and Sofia filled up plates for the girls. They filled their own plates and sat down to eat. Emmy prayed and the girls began eating.

"Do you remember that white minivan?" Jennifer asked Emmy as she and Ryan sat down with their food. "The one you bought for me back in Indianapolis, I think."

Liz looked at Emmy. "You've been giving away your money for a long time, huh?"

"Hush." Emmy nudged Liz. "I remember it."

"We put over 500,000 miles on it. We used it until we got our bus. Thank you, Emmy."

Liz leaned closer to Emmy. "Did you buy their bus?"

"No, now hush, and let me eat."

Jennifer ate quickly and then motioned to her band. "Hate to eat and run, Emmy, but we gotta get ready to earn our money."

"I'll try to talk to you later," Emmy said.

"I'll try, but we gotta leave real quick. We have to be in Ft. Worth tomorrow, and it's a long drive."

Emmy, Sofia and Liz waited at the table while the girls finished.

"She sounds real southern," Liz mentioned.

"She was born in the mountains of North Carolina, but moved to Knoxville. I guess she still lives there. We've kinda lost touch over the years."

The girls finished eating, and Emmy led everyone back to

383

their spot at the side of the stage. Jennifer saw them as she ended a song. She motioned for Emmy to come out on stage.

"Jennifer, what are you doing?" Emmy whispered.

"Don't worry. I won't make you sing with me. I just want to say something to the crowd." Jennifer pulled Emmy to the middle of the stage. "I'm sure you recognize this little lady," she waited for the applause to die down. "You probably aren't aware of how she supported me early in my career. I want you to know that Emmy is the kindest and most generous person I have ever met. Thank you for your support over the years. If it wasn't for you, I wouldn't be doing what I love to do. Well, I might be singing for twenty-five dollars, a cheeseburger and a Coke back in Bryson City, but I sure wouldn't be standin' here today." Jennifer grinned at Emmy as she referenced a remark Emmy once teased her about.

Emmy bit her lip as Jennifer hugged her.

"I hope that didn't embarrass you too much. Take care, Emmy." Jennifer resumed her set.

Emmy ran back over to Liz and the girls. Tyler and Grayson had joined them.

"I'm sorry, but I need to go get ready. Will you guys be all right?"

"I'll keep an eye on them," Tony Bertucci said.

"How did you get in here, creep?"

"I told them I was your bodyguard, brat. Sofia ran back to the van to get jackets in case it gets cold." Tony laughed and picked up Heather and Isabella and put them over his shoulders as they squealed.

"Uncle Tony, you better put us down, and don't try to tickle us," Isabella said.

"I would never tickle you. Are you ticklish there?" He tickled Isabella behind her knee.

She giggled and squirmed to get down. "Tickle me again."

"Does this tickle?" He did the other knee.

"Tickle me now," Heather said and then giggled.

"One time, but then I have to set you down." He tickled Heather and set the girls down.

"Are you here by yourself?" Tyler picked Grayson up and

set him on his shoulders. "Hold on, buddy."

"I came with John and Kristen. They're sitting out front. Sloane stayed home with Mama to watch all the kids. I saw Diane and Brady back there somewhere." Tony pointed to the backstage area.

Jennifer Sinclaire ended her set, and glanced around for Emmy. When she didn't see Emmy, Jennifer turned to her guys. "Let's hit the road. It's a long way to Ft. Worth."

The crews removed her band's gear from the stage, and it was hauled to their bus and stowed away.

"Is Mommy going to sing next?" Heather asked Liz.

Liz checked her cell phone for the time. "She should be going on in twenty minutes."

"I gotta go potty," Heather said.

"Me, too," Natalie whispered.

Tony picked up the twins. "Let's go together."

Liz held Natalie's hand, and Tyler carried Grayson.

Tony pointed. "There are porta-potties over there."

"We don't like those," Heather said.

"They smell funny. We want to use the bathroom under there by the dressing rooms." Isabella pointed.

"Don't move! Get on your knees and put your hands on top of your head." Detective Warren Sanders shouted.

Six other SoHam officers in shorts and t-shirts trained their weapons on the man in a running suit. The man looked around for an escape route.

"Don't do it," Detective Sanders said.

The man backed up toward the line of porta-potties, watched the six officers closing in, sighed and dropped to his knees. He placed his hands on his head.

"Cuff him," Detective Sanders ordered.

One of the officers did.

"We've been looking for you for a few months, Ronald," Detective Sanders said.

"You got the wrong guy. I ain't done nothin'."

"And it's going to stay that way in my city. Get him out of

385

here before anyone sees him. I don't want to create a disturbance," Detective Sanders ordered. *He's a piece of crap like his brother.*

The officers quickly hauled him away to a waiting squad car.

Detective Sanders turned and waved to a man standing a hundred feet away next to the exit of the south stands.

The man waved back and whispered to Diane. "It's over. He's in custody."

Thank you, Rosco." Diane looked back toward the area and the scene looked perfectly normal as a few people waited in lines. "So that was Ronald Delaney?"

"Yes, Todd's older brother. He was wanted in three states out west."

Brady put his hands on Diane's shoulders. "What will they do with him?"

"Send him to Arizona. The U.S. Marshals should have him in Phoenix about the time this concert ends."

"Do you think Emmy suspects anything?" Diane asked.

"I certainly hope not. If we're lucky, she'll never know this incident ever happened."

Diane looked up and decided to hug him. "Will I ever know your real name?"

The man she knew as Rosco Sandchek, and who looked like Tommy Lee Jones, smiled. "Not if I do my job properly."

"And you are very good at your job, right?"

"Yes, Mrs. Diane, I am," he said with a straight face and walked away.

Tyler took Grayson into a room and changed his diaper.

"Liz, will you take the girls? I will wait right here," Tony said. He leaned against the concrete wall and looked around at the crowd as the kids did their business.

"Hey, Tony Bertucci, beautiful day for a concert, right?"

"You better believe it," Tony smiled at one of the Friday crew members as he rolled a case toward the stage.

"Did everyone go?" Tony asked the kids when they returned.

386

"Uncle Tony, you can't ask that." Heather frowned at him with her hands on her hips. "We're not babies. We're big girls."

"Excuse me!" Tony grinned.

They went back to their spot on the side of the stage.

Frankie Hanna met them. "I brought out some chairs. Emmy thought you might want to sit."

"Thank you, Frankie," Tony said.

Frankie nodded and went back to work.

"He doesn't say much, does he?" Tyler chuckled.

"No, but he adores the girls."

Emmy's band walked onto the stage five minutes later to get ready. Emmy and Sofia walked over to the girls. Sofia set the jackets on a chair.

"Mommy, Miss Liz took us to the potty, and Uncle Tony helped."

Emmy looked at Tony.

"I waited outside," he explained.

"I have to go sing. You can stay here if you want. Daddy and Kevin might come out. He's been very busy today."

"Can we have a snack after you sing?" Heather asked.

"Okay, but only one snack." Emmy took her mic from Frankie and dashed out onto the stage as the crowd roared.

Heather, Isabella and Natalie covered their ears and giggled.

Emmy finished her set and walked over to the girls.

"You did a good job, Mommy. Can we have our snack now?" Heather asked.

Emmy laughed. *You certainly are a little stinker.* She looked up at Tyler. "Did you enjoy it?"

Tyler chuckled. "Amazing! I've heard stories about how shy you were as a young lady, and look at you now."

"I'm still shy," Emmy said and then bit her lip.

"Kenny and Kevin Michael stopped by for a few minutes, but then he had to run. Kenny, I mean. Kevin and Grayson are with Tony."

"Where did Tony go?" Emmy asked while looking around.

"He took Grayson and Kevin to watch the street performers

387

back by the catering tent. Tony said something about hearing you sing a gazillion times."

"He's such a creep." Emmy laughed and said, "How about I meet you at the catering tent. I want to change. I'm soaked."

"We'll meet you there," Tyler said. He picked up Natalie, and Liz and Sofia took Heather and Isabella.

Emmy changed in her dressing room under the stands and hurried back to the tent. She almost ran into Brady. "I didn't know you guys were here."

Diane walked over. "We decided to come at the last minute." Diane looked at her younger sister, and then hugged her tightly.

"Are you okay?" Emmy asked after being released.

"Yes, everything is all right. Now."

"If you say so." Emmy tilted her head and stared up at Diane for a moment.

Sofia stayed with the kids in a room under the stands behind the stage. Grayson fell asleep on a couch. Kevin and the girls sang songs and pretended to be having their own concert. Tyler and Liz joined Dany and Darian in the fifth row, center section to watch Fridays At Five for the first time. Emmy and Tony stood at the side of the stage. The lights used for football faded into darkness, and the stage instantly went black.

"I've seen this happen a gazillion times, but I still get chills," Emmy yelled at Tony.

"Yeah, big deal. Lights, lasers, pyrotechnics and loud music," Tony said as he shrugged.

She watched as Frankie Hanna and some of the other crew members used flashlights to lead Kenny and the band to their spots on stage.

"Get ready, Tony!" Emmy covered her ears.

Dave banged his sticks together four times and the stage exploded in a flash of light and sound.

Chapter Thirty-Nine

"Happy birthday, Em." Kenny put an arm around her, drew her closer and kissed her. "Do you have plans for today? It is a special birthday, remember?"

"She stretched her arms over her head as she yawned. "And what makes this one special?"

"It's the only time you will turn thirty-three," he said.

She looked at him and rolled her eyes. "You are such a dork, but I love you anyway."

They heard a soft knock on the door.

"Yes?" Kenny said.

"Can we come in?" Isabella asked.

"Yes, Mommy is awake."

Heather pushed the door open and the kids rushed into the bedroom and climbed onto the bed.

"Happy birthday, Mommy." Kevin Michael lay next to her.

She looked into his eyes, which reminded her so much of Kenny's. "Thank you, little man."

"I brought a police car for you to play with. But you can't lose it, and I want it back." He showed her the police car.

Emmy turned onto her back and scooted up in the bed. She ran her hands through her hair.

"Should we sing 'Happy Birthday' now, or wait until you open your presents?" Isabella asked.

"Why don't we wait, Isa," Kenny said.

"Okay. What do you want for breakfast? I will help Daddy make it."

"Thank you, Isa." Emmy put a finger to her mouth. "Hmmm, what do I have a taste for?"

"I think you need pancakes." Kevin pushed his police car around on the bed.

"Pancakes with blueberries?" Emmy asked.

Heather scooted closer to Kenny and ran a hand over his cheek and chin. "You need to shave, Daddy." Then she looked at Emmy. "I like pancakes with blueberries. I could eat them everyday."

Kenny chuckled and reached over to tickle Emmy's side. "I know someone else who could eat them for breakfast everyday."

"Stop that!" Emmy said but with a smile.

"I want five pancakes." Kevin held up his hand with his fingers extended. "And I want sausage, too."

"You must be very hungry," Kenny said.

"I'm a growing man. I need to eat a lot." He fell off of the bed but popped back up. "I'm okay."

"Should we go downstairs and let Mommy get dressed? We can get breakfast ready and watch her open her presents," Kenny suggested. "I need to get dressed, too."

"Okay, but don't take too long. We have a busy day ahead of us," Heather said. "We're 'posed to play with Dotty and Noemi."

"I'll hurry," Emmy promised. "Let me take a quick shower, and I'll come downstairs." She pointed to the door. "Now scoot."

The girls kissed Emmy and held hands as they scrambled off of the bed and dashed out of the room. Kevin ran after them, but then hustled back. "I need this police car. I'll let you play with it later, Mommy." He grabbed his car and sprinted after his sisters.

Kenny leaned over, kissed Emmy again, smiled and said, "Happy birthday. I have a present for you."

"Hurry, Mommy! We're hungry," Kevin shouted from the hallway.

Emmy and Kenny looked toward the door and heard two girls giggling.

"We're coming." Kenny sighed as he got out of bed.

Emmy grinned. "I'll take a raincheck."

Later that morning Emmy sat behind the recording console in the basement studio and listened to a newly recorded vocal track. *I need to redo that line.* She listened to the end of the track and then closed her eyes. She waited for a moment and then began to pray out loud. "Lord, thank you for your many blessings." She prayed for the people on her prayer list, the church and then asked for direction for her life. "Lord, guide me. Show me if there is anything I need to change." Then she paused. She cleared her mind and listened for the Holy Spirit to talk to her heart, just like Pastor Tyler had taught the people at church. She felt her heart slow down as she took deep breaths. For four minutes she sat with her eyes closed and her mind clear without making a sound. Then suddenly she opened her eyes and sat up. She put her feet on the floor and grabbed the arms of the recliner.

"Really, Lord!? Are you sure? I don't know if I can do that." She paused again and listened. "Okay," she thought about one of her favorite verses. "In Psalms 28:7, it says 'The Lord is my strength and my shield; my heart trusts in him and he helps me. My heart leaps for joy, and with my song I praise him.' My song, Lord. That's what I do. I write songs, not what you are telling me." She closed her eyes and tried to fight back the tears. "Songs, I write songs," she wept until Philippians 4:13 popped into her head. "I can do all this through him who gives me strength." She sighed and took a deep breath. "Fine! I won't fight you because you always win."

At that moment Kenny entered the control room. "You okay, Em. I thought I heard something."

"That was me fighting against God," she said.

"Did you win?"

"Of course not." She sighed. "But this is crazy."

He tilted his head. "What? Why would you fight God?"

"Because I'm stubborn and because of what He wants me to do," she said and then bit her lip.

"What is He asking you to do?"

"The Holy Spirit told me to write a book."

"A book? Are you sure? You write songs." He pulled her out of the chair and held her hands.

She looked up at Kenny, and he saw the sparkle in her eyes. "That's what I tried to tell Him, but He won't listen."

Kenny let go of her hands. "What will you do?"

She shrugged. "I'll do what He told me to. I don't know what good it will do, but I'll do it. I'll write a book about my life. Like anyone will want to read that." She laughed and said, "This is crazy. Where in the world would I start?"

Kenny kissed her cheek. "I'm sure you will figure it out, m'lady."

Check out these other titles by the author. Visit the website:
kennethleemcgee.com

The Emmy's Story Series

1. We We're 'posed to Get Married
2. One Of The Guys
3. A New Friend
4. Did You Like the Ravioli Tonight?
5. Completely and Forever: A Wedding
6. It's Time To Go!
7. How Difficult Can It Be?
8. Forever... Isabella... Forever
9. The Forgettable Year
10. Turning Thirty
11. Hello, I'm James

The Annie Mercer O'Dell Series

1. Roosevelt High
2. North Park College
3. Smoky Mountain Summer

Stand Alone Books

1. Growing Up In Kinmundy Junction
2. Grandpa, Lions and Kitty Cats: A Collection Of Short Stories For Children Of All Ages